The Literary Dog

The Literary Dog

GREAT CONTEMPORARY DOG STORIES

Edited and with an Introduction by
Jeanne Schinto

THE ATLANTIC MONTHLY PRESS
NEW YORK

♦

Copyright © 1990 by Jeanne Schinto

Heartfelt thanks to all the authors, publishers, and agents
who kindly gave me permission to reprint these stories.
Thanks, especially, to my own agent, Faith Hornby Hamlin,
for her energy, good humor, and good sense.
A complete list of acknowledgments appears on pp. 371–73.

Library of Congress Cataloging-in-Publication Data

The literary dog: great contemporary dog stories / edited and with an
   introduction by Jeanne Schinto.—1st ed.
   ISBN 0-87113-383-0
   1. Dogs—Fiction.   2. Short stories, American.   3. Short stories,
English.
PS648.D64L5   1990   813'.010836—dc20   90-34834

Published simultaneously in Canada
Printed in the United States of America
FIRST EDITION

The Atlantic Monthly Press
19 Union Square West
New York, NY 10003

FIRST PRINTING

Contents

CONTENTS

CONTENTS

CONTENTS

CONTENTS

JEANNE SCHINTO

Introduction

I was afraid of dogs when I was little. Pedaling my bike around the neighborhood, I hoped to sneak past certain foul-tempered beasts who seemed to live only to lunge out of their yards and chase cars and other fast-moving objects down the street. I learned that to pedal as slowly as I could was the best way to travel. Once, however, despite my stealth, a Chihuahua sprang out of a hedge and nipped my calf. The dog was patterned black and white, like a tiny trembling pinto, and I remember the insult, the bubbling anger I felt. I wasn't hurt. The nip was only a pinch—it had barely broken the skin. There was no trickle of blood (as, even then, I knew I secretly wished for). A scratch, traced in a flash onto my cheek by a cat, had hurt more. Still, I wanted to throw down my bike and march up to the front door of that ratty dog's family (Bianchi was their name—oh, yes, I remember!) and give them a piece of my mind. I didn't, though. The dog, quivering, continued to threaten me, all four of its legs off the ground each time it wheezed out another venomous yip. So, grumbling, I rode my bike on home, gingerly. How I resented and envied those dogs who so ably kept me in line, dogs large and small who knocked me out of my daydreams, who kept my mind an innocent's because they kept it clear.

I suppose this is by way of saying that I do not think all dogs are angels. In fact, I don't think any are, not even my own. That is, I think dogs are simply themselves, which, in my opinion, is something quite adequate. For example, I am as bored (and doubtful) as I hope you are, hearing how somebody's Fifi or Muffin is "just like a little person." Dogs are not people dressed up in fur

1

coats, and to deny them their nature is to do them great harm. Because of the way their wolf forebears lived—in packs, in *families*—dogs are much *like* us, but beyond that there are many thankful dissimilarities, and their lack of language is only one of them.

To begin this book by mentioning the snapping teeth of the Bianchis' live gargoyle is also to say two other things, albeit obliquely, so I'll translate. One, I view dogs as I view all of the material world: not only as the things themselves but as symbols of other, hidden (or intangible) "things"—that is, all the things (and more) that the stories in this book are really "about" and which first-class fiction is always "about," the "subject matter" notwithstanding. Two, this opening is also designed to be a slant-wise warning. Dog lovers, beware! If you are looking to this volume for sentimental sap about "our four-footed friends," you'd do better to look elsewhere. Indeed, I think a dog lover would be downright puzzled by some of my selections. Some might even be outraged. But maybe the idea of a dog lover is apocryphal, anyway. As Thurber said: "I am not a dog-lover. To me, a dog-lover is a dog who is in love with another dog." This book is, rather, for lovers of good fiction, with, let us say, a healthy side interest in dogs. And fiction lovers are no myth. They exist, I know, because I am one.

So then you might suppose, since I have undertaken this project, that I am at least a *liker* of dogs. "You must really like dogs," someone said to me while I was in the midst of searching out stories for this book. "I like *certain* dogs. . . ." I hesitated, only later thinking of the better, truer, reply: I am never indifferent to a dog. I notice dogs. I have strong opinions about dogs. I have lived with dogs now for half my life, though I often still fear *strange* dogs. For no matter how you may think it otherwise, this master of showing, not telling—the first animal (even before cats) we humans brought into our homes (c. 10,000 B.C.)—is still only capable of purely animal behavior.

The traditional dog story, of course, attempts to debunk that basic truth. A dog story of the predictable kind usually recounts some heroic dog deed, not always believable, though the teller swears it is true. And books filled with that sort of, well, doggerel are part of a long tradition. Beyond that, however, short-fiction writers have a history of using the dog as a subject for the highest and purest literary aims. Witness just two examples: Stephen Crane's "A Dark-Brown Dog" and Kafka's "Investigations of a Dog."

Nor are dog story *anthologies* anything new, though I believe this one is unique for reasons upcoming. *Famous Dogs in Fiction* (1921, 1930) was edited by J. Walker McSpadden, who boasted that "so far as the present editor is aware, this is the first attempt to gather together a group of diverse stories in honor of man's best friend." But McSpadden was obviously unaware of Edward Jesse's *Anecdotes of Dogs* (1846), *Dog Stories from the 'Spectator,'* edited by J. St. L. Strachey (1895), and Jerome K. Jerome's *Dog Stories by Zola and Others* (1904)—to name only three. At any rate, McSpadden's aim, like many of those before him, was "a sort of stroll through a literary bench show" exhibiting "outstanding examples which no canine lover can afford to miss." McSpadden's selections included stories by Sir Walter Scott, Jack London, Dickens, Tolstoy, and Albert Payson Terhune, whose Lad "had a heart that did not know the meaning of fear or of disloyalty or meanness."

Jack Goodman, editor of the well-known *Fireside Book of Dog Stories* (1943), likewise included London and Terhune but also four Thurber pieces, three by E. B. White, an O. Henry, a Rudyard Kipling, a Thomas Mann, the previously mentioned Stephen Crane, D. H. Lawrence, John Galsworthy, Alexander Woollcott, Anatole France, a portion of *Lassie Come-Home* by Eric Knight, and an essay by Robert Louis Stevenson titled "The Character of Dogs." When Goodman made his selection, he asked himself: "If I were a dog, would I want that one in?" And though he bypassed Kafka and Virginia Woolf (whose *Flush* was published in 1933), he seems to have been otherwise fairly well guided.

In the volume in your hands you will find no Thurber, no London, no Kipling, and certainly no Terhune or Knight. But also, sadly, no Crane, no Kafka, and no Woolf. I have limited my choices to only the very best fiction, yes, but have restricted myself in other ways too. I've included only contemporary pieces (the earliest was published in 1963, the bulk are from the eighties, and—here is the unique part—I don't believe any have been included in a dog story anthology until now). Nor will you find any works first published in anything other than English (in other words, no translations). And finally, you'll find here only wholes (all short stories, no novel excerpts). And doesn't it go without saying (though I'll say it, anyway) that I've passed up nonfiction, no matter how good? For example, I was sorely tempted to bend the definition of "story" by a compelling piece that first appeared in *The Threepenny Review*, called "Vital Signs," a memoir by Natalie Kusz, who was attacked by hungry huskies when she was a child in Alaska.

To some readers a few of these pieces may not seem "doggy" enough. In certain cases, waiting for the entrance of the dog may feel like waiting for the other shoe to drop. I don't mean it to be distracting. I believe these are all stories in which the dog is necessary to the effect that the author wishes to create. I also believe that none of these stories would "work" without the canine component, no more than would "Dawn After the Wreck"—the J. M. W. Turner painting with the dog on the beach barking at the nub of the sinking ship (at least *my* imagination supplies the bark). Technically it is not a very "doggy" painting, square inch for square inch, if you are comparing it to, say, Victorian dog portraiture. But which makes the stronger narrative statement? And where would Turner's painting be *without* the dog?

I have roughly arranged the selections according to setting. I begin with a primitive scene and proceed to so-called civilization. From the Australian bush, then, we move to the farm, on to the suburbs, the city, and finally outer space. In any setting, much is revealed by the relationship that develops between the two: dog and master.

Though toy dogs have been bred since Neolithic times for companionship, today companionship is the primary role of dogs of all sizes. No longer hunters or herders or beasts of burden, most now have a much more serious social function to fill. Some dogs, like a certain golden retriever I saw being reprimanded in the park, may be asked to fill roles they couldn't possibly. "You listen to your father!" bellowed the woman when the golden misbehaved for her boyfriend. "This is my empty-nest dog," said a woman of her Welsh corgi at a dog obedience class I attended recently.

Evidently, however, dogs are performing adequately enough, for there are more and more companion dogs today—the dog population is growing out of bounds, some say. Some scientific studies claim that people's affection for pets reduces the amount of available affection for other people, that pets use up valuable resources, and that pet owners are of poorer mental health than nonowners. Yet more of the research demonstrates opposite findings: pets lower human blood pressure, increase longevity, are good for mental health because they curb the effects of prolonged loneliness. Studies have even claimed, in the bulky language they use, that people who have low affection for pets are low in affection for others, while those with a high affection for pets are high in affection for others.

As the dogs in our midst multiply, so, too, do the dog stories. For every one collected here I have read four more. And I'm still reading. Surely I have omitted some winners either because they never came to my attention or for some other, arbitrary reason. For example, Stephen Dixon's "The Dat"— about a cat who turns into a dog—was reluctantly set aside because it was a cat story as well as a dog story. Beyond that, the book reflects purely personal preferences, as well as an attempt to show as many aspects of companion dogs as possible. There is one story about a working dog, but as you will see, he did very little work. This book features good and bad dogs but only great fiction.

B. WONGAR

Warand, *the Dingo*

I'm taking you to bare and waterless country.
—wailing chant, northern Australia

I have never heard what a trap looks like. It is set for animals, perhaps people as well, and whoever it snaps shut on does not live to tell how it was. It is a man-made beast, not so big: two steel jaws each with a row of teeth—I can feel them with my fingertips. They are ghastly; it will be a struggle to break away from their grip.

It must hurt, that caught leg; Warand does not show much of it now. The animal has given up struggling to break free and licks his front limb at the knee where the steel teeth must have gone through the skin. Yes, he licks my hand as well; perhaps he thinks I am caught in the trap too. What can I do, I wonder. My *mauwulan,* walking stick, has been broken into pieces; I tried to force it inside the trap and push the jaws apart but wood is weak against steel. Maybe there is something better to be found than a piece of wood. My *duwei,* my late husband, used stone: "With tough rock you can wreck the trap with one blow, it rips the guts out of it," he told me. A pity there are no rocks here; maybe there are some farther up in the bush but it is hard to find anything when you are blind.

I won't go far away; with no one to lead me now, I could wander off into the bush and never find my way back. Before, whenever I felt lost, I only had to whistle—Warand always came on my call. Even if the dingo was a voice away from me, he would rush back and lead me to the right track. Duwei says the dingoes are our own people reborn—they come back to life as animals, hoping they might do better that way. They have thick fur to keep them warm at night, and when they are out looking for tucker, they will catch up with a wallaby much quicker than any of our fellows with their spears, but . . . yes, whatever

6

luck the dingoes had did not last; the country has lately gone hard on all of us. Whether you are a human or an animal, the whites are out to trap you just the same.

Warand yaps; perhaps as I am moving away the animal is warning me not to wander far off and . . . I might never find my way back. Dingoes not only stick to you for life but follow your mind as well. We had a whole pack of them long ago when we lived near the Homestead, about a couple of camps away down the plain. The animals used to clear out at dawn so they wouldn't be seen by the stockmen, but even if they went to the far end of the country, they always returned at evening to lie curled up against us when the night grew cold. They slept with their ears pricked up, not so much out of fear—the whites do not hunt during the night, but my husband talked in his sleep and the animals were keen not to miss a single word. The dingoes would have been right: when one talks in his dreams he is not only telling what is on his mind but brings us a message from our spirits.

Warand still yaps, though the call sounds a bit faint now. I should go back and give the poor fellow a cuddle . . . no, I'd better look for a branch or two with some leaves and hurry to make a bit of shade over him. The sun is getting very hot and the sandy ground will soon be . . . it will feel like treading over hot ashes. On a day like this it will not take long for the heat to finish you off. What will I do if he goes? We stick to each other as two do when there is no one else in the whole country left to cling to.

I'll wave the branch over Warand to cool him a bit. . . . He sighs, throwing out a whole load of pain, then licks my leg. Duwei told me that dingoes are like humans: when hurt, they suffer just the same as we do. Once a dingo bitch did not turn up in camp at the end of the day but instead showed up the next afternoon. She came on three legs, followed by a swarm of flies, and crawled up to lie beside us. Duwei gave her some water and went to look for tucker, but she had no strength to open her mouth; only her eyes tracked us about trying to tell us something. . . . Yes, the wound was a bit much and she gave up. No, I don't think Warand will quit like that; he is a tough hunter, used to wandering through the country every day. He has dodged more traps than there are trees around and has always made it back to camp with a catch—a small goanna in his mouth if nothing else.

Poor Warand leans his head against my leg and sighs; I can feel his heart beating fast as though fighting for breath. I wonder how he let himself be caught today—he knows every single bush around here. There is a water hole down at the gully, about a voice away from here, and he leads me there and back every day. Before, we had to sneak in only at dusk or dawn for a quick drink and to fill our billycan while the stockmen were not around and then follow the track back up the gully. There is a rock shelter high up at the foot of the hills, the shadiest spot in the whole country for animals and people alike. No, the whites hardly ever came that way; they don't like to struggle over the craggy slopes. Perhaps they were afraid that our spirits might still be hiding behind the cliffs and would push the rocks down on them. From the cave we used to hear the stockmen on their horses galloping across the plain beyond the water hole mustering their herds or . . . yes, the whining sound of the truck struggling through the bush. Whatever it was—animal or machine—Duwei always kept his eyes on the trail of dust the stockmen left behind, and if it was headed this way he and the dingoes would dash from the shelter and sneak out farther into the hills.

The end of the trap is chained and bolted to a tree stump—no hope of taking that off and letting Warand drag the steel jaws about. I had better go and look for some water before the dingo pants away. The sun is like a boiling billy resting on top of our heads. The water hole should not be far off—I can hear a flock of *lindaridj,* galahs, busily chatting at the drinking place. The birds are never tired of making a noise, and the sound will show me the right way to move. I should find a new *mauwulan*—a small branch will do if nothing better—just to have something in front of me so I can feel where to step. I wish this were only a dream, long and hard—the same as those Duwei often had when he struggled in his sleep and the dingoes' ears were up like spears to catch every word. He never told me what the dreams were all about and I don't think the dingoes learned the secrets either. It was about us I reckon; this water hole is the only one for many camps around. It used to hold enough water for a much bigger *babaru** than the two of us and all those birds and

*family—Ed.

8

animals that called in from the far bush, even many voices away, until the cows were brought here. The white man's beasts drank most of it and we always feared that next time we came around looking for water, there might be nothing left but a muddy patch.

The dingo howls; maybe he is trying to let me know how far away I have gone, or perhaps he wants me to hurry back with a drink. On a day like this you could not hold out for long; Duwei did hold out for a finger-count of days, however, but he did not have the whole of his body in the sun. The stockmen chained him to a large boulder, there beyond the Homestead, and there was a shady patch under it for shelter, but only big enough for him to squeeze his head and chest underneath. I wonder why they chained him; they say he stole a horse, but it is not one of our animals and you never go close to a beast of that size; it gallops through the country like a willy-willy, and even if a whole tribe of our fellows were around, the spears would not be fast enough to catch up with it. Yes, Duwei might have tried to scare the beast off and not let it hang around the water hole, but . . . no, I don't think they got him because of that animal. When the whites left the Homestead not long ago, a whole pack of horses was left behind to do good to no one. I could not see them, but now and then I can hear a thundering in the bush and I can't help fearing that the stockmen are back, but as the sound of hooves fades away like a wild wind you soon come to know—no man is around, only the beasts left behind and gone astray.

There is plenty of water in the hole; it is not hard to dip in the billycan now. Before, with the cows around, the hole was half full at its best and I always had to struggle through thick mud to scoop it up and then plunge my hand into the billycan to feel how much silt was in it too. No, I will not lose myself here, I know every bit of this ground and move about touching it like my own skin, and . . . there should be a few stones around the edge of the water. I remember them before, covered with mud and often splashed with dung, but they should be well dry now, and one of them will not be hard to carry back, if I can only find it. No, I will not wander off from this place; the *lindaridj* are around, screeching all the time—a whole flock of them and much noisier than ever before. Perhaps the birds are trying to tell me how good it must be to have the water hole to ourselves again. A wild horse or a donkey might come now and then, but not those herds of cows to muddy the place and make the water's edge slide down to the bottom.

The dingo howls again; it sounds more like a cry now than a call, worn out and faint. Perhaps I should hurry back, but the stone is a bit heavy to carry. I will get it there moving a few steps at a time; the bigger the stone, the better blow it will give to the trap. It will be just as Duwei did it when he was around. I went to see him every day when he was chained down to that boulder and brought him water and tucker. I was still able then to plunge my digging stick in the ground and gather some roots. I even often got a handful of witchetty grubs from around the wattletree stumps. He liked that tucker better than anything gathered from the bush.

There is no howl to be heard now. Warand must have given up, or perhaps he is resting for a while and will call out again. I know the part around here well, and I should be getting closer; he might have seen me coming already and maybe he is wagging his tail now. If I can't manage to wreck that trap I will have to rub the chain against the stone and break it. I tried to free Duwei that way, too, though the links were much heavier, but we did it in turn, each of us having a go and then resting while the other rubbed the steel against the sharp edge of the rock. We made quite a groove, halfway through the link, but . . . I had to go and bring a billy of water, leaving him behind. He seemed not so keen to struggle when he was left alone. Perhaps he feared that even if he did break free, it would not be long before he would be caught again and brought back to the boulder and . . . yes, the more you struggle, the harder they press on you. He came to see me the following night in my sleep: "I'm off to Dreaming; our fellows have come and freed me."

The spirits whisked Duwei away; once they see that you are stuck hard they do not sit and watch you suffer forever.

The stump is here all right and the pieces of chain that were bound to that trap. The steel is terribly hot, lying on the sand; I have almost taken the skin off my fingers by touching it. How poor Warand must feel; perhaps . . . no, only the leg is left, with flies buzzing around it and blood splashed over the steel jaws. He has bitten off his limb and wandered off to the bush. I had better sound out a few calls to tell him I am back, give him some water and get a leafy branch to keep those flies off. Later we can go back down the gully and camp there—it is all our country again, and although it might not bring much good now to either of us, it will ease our wounds to know the land is ours.

I'll sound out more calls, and if he is not back by the end of the day, Warand will turn up in my dreams for sure.

MARK RICHARD

Strays

At night, stray dogs come up underneath our house to lick our leaking pipes. Beneath my brother and my's room we hear them coughing and growling, scratching their ratted backs against the boards beneath our beds. We lie awake, listening, my brother thinking of names to name the one he is setting out to catch. Salute and Topboy are high on his list.

I tell my brother these dogs are wild and cowering. A bare-heeled stomp on the floor off our beds sends them scuttling spine-bowed out the crawl space beneath our open window. Sometimes, when my brother is quick, he leans out and touches one slipping away.

Our father has meant to put the screens back on the windows for spring. He has even hauled them out of the storage shed and stacked them in the drive. He lays them one by one over sawhorses to tack in the frames tighter and weave patches against mosquitoes. This is what he means to do, but our mother that morning pulls all the preserves off the shelves onto the floor, sticks my brother and my's Easter Sunday drawings in her mouth, and leaves the house through the field next door, cleared the week before for corn.

Uncle Trash is our nearest relative with a car and our mother has a good half-day head start on our father when Uncle Trash arrives. Uncle Trash runs his car up the drive in a big speed, splitting all the screens stacked there from their frames. There is an exploded chicken in the grille of Uncle Trash's car. They don't even turn the motor off as Uncle Trash slides out and our father gets behind the wheel, backing back over the screens, setting out in search of our mother.

Uncle Trash finds out that he has left his bottle under the seat of his car. He goes into our kitchen, pulling out all the shelves our mother missed. Then he is in the towel box in the hall, looking, pulling out stuff in stacks. He is in our parents' room, opening short doors. He is in the storage shed, opening and sniffing a mason jar of gasoline for the power mower. Uncle Trash comes up and asks, Which way it is to town for a drink. I point up the road. Uncle Trash sets off, saying, Don't y'all burn the house down.

My brother and I hang out in the side yard, doing handstands until dark. We catch handfuls of lightning bugs and smear bright yellow on our shirts. It is late. I wash our feet and put us to bed. We wait for somebody to come back home but nobody ever does. Lucky for me when my brother begins to whine for our mother the stray dogs show up under the house. My brother starts making up lists of new names for them, naming himself to sleep.

Hungry, we wake up to something sounding in the kitchen not like our mother fixing us anything to eat.

It is Uncle Trash. He is throwing up and spitting blood into the pump-handled sink. I ask him did he have an accident and he sends my brother upstairs for merthiolate and Q-tips. His face is angled out from his head on one side so that-sided eye is shut. His good eye waters when he wiggles loose teeth with cut-up fingers.

Uncle Trash says he had an accident, all right. He says he was up in a card game and then he was real up in a card game, so up he bet his car, accidentally forgetting that our father had driven off with it in search of our mother. Uncle Trash says the man who won the card game went ahead and beat up Uncle Trash on purpose anyway.

All day Uncle Trash sleeps in our parents' room. We in the front yard can hear him snoring. My brother and I dig in the dirt with spoons, making roadbeds and highways for my tin metal trucks. In the evening, Uncle Trash comes down in one of our father's shirts, dirty, but cleaner than the one he had gotten beat up in. We have banana sandwiches for supper. Uncle Trash asks do we have a deck of cards in the house. He says he wants to see do his tooth-cut fingers still bend enough to work. I have to tell him how our mother disallows card-playing in the house but that my brother has a pack of Old Maid somewhere in the toy box. While my brother goes out to look I brag at how I always beat my brother out, leaving him the Old Maid, and Uncle Trash says, Oh, yeah? and digs around in his pocket for a nickel he puts on the table. He says, We'll play a nickel a game. I go into my brother and my's room to get the Band-Aid box of nickels and dimes I sometimes short from the collection plate on Sunday.

Uncle Trash is making painful faces, flexing his red-painted fingers around the Old Maid deck of circus-star cards, but he still shuffles, cuts, and deals a three-way hand one-handed—and not much longer, I lose my Band-Aid box of money and all the tin metal trucks of mine out in the front yard. Uncle Trash makes me go out and get them and put them on his side of the table. My brother loses a set of bowling pins and a stuffed beagle. In two more hands, we stack up our winter boots and coats with the hoods on Uncle Trash's side of the table. In the last hand, my brother and I step out of our shorts and underdrawers while Uncle Trash smiles, saying, And now, gentlemen, if you please, the shirts off y'all's backs.

Uncle Trash rakes everything my brother and I owned into the pillow-cases off our bed and says let that be a lesson to me. He is off through the front porch door, leaving us buck-naked at the table, his last words as he goes up the road, shoulder-slinging his loot, Don't y'all burn the house down.

I am burning hot at Uncle Trash.

Then I am burning hot at our father for leaving us with him to look for our mother.

Then I am burning hot at my mother for running off, leaving me with my brother, who is rubber-chinning and face-pouting his way into a good cry.

There is only one thing left to do, and that is to take all we still have left that we own and throw it at my brother—and I do—and Old Maid cards explode on his face, setting him off on a really good howl.

I tell my brother that making so much noise will keep the stray dogs away, and he believes it, and then I start to believe it when it gets later than usual, past the crickets and into a long moon over the trees, but they finally do come after my brother finally does fall asleep, so I just wait until I know there are several strays beneath the bed boards, scratching their rat-matted backs and growling, and I stomp on the floor, what is my favorite part about the dogs, stomping and then watching them scatter in a hundred directions and then seeing them one by one collect in a pack at the edge of the field near the trees.

In the morning right off I recognize the bicycle coming wobble-wheeling into the front yard. It's the one the colored boy outside Cuts uses to run lunches and ice water to the pulpwood truck Mr. Cuts has working cut-over timber on the edge of town. The colored boy that usually drives the bicycle snaps bottlecaps off his fingers at my brother and I when we go to Cuts with our mother to make groceries. We have to wait outside by the kerosene pump, out by the tar-papered lean-to shed, the pop-crate place where the men sit around and Uncle Trash does his card work now. White people generally don't go into Cuts unless they have to buy on credit.

We at school know Mr. and Mrs. Cuts come from a family that eats children. There is a red metal tree with plastic-wrapped toys in the window and a long candy counter case inside to lure you in. Mr. and Mrs. Cuts have no children of their own. They ate them during a hard winter and salted the rest down for sandwiches the colored boy runs out to the pulpwood crew at noon. I count colored children going in to buy some candy to see how many make it back out, but generally our mother is ready to go home way before I can tell. Our credit at Cuts is short.

The front tire catches in one of our tin metal truck's underground tunnels and Uncle Trash takes a spill. The cut crate bolted to the bicycle handlebars spills brown paper packages sealed with electrical tape out into the yard along with a case of Champale and a box of cigars. Uncle Trash is down where he falls. He lays asleep all day under the tree in the front yard, moving only just to crawl back into the wandering shade.

We have for supper sirloins, Champale, and cigars. Uncle Trash teaches how to cross our legs up on the table after dinner, but says he'll go ahead and leave my brother and my's cigars unlit. There is no outlook for our toys and my Band-Aid can of nickels and dimes, checking all the packages, even checking twice again the cut crate bolted on the front of the bicycle. Uncle Trash shows us a headstand on the table while drinking a bottle of Champale, then

15

he stands in the sink and sings "Gather My Farflung Thoughts Together." My brother and I chomp our cigars and clap but in our hearts we are low and lonesome.

Don't y'all burn down the house, says Uncle Trash, pedaling out the yard to Cuts.

My brother leans out our window with a rope coil and sirloin scraps strung on strings. He is in a greasy-fingered sleep when the strings slither like white snakes off our bed, over the sill, out into the fields beyond.

There's July corn and no word from our parents.

Uncle Trash doesn't remember the Fourth of July or the Fourth of July parade. Uncle Trash bunches cattails in the fenders of his bicycle and clips our Old Maid cards in the spokes and follows the fire engine through town with my brother and I in the front cut-out crate throwing penny candy to the crowds. What are you trying to be? the colored men at Cuts ask Uncle Trash when we end up the parade there. I spot a broken-wheeled tin metal truck of mine in a colored child's hand, driving it in circles by the Cuts front steps. Foolish, says Uncle Trash.

Uncle Trash doesn't remember winning Mrs. Cuts in a card game for a day to come out and clean the house and us in the bargain. She pushes the furniture around with a broom and calls us abominations. There's a bucket of soap to wash our heads and a jar of sour-smelling cream for our infected bites, fleas from under the house, and mosquitoes through the windows. The screens are rusty squares in the driveway dirt. Uncle Trash leaves her his razor opened as long as my arm. She comes after my brother and I with it to cut our hair, she says. We know better. My brother dives under the house and I am up a tree.

Uncle Trash doesn't remember July, but when we tell him about it, he says it sounds like July was probably a good idea at the time.

It is August with the brown, twisted corn in the fields next to the house. There is word from our parents. They are in the state capital. One of them has been in jail. Uncle Trash is still promising screens. We get from Cuts bug spray instead.

I wake up in the middle of a night. My brother floats through the window. Out in the yard, he and a stray have each other on the end of a rope. He reels her in and I make the tackle. Already I feel the fleas leave her rag-matted coat and crawl over my arms and up my neck. We spray her down with a whole can of bug spray until her coat lathers like soap. My brother gets some matches to burn a tick like a grape out of her ear. The touch of the match covers her like a blue-flame sweater. She's a fireball shooting beneath the house.

By the time Uncle Trash and the rest of town get there, the Fire Warden says the house is Fully Involved.

In the morning I see our parents drive past where our house used to be. I see them go by again until they recognize the yard. Uncle Trash is trying to bring my brother out of the trance he is in by showing him how some tricks work on the left-standing steps of the stoop. Uncle Trash shows Jack-Away, Queen in the Whorehouse, and No Money Down. Our father says for Uncle Trash to stand up so he can knock him down. Uncle Trash says he deserves that one. Our father knocks Uncle Trash down again and tells him not to get up. If you get up I'll kill you, our father says.

Uncle Trash crawls on all fours across our yard out to the road.

Goodbye, Uncle Trash, I say.

Goodbye, men! Uncle Trash says. Don't y'all burn the house down! he says, and I say, We won't.

During the knocking-down nobody notices our mother. She is a flat-footed running rustle through the corn all burned up by the summer sun.

DORIS LESSING

The Story of Two Dogs

Getting a new dog turned out to be more difficult than we thought, and for reasons rooted deep in the nature of our family. For what, on the face of it, could have been easier to find than a puppy once it had been decided: "Jock needs a companion, otherwise he'll spend his time with those dirty Kaffir dogs in the compound"? All the farms in the district had dogs who bred puppies of the most desirable sort. All the farm compounds owned miserable beasts kept hungry so that they would be good hunters for their meat-starved masters; though often enough puppies born to the cage-ribbed bitches from this world of mud huts were reared in white houses and turned out well. Jacob our builder heard we wanted another dog, and came up with a lively puppy on the end of a bit of rope. But we tactfully refused. The thin flea-bitten little object was not good enough for Jock, my mother said; though we children were only too ready to take it in.

Jock was a mongrel himself, a mixture of Alsatian, Rhodesian ridgeback, and some other breed—terrier?—that gave him ears too cocky and small above a long melancholy face. In short, he was nothing to boast of, outwardly: his qualities were all intrinsic or bestowed on him by my mother who had given this animal her heart when my brother went off to boarding school.

In theory Jock was my brother's dog. Yet why give a dog to a boy at that moment when he departs for school and will be away from home two-thirds of the year? In fact my brother's dog was his substitute; and my poor mother, whose children were always away being educated, because we were farmers, and farmers' children had no choice but to go to the cities for their schooling—my poor mother caressed Jock's too-small intelligent ears and crooned: "There, Jock! There, old boy! There, good dog, yes, you're a *good* dog, Jock, you're such a *good* dog. . . ." While my father said, uncomfortably: "For goodness sake, old girl, you'll ruin him, that isn't a house pet, he's not a lapdog, he's a farm dog." To which my mother said nothing, but her face put on a most familiar look of misunderstood suffering, and she bent it down close so that the flickering red tongue just touched her cheeks, and sang to him: "Poor old Jock then, yes, you're a poor old dog, you're not a rough farm dog, you're a good dog, and you're not strong, no you're delicate."

At this last word my brother protested; my father protested; and so did I. All of us, in our different ways, had refused to be "delicate"—had escaped from being "delicate"—and we wished to rescue a perfectly strong and healthy young dog from being forced into invalidism, as we all, at different times, had been. Also of course we all (and we knew it and felt guilty about it) were secretly pleased that Jock was now absorbing the force of my mother's pathetic need for something "delicate" to nurse and protect.

Yet there was something in the whole business that was a reproach to us. When my mother bent her sad face over the animal, stroking him with her beautiful white hands on which the rings had grown too large, and said: "There, good dog, yes Jock, you're such a gentleman—" well, there was something in all this that made us, my father, my brother and myself, need to explode with fury, or to take Jock away and make him run over the farm like the tough young brute he was, or go away ourselves forever so that we didn't have to hear the awful yearning intensity in her voice. Because it was entirely our fault that note was in her voice at all; if we had allowed ourselves to be delicate, and good, or even gentlemen or ladies, there would have been no need for Jock to sit between my mother's knees, his loyal noble head on her lap, while she caressed and yearned and suffered.

It was my father who decided there must be another dog, and for the expressed reason that otherwise Jock would be turned into a "sissy." (At this word, reminder of a hundred earlier battles, my brother flushed, looked sulky, and went right out of the room.) My mother would not hear of another dog until her Jock took to sneaking off to the farm compound to play with the

Kaffir dogs. "Oh you bad dog, Jock," she said sorrowfully, "playing with those nasty dirty dogs, how could you, Jock!" And he would playfully, but in an agony of remorse, snap and lick at her face, while she bent the whole force of her inevitably betrayed self over him, crooning: "How could you, oh how could you, Jock?"

So there must be a new puppy. And since Jock was (at heart, despite his temporary lapse) noble and generous and above all well-bred, his companion must also possess these qualities. And which dog, where in the world, could possibly be good enough? My mother turned down a dozen puppies; but Jock was still going off to the compound, slinking back to gaze soulfully into my mother's eyes. This new puppy was to be my dog. I decided this: if my brother owned a dog, then it was only fair that I should. But my lack of force in claiming this puppy was because I was in the grip of abstract justice only. The fact was I didn't want a good noble and well-bred dog. I didn't know what I did want, but the idea of such a dog bored me. So I was content to let my mother turn down puppies, provided she kept her terrible maternal energy on Jock, and away from me.

Then the family went off for one of our long visits in another part of the country, driving from farm to farm to stop a night, or a day, or a meal, with friends. To the last place we were invited for the weekend. A distant cousin of my father, "a Norfolk man" (my father was from Essex), had married a woman who had nursed in the war (First World War) with my mother. They now lived in a small brick and iron house surrounded by granite *kopjes* that erupted everywhere from thick bush. They were as isolated as any people I've known, eighty miles from the nearest railway station. As my father said, they were "not suited," for they quarreled or sent each other to Coventry all the weekend. However, it was not until much later that I thought about the pathos of these two people, living alone on a minute pension in the middle of the bush, and "not suited"; for that weekend I was in love.

It was night when we arrived, about eight in the evening, and an almost full moon floated heavy and yellow above a stark granite-bouldered *kopje*. The bush around was black and low and silent, except that the crickets made a small incessant din. The car drew up outside a small boxlike structure whose iron roof glinted off moonlight. As the engine stopped, the sound of crickets swelled up, the moonlight's cold came in a breath of fragrance to our faces; and there was the sound of a mad wild yapping. Behold, around the corner of the house came a small black wriggling object that hurled itself towards the car, changed course almost on touching it, and hurtled off again, yapping in a high delirious yammering which, while it faded behind the house, continued faintly, our ears, or at least mine, straining after it.

"Take no notice of that puppy," said our host, the man from Norfolk. "It's been stark staring mad with the moon every night this last week."

We went into the house, were fed, were looked after; I was put to bed so that the grown-ups could talk freely. All the time came the mad high yapping. In my tiny bedroom I looked out onto a space of flat white sand that reflected the moon between the house and the farm buildings, and there hurtled a mad wild puppy, crazy with joy of life, or moonlight, weaving back and forth, round and round, snapping at its own black shadow and tripping over its own clumsy feet—like a drunken moth around a candle flame, or like . . . like nothing I've ever seen or heard of since.

The moon, large and remote and soft, stood up over the trees, the empty white sand, the house which had unhappy human beings in it; and a mad little dog yapping and beating its course of drunken joyous delirium. That, of course, was my puppy; and when Mr. Barnes came out from the house saying: "Now, now, come now, you lunatic animal . . ." finally almost throwing himself on the crazy creature, to lift it in his arms still yapping and wriggling and flapping around like a fish, so that he could carry it to the packing case that was its kennel, I was already saying, as anguished as a mother watching a stranger handle her child: Careful now, careful, that's my dog.

Next day, after breakfast, I visited the packing case. Its white wood oozed out resin that smelled tangy in hot sunlight, and its front was open and spilling out soft yellow straw. On the straw a large beautiful black dog lay with her head on outstretched forepaws. Beside her a brindled pup lay on its fat back, its four paws sprawled every which way, its eyes rolled up, as ecstatic with heat and food and laziness as it had been the night before from the joy of movement. A crust of mealie porridge was drying on its shining black lips that were drawn slightly back to show perfect milk teeth. His mother kept her eyes on him, but her pride was dimmed with sleep and heat.

I went inside to announce my spiritual ownership of the puppy. They were all around the breakfast table. The man from Norfolk was swapping boyhood reminiscences (shared in space, not time) with my father. His wife, her eyes still red from the weeping that had followed a night quarrel, was gossiping with my mother about the various London hospitals where they had ministered to the wounded of the War they had (apparently so enjoyably) shared.

My mother at once said: "Oh my dear, no, not that puppy, didn't you see him last night? We'll never train him."

The man from Norfolk said I could have him with pleasure.

My father said he didn't see what was wrong with the dog, if a dog was healthy that was all that mattered: my mother dropped her eyes forlornly, and sat silent.

The man from Norfolk's wife said she couldn't bear to part with the silly little thing, goodness knows there was little enough pleasure in her life.

The atmosphere of people at loggerheads being familiar to me, it was not necessary for me to know *why* they disagreed, or in what ways, or what criticisms they were going to make about my puppy. I only knew that inner logics would in due course work themselves out and the puppy would be mine. I left the four people to talk about their differences through a small puppy, and went to worship the animal, who was now sitting in a patch of shade beside the sweet-wood-smelling packing case, its dark brindled coat glistening, with dark wet patches on it from its mother's ministering tongue. His own pink tongue absurdly stuck out between white teeth, as if he had been too careless or lazy to withdraw it into its proper place under his equally pink wet palate. His brown buttony beautiful eyes . . . but enough, he was an ordinary mongrelly puppy.

Later I went back to the house to find out how the battle balanced: my mother had obviously won my father over, for he said he thought it was wiser not to have that puppy: "Bad blood tells, you know."

The bad blood was from the father, whose history delighted my fourteen-year-old imagination. This district being wild, scarcely populated, full of wild animals, even leopards and lions, the four policemen at the police station had a tougher task than in places nearer town; and they had bought half a dozen large dogs to (a) terrorize possible burglars around the police station itself and (b) surround themselves with an aura of controlled animal savagery. For the dogs were trained to kill if necessary. One of these dogs, a big ridgeback, had "gone wild." He had slipped his tether at the station and taken to the bush, living by himself on small buck, hares, birds, even stealing farmers' chickens. This dog, whose proud lonely shape had been a familiar one to farmers for years, on moonlit nights, or in gray dawns and dusks, standing aloof from human warmth and friendship, had taken Stella, my puppy's mother, off with him for a week of sport and hunting. She simply went away with him one morning; the Barneses had seen her go; had called after her; she had not even looked back. A week later she returned home at dawn and gave a low whine outside their bedroom window, saying: I'm home; and they woke to see their errant Stella standing erect in the paling moonlight, her nose pointed outwards and away from them towards a great powerful dog who seemed to signal to her with his slightly moving tail before fading into the bush. Mr. Barnes fired some futile shots into the bush after him. Then they both scolded Stella who in due time produced seven puppies, in all combinations of black, brown and gold. She was no pure-bred herself, though of course her owners thought she was or ought to be, being their dog. The night the puppies were born, the man from Norfolk and his wife heard a sad wail or cry, and arose from their beds to see the wild police dog bending his head in at the packing-case door. All the bush was flooded with a pinkish-gold dawn light, and the dog looked as if he had an aureole of gold around him. Stella was half wailing, half growling her welcome, or protest, or fear at his great powerful reappearance and his thrusting muzzle so close to her seven helpless pups. They called out, and he turned his outlaw's head to the window where they stood side by side in striped pajamas and embroidered pink silk. He put back his head and howled, he howled, a mad wild sound that gave them gooseflesh, so they said; but I did not understand that until years later when Bill the puppy "went wild" and I saw him that day on the antheap howling his pain of longing to an empty listening world.

The father of her puppies did not come near Stella again; but a month

23

later he was shot dead at another farm, fifty miles away, coming out of a chicken run with a fine white Leghorn in his mouth; and by that time she had only one pup left, they had drowned the rest. It was bad blood, they said, no point in preserving it, they had only left her that one pup out of pity.

I said not a word as they told this cautionary tale, merely preserved the obstinate calm of someone who knows she will get her own way. Was right on my side? It was. Was I owed a dog? I was. Should anybody but myself choose my dog? No, but . . . very well then, I had chosen. I chose this dog. I chose it. Too late, I *had* chosen it.

Three days and three nights we spent at the Barneses' place. The days were hot and slow and full of sluggish emotions; and the two dogs slept in the packing case. At nights, the four people stayed in the living room, a small brick place heated unendurably by the paraffin lamp whose oily yellow glow attracted moths and beetles in a perpetual whirling halo of small moving bodies. They talked, and I listened for the mad far yapping, and then I crept out into the cold moonlight. On the last night of our stay the moon was full, a great perfect white ball, its history marked on a face that seemed close enough to touch as it floated over the dark cricket-singing bush. And there on the white sand yapped and danced the crazy puppy, while his mother, the big beautiful animal, sat and watched, her intelligent yellow eyes slightly anxious as her muzzle followed the erratic movements of her child, the child of her dead mate from the bush. I crept up beside Stella, sat on the still-warm cement beside her, put my arm around her soft furry neck, and my head beside her alert moving head. I adjusted my breathing so that my rib cage moved up and down beside hers, so as to be closer to the warmth of her barrelly furry chest, and together we turned our eyes from the great staring floating moon to the tiny black hurtling puppy who shot in circles from near us, so near he all but crashed into us, to two hundred yards away where he just missed the wheels of the farm wagon. We watched, and I felt the chill of moonlight deepen on Stella's fur, and on my own silk skin, while our ribs moved gently up and down together, and we waited until the man from Norfolk came to first shout, then yell, then fling himself on the mad little dog and shut him up in the wooden box where yellow bars of moonlight fell into black dog-smelling shadow.

24

"There now, Stella girl, you go in with your puppy," said the man, bending to pat her head as she obediently went inside. She used her soft nose to push her puppy over. He was so exhausted that he fell and lay, his four legs stretched out and quivering like a shot dog, his breath squeezed in and out of him in small regular wheezy pants like whines. And so I left them, Stella and her puppy, to go to my bed in the little brick house which seemed literally crammed with hateful emotions. I went to sleep, thinking of the hurtling little dog, now at last asleep with exhaustion, his nose pushed against his mother's breathing black side, the slits of yellow moonlight moving over him through the boards of fragrant wood.

We took him away next morning, having first locked Stella in a room so that she could not see us go.

It was a three-hundred-mile drive, and all the way Bill yapped and panted and yawned and wriggled idiotically on his back on the lap of whoever held him, his eyes rolled up, his big paws lolling. He was a full-time charge for myself and my mother, and, after the city, my brother, whose holidays were starting. He, at first sight of the second dog, reverted to the role of Jock's master, and dismissed my animal as altogether less valuable material. My mother, by now Bill's slave, agreed with him, but invited him to admire the adorable wrinkles on the puppy's forehead. My father demanded irritably that both dogs should be "thoroughly trained."

Meanwhile, as the nightmare journey proceeded, it was noticeable that my mother talked more and more about Jock, guiltily, as if she had betrayed him. "Poor little Jock, what will he say?"

Jock was in fact a handsome young dog. More Alsatian than anything, he was a low-standing, thick-coated animal of a warm gold color, with a vestigial "ridge" along his spine, rather wolflike, or foxlike, if one looked at him frontways, with his sharp cocked ears. And he was definitely not "little." There was something dignified about him from the moment he was out of puppyhood, even when he was being scolded by my mother for his visits to the compound.

The meeting, prepared for by us all with trepidation, went off in a way which was a credit to everyone, but particularly Jock, who regained my mother's heart at a stroke. The puppy was released from the car and carried to where Jock sat, noble and restrained as usual, waiting for us to greet him. Bill at once began weaving and yapping around the rocky space in front of the house. Then he saw Jock, bounded up to him, stopped a couple of feet away, sat down on his fat backside and yelped excitedly. Jock began a yawning, snapping movement of his head, making it go from side to side in half-snarling, half-laughing protest, while the puppy crept closer, right up, jumping at the older dog's lifted wrinkling muzzle. Jock did not move away; he forced himself to remain still, because he could see us all watching. At last he lifted up his paw, pushed Bill over with it, pinned him down, examined him, then sniffed and licked him. He had accepted him, and Bill had found a substitute for his mother who was presumably mourning his loss. We were able to leave the child (as my mother kept calling him) in Jock's infinitely patient care. "You are such a good dog, Jock," she said, overcome by this scene, and the other touching scenes that followed, all marked by Jock's extraordinary forbearance for what was, and even I had to admit it, an intolerably destructive little dog.

Training became urgent. But this was not at all easy, due, like the business of getting a new puppy, to the inner nature of the family.

To take only one difficulty: dogs must be trained by their masters, they must owe allegiance to one person. And who was Jock to obey? And Bill: I was his master, in theory. In practice, Jock was. Was I to take over from Jock? But even to state it is to expose its absurdity: what I adored was the graceless puppy, and what did I want with a well-trained dog? Trained for *what*?

A watchdog? But all our dogs were watchdogs. "Natives"—such was the article of faith—were by nature scared of dogs. Yet everyone repeated stories about thieves poisoning fierce dogs, or making friends with them. So apparently no one really believed that watchdogs were any use. Yet every farm had its watchdog.

Throughout my childhood I used to lie in bed, the bush not fifty yards away all around the house, listening to the cry of the nightjar, the owls, the frogs and the crickets; to the tom-toms from the compound; to the mysterious rustling in the thatch over my head, or the long grass it had been cut from down the hill; to all the thousand noises of the night on the veld; and every one of these noises was marked also by the house dogs, who would bark and sniff and investigate and growl at all these; and also at starlight on the polished surface of a leaf, at the moon lifting itself over the mountains, at a branch cracking behind the house, at the first rim of hot red showing above the horizon—in short at anything and everything. Watchdogs, in my experience, were never asleep; but they were not so much a guard against thieves (we never had any thieves that I can remember) as a kind of instrument designed to measure or record the rustlings and movements of the African night that seemed to have an enormous life of its own, but a collective life, so that the falling of a stone, or a star shooting through the Milky Way, the grunt of a wild pig, and the wind rustling in the mealie field were all evidences and aspects of the same truth.

How did one "train" a watchdog? Presumably to respond only to the slinking approach of a human, black or white. What use is a watchdog otherwise? But even now, the most powerful memory of my childhood is of lying awake listening to the sobbing howl of a dog at the inexplicable appearance of the yellow face of the moon; of creeping to the window to see the long muzzle of a dog pointed black against a great bowl of stars. We needed no moon calendar with those dogs, who were like traffic in London: to sleep at all, one had to learn not to hear them. And if one did not hear them, one would not hear the stiff warning growl that (presumably) would greet a marauder.

At first Jock and Bill were locked up in the dining room at night. But there were so many stirrings and yappings and rushings from window to window after the rising sun or moon, or the black shadows which moved across whitewashed walls from the branches of the trees in the garden, that soon we could no longer stand the lack of sleep, and they were turned out onto the verandah. With many hopeful injunctions from my mother that they were to be "good dogs": which meant that they should ignore their real natures and sleep from sundown to sunup. Even then, when Bill was just out of puppyhood, they might be missing altogether in the early mornings. They would come guiltily up the road from the lands at breakfast time, their coats full of grass seeds, and we knew they had rushed down into the bush after an owl, or a grazing animal, and, finding themselves farther from home than they had expected in a strange nocturnal world, had begun nosing and sniffing and exploring in practice for their days of wildness soon to come.

So they weren't watchdogs. Hunting dogs perhaps? My brother undertook to train them, and we went through a long and absurd period of "Down, Jock," "To heel, Bill," while sticks of barley sugar balanced on noses, and paws were offered to be shaken by human hands, etc., etc. Through all this Jock suffered, bravely, but saying so clearly with every part of him that he would do anything to please my mother—he would send her glances half proud and half apologetic all the time my brother drilled him, that after an hour of training my brother would retreat, muttering that it was too hot, and Jock bounded off to lay his head on my mother's lap. As for Bill, he never achieved anything. Never did he sit still with the golden lumps on his nose, he ate them at once. Never did he stay to heel. Never did he remember what he was supposed to do with his paw when one of us offered him a hand. The truth was, I understood then, watching the training sessions, that Bill was stupid. I pretended of course that he despised being trained, he found it humiliating; and that Jock's readiness to go through with the silly business showed his lack of spirit. But alas, there was no getting around it, Bill simply wasn't very bright.

Meanwhile he had ceased to be a fat charmer; he had become a lean young dog, good-looking, with his dark brindled coat, and his big head that had a touch of Newfoundland. He had a look of puppy about him still. For just as Jock seemed born elderly, had respectable white hairs on his chin from the start; so Bill kept something young in him; he was a young dog until he died.

The training sessions did not last long. Now my brother said the dogs would be trained on the job: this to pacify my father, who kept saying that they were a disgrace and "not worth their salt."

There began a new regime, my brother, myself, and the two dogs. We set forth each morning, first my brother, earnest with responsibility, his rifle swinging in his hand, at his heels the two dogs. Behind this time-honored unit, myself, the girl, with no useful part to play in the serious masculine business, but necessary to provide admiration. This was a very old role for me indeed:

to walk away on one side of the scene, a small fierce girl, hungry to be part of it, but knowing she never would be, above all because the heart that had been put to pump away all her life under her ribs was not only critical and intransigent, but one which longed so bitterly to melt into loving acceptance. An uncomfortable combination, as she knew even then—yet I could not remove the sulky smile from my face. And it *was* absurd: there was my brother, so intent and serious, with Jock the good dog just behind him; and there was Bill the bad dog intermittently behind him, but more often than not sneaking off to enjoy some side path. And there was myself, unwillingly following, my weight shifting from hip to hip, bored and showing it.

I knew the route too well. Before we reached the sullen thickets of the bush where game and birds were to be found, there was a long walk up the back of the *kopje* through a luxuriant pawpaw grove, then through sweet potato vines that tangled our ankles, and tripped us, then past a rubbish heap whose sweet rotten smell was expressed in a heave of glittering black flies, then the bush itself. Here it was all dull green stunted trees, miles and miles of the smallish, flattish *msasa* trees in their second growth: they had all been cut for mine furnaces at some time. And over the flat ugly bush a large overbearing blue sky.

We were on our way to get food. So we kept saying. Whatever we shot would be eaten by "the house," or by the house's servants, or by "the compound." But we were hunting according to a newer law than the need for food, and we knew it and that was why we were always a bit apologetic about these expeditions, and why we so often chose to return empty-handed. We were hunting because my brother had been given a new and efficient rifle that would bring down (infallibly, if my brother shot) birds, large and small; and small animals, and very often large game like koodoo and sable. We were hunting because we owned a gun. And because we owned a gun, we should have hunting dogs, it made the business less ugly for some reason.

We were on our way to the Great Vlei, as distinct from the Big Vlei, which was five miles in the other direction. The Big Vlei was burnt out and eroded, and the waterholes usually dried up early. We did not like going there. But to reach the Great Vlei, which was beautiful, we had to go through the ugly bush "at the back of the *kopje.*" These ritual names for parts of the farm seemed rather to be names for regions in our minds. "Going to the Great Vlei" had a fairy-tale quality about it, because of having to pass through the region of sour ugly frightening bush first. For it did frighten us, always, and without reason: we felt it was hostile to us and we walked through it quickly, knowing that we were earning by this danger the water-running peace of the Great Vlei. It was only partly on our farm; the boundary between it and the next farm ran invisibly down its center, drawn by the eye from this outcrop to that big tree to that pothole to that antheap. It was a grassy valley with trees standing tall and spreading on either side of the watercourse, which was a half-mile width of intense greenness broken by sky-reflecting brown pools. This was old bush, these trees had never been cut: the Great Vlei had the inevitable look of natural bush—that no branch, no shrub, no patch of thorn, no outcrop, could have been in any other place or stood at any other angle.

The potholes here were always full. The water was stained clear brown, and the mud bottom had a small movement of creatures, while over the brown ripples skimmed blue jays and hummingbirds and all kinds of vivid flashing birds we did not know the names of. Along the lush verges lolled pink and white water lilies on their water-gemmed leaves.

This paradise was where the dogs were to be trained.

During the first holidays, long ones of six weeks, my brother was indefatigable, and we set off every morning after breakfast. In the Great Vlei I sat on a pool's edge under a thorn tree, and daydreamed to the tune of the ripples my swinging feet set moving across the water, while my brother, armed with the rifle, various sizes of stick, and lumps of sugar and biltong, put the two dogs through their paces. Sometimes, roused perhaps because the sun that fell through the green lace of the thorn was burning my shoulders, I turned to watch the three creatures, hard at work a hundred yards off on an empty patch of sand. Jock, more often than not, would be a dead dog, or his nose would be on his paws while his attentive eyes were on my brother's face. Or he would be sitting up, a dog statue, a golden dog, admirably obedient. Bill, on the other hand, was probably balancing on his spine, all four paws in the air, his throat back so that he was flat from nose to tail tip, receiving the hot sun equally over his brindled fur. I would hear, through my own lazy thoughts: "Good dog, Jock, yes, good dog. Idiot Bill, fool dog, why don't you work like Jock?" And my brother, his face reddened and sweaty, would come over to flop beside me, saying: "It's all Bill's fault, he's a bad example. And of course Jock doesn't see why he should work hard when Bill just plays all the time." Well, it probably was my fault that the training failed. If my earnest and undivided attention had been given, as I knew quite well was being demanded of me, to this business of the boy and the two dogs, perhaps we would have ended up with a brace of efficient and obedient animals, ever ready to die, to go to heel, and to fetch it. Perhaps.

By next holidays, moral disintegration had set in. My father complained the dogs obeyed nobody, and demanded training, serious and unremitting. My brother and I watched our mother petting Jock and scolding Bill, and came to an unspoken agreement. We set off for the Great Vlei but once there we loafed up and down the waterholes, while the dogs did as they liked, learning the joys of freedom.

The uses of water, for instance. Jock, cautious as usual, would test a pool with his paw, before moving in to stand chest deep, his muzzle just above the ripples, licking at them with small yaps of greeting or excitement. Then he walked gently in and swam up and down and around the brown pool in the green shade of the thorn trees. Meanwhile Bill would have found a shallow pool and be at his favorite game. Starting twenty yards from the rim of a pool he would hurl himself, barking shrilly, across the grass, then across the pool, not so much swimming across it as bouncing across it. Out the other side, up the side of the vlei, around in a big loop, then back, and around again . . . and again and again and again. Great sheets of brown water went up into the sky above him, crashing back into the pool while he barked his exultation.

That was one game. Or they chased each other up and down the four-mile-long valley like enemies, and when one caught the other there was a growling and a snarling and a fighting that sounded genuine enough. Sometimes we went to separate them, an interference they suffered; and the moment we let them go one or another would be off, his hindquarters pistoning, with the other in pursuit, fierce and silent. They might race a mile, two miles, before one leaped at the other's throat and brought him down. This game, too, over and over again, so that when they did go wild, we knew how they killed the wild pig and the buck they lived on.

On frivolous mornings they chased butterflies, while my brother and I dangled our feet in a pool and watched. Once, very solemnly, as it were in parody of the ridiculous business (now over, thank goodness) of "fetch it" and "to heel," Jock brought us in his jaws a big orange-and-black butterfly, the delicate wings all broken, and the orange bloom smearing his furry lips. He laid it in front of us, held the still fluttering creature flat with a paw, then lay down, his nose pointing at it. His brown eyes rolled up, wickedly hypocritical, as if to say: "Look, a butterfly, I'm a *good* dog." Meanwhile, Bill leaped and barked, a small brown dog hurling himself up into the great blue sky after floating colored wings. He had taken no notice at all of Jock's captive. But we both felt that Bill was much more likely than Jock to make such a seditious comment, and in fact my brother said: "Bill's corrupted Jock. I'm sure Jock would never go wild like this unless Bill was showing him. It's the blood coming out." But alas, we had no idea yet of what "going wild" could mean. For a couple of years yet it still meant small indisciplines, and mostly Bill's.

For instance, there was the time Bill forced himself through a loose plank in the door of the store hut, and there ate and ate, eggs, cake, bread, a joint of beef, a ripening guinea fowl, half a ham. Then he couldn't get out. In the morning he was a swollen dog, rolling on the floor and whining with the agony of his overindulgence. "Stupid dog, Bill, Jock would never do a thing like that, he'd be too intelligent not to know he'd swell up if he ate so much."

Then he ate eggs out of the nest, a crime for which on a farm a dog gets shot. Very close was Bill to this fate. He had actually been seen sneaking out of the chicken run, feathers on his nose, egg smear on his muzzle. And there was a mess of oozing yellow and white slime over the straw of the nests. The fowls cackled and raised their feathers whenever Bill came near. First he was beaten, by the cook, until his howls shook the farm. Then my mother blew eggs and filled them with a solution of mustard and left them in the nests. Sure enough, next morning, a hell of wild howls and shrieks: the beatings had taught him nothing. We went out to see a brown dog running and racing in agonized circles with his tongue hanging out, while the sun came up red over black mountains—a splendid backdrop to a disgraceful scene. My mother took the poor inflamed jaws and washed them in warm water and said: "Well now, Bill, you'd better learn, or it's the firing squad for you."

He learned, but not easily. More than once my brother and I, having arisen early for the hunt, stood in front of the house in the dawn hush, the sky a high, far gray above us, the edge of the mountains just reddening, the great spaces of silent bush full of the dark of the night. We sniffed at the small sharpness of the dew, and the heavy somnolent night-smell off the bush, felt the cold heavy air on our cheeks. We stood, whistling very low, so that the dogs would come from wherever they had chosen to sleep. Soon Jock would appear, yawning and sweeping his tail back and forth. No Bill—then we saw him, sitting on his haunches just outside the chicken run, his nose resting in a loop of the wire, his eyes closed in, yearning for the warm delicious ooze of fresh egg. And we would clap our hands over our mouths and double up with heartless laughter that had to be muffled so as not to disturb our parents.

On the mornings when we went hunting, and took the dogs, we knew that before we'd gone half a mile either Jock or Bill would dash off barking into the bush; the one left would look up from his own nosing and sniffing and rush away too. We would hear the wild double barking fade away with the crash and the rush of the two bodies, and, often enough, the subsidiary rushings away of other animals who had been asleep or resting and just waiting until we had gone away. Now we could look for something to shoot, which probably we would never have seen at all had the dogs been there. We could settle down for long patient stalks, circling around a grazing koodoo, or a couple of duikers. Often enough we would lie watching them for hours, afraid only that Jock and Bill would come back, putting an end to this particular pleasure. I remember once we caught a glimpse of a duiker grazing on the edge of a farmland that was still half dark. We got onto our stomachs and wriggled through the long grass, not able to see if the duiker was still there. Slowly the field opened up in front of us, a heaving mass of big black clods. We carefully raised our heads, and there, at the edge of the clod sea, a couple of arm's lengths away, were three little duikers, their heads turned away from us to where the sun was about to rise. They were three black, quite motionless silhouettes. Away over the other side of the field, big clods became tinged with reddish gold. The earth turned so fast toward the sun that the light came running from the tip of one clod to the next across the field like flames leaping along the tops of long grasses in front of a strong wind. The light reached the duikers and outlined them with warm gold. They were three glittering little beasts on the edge of an imminent sunlight. They then began to butt each other, lifting their hindquarters and bringing down their hind feet in clicking leaps like dancers. They tossed their sharp little horns and made short half-angry rushes at each other. The sun was up. Three little buck danced on the edge of the deep green bush where we lay hidden, and there was a weak sunlight warming their gold hides. The sun separated itself from the line of the hills, and became calm and big and yellow; a warm yellow color filled the world, the little buck stopped dancing, and walked slowly off, frisking their white tails and tossing their pretty heads, into the bush.

We would never have seen them at all, if the dogs hadn't been miles away.

In fact, all they were good for was their indiscipline. If we wanted to be sure of something to eat, we tied ropes to the dogs' collars until we actually heard the small clink-clink-clink of guinea fowl running through the bush. Then we untied them. The dogs were at once off after the birds, who rose clumsily into the air, looking like flying shawls that sailed along, just above grass level, with the dogs' jaws snapping underneath them. All they wanted was to land unobserved in the long grass, but they were always forced to rise painfully into the trees, on their weak wings. Sometimes, if it was a large flock, a dozen trees might be dotted with the small black shapes of guinea fowl outlined against dawn or evening skies. They watched the barking dogs, took no notice of us. My brother or I—for even I could hardly miss in such conditions—planted our feet wide for balance, took aim at a chosen bird and shot. The carcass fell into the worrying jaws beneath. Meanwhile a second bird would be chosen and shot. With the two birds tied together by their feet, the rifle, justified by utility, proudly swinging, we would saunter back to the house through the sun-scented bush of our enchanted childhood. The dogs, for politeness' sake, escorted us part of the way home, then went off hunting on their own. Guinea fowl were very tame sport for them, by then.

It had come to this, that if we actually wished to shoot something, or to watch animals, or even to take a walk through bush where every animal for miles had not been scared away, we had to lock up the dogs before we left, ignoring their whines and their howls. Even so, if let out too soon, they would follow. Once, after we had walked six miles or so, a leisurely morning's trek toward the mountains, the dogs arrived, panting, happy, their pink wet tongues hot on our knees and forearms, saying how delighted they were to have found us. They licked and wagged for a few moments—then off they went, they vanished, and did not come home until evening. We were worried. We had not known that they went so far from the farm by themselves. We spoke of how bad it would be if they took to frequenting other farms—perhaps other chicken runs? But it was all too late. They were too old to train. Either they had to be kept permanently on leashes, tied to trees outside the house, and for dogs like these it was not much better than being dead—either that, or they must run free and take their chances.

We got news of the dogs in letters from home and it was increasingly bad. My brother and I, at our respective boarding schools where we were supposed to be learning discipline, order, and sound characters, read: "The dogs went away a whole night, they only came back at lunchtime." "Jock and Bill have been three days and nights in the bush. They've just come home, worn out." "The dogs must have made a kill this time and stayed beside it like wild animals, because they came home too gorged to eat, they just drank a lot of water and fell off to sleep like babies. . . ." "Mr. Daly rang up yesterday to say he saw Jock and Bill hunting along the hill behind his house. They've been chasing his oxen. We've got to beat them when they get home because if they don't learn, they'll get themselves shot one of these dark nights. . . ."

They weren't there at all when we went home for the holidays. They had already been gone for nearly a week. But, or so we flattered ourselves, they sensed our return, for back they came, trotting gently side by side up the hill in the moonlight, two low black shapes moving above the accompanying black shapes of their shadows, their eyes gleaming red as the shafts of lamplight struck them. They greeted us, my brother and me, affectionately enough, but at once went off to sleep. We told ourselves that they saw us as creatures like them, who went off on long exciting hunts: but we knew it was sentimental nonsense, designed to take the edge off the hurt we felt because our animals, *our* dogs, cared so little about us. They went away again that night, or rather, in the first dawnlight. A week later they came home. They smelled foul, they must have been chasing a skunk or a wildcat. Their fur was matted with grass seeds and their skin lumpy with ticks. They drank water heavily, but refused food: their breath was foetid with the smell of meat.

They lay down to sleep and remained limp while we, each taking an animal, its sleeping head heavy in our laps, removed ticks, grass seeds, black-jacks. On Bill's forepaw was a hard ridge which I thought was an old scar. He sleep-whimpered when I touched it. It was a noose of plaited grass, used by Africans to snare birds. Luckily it had snapped off. "Yes," said my father, "that's how they'll end, both of them, they'll die in a trap, and serve them both right, they won't get any sympathy from me!"

We were frightened into locking them up for a day; but we could not stand their misery, and let them out again.

We were always springing gametraps of all kinds. For the big buck, the sable, the eland, the koodoo, the Africans bent a sapling across a path, held it by light string, and fixed on it a noose of heavy wire cut from a fence. For the smaller buck there were low traps with nooses of fine baling wire or plaited tree fiber. And at the corners of the cultivated fields or at the edges of waterholes, where the birds and hares came down to feed, were always a myriad tiny tracks under the grass, and often across every track hung a small noose of plaited grass. Sometimes we spent whole days destroying these snares.

In order to keep the dogs amused, we took to walking miles every day. We were exhausted, but they were not, and simply went off at night as well. Then we rode bicycles as fast as we could along the rough farm tracks, with the dogs bounding easily beside us. We wore ourselves out, trying to please Jock and Bill, who, we imagined, knew what we were doing and were trying to humor us. But we stuck at it. Once, at the end of a glade, we saw the skeleton of a large animal hanging from a noose. Some African had forgotten to visit his traps. We showed the skeleton to Jock and Bill, and talked and warned and threatened, almost in tears, because human speech was not dogs' speech. They sniffed around the bones, yapped a few times up into our faces—out of politeness, we felt; and were off again into the bush.

At school we heard that they were almost completely wild. Sometimes they came home for a meal, or a day's sleep, "treating the house," my mother complained, "like a hotel."

Then fate struck, in the shape of a bucktrap.

One night, very late, we heard whining, and went out to greet them. They were crawling toward the front door, almost on their bellies. Their ribs stuck out, their coats stared, their eyes shone unhealthily. They fell on the food we gave them; they were starved. Then on Jock's neck, which was bent over the food bowl, showed the explanation: a thick strand of wire. It was not solid wire, but made of a dozen twisted strands, and had been chewed through, near the collar. We examined Bill's mouth: chewing the wire through must have taken a long time, days perhaps: his gums and lips were scarred and bleeding, and his teeth were worn down to stumps, like an old dog's teeth. If the wire had not been stranded, Jock would have died in the trap. As it was, he fell ill, his lungs were strained, since he had been half strangled with the wire. And Bill could no longer chew properly, he ate uncomfortably, like an old person. They stayed at home for weeks, reformed dogs, barked around the house at night, and ate regular meals.

Then they went off again, but came home more often than they had. Jock's lungs weren't right: he would lie out in the sun, gasping and wheezing, as if trying to rest them. As for Bill, he could only eat soft food. How, then, did they manage when they were hunting?

One afternoon we were shooting, miles from home, and we saw them. First we heard the familiar excited yapping coming toward us, about two miles off. We were in a large vlei, full of tall whitish grass which swayed and bent along a fast regular line: a shape showed, it was a duiker, hard to see until it was close because it was reddish brown in color, and the vlei had plenty of the pinkish feathery grass that turns a soft intense red in strong light. Being near sunset, the pale grass was on the verge of being invisible, like wires of white light; and the pink grass flamed and glowed; and the fur of the little buck shone red. It swerved suddenly. Had it seen us? No, it was because of Jock who had made a quick maneuvering turn from where he had been lying in the pink grass, to watch the buck, and behind it, Bill, pistoning along like a machine. Jock, who could no longer run fast, had turned the buck into Bill's jaws. We saw Bill bound at the little creature's throat, bring it down and hold it until Jock came in to kill it: his own teeth were useless now.

We walked over to greet them, but with restraint, for these two growling snarling creatures seemed not to know us, they raised eyes glazed with savagery, as they tore at the dead buck. Or rather, as Jock tore at it. Before we went away we saw Jock pushing over lumps of hot steaming meat toward Bill, who otherwise would have gone hungry.

They were really a team now; neither could function without the other. So we thought.

But soon Jock took to coming home from the hunting trips early, after one or two days, and Bill might stay out for a week or more. Jock lay watching the bush, and when Bill came, he licked his ears and face as if he had reverted to the role of Bill's mother.

Once I heard Bill barking and went to see. The telephone line ran through a vlei near the house to the farm over the hill. The wires hummed and sang and twanged. Bill was underneath the wires, which were a good fifteen feet over his head, jumping and barking at them: he was playing, out of exuberance, as he had done when a small puppy. But now it made me sad, seeing the strong dog playing all alone, while his friend lay quiet in the sun, wheezing from damaged lungs.

And what did Bill live on, in the bush? Rats, bird's eggs, lizards, anything *soft* enough? That was painful, too, thinking of the powerful hunters in the days of their glory.

Soon we got telephone calls from neighbors: Bill dropped in, he finished off the food in our dog's bowl. . . . Bill seemed hungry, so we fed him. . . . Your dog Bill is looking very thin, isn't he? . . . Bill was around our chicken run—I'm sorry, but if he goes for the eggs, then . . .

Bill had puppies with a pedigreed bitch fifteen miles off: her owners were annoyed: Bill was not good enough for them, and besides there was the question of his "bad blood." All the puppies were destroyed. He was hanging around the house all the time, although he had been beaten, and they had even fired shots into the air to scare him off. Was there anything we could do to keep him at home? they asked; for they were tired of having to keep their bitch tied up.

No, there was nothing we could do. Rather, there was nothing we *would* do; for when Bill came trotting up from the bush to drink deeply out of Jock's bowl, and to lie for a while nose to nose with Jock, well, we could have caught him and tied him up, but we did not. "He won't last long anyway," said my father. And my mother told Jock that he was a sensible and intelligent dog; for she again sang praises of his nature and character, just as if he had never spent so many glorious years in the bush.

I went to visit the neighbor who owned Bill's mate. She was tied to a post on the verandah. All night we were disturbed by a wild sad howling from the bush, and she whimpered and strained at her rope. In the morning I walked out into the hot silence of the bush, and called to him: Bill, Bill, it's me. Nothing, no sound. I sat on the slope of an antheap in the shade, and waited. Soon Bill came into view, trotting between the trees. He was very thin. He looked gaunt, stiff, wary—an old outlaw, afraid of traps. He saw me, but stopped about twenty yards off. He climbed halfway up another anthill and sat there in full sunlight, so I could see the harsh patches on his coat. We sat in silence, looking at each other. Then he lifted his head and howled, like the howl dogs give to the full moon, long, terrible, lonely. But it was morning, the sun calm and clear, and the bush without mystery. He sat and howled his heart out, his muzzle pointed away toward where his mate was chained. We could hear the faint whimperings she made, and the clink of her metal dish as she moved about. I couldn't stand it. It made my flesh cold, and I could see the hairs standing up on my forearm. I went over to him and sat by him and put my arm around his neck as once, so many years ago, I had put my arm around his mother that moonlit night before I stole her puppy away from her. He put his muzzle on my forearm and whimpered, or rather cried. Then he lifted it and howled. . . . "Oh, my God, Bill, don't do that, please don't, it's not the slightest use, please, dear Bill. . . ." But he went on, until suddenly he leaped up in the middle of a howl, as if his pain were too strong to contain in sitting, and he sniffed at me, as if to say: That's you, is it, well, good-bye—then he turned his wild head to the bush and trotted away.

Very soon he was shot, coming out of a chicken run early one morning with an egg in his mouth.

Jock was quite alone now. He spent his old age lying in the sun, his nose pointed out over the miles and miles of bush between our house and the mountains where he had hunted all those years with Bill. He was really an old dog, his legs were stiff, and his coat was rough, and he wheezed and gasped. Sometimes, at night, when the moon was up, he went out to howl at it, and we would say: He's missing Bill. He would come back to sit at my mother's knee, resting his head so that she could stroke it. She would say: "Poor old Jock, poor old boy, are you missing that bad dog Bill?"

Sometimes, when he lay dozing, he started up and went trotting on his stiff old legs through the house and the outhouses, sniffing everywhere and anxiously whining. Then he stood, upright, one paw raised, as he used to do when he was young, and gazed over the bush and softly whined. And we would say: "He must have been dreaming he was out hunting with Bill."

He got ill. He could hardly breathe. We carried him in our arms down the hill into the bush, and my mother stroked and patted him while my father put the gun barrel to the back of his head and shot him.

ALISTAIR MACLEOD

Winter Dog

I am writing this in December. In the period close to Christmas, and three days after the first snowfall in this region of southwestern Ontario. The snow came quietly in the night or in the early morning. When we went to bed near midnight, there was none at all. Then early in the morning we heard the children singing Christmas songs from their rooms across the hall. It was very dark and I rolled over to check the time. It was four-thirty A.M. One of them must have awakened and looked out the window to find the snow and then eagerly awakened the others. They are half crazed by the promise of Christmas, and the discovery of the snow is an unexpected giddy surprise. There was no snow promised for this area, not even yesterday.

"What are you doing?" I call, although it is obvious.

"Singing Christmas songs," they shout back with equal obviousness, "because it snowed."

"Try to be quiet," I say, "or you'll wake the baby."

"She's already awake," they say. "She's listening to our singing. She likes it. Can we go out and make a snowman?"

I roll from my bed and go to the window. The neighboring houses are muffled in snow and silence and there are as yet no lights in any of them. The snow has stopped falling and its whitened quietness reflects the shadows of the night.

"This snow is no good for snowmen," I say. "It is too dry."

"How can snow be dry?" asks a young voice. Then an older one says, "Well, then can we go out and make the first tracks?"

41

They take my silence for consent and there are great sounds of rustling and giggling as they go downstairs to touch the light switches and rummage and jostle for coats and boots.

"What on earth is happening?" asks my wife from her bed. "What are they doing?"

"They are going outside to make the first tracks in the snow," I say. "It snowed quite heavily last night."

"What time is it?"

"Shortly after four-thirty."

"Oh."

We ourselves have been nervous and restless for the past weeks. We have been troubled by illness and uncertainty in those we love far away on Canada's east coast. We have already considered and rejected driving the fifteen hundred miles. Too far, too uncertain, too expensive, fickle weather, the complications of transporting Santa Claus.

Instead, we sleep uncertainly and toss in unbidden dreams. We jump when the phone rings after ten P.M. and are then reassured by the distant voices.

"First of all, there is nothing wrong," they say. "Things are just the same."

Sometimes we make calls ourselves, even to the hospital in Halifax, and are surprised at the voices which answer.

"I just got here this afternoon from Newfoundland. I'm going to try to stay a week. He seems better today. He's sleeping now."

At other times we receive calls from farther west, from Edmonton and Calgary and Vancouver. People hoping to find objectivity in the most subjective of situations. Strung out in uncertainty across the time zones from British Columbia to Newfoundland.

Within our present city, people move and consider possibilities:

If he dies tonight we'll leave right away. Can you come?

We will have to drive as we'll never get air reservations at this time.

I'm not sure if my car is good enough. I'm always afraid of the mountains near Cabano.

If we were stranded in Rivière du Loup we would be worse off than being here. It would be too far for anyone to come and get us.

My car will go but I'm not so sure I can drive it all the way. My eyes are not so good anymore, especially at night in drifting snow.

Perhaps there'll be no drifting snow.

There's always drifting snow.

We'll take my car if you'll drive it. We'll have to drive straight through.

John phoned and said he'll give us his car if we want it or he'll drive—either his own car or someone else's.

He drinks too heavily, especially for long-distance driving, and at this time of year. He's been drinking ever since this news began.

He drinks because he cares. It's just the way he is.

Not everybody drinks.

Not everybody cares, and if he gives you his word, he'll never drink until he gets there. We all know that.

But so far nothing has happened. Things seem to remain the same.

Through the window and out on the white plane of the snow, the silent, laughing children now appear. They move in their muffled clothes like mummers on the whitest of stages. They dance and gesture noiselessly, flopping their arms in parodies of heavy, happy, earthbound birds. They have been warned by the eldest to be aware of the sleeping neighbors so they cavort only in pantomime, sometimes raising mittened hands to their mouths to suppress their joyous laughter. They dance and prance in the moonlight, tossing snow in one another's direction, tracing out various shapes and initials, forming lines which snake across the previously unmarked whiteness. All of it in silence, unknown and unseen and unheard to the neighboring world. They seem unreal even to me, their father, standing at his darkened window. It is almost as if they have danced out of the world of folklore like happy elves who cavort and mimic and caper through the private hours of this whitened dark, only to vanish with the coming of the morning's light and leaving only the signs of their activities behind. I am tempted to check the recently vacated beds to confirm what perhaps I think I know.

Then out of the corner of my eye I see him. The golden collie-like dog.

He appears almost as if from the wings of the stage or as a figure newly noticed in the lower corner of a winter painting. He sits quietly and watches the playful scene before him and then, as if responding to a silent invitation, bounds into its midst. The children chase him in frantic circles, falling and rolling as he doubles back and darts and dodges between their legs and through their outstretched arms. He seizes a mitt loosened from its owner's hand, and tosses it happily in the air and then snatches it back into his jaws an instant before it reaches the ground and seconds before the tumbling bodies fall on the emptiness of its expected destination. He races to the edge of the scene and lies facing them, holding the mitt tantalizingly between his paws, and then as they dash towards him, he leaps forward again, tossing and catching it before him and zigzagging through them as the Sunday football player might return the much sought-after ball. After he has gone through and eluded them all, he looks back over his shoulder and again, like an elated athlete, tosses the mitt high in what seems like an imaginary end zone. Then he seizes it once more and lopes in a wide circle around his pursuers, eventually coming closer and closer to them until once more their stretching hands are able to actually touch his shoulders and back and haunches, although he continues always to wriggle free. He is touched but never captured, which is the nature of the game. Then he is gone. As suddenly as he came. I strain my eyes in the direction of the adjoining street, towards the house where I have often seen him, always within a yard enclosed by woven links of chain. I see the flash of his silhouette, outlined perhaps against the snow or the light cast by the street lamps or the moon. It arcs upwards and seems to hang for an instant high above the top of the fence and then it descends on the other side. He lands on his shoulder in a fluff of snow and with a half roll regains his feet and vanishes within the shadow of his owner's house.

"What are you looking at?" asks my wife.

"That golden collie-like dog from the other street was just playing with the children in the snow."

"But he's always in that fenced-in yard."

"I guess not always. He jumped the fence just now and went back in. I guess the owners and the rest of us think he's fenced in but he knows he's not. He probably comes out every night and leads an exciting life. I hope they don't see his tracks or they'll probably begin to chain him."

"What are the children doing?"

"They look tired now from chasing the dog. They'll probably soon be back in. I think I'll go downstairs and wait for them and make myself a cup of coffee."

"Okay."

I look once more towards the fenced-in yard but the dog is nowhere to be seen.

I first saw such a dog when I was twelve and he came as a pup of about two months in a crate to the railroad station which was about eight miles from where we lived. Someone must have phoned or dropped in to say: "Your dog's at the station."

He had come to Cape Breton in response to a letter and a check which my father had sent to Morrisburg, Ontario. We had seen the ads for "cattle collie dogs" in the *Family Herald,* which was the farm newspaper of the time, and we were in need of a good young working dog.

His crate was clean and neat and there was still a supply of dog biscuits with him and a can in the corner to hold water. The baggage handlers had looked after him well on the trip east, and he appeared in good spirits. He had a white collar and chest and four rather large white paws and a small white blaze on his forehead. The rest of him was a fluffy, golden brown, although his eyebrows and the tips of his ears as well as the end of his tail were darker, tingeing almost to black. When he grew to his full size the blackish shadings became really black, and although he had the long, heavy coat of a collie, it was in certain areas more gray than gold. He was also taller than the average collie and with a deeper chest. He seemed to be at least part German shepherd.

It was winter when he came and we kept him in the house where he slept behind the stove in a box lined with an old coat. Our other dogs slept mostly in the stables or outside in the lees of woodpiles or under porches or curled up on the banking of the house. We seemed to care more for him because he was smaller and it was winter and he was somehow like a visitor, and also because more was expected of him and also perhaps because we had paid money for him and thought about his coming for some time—like a "planned" child. Skeptical neighbors and relatives who thought the idea of paying money for a dog was rather exotic or frivolous would ask: "Is that your Ontario dog?" or "Do you think your Ontario dog will be any good?"

He turned out to be no good at all and no one knew why. Perhaps it was because of the suspected German shepherd blood. But he could not "get the hang of it." Although we worked him and trained him as we had other dogs, he seemed always to bring panic instead of order and to make things worse instead of better. He became a "head dog," which meant that instead of working behind the cattle he lunged at their heads, impeding them from any forward motion and causing them to turn in endless, meaningless bewildered circles. On the few occasions when he did go behind them, he was "rough," which meant that instead of being a floating, nipping, suggestive presence, he actually bit them and caused them to gallop, which was another sin. Some-times in the summer the milk cows suffering from his misunderstood pursuit would jam pell-mell into the stable, tossing their wide horns in fear, and with their great sides heaving and perspiring while down their legs and tails the wasted milk ran in rivulets mingling with the blood caused by his slashing wounds. He was, it was said, "worse than nothing."

Gradually everyone despaired, although he continued to grow gray and golden and was, as everyone agreed, a "beautiful-looking dog."

He was also tremendously strong and in the winter months I would hitch him to a sleigh which he pulled easily and willingly on almost any kind of surface. When he was harnessed I used to put a collar around his neck and attach a light line to it so that I might have some minimum control over him, but it was hardly ever needed. He would pull home the Christmas tree or the bag of flour or the deer which was shot far back in the woods, and when we visited our winter snares he would pull home the gunnysacks which contained the partridges and rabbits which we gathered. He would also pull us, especially on the flat windswept stretches of land beside the sea. There the snow was never really deep and the water that oozed from a series of freshwater springs and ponds contributed to a glaze of ice and crisply crusted snow which the sleigh runners seemed to sing over without ever breaking through. He would begin with an easy lope and then increase his swiftness until both he and the sleigh seemed to touch the surface at only irregular intervals. He would stretch out then with his ears flattened against his head and his shoulders bunching and contracting in the rhythm of his speed. Behind him on the sleigh we would cling tenaciously to the wooden slats as the particles of ice and snow dislodged by his nails hurtled towards our faces. We would avert our heads and close our eyes and the wind stung so sharply that the difference between freezing and burning could not be known. He would do that until late in the afternoon when it was time to return home and begin our chores.

On the sunny winter Sunday that I am thinking of, I planned to visit my snares. There seemed no other children around that afternoon and the adults were expecting relatives. I harnessed the dog to the sleigh, opened the door of the house and shouted that I was going to look at my snares. We began to climb the hill behind the house on our way to the woods when we looked back and out towards the sea. The "big ice," which was what we called the major pack of drift ice, was in solidly against the shore and stretched out beyond the range of vision. It had not been "in" yesterday, although for the past weeks we had seen it moving offshore, sometimes close and sometimes distant, depending on the winds and tides. The coming of the big ice marked the official beginning of the coldest part of winter. It was mostly drift ice from the Arctic and Labrador, although some of it was freshwater ice from the estuary of the St. Lawrence. It drifted down with the dropping temperatures, bringing its own mysterious coldness and stretching for hundreds of miles in craters and pans, sometimes in grotesque shapes and sometimes in dazzling architectural forms. It was blue and white and sometimes gray and at other times a dazzling emerald green.

The dog and I changed our direction towards the sea, to find what the ice might yield. Our land had always been beside the sea and we had always gone towards it to find newness and the extraordinary; and over the years we, as others along the coast, had found quite a lot, although never the pirate chests of gold which were supposed to abound or the reasons for the mysterious lights that our elders still spoke of and persisted in seeing. But kegs of rum had washed up, and sometimes bloated horses and various fishing paraphernalia and valuable timber and furniture from foundered ships. The door of my room was apparently the galley door from a ship called the *Judith Franklin*, which was wrecked during the early winter in which my great-grandfather was building his house. My grandfather told of how they had heard the cries and seen the lights as the ship neared the rocks and of how they had run down in the dark and tossed lines to the people while tying themselves to trees on the shore. All were saved, including women clinging to small children. The next day the builders of the new house went down to the shore and salvaged what they could from the wreckage of the vanquished ship. A sort of symbolic marriage of the new and the old: doors and shelving, stairways, hatches, wooden chests and trunks and various glass figurines and lanterns which were miraculously never broken.

People came too. The dead as well as the living. Bodies of men swept overboard and reported lost at sea and the bodies of men still crouched within the shelter of their boats' broken bows. And sometimes in late winter young sealers who had quit their vessels would walk across the ice and come to our doors. They were usually very young—some still in their teens—and had signed on for jobs they could not or no longer wished to handle. They were often disoriented and did not know where they were, only that they had seen land and had decided to walk towards it. They were often frostbitten and with little money and uncertain as to how they might get to Halifax.

The dog and I walked towards the ice upon the sea. Sometimes it was hard to "get on" the ice, which meant that at the point where the pack met the shore there might be open water or irregularities caused by the indentations of the coastline or the workings of the tides and currents, but for us on that day there was no difficulty at all. We were on easily and effortlessly and enthused in our new adventure. For the first mile there was nothing but the vastness of the white expanse. We came to a clear stretch where the ice was as smooth and unruffled as that of an indoor arena and I knelt on the sleigh while the dog loped easily along. Gradually the ice changed to an uneven terrain of pressure ridges and hummocks, making it impossible to ride farther; and then suddenly, upon rounding a hummock, I saw the perfect seal. At first I thought it was alive, as did the dog who stopped so suddenly in his tracks that the sleigh almost collided with his legs. The hackles on the back of his neck rose and he growled in the dangerous way he was beginning to develop. But the seal was dead, yet facing us in a frozen perfection that was difficult to believe. There was a light powder of snow over its darker coat and a delicate rime of frost still formed the outline of its whiskers. Its eyes were wide open and it stared straight ahead towards the land. Even now in memory it seems more real than reality—as if it were transformed by frozen art into something more arresting than life itself. The way the sudden seal in the museum exhibit freezes your eyes with the touch of truth. Immediately I wanted to take it home.

It was frozen solidly in a base of ice so I began to look for something that might serve as a pry. I let the dog out of his harness and hung the sleigh and harness on top of the hummock to mark the place and began my search. Some distance away I found a pole about twelve feet long. It is always surprising to find such things on the ice field but they are, often amazingly, there, almost in the same way that you might find a pole floating in the summer ocean. Unpredictable but possible. I took the pole back and began my work. The dog went off on explorations of his own.

Although it was firmly frozen, the task did not seem impossible and by inserting the end of the pole under first one side and then the other and working from the front to the back, it was possible to cause a gradual loosening. I remember thinking how very warm it was because I was working hard and perspiring heavily. When the dog came back he was uneasy, and I realized it was starting to snow a bit but I was almost done. He sniffed with disinterest at the seal and began to whine a bit, which was something he did not often do. Finally, after another quarter of an hour, I was able to roll my trophy onto the sleigh and with the dog in harness we set off. We had gone perhaps two hundred yards when the seal slid free. I took the dog and the sleigh back and once again managed to roll the seal on. This time I took the line from the dog's collar and tied the seal to the sleigh, reasoning that the dog would go home anyway and there would be no need to guide him. My fingers were numb as I tried to fasten the awkward knots and the dog began to whine and rear. When I gave the command he bolted forward and I clung at the back of the sleigh to the seal. The snow was heavier now and blowing in my face but we were moving rapidly and when we came to the stretch of arena-like ice we skimmed across it almost like an iceboat, the profile of the frozen seal at the front of the sleigh like those figures at the prows of Viking ships. At the very end of the smooth stretch, we went through. From my position at the end of the sleigh I felt him drop almost before I saw him, and rolled backwards seconds before the sleigh and seal followed him into the blackness of the water. He went under once carried by his own momentum but surfaced almost immediately with his head up and his paws scrambling at the icy, jagged edge of the hole; but when the weight and momentum of the sleigh and its burden struck, he went down again, this time out of sight.

I realized we had struck a "seam" and that the stretch of smooth ice had been deceivingly and temporarily joined to the rougher ice near the shore and now was in the process of breaking away. I saw the widening line before me and jumped to the other side just as his head miraculously came up once more. I lay on my stomach and grabbed his collar in both my hands and then in a moment of panic did not know what to do. I could feel myself sliding towards him and the darkness of the water and was aware of the weight that pulled me forward and down. I was also aware of his razor-sharp claws flailing violently before my face and knew that I might lose my eyes. And I was aware that his own eyes were bulging from their sockets and that he might think I was trying to choke him and might lunge and slash my face with his teeth in desperation. I knew all of this but somehow did nothing about it; it seemed almost simpler to hang on and be drawn into the darkness of the gently slopping water, seeming to slop gently in spite of all the agitation. Then suddenly he was free, scrambling over my shoulder and dragging the sleigh behind him. The seal surfaced again, buoyed up perhaps by the physics of its frozen body or the nature of its fur. Still looking more genuine than it could have in life, its snout and head broke the open water and it seemed to look at us curiously for an instant before it vanished permanently beneath the ice. The loose and badly tied knots had apparently not held when the sleigh was in a near-vertical position and we were saved by the ineptitude of my own numbed fingers. We had been spared for a future time.

He lay gasping and choking for a moment, coughing up the icy salt water, and then almost immediately his coat began to freeze. I realized then how cold I was myself and that even in the moments I had been lying on the ice, my clothes had begun to adhere to it. My earlier heated perspiration was now a cold rime upon my body and I imagined it outlining me there, beneath my clothes, in a sketch of frosty white. I got on the sleigh once more and crouched low as he began to race towards home. His coat was freezing fast, and as he ran the individual ice-coated hairs began to clack together like rhythmical castanets attuned to the motion of his body. It was snowing quite heavily in our faces now and it seemed to be approaching dusk, although I doubted if it were so on the land which I could now no longer see. I realized all the obvious things I should have considered earlier. That if the snow was blowing in our faces, the wind was off the land, and if it was off the land, it was blowing the ice pack back out to sea. That was probably one reason why the seam had opened. And also that the ice had only been in one night and had not had a chance to set. I realized other things as well. That it was the time of the late afternoon when the tide was falling. That no one knew where we were. That I had said we were going to look at snares, which was not where we had gone at all. And I remembered now that I had received no answer even to that misinformation, so perhaps I had not even been heard. And also if there was drifting snow like this on land, our tracks would by now have been obliterated.

We came to a rough section of ice: huge slabs on their sides and others piled one on top of the other as if they were in some strange form of storage. It was no longer possible to ride the sleigh but as I stood up I lifted it and hung on to it as a means of holding on to the dog. The line usually attached to his collar had sunk with the vanished seal. My knees were stiff when I stood up; and deprived of the windbreak effect which the dog had provided, I felt the snow driving full into my face, particularly my eyes. It did not merely impede my vision, the way distant snow flurries might, but actually entered my eyes, causing them to water and freeze nearly shut. I was aware of the weight of ice on my eyelashes and could see them as they gradually lowered and became heavier. I did not remember ice like this when I got on, although I did not find that terribly surprising. I pressed the soles of my numbed feet firmly down upon it to try to feel if it was moving out, but it was impossible to tell because there was no fixed point of reference. Almost the sensation one gets on a conveyor belt at airports or on escalators; although you are standing still you recognize motion, but should you shut your eyes and be deprived of sight, even that recognition may become ambiguously uncertain.

The dog began to whine and to walk around me in circles, binding my legs with the traces of the harness as I continued to grasp the sleigh. Finally I decided to let him go as there seemed no way to hold him and there was nothing else to do. I unhitched the traces and doubled them up as best I could and tucked them under the backpad of his harness so they would not drag behind him and become snagged on any obstacles. I did not take off my mitts to do so as I was afraid I would not be able to get them back on. He vanished into the snow almost immediately.

The sleigh had been a gift from an uncle, so I hung on to it and carried it with both hands before me like an ineffectual shield against the wind and snow. I lowered my head as much as I could and turned it sideways so the wind would beat against my head instead of directly into my face. Sometimes I would turn and walk backwards for a few steps. Although I knew it was not the wisest thing to do, it seemed at times the only way to breathe. And then I began to feel the water sloshing about my feet.

Sometimes when the tides or currents ran heavily and the ice began to separate, the water that was beneath it would well up and wash over it almost as if it were reflooding it. Sometimes you could see the hard ice clearly beneath the water but at other times a sort of floating slush was formed mingling with snow and "slob" ice which was not yet solid. It was thick and dense and soupy and it was impossible to see what lay beneath it. Experienced men on the ice sometimes carried a slender pole so they could test the consistency of the footing which might or might not lie before them, but I was obviously not one of them, although I had a momentary twinge for the pole I had used to dislodge the seal. Still, there was nothing to do but go forward.

When I went through, the first sensation was almost of relief and relaxation for the water initially made me feel much warmer than I had been on the surface. It was the most dangerous of false sensations for I knew my clothes were becoming heavier by the second. I clung to the sleigh somewhat as a raft and lunged forward with it in a kind of up-and-down swimming motion, hoping that it might strike some sort of solidity before my arms became so weighted and sodden that I could no longer lift them. I cried out then for the first time into the driving snow.

He came almost immediately, although I could see he was afraid and the slobbing slush was up to his knees. Still, he seemed to be on some kind of solid footing for he was not swimming. I splashed towards him and when almost there, desperately threw the sleigh before me and lunged for the edge of what seemed like his footing, but it only gave way as if my hands were closing on icy insubstantial porridge. He moved forward then, although I still could not tell if what supported him would be of any use to me. Finally I grasped the breast strap of his harness. He began to back up then, and as I said, he was tremendously strong. The harness began to slide forward on his shoulders but he continued to pull as I continued to grasp and then I could feel my elbows on what seemed like solid ice and I was able to hook them on the edge and draw myself, dripping and soaking, like another seal out of the black water and onto the whiteness of the slushy ice. Almost at once my clothes began to freeze. My elbows and knees began to creak when I bent them as if I were a robot from the realm of science fiction and then I could see myself clothed in transparent ice as if I had been coated with shellac or finished with clear varnish.

As the fall into the winter sea had at first seemed ironically warm, so now my garments of ice seemed a protection against the biting wind, but I knew it was a deceptive sensation and that I did not have much time before me. The dog faced into the wind and I followed him. This time he stayed in sight, and at times even turned back to wait for me. He was cautious but certain and gradually the slush disappeared, and although we were still in water, the ice was hard and clear beneath it. The frozen heaviness of my clothes began to weigh on me and I could feel myself, ironically, perspiring within my suit of icy armor. I was very tired, which I knew was another dangerous sensation. And then I saw the land. It was very close and a sudden surprise. Almost like coming upon a stalled and unexpected automobile in a highway's winter storm. It was only yards away, and although there was no longer any ice actually touching the shore, there were several pans of it floating in the region between. The dog jumped from one to the other and I followed him, still clutching the sleigh, and missing only the last pan which floated close to the rocky shore. The water came only to my waist and I was able to touch the bottom and splash noisily on land. We had been spared again for a future time and I was never to know whether he had reached the shore himself and come back or whether he had heard my call against the wind.

We began to run towards home and the land lightened and there were touches of evening sun. The wind still blew but no snow was falling. Yet when I looked back, the ice and the ocean were invisible in the swirling squalls. It was like looking at another far and distant country on the screen of a snowy television.

I became obsessed, now that I could afford the luxury, with not being found disobedient or considered a fool. The visitors' vehicles were still in the yard so I imagined most of the family to be in the parlor or living room, and I circled the house and entered through the kitchen, taking the dog with me. I was able to get upstairs unnoticed and get my clothes changed and when I came down I mingled with everybody and tried to appear as normal as I could. My own family was caught up with the visitors and only general comments came my way. The dog, who could not change his clothes, lay under the table with his head on his paws and he was also largely unnoticed. Later as the ice melted from his coat, a puddle formed around him, which I casually mopped up. Still later someone said, "I wonder where that dog has been, his coat is soaking wet." I was never to tell anyone of the afternoon's experience or that he had saved my life.

Two winters later I was sitting at a neighbor's kitchen table when I looked out the window and saw the dog as he was shot. He had followed my father and also me and had been sitting rather regally on a little hill beside the house and I suppose had presented an ideal target. But he had moved at just the right or wrong time and instead of killing him the high-powered bullet smashed into his shoulder. He jumped into the air and turned his snapping teeth upon the wound, trying to bite the cause of the pain he could not see. And then he turned towards home, unsteady but still strong on his three remaining legs.

No doubt he felt, as we all do, that if he could get home he might be saved, but he did not make it, as we knew he could not, because of the amount of blood on the snow and the wavering pattern of his three-legged tracks. Yet he was, as I said, tremendously strong and he managed almost three quarters of a mile. The house he sought must have been within his vision when he died for we could see it quite clearly when we came to his body by the roadside. His eyes were open and his tongue was clenched between his teeth and the little blood he had left dropped red and black on the winter snow. He was not to be saved for a future time anymore.

I learned later that my father had asked the neighbor to shoot him and that we had led him into a kind of ambush. Perhaps my father did so because the neighbor was younger and had a better gun or was a better shot. Perhaps because my father did not want to be involved. It was obvious he had not planned on things turning out so messy.

The dog had become increasingly powerful and protective, to the extent that people were afraid to come into the yard. And he had also bitten two of the neighbor's children and caused them to be frightened of passing our house on their journeys to and from school. And perhaps there was also the feeling in the community that he was getting more than his share of the breeding: that he traveled farther than other dogs on his nightly forays and that he fought off and injured the other smaller dogs who might compete with him for female favors. Perhaps there was fear that his dominance and undesirable characteristics did not bode well for future generations.

This has been the writing down of a memory triggered by the sight of a golden dog at play in the silent snow with my own excited children. After they came in and had their hot chocolate, the wind began to blow; and by the time I left for work, there was no evidence of their early-morning revels or any dog tracks leading to the chain-link fence. The "enclosed" dog looked impassively at me as I brushed the snow from the buried windshield. What does he know? he seemed to say.

The snow continues to drift and to persist as another uncertainty added to those we already have. Should we be forced to drive tonight, it will be a long, tough journey into the wind and the driving snow which is pounding across Ontario and Quebec and New Brunswick and against the granite coast of Nova Scotia. Should we be drawn by death, we might well meet our own. Still, it is only because I am alive that I can even consider such possibilities. Had I not been saved by the golden dog, I would not have these tight concerns or children playing in the snow or of course these memories. It is because of him that I have been able to come this far in time.

It is too bad that I could not have saved him as well and my feelings did him little good as I looked upon his bloodied body there beside the road. It was too late and out of my control and even if I had known the possibilities of the future it would not have been easy.

He was with us only for a while and brought his own changes, and yet he still persists. He persists in my memory and in my life and he persists physically as well. He is there in this winter storm. There in the golden-gray dogs with their black-tipped ears and tails, sleeping in the stables or in the lees of woodpiles or under porches or curled beside the houses which face towards the sea.

LYNNE SHARON SCHWARTZ

Sound Is Second Sight

A farmer of austere habits lived some ways from town in a ramshackle farmhouse, and he looked as forlorn and ramshackle as his house with its weather-beaten wooden slats and cracked shingles. Tall, taciturn, dressed in drab, loose-fitting clothes, he would gaze down at the ground as he walked. He carried a gnarled walking stick and let his mud-colored hair droop around his face, and so he appeared older than he was. Actually he was not old at all, nor crabbed as some believed, merely a solitary. Out of habit he kept his distance, and the people of the town thought it best to keep their distance as well.

His only companion was a greyhound dog, slender, blond, and frolicsome after the manner of her kind. She was fiercely devoted to the farmer and, unlike the townspeople, not frightened off by his gnarled walking stick or his silence or his gaunt, shielded face. Outdoors, in the fields or in town, the farmer and his dog were silent and undemonstrative, yet they had the air of creatures very much attuned and in comfort together. The townspeople were puzzled by the dog. Not a farm dog by any means. Not a dog that could be useful. Her very prettiness and uselessness seemed out of place in that stony countryside, and when she strutted down the main street she drew hostile glances. Rumors sprang up that the dog, for all her prettiness, had sinister powers; possibly even the farmer did. Her origins were mysterious: all anyone knew was that after vanishing for several days the farmer had returned with the dog perched in the front seat of his truck, sniffing in her disdainful way.

In fact he had found her in a nearby and larger market town. The dogcatcher had seemed hesitant to sell her: a well-meaning fellow, he hinted that the dog had brought bad luck to former owners, best leave her to her fate. But the farmer had a sudden craving for the pretty creature, whom he had spied standing in a corner of the yard apart from the pack of other animals; she reminded him of himself, isolated, the butt of nasty tall tales, perhaps even ill treated when young, as he had been. She had an unearthly howl, the dogcatcher also warned, wild enough to rouse the dead. But she made no sound at all in her corner of the cluttered yard, so the farmer paid no heed and bought her.

Evenings, alone in the house, they romped together in front of the fire, the farmer bellowing and laughing, the dog yelping and snapping playfully. She barked seldom. Her bark was indeed loud and piercing, almost a howl, and it was as if she held it in out of deference to human ears. Despite his carelessness about the outside of the house, the farmer kept the inside pleasant and tidy: the wood floors, with their wide planks, were swept clean, the logs piled near the fireplace had a sweet smoky smell, and the soft cushions on the floor were inviting. Besides all that, the dog got good food to eat; she made a contented, obedient housemate.

And then one day after spending almost a week away at the nearby market town, the farmer and his dog came home with a bright-eyed wife, who also excited curiosity among the townspeople, and a few of the more outspoken wondered slyly whether he had found her in the same mysterious way as he had found the dog. She was small and rounded, with rosy cheeks, milky skin, and black curls. She smiled indulgently at the confusion of the dog, who bristled when she stroked her blond fur. She laughed at the farmer's long shield of hair and brushed it off his really rather handsome face with a tender gesture. Nor was she much bothered by the ramshackle appearance of the house, for she saw that the inside was cheerful and tidy. The vegetable garden behind the house was her delight: under the farmer's care, tomatoes and beans and peas were flourishing in such abundance she could hardly pick them fast enough. The people of the town, who could find nothing to fault her with since she was unfailingly courteous and proper, were astonished that so sprightly a creature could be happy living with the taciturn farmer, yet she appeared quite

58

happy. When the three of them walked down the main street, it was the farmer and his wife, now, who were silent and undemonstrative, yet seemed very much attuned and in comfort together. The dog fretted alongside. Occasionally she gave out her lacerating howl, which made passersby start, and startled even the farmer, who hastened to quiet her. The dog was not neglected—the farmer still stroked her and spoke kindly to her and took her along daily to the fields, but in the nature of things it was not the same.

Evenings, in the broken-down house, the farmer and his wife lay on rugs in front of the fire, while the dog fussed in a cold corner, ignoring their beckonings. The farmer had never been so happy in his life. He had grown up lonely and lived lonely, and, given the awkward shyness that no one till now had found appealing, had never expected to be other than lonely till the day he died. He was no less astonished than the townspeople that this pretty, loving wife welcomed his company and settled so easily into his house. It was a gift he could not fathom, dared not even question, and while it did not change his appearance—he still dressed in drab, nondescript clothing—or the appearance of his house—still forlorn and ramshackle—he felt himself a changed man. For this his heart was full of gratitude to his wife, and in his innocence, he envisioned living with her serenely to the end of his days.

What the farmer loved most about his wife was not her prettiness or her sweet nature, but her voice. It was like music; it could sing out low like a cello or high like a flute, and flit through the whole range in between. When she called to him in the fields, midday, her pure long-lasting note cut a path through the air. When she rushed to greet him or tell him news of the garden her voice was full, impelled by energy. And when she lay with him before the fire its timbre was more than deep—dense, as if the sound itself might be grasped and held, caressed. To the farmer her voice expressed all moods and possibilities; living with her after living silent for so long with the dog was like embracing another dimension, having a sixth sense.

The dog clearly did not love the sound of the wife's voice, although it was never anything but gentle and cajoling, in a futile effort to win her trust. The dog still bristled at her touch and took food grudgingly from her hands. If the farmer whistled her over while his wife was nearby, she hung back and needed to be coaxed. And when the two were alone, the dog would snap at her skirts, or snarl, or set up a howling the wife could not stop. In the garden she stepped across the wife's path to trip her up. In the kitchen she knocked over a tureen of soup—the wife had to jump aside so as not to be scalded. She reproached the dog softly, in dismay more than anger. The wife did not mention these incidents to the farmer—they seemed, after all, so petty. She was a tolerant soul who took what came along. She too had been lonely and ill treated as a child, and also, because of her prettiness, suspected of evils she did not commit, so she found herself fortunate in her new life; her thoughts were rooted in its daily pleasures. She was hardly one to brood over the fussing of a dog: surely the creature would come round in time.

This happy period in the farmer's life lasted for three years, and then the wife took sick with a mysterious illness, not painful but enervating. It had never been seen before in that region, and there seemed nothing anyone could do to save her. The farmer fed her with his own hands and pleaded with her to rally, if only for his sake, but she shook her head gravely, like one already past the threshold. In despair he wanted to take the very strength from his own body and feed it to her. But she was doomed. Stunned with grief, he buried her some distance from the house. After a time, though his grief remained acute, there mingled with it a feeling that, just as he had grown up lonely and lived lonely, so he was to remain lonely till the day he died, and that the time with his wife was a fleeting interlude given to him unfathomably. He sought solace in the company of his dog, who became frolicsome and good-tempered as in the early days. When they walked together in the town they once again had the air of creatures very much attuned and in comfort together. As for the townspeople, after paying their condolences they kept their distance as before.

One moonlit summer night as he lay awake with the windows wide open, the farmer heard his wife's voice calling his name far out across the fields. He rushed to the window and called back into the night. Over and over her voice called, now closer, now farther off, as if it were drifting about, seeking him in the dark but powerless to find the way. Then the dog went to the window and began to bark. As the shrill howling persisted, the voice came closer and closer until at last it was there in the room, that voice he used to feel was almost palpable. The farmer was overjoyed. All night long his wife's voice talked with him and kept him company, while the dog crouched silent in a corner. They talked, as always, of small daily things—the farm and the town, the vegetable garden—and of love. The range and timbre of the wondrous voice were unaltered by death. As day broke she left.

She came often after that. Each time, the farmer passed the whole night with her, talking of daily things and feeling joyful, if baffled, at this great gift given back to him, at least in part. Whenever her voice sounded from far off, the dog would go to the open window to help her find her way. For only that horrible howling, puncturing the night like an arrow, could guide her; the farmer's own, human, voice was of no avail.

For a long time the farmer lived thus, enjoying the mild companionship of the dog by day and the beloved voice of his dead wife by night. But the dog was growing old. During their walks through the fields he noticed that she trudged ever more slowly, breathing with effort. Yet fiercely devoted, she strove to keep up with him, would not desert his path. One day the farmer sensed she was no longer behind him; he went back a short distance and found her collapsed on the ground. He carried her back to the house, settled her on a rug in front of the fire, and gave her water from his cupped hand till she closed her eyes and died. He buried her under a tree near the barn.

Now the farmer suffered an excruciating loneliness. In daylight he walked alone and in the dark he knew the agony of hearing his wife's voice calling out there, unable to find him without the howling to guide her. Many nights the voice called, raw with pleading, while the farmer shouted out the window to no avail. As the voice despaired and faded he would shut the window with bitter tears in his throat. The voice stopped seeking him. He pondered whether it was worse to have no gifts at all, or to have gifts given and so cruelly withdrawn.

Then one night as he lay sleepless, there came the awful voice of the dog, howling far across the fields. The farmer rushed to the window. The dog's voice came steadily closer, finding its way with ease. Although he could neither stroke her nor play with her, and although she kept silent once in the room, the farmer took comfort and rested more calmly, feeling her presence. He reflected, though, how strange it was to have as companion a voice that had best not make itself heard, for very ugliness.

On a moonlit night when the dog had come, the farmer was sitting at the window when he heard his wife's voice again, calling over the fields. He leaped to his feet and called back as loudly as he could. Suddenly from right beside him came the lacerating howl of the dog, slicing into the still night. He longed to hug her in gratitude, but there was nothing to the touch. Just as before, the dog's voice howled until the wife's voice found its way into the room. The farmer was trembling with emotion; he longed to embrace her, but again he had to content himself with what he was given.

His wife's voice was joyous too; but scarcely had she begun to speak of this recovery of each other than her voice was overpowered by the dog's insistent howl. Sternly, the farmer commanded the animal to be silent, but for the first time she refused to obey him. The wife's voice grew higher, urgent: she was calling for help. Her words became screams, then pure shrieks of sound swooping through the air; meanwhile the howling reached an unearthly pitch, filling up the room, exulting in its rough, wild fury kept at bay so long. The farmer veered about in a frenzy of helplessness, arms outstretched and flailing for something to touch. The wife's terrified shrieks got short and staccato, like the plucking of a taut string against the prolonged howls tearing into the dark. Madly, the farmer raced about, hands plunging and stabbing at the empty night. Till at last there was one drawn-out, descending note wailed in unison with the dog's rapid panting, and then both voices sank and subsided, and there was nothing.

When the townspeople came to investigate they found the farmer gone, the house abandoned. The bedroom was all in disorder, as if a rampaging wind had whipped things up and left them to fall where they might. From near the window, reported some, came now and then a hoarse, panting noise, like a beast out of breath.

T. CORAGHESSAN BOYLE

Heart of a Champion

We scan the cornfields and the wheat-
fields winking gold and goldbrown and yellowbrown in the midday sun, on up
the grassy slope to the barn redder than red against the sky bluer than blue,
across the smooth stretch of the barnyard with its pecking chickens, and then
right on up to the screen door at the back of the house. The door swings open,
a black hole in the sun, and Timmy emerges with his corn-silk hair, corn-fed
face. He is dressed in crisp overalls, striped T-shirt, stubby blue Keds. There'd
have to be a breeze—and we're not disappointed—his clean fine cup-cut hair
waves and settles as he scuffs across the barnyard and out to the edge of the
field. The boy stops there to gaze out over the nodding wheat, eyes unsquinted
despite the sun, and blue as tinted lenses. Then he brings three fingers to his
lips in a neat triangle and whistles long and low, sloping up sharp to cut off
at the peak. A moment passes: he whistles again. And then we see it—way out
there at the far corner of the field—the ripple, the dashing furrow, the blur
of the streaking dog, white chest, flashing feet.

They're in the woods now. The boy whistling, hands in pockets, kicking
along with his short baby-fat strides; the dog beside him wagging the white tip
of her tail like an all-clear flag. They pass beneath an arching old black-barked
oak. It creaks. And suddenly begins to fling itself down on them: immense,
brutal: a panzer strike. The boy's eyes startle and then there's a blur, a smart
snout clutching his pantleg, the thunderblast of the trunk, the dust and
spinning leaves. "Golly, Lassie . . . I didn't even see it," says the boy, sitting

safe in a mound of moss. The collie looks up at him (the svelte snout, the deep gold logician's eyes) and laps at his face.

And now they're down by the river. The water is brown with angry suppurations, spiked with branches, fence posts, tires and logs. It rushes like the sides of boxcars—and chews deep and insidious at the bank under Timmy's feet. The roar is like a jetport: little wonder he can't hear the dog's warning bark. We watch the crack appear, widen to a ditch; then the halves separating (snatch of red earth, writhe of worm), the poise and pitch, and Timmy crushing down with it. Just a flash—but already he's way downstream, his head like a plastic jug, dashed and bobbed, spinning toward the nasty mouth of the falls. But there's the dog—fast as a struck match—bursting along the bank all white and gold melded in motion, hair sleeked with the wind of it, legs beating time to the panting score. . . . Yet what can she hope to do?—the current surges on, lengths ahead, sure bet to win the race to the falls. Timmy sweeps closer, sweeps closer, the falls loud now as a hundred timpani, the war drums of the Sioux, Africa gone bloodlust mad! The dog strains, lashing over the wet earth like a whipcrack; strains every last ganglion and dendrite until finally she draws abreast of him. Then she's in the air, the foaming yellow water. Her paws churning like pistons, whiskers chuffing with the exertion—oh, the roar!—and there, she's got him, her sure jaws clamping down on the shirt collar, her eyes fixed on the slip of rock at the falls' edge. Our blood races, organs palpitate. The black brink of the falls, the white paws digging at the rock—and then they're safe. The collie sniffs at Timmy's inert little form, nudges his side until she manages to roll him over. Then clears his tongue and begins mouth-to-mouth.

Night: the barnyard still, a bulb burning over the screen door. Inside, the family sits at dinner, the table heaped with pork chops, mashed potatoes, applesauce and peas, a pitcher of clean white milk. Home-baked bread. Mom and Dad, their faces sexless, bland, perpetually good-humored and sympathetic, poise stiff-backed, forks in midswoop, while Timmy tells his story: "So then Lassie grabbed me by the collar and golly, I musta blanked out cause I don't remember anything more till I woke up on the rock—"

"Well I'll be," says Mom.

"You're lucky you've got such a good dog, son," says Dad, gazing down at the collie where she lies patiently, snout over paw, tail wapping the floor. She is combed and washed and fluffed, her lashes mascaraed and curled, her chest and paws white as dish soap. She looks up humbly. But then her ears leap, her neck jerks round—and she's up at the door, head cocked, alert. A high yipping yowl like a stuttering fire whistle shudders through the room. And then another. The dog whines.

"Darn," says Dad. "I thought we were rid of those coyotes—next thing they'll be after the chickens again."

The moon blanches the yard, leans black shadows on the trees, the barn. Upstairs in the house, Timmy lies sleeping in the pale light, his hair fastidiously mussed, his breathing gentle. The collie lies on the throw rug beside the bed. We see that her eyes are open. Suddenly she rises and slips to the window, silent as a shadow. And looks down the long elegant snout to the barnyard below, where the coyote slinks from shade to shade, a limp pullet dangling from his jaws. He is stunted, scabious, syphilitic, his forepaw trap-twisted, his eyes running. The collie whimpers softly from behind the window. And the coyote stops in mid-trot, frozen in a cold shard of light, ears high on his head. Then drops the chicken at his feet, leers up at the window and begins a soft, crooning, sad-faced song.

The screen door slaps behind Timmy as he bolts from the house, Lassie at his heels. Mom's head emerges on the rebound. "Timmy!" (He stops as if jerked by a rope, turns to face her.) "You be home before lunch, hear?"

"Sure, Mom," he says, already spinning off, the dog by his side. We get a close-up of Mom's face: she is smiling a benevolent boys-will-be-boys smile. Her teeth are perfect.

In the woods Timmy steps on a rattler and the dog bites its head off. "Gosh," he says. "Good girl, Lassie." Then he stumbles and slips over an embankment, rolls down the brushy incline and over a sudden precipice, whirling out into the breathtaking blue space like a sky diver. He thumps down on a narrow ledge twenty feet below. And immediately scrambles to his feet, peering timorously down the sheer wall to the heap of bleached bone at its base. Small stones break loose, shoot out like asteroids. Dirt slides begin. But Lassie yarps reassuringly from above, sprints back to the barn for a winch and cable, hoists the boy to safety.

On their way back for lunch Timmy leads them through a still and leaf-darkened copse. We remark how odd it is that the birds and crickets have left off their cheeping, how puzzling that the background music has begun to rumble so. Suddenly, round a bend in the path before them, the coyote appears. Nose to the ground, intent, unaware of them. But all at once he jerks to a halt, shudders like an epileptic, the hackles rising, tail dipping between his legs. The collie too stops short, just yards away, her chest proud and shaggy and white. The coyote cowers, bunches like a cat, glares at them. Timmy's face sags with alarm. The coyote lifts his lip. But then, instead of leaping at her adversary's throat, the collie prances up and stretches her nose out to him, her eyes soft as a leading lady's, round as a doe's. She's balsamed and perfumed; her full chest tapers a lovely S to her sleek haunches and sculpted legs. He is puny, runted, half her size, his coat like a discarded doormat. She circles him now, sniffing. She whimpers, he growls: throaty and tough, the bad guy. And stands stiff while she licks at his whiskers, noses at his rear, the bald black scrotum. Timmy is horror-struck. Then, the music sweeping off in birdtrills of flute and harpstring, the coyote slips round behind, throat thrown back, black lips tight with anticipation.

"What was she doing, Dad?" Timmy asks over his milk and sandwich.

"The sky was blue today, son," he says.

"But she had him trapped, Dad—they were stuck together end to end and I thought we had that wicked old coyote but then she went and let him go—what's got into her, Dad?"

"The barn was red today, son," he says.

Late afternoon: the sun mellow, more orange than white. Purpling clots of shadow hang from the branches, ravel out from the tree trunks. Bees and wasps and flies saw away at the wet full-bellied air. Timmy and the dog are far out beyond the north pasture, out by the old Indian burial mound, where the boy stoops now to search for arrowheads. Oddly, the collie is not watching him: instead she's pacing the crest above, whimpering softly, pausing from time to time to stare out across the forest, her eyes distant and moonstruck. Behind her, storm clouds squat on the horizon like dark kidneys or brains.

We observe the wind kicking up: leaves flapping like wash, saplings quivering, weeds whipping. It darkens quickly now, the clouds scudding low and smoky over the treetops, blotting the sun from view. Lassie's white is whiter than ever, highlighted against the dark horizon, the wind-whipped hair foaming around her. Still she doesn't look down at the boy: he digs, dirty-kneed, stoop-backed, oblivious. Then the first fat random drops, a flash, the volcanic blast of thunder. Timmy glances over his shoulder at the noise: he's just in time to watch the scorched pine plummeting toward the constellated freckles in the center of his forehead. Now the collie turns—too late!—the swoosh-whack! of the tree, the trembling needles. She's there in an instant, tearing at the green welter, struggling through to his side. He lies unconscious in the muddying earth, hair artistically arranged, a thin scratch painted on his cheek. The trunk lies across the small of his back like the tail of a brontosaurus. The rain falls.

Lassie tugs doggedly at a knob in the trunk, her pretty paws slipping in the wet—but it's no use—it would take a block and tackle, a crane, an army of Bunyans to shift that stubborn bulk. She falters, licks at his ear, whimpers. We observe the troubled look in her eye as she hesitates, uncertain, priorities warring: should she stand guard, or dash for help? The decision is sure and swift—her eyes firm with purpose and she's off like a shard of shrapnel, already up the hill, shooting past the dripping trees, over the river, already cleaving through the high wet banks of wheat.

A moment later she's dashing through the puddled and rain-screened barnyard, barking right on up to the back door, where she pauses to scratch daintily, her voice high-pitched and insistent. Mom swings open the door and the collie pads in, claws clacking on the shiny linoleum. "What is it girl? What's the matter? Where's Timmy?"

"Yarf! Yarfata-yarf-yarf!"

"Oh my! Dad! Dad, come quickly!"

Dad rushes in, his face stolid and reassuring as the Lincoln Memorial. "What is it, dear? . . . Why, Lassie?"

"Oh Dad, Timmy's trapped under a pine tree out by the old Indian burial ground—"

"Arpit-arp."

"—a mile and a half past the north pasture."

Dad is quick, firm, decisive. "Lassie—you get back up there and stand watch over Timmy . . . Mom and I'll go for Doc Walker. Hurry now!"

The collie hesitates at the door: "Rarf-arrar-ra!"

"Right," says Dad. "Mom, fetch the chain saw."

We're back in the woods now. A shot of the mud-running burial mound locates us—yes, there's the fallen pine, and there: Timmy. He lies in a puddle, eyes closed, breathing slow. The hiss of the rain is loud as static. We see it at work: scattering leaves, digging trenches, inciting streams to swallow their banks. It lies deep now in the low areas, and in the mid areas, and in the high areas. Then a shot of the dam, some indeterminate (but short we presume) distance off, the yellow water churning over its lip like urine, the ugly earthen belly distended, blistered with the pressure. Raindrops pock the surface like a plague.

Suddenly the music plunges to those thunderous crouching chords— we're back at the pine now—what is it? There: the coyote. Sniffing, furtive, the malicious eyes, the crouch and slink. He stiffens when he spots the boy— but then slouches closer, a rubbery dangle drooling from between his mis-meshed teeth. Closer. Right over the prone figure now, those ominous chords setting up ominous vibrations in our bowels. He stoops, head dipping between his shoulders, irises caught in the corners of his eyes: wary, sly, predatory: the vulture slavering over the fallen fawn.

But wait!—here comes the collie, sprinting out of the wheatfield, bounding rock to rock across the crazed river, her limbs contourless with sheer speed and purpose, the music racing in a mad heroic prestissimo!

* * *

The jolting front seat of a Ford. Dad, Mom and the Doctor, all dressed in rain slickers and flap-brimmed rain hats, sitting shoulder to shoulder behind the clapping wipers. Their jaws set with determination, eyes aflicker with pioneer gumption.

The coyote's jaws, serrated grinders, work at the tough bone and cartilage of Timmy's left hand. The boy's eyelids flutter with the pain, and he lifts his head feebly—but almost immediately it slaps down again, flat and volitionless, in the mud. At that instant Lassie blazes over the hill like a cavalry charge, show-dog indignation aflame in her eyes. The scrag of a coyote looks up at her, drooling blood, choking down frantic bits of flesh. Looks up at her from eyes that go back thirty million years, savage and bloodlustful and free. Looks up unmoved, uncringing, the bloody snout and steady yellow eyes less a physical challenge than philosophical. We watch the collie's expression alter in mid-bound—the look of offended AKC morality giving way, dissolving. She skids to a halt, drops her tail and approaches him, a buttery gaze in her golden eyes. She licks the blood from his lips.

The dam. Impossibly swollen, rain festering the yellow surface, a hundred new streams a minute rampaging in, the pressure of those millions of gallons hard-punching those millions more. There! the first gap, the water spewing out, a burst bubo. And now the dam shudders, splinters, falls to pieces like so much cheap pottery. The roar is devastating.

The two animals start at that terrible rumbling, and still working their gummy jaws, they dash up the far side of the hill. We watch the white-tipped tail retreating side by side with the hacked and tick-blistered gray one—wagging like raggled banners as they disappear into the trees at the top of the rise. We're left with a tableau: the rain, the fallen pine in the crotch of the valley's V, the spot of the boy's head. And that chilling roar in our ears. Suddenly the wall of water appears at the far end of the V, smashing through the little declivity like a god-sized fist, prickling with shattered trunks and boulders, grinding along like a quick-melted glacier, like planets in collision.

We cut to Timmy: eyes closed, hair plastered, his left arm looking as though it should be wrapped in butcher's paper. How? we wonder. How will they ever get him out of this? But then we see them—Mom, Dad and the Doctor— struggling up that same rise, rushing with the frenetic music now, the torrent seething closer, booming and howling. Dad launches himself in full charge down the hillside—but the water is already sweeping over the fallen pine, lifting it like paper—there's a blur, a quick clip of a typhoon at sea (is that a flash of blond hair?), and it's over. The valley is filled to the top of the rise, the water ribbed and rushing like the Colorado in adolescence. Dad's pants are wet to the crotch.

Mom's face, the Doctor's. Rain. And then the opening strains of the theme song, one violin at first, swelling in mournful mid-American triumph as the full orchestra comes in, tearful, beautiful, heroic, sweeping us up and out of the dismal rain, back to the golden wheatfields in the midday sun. The boy cups his hands to his mouth and pipes: "Laahh-sie! Laahh-sie!" And then we see it—way out there at the end of the field—the ripple, the dashing furrow, the blur of the streaking dog, white chest, flashing feet.

MADISON SMARTT BELL

Black and Tan

Up until his family died out from under him, Peter Jackson used to grow tobacco. His place was a long ways out from town, up on the hillside above Keyhole Lake—you had a nice view of the lake from up there. It was forty or fifty acres that he owned, and an easement down to the lakeshore. Maybe a third of that land was too rocky to farm, and another third was grown up in cedars, fine old trees he never cared to cut down. There was the place his house was set, and what was left you could grow tobacco on. He did just about all the work himself, hiring a couple of hands only once in a while—at cutting and drying time, for instance.

"Tobacco," he was known to say, and then he'd pause and spit a splash of it to one side of the courthouse steps. "Tobacco, now, that's eight days a week. . . ." Like most farmers, he'd come to town on Saturday, visit the Co-op or the Standard Farm Store, maybe get a few things at the supermarket. When he got done his errands, he might wander through the courthouse square and talk a while with this one and that one. One Sunday a month, more or less, he'd drive in with his wife and they'd both go to church, and two, three times a year, he'd come in by himself and get falling-down drunk. At the end of his evening he'd just go to sleep in the cab of his truck, then in the morning hitch himself straight and drive on out home. Never caused anybody any more trouble than that. Later on, after he'd got the dogs, he cut out the drinking and the church along with it, right about at the same time.

A steady fellow, then, and mostly known as a hard worker. Quiet, never had a whole lot to say, but what he said was reasonable. Whatever he told you he would do would get done, if nothing serious kept him from it. That was the kind of thing any of us might have said of him, supposing we'd been asked.

Amy was the name of his wife, who'd been a Puckett before she married. Never raised any objection to living so far out from town. She was fond of the woods and fond of the lake, so maybe that made up for whatever loneliness there may have been to it. They didn't have any neighbors near, though a couple of Nashville people had built summer houses on the far side of the lake. Like Peter Jackson, Amy was a worker; she grew a garden, put up food for the winter. They were both in the garden picking tomatoes on the late September evening when she all of a sudden fell over dead. Heart attack was what did her in, faster than a bullet. Jackson said he spent a minute twirling around to see where the shot might have come from, before he went to her. They had been working opposite ends of the row, and she was already getting cold by the time he got to her, he said. And she not more than fifty, fifty-five.

Jackson wasn't as broke up about it as you could have thought a man might be, losing his wife in her prime that way. Or if he was, he didn't show it much. There was a good turnout at the funeral, for Amy was well liked around the town. The old hens were forever coming up to him and saying how *terrible* they thought it was, and every time he told them, *No. No, it ain't so terrible, not really. If her time had come to go, then better she went quickly, with no pain.* So everybody said how well he was bearing it. And then his children started to die.

They had two children, son and daughter; June and Richard were their names. Both of them looked fair to rise above their raising, both going on past high school, which neither of their parents had. The boy was putting himself through U.T. Knoxville on an ROTC scholarship, and then one summer he got himself killed in a training accident, some kind of a foolish, avoidable thing. Well, he went quick, too, did Richard. It put Peter Jackson back at the graveside just under a year after they buried Amy. He was dry-eyed again but tight around the mouth, and whatever people spoke to him, he didn't have much to say back. June stood with him the whole time through, hanging onto his elbow and kind of fending people off. It might have been she was already sick herself by that time, though nobody knew anything of it yet.

June was the older of the two; she'd gone to nursing school in Nashville and kept living there once she was done, had herself a job at the Baptist Hospital. After she got that cancer she stayed on as a patient a while but there wasn't anything they could do for her, and in the end she came home to Keyhole Lake to die. Peter Jackson nursed her right on through it, never had any other help at all. It wasn't quick or anything like it; it kept on for five or six months, and you didn't have to hear a whole lot about it to know there must have been pain to spare.

It was mid-March or so when they buried her; there'd been a hard winter and there was still some thin snow on the ground. Peter Jackson stood alone this time, grim and silent for most part. Nobody had a lot to say to him, either. He had gone lean under his hardship, but he was still a fine-looking man, and people said he looked well in his funeral suit. Of course he'd had his share of opportunity to get the hang of wearing it. As a young man he'd had deep red hair, and now it was rust-colored, patched with gray. His eyebrows were thick and bushy, turning out in devilish points at the sides, and underneath, his deep-set eyes surprised you with the brightness of their green. This time he wouldn't turn back from the grave once they had filled it, and after a minute the priest walked over to stand with him. Shoulder to shoulder, they looked like a matched pair, Mr. Chalk in his black cassock and Jackson in the suit.

Mr. Chalk was fairly new to the town; he'd done a lot of work in the prisons and he wasn't known for wasting his words. A few people crept up near, to listen for what he'd find to say to a man like Jackson, which was this:

"Well, you're still here," Mr. Chalk was heard to say.

Jackson spat on the snow and said, "What of it?"

"You're surviving," Mr. Chalk said. "Today's today and then there'll be tomorrow."

"That's right, and it's a curse," Peter Jackson said, and turned on the priest with the tunnels of his eyes. "I been cursed with survival," he said then, speaking in a different tone than before, as if, after all, it were a new discovery.

That spring he didn't plant tobacco. Round about the time he should have been, he was driving all around the county looking at dogs and going clear to Nashville too. He looked at all the good-sized breeds: collies, Great

Danes, German shepherds. There was a story that went along with it, which got out and made the rounds. Funny how many people got to hear of it, because it was a personal kind of a thing for a man like Peter Jackson to go telling.

It appeared that when Peter Jackson was born, his parents had a big old dog that they let live in the house and all. Jackson, himself, didn't recall what kind of a dog it might have been, and there wasn't anybody for him to ask, because his parents were long dead and he never had any brothers or sisters. Anyway, they had worried the dog might eat the baby when they brought him home, but it turned out the opposite; the dog loved the child. So much so that in the long run they trusted the dog to watch the baby. They might go out and work their land or even leave the place altogether for a short spell, knowing the dog would see everything was all right. This all happened at that same place at Keyhole Lake, and one time, so the story went, little Peter Jackson, only two or three years old, let himself out of the house somehow and went wandering all the way down to the shore. This old dog went right along with him, saw he didn't drown himself or get any other kind of hurt, and in the end when the child was tired, the dog brought him on back home.

So Peter Jackson spent that spring driving practically all over creation looking at different kinds of dogs, and when people wondered how he could be so choosy when he didn't even appear to know what it was he wanted, that was the tale he would tell them. Finally he ended up at the place of this woman way out the Lebanon Road who bred Dobermans. He went out and looked at her dogs a while and went home and came back another day and told her, "Let me have two of them."

"What do you mean, 'two'?" she said. "Do you even know if you want one? Which two did you have in mind, anyway?"

"Pick me out two likely ones," Peter Jackson said. "A male and a female. Ones that ain't too close related." And the next thing anybody knew, he was breeding Dobermans himself. Rebuilt his old drying barn into kennels and fenced in some pens out in front of it. Told anybody who cared to know that Dobermans weren't naturally mean like they had the name for, but that they were smart and naturally loyal and would be inclined to protect you and your house and land without any special training. Although he could supply the training, too, if that was what you wanted. He started selling a good many as pets and maybe an equal number as guard dogs. That was about the time the K-9 patrols came into style, so he drew business from the police, and in a year or so people were coming good long distances, even from out of state at times, to buy their dogs from Peter Jackson. He was thought to be so good at it that eventually people began to bring him dogs that other trainers couldn't handle. Which may have been what first gave him the notion of taking in those boys.

Maynard Ferguson, the county judge, was the man Jackson had to go see about this idea. In Franklin the county judge doubles up as juvenile judge, too, so Ferguson had the management of whatsoever people under seventeen or eighteen couldn't seem to keep themselves out of trouble. Of which there were always a few that he couldn't quite figure out what to do with. It was kind of left-handed work for him to be doing, anyway. Still, he was leery of Jackson's idea at first. Because Jackson wasn't getting any younger, was he? And his place was clear the hell and gone from anywhere else to speak of, and who knew just how bone-mean some of those boys might turn out to be? But after they had talked a while they arrived at an understanding. When Peter Jackson had gone on home, Judge Ferguson pulled his file on a boy named Willard Clement, and pretty soon he was on the phone arranging for a deputy to drive the boy out to Jackson's place.

The highway runs on the near side of the ridge from the lake, and you got to Peter Jackson's by turning off on a little old dirt driveway that came up over the crest of the hill and dipped down on the other side to stop in front of Jackson's house, an old log house that had been clapboarded over and added onto a couple or three times. A ways below the house were the dog pens, and anytime a car turned in, all those dogs would start in barking. Past the kennels a trail went winding down the hill and twisted in amongst the cedars; you couldn't see quite how it got there from above, but way on down it came out near the little dock where Jackson kept a pirogue tied, for when he wanted to paddle out on the lake and fish.

But the first thing a stranger would be apt to notice, coming over that rise, would be the lake itself. It always looked sort of surprising from the ridge top. It isn't really keyhole-shaped, just narrow at one end and wide at the other; how come they give it that name is that the middle of the wide part is so deep, nobody ever found the bottom, and somebody had the idea it was like that part of a keyhole that just goes clear through the door. From up by Peter Jackson's house you could always see how the color of the water would change as it neared the middle, homing in on that deep dark circle of blue.

Jackson's dogs stayed in the pens, all but two that were his pets; them he let live in the house and have the run of the whole place. Bronwen he called one of them, and the other was Caesar. All his dogs had peculiar names like that, which he looked up in books. When the deputy pulled in to deliver Willard Clement, he found Jackson waiting out in the yard, the two dogs on either side of him. The deputy unlocked Willard out of that caged-up backseat and brought him on down to get introduced. Jackson said hello and then made both of the dogs put up their paws to shake, they were that well trained, almost like folks. Then he turned around all of a sudden and pointed back up the hill and called out, "Hit it, Bronwen," and snapped his fingers twice. The dog went bounding up the hill and jumped up in the air and locked her jaws on a piece of two-by-four Jackson had nailed between two cedar trunks about five feet off of the ground, and she just kept right on hanging there, her whole weight on her teeth so to speak, until Jackson said, "All right, leggo, Bronwen," and then she dropped down. Willard Clement was staring googly-eyed, and you could just practically see it, the deputy said, how any thought he might have had of causing Peter Jackson some type of trouble was evaporating clean out of his mind.

Jackson put Willard Clement up in what had been Richard's room, and that's where he put all the others that came along after him. He kept them busy working with the dogs, first just putting the food out and cleaning the pens and later on taking them for exercise and helping with the training some. The boys mostly stayed out there six weeks to two months, which was long enough to learn a little something about how to train a dog. And the work told on them, gentled them down some. A number kept on working with animals, one way or another, after they were done their stay at Jackson's. Willard Clement, I believe, finally became a vet.

You couldn't miss the difference in those boys, between the time they got dropped off out there and the time they got picked up again. You'd drive one of them out there, locked into the back like something that had rabies maybe, but when you went to go get him again, likely he'd look like somebody you could trust to ride in the front seat alongside of you. He would be saying *yes sir* and *no sir* and standing up straight and looking you in the eye. Nobody quite knew what Jackson practiced on those boys, but whatever it was, it seemed to work. And a good few of them seemed to really be grateful for it too. There were some that tried going back out to visit him, a lot later on once they were grown, but the funny thing was that Jackson himself never seemed to care too much about seeing any of them again.

There must have been eight or ten of those boys between Clement and Don Bantry. Anyway, he'd been having them out there for near about two years. There hadn't been a one of them he'd failed to turn around, either, else they probably never would have thought of sending Bantry out there, because that boy was a tough nut to crack. He was about sixteen at that time, but already big as a man. What he was most recently in trouble for was beating up a teacher at the high school and breaking his arm, but there was a long string of things leading up to that: liquor and pot, some car stealing, a burglary, suspicion of a rape he never got tried on. They wouldn't have him at the reform school again, just flat out wouldn't. Ferguson was in a toss-up whether to try and figure some way to get him tried as an adult or send him out to Jackson's awhile, and what he decided shows you how he'd come to think that Peter Jackson was magic.

Bantry had kind of short bowlegs, but big shoulders and longish arms. He had a pelt of heavy black hair all over him, and even his eyebrows met in the middle. He looked a good deal like an ape, and he wasn't above acting like one too. Well, the deputy turned him out of the car, and Jackson had Bronwen and Caesar put up their paws, but Bantry wasn't having any of that. "Ain't shaking hands with no goddamn dog," he said. But it wasn't the first time one of them had said it. Jackson had Caesar run and hit that two-by-four and hang by his jaws a half minute or so. You couldn't have told what Bantry thought, his face never showed a thing, but that trick had always worked before, so the deputy left on out of there. And right from the start, it was war.

Jackson went and got a shovel and handed it to Bantry. Explained to him how to go about cleaning out those dog pens, where he'd find the wheelbarrow at, where to go dump all he shoveled up. Bantry didn't reach to take hold of the shovel, so Jackson finally just let it drop and lean against his shoulder.

"Better get a move on," Jackson said, or something about like it, and then he started walking back down toward the house. He was halfway there when he heard some kind of a noise or shout and turned around in time to see Bantry flinging the shovel like a spear, not quite at him but close enough in his general direction that Bronwen and Caesar started growling. Jackson told the dogs to stay. Bantry had turned and started walking up the drive, where the dust of the deputy's car had not yet even settled, like he didn't know it was at least twenty miles to anywhere else or didn't care, either one.

"Come on back here before I have the dogs bring you," Peter Jackson called after him. Bantry kept walking, didn't even glance back. He was near the top of the hill when the dogs got to him, and he swung around and tried to get off a kick, but before he could land one, Bronwen had him by the one arm and Caesar by the other. They clamped onto to him just short of breaking his skin and starting dragging him on back down the drive to where the shovel had landed, just like Jackson had said they would. He came along with them, had no choice, as long as he didn't want his arms torn off. His face was fish-white, but Peter Jackson thought it was anger more than fear. Bantry was not the kind that scared easy, though he was sharp enough to know a fight he couldn't win. This time when Jackson offered him the shovel he took it, and he went on and cleaned out the dog runs. For the next week, ten days or so, whatever Jackson told him to do, he did it, but did it like a slave, not looking at him or speaking, either. He never said anything at all unless he was asked a question, not even at the supper table.

Jackson had a dog named Olwen, with seven pups near ready to wean. He had Bantry feeding the puppies their oatmeal and all. One day when Bantry was coming out of Olwen's run, Jackson snapped his fingers to Caesar. The dog hit Bantry square in the chest, knocked him over square on his back, and stood over him with that whole mouthful of teeth showing white and needle-sharp. With all that, Bantry kept most of his cool. He turned his head to one side slowly and called out to Peter Jackson.

"What I do now?"

"You been doing something to Olwen's puppies," Jackson told him, walking up closer.

"You never seen me," Bantry said.

"But I still know it," Jackson said. "And if you don't stop, I'll know that too." And he let Bantry lay and think on that a minute, before he called Caesar to leave him get back up.

Another week or so went by, Bantry doing his work with his head bowed down, not speaking until he was spoken to, and then answering short as he could. Till one evening when Jackson was starting to cook supper and felt like he had a headache coming on. Bantry had just fed Bronwen and Caesar on the kitchen floor, so they were busy over their pans. Jackson stepped into his bedroom to get himself an aspirin, and then Bantry was in there right behind him, already shutting and bolting the door.

"You been waiting your chance quite a while, hadn't you, boy?" Jackson said. And straightaway he hit Bantry over the eye, twisting his fist so it would cut. He thought if he surprised him, he might win, or anyway get a chance to open the door back up. But Bantry didn't have his reputation for nothing. Jackson got in a couple more shots and thought maybe he was doing all right, when next thing he knew, he was lying on the floor, not able to get up again. Then it was quiet for a minute or two, except for the two dogs scrabbling at the outside of the door. Every so often one or the other would back off and get a running start and throw himself up against it.

"You fight okay for an old man," Bantry said, panting. It was about his first volunteer word since he got there. "But you still lost." Jackson didn't answer him. It was hurting him too much to breathe right then. Bantry reached a handkerchief off the dresser and dabbed at the cut above his eye. Then he picked up the keys of Jackson's truck and twirled the ring around his finger.

"You won't never make it," Jackson said. They were both still again for a minute, listening to the dogs trying to come through the door.

"I could always kill you," Bantry said.

"You'll still come out behind," Jackson said. "I already lived a lot longer than you."

Bantry sat down on the edge of Jackson's bed, looking down at the floor.

He still had to hold the handkerchief over his cut to keep the blood from running in his eye.

"What say we just call it a draw?" Jackson said. "We could just go on in the kitchen and eat supper and forget the whole thing."

Bantry looked over at him.

"How I know you're telling the truth?" he said.

"Hell, you don't," Peter Jackson said. "But there's always a chance of it. And some chance is better than no chance at all."

Bantry sat and thought a while longer. Then he reached over and un-latched the door. The dogs came in fast, spinning around, slipping a little on the slick board floor. They were in such a hurry to find Bantry and eat him alive, they were just about falling over themselves.

"Let him alone," Jackson called out, and both dogs simmered down right away. Then to Bantry, "You come on here and help me up. And let me have that aspirin bottle, that's what I was after in here in the first place."

Another week or so went by. Bantry's cut was healing up; it was not so bad as it looked at first. Jackson had thought his ribs were cracked, but it turned out they were only bruised and soon enough they started feeling better. Bantry went on about the same as before, doing what he was told and not saying much, yet Jackson didn't think he was quite so sullen and angry as he had been. Then one afternoon Bantry came up to him and said, "I'm done with the dog runs. All right I go down by the lake a while?"

"Go ahead on," Jackson said. He was kind of pleased because it was the first time Bantry had asked him for anything, and for that matter it was the first time he'd acted like he knew the lake was even there.

So Bantry went on down the trail and Jackson went and turned out a dog named Theodore he was training for K-9. He had on all the pads he wore whenever he was going to let a dog have at him. After twenty minutes or so he took a break and walked around the low side of the kennels where he could see out to the lake, and that was when he saw Bantry out paddling in the pirogue.

Later on Jackson couldn't tell just why the sight of it hit him so hard. He hadn't told Bantry he could use the boat, but then he hadn't told him he couldn't, either. He might have been trying to run off again; there were people in the houses on the far side of the lake, and Bantry might have thought he could get over there and steal one of their cars. But even from that far distance Jackson could see that Bantry didn't know much at all about how to handle a boat; he couldn't keep it headed straight, and he kept heeling it way over to one side or the other.

Whatever his reason was, Jackson decided he wanted to get down there quick. He took out running down the trail, shedding his pads as he went along. Bronwen and Caesar came along with him, and Theodore, who was still out loose, was frisking along after all of them, not taking it too seriously, just having a good time. The trail takes a zig and a zag through the cedar grove, and for the last leg or two Jackson couldn't see the lake at all. When he finally came out at the foot of the path, he saw Bantry had turned the boat over somehow and was thrashing around a good way from it. You could tell by one quick look he didn't know how to swim a stroke. And what kind of a fool would overset a flat-bottom boat, anyway? He wasn't over the deep part of the lake; if he had been, the way things fell out, he would probably be there yet.

Jackson took off his knee pads, which he hadn't been able to get rid of while he was running. He took off his shoes and some more of his clothes and waded out into the lake. The dogs ran up and down the shoreline barking like crazy, and now and then one of them would put a paw in the water, but they were not dogs that liked to swim. Without thinking, Jackson swam straight out to where Bantry was at and laid a hold to him, only Bantry got a better hold on him first and dragged him right on under. It was not anything he meant to be doing exactly, just how any drowning man behaves. He was trying to climb out of the lake over Jackson's back, but Jackson was going down underneath him, getting light-headed, for no matter what he tried, he couldn't raise his head clear for a breath. Then it came to him he had better swim for the bottom. When he dove down, he felt Bantry come loose from him and he kept going down till he was free, then out a ways, swimming as far as he could underwater before he came back up.

He was tired then, and his banged ribs had started to hurt from that long time he'd been down and holding his breath. For a minute or two he had to lie in a dead man's float to rest, and then he raised his head and started treading water, slow. It was a cloudy day, no sun at all, and he could feel the cold cutting through to his bones. The surface of the lake was black as oil. Bantry was still struggling about twenty feet from him, but he was near done in by that time. He stared at Jackson, his eyes rolling white. Jackson trod water and looked right back at him, until Bantry gave it up and slid down under the lake.

Ripples were widening out from the place where Bantry's head went down, and Peter Jackson kept on treading water. He counted up to twenty-five before he dove. It was ten feet deep, maybe twelve, at the point where they were at, colder yet along the bottom, and dark with silt. He didn't find Bantry the first dive he made, though he stayed down until his head was pounding. It took him a count of thirty to get the breath back for another try, and he was starting to think he might have miscalculated. But on the second time he found him and hauled him back up. Bantry was not putting up any fight now; he was not any more than a deadweight. Jackson got him in a cross-chest carry and swam him into the shore.

The dogs were going wild there on the bank, yapping and jumping up and down. Jackson dumped Bantry facedown on the gravel and swatted the dogs away. He knelt down and started mashing Bantry's shoulders. There was plenty of water coming out of him, but he was cold and not moving a twitch, and Jackson was thinking he had miscalculated sure enough, when Bantry shuddered and coughed and puked a little and then raised up on his elbows. Jackson got off of him and watched him start to breathe. After a little bit Bantry's eyes came clear.

"You'da let me drown," Bantry said. "You'da just let me . . ."

"You never left me much of a choice," Jackson said.

"You was just setting there watching me drown," Bantry said. He sat up one joint at a time and then let his head drop down and hang over his folded knees. The cut above his eye had opened back up and was bleeding some. In a minute he had started to cry.

Peter Jackson never had seen anybody carrying on the way Bantry was, not any pretty near grown man, at least. He didn't feel any too sorry for Bantry, but it was unpleasant watching him cry like that. It was like watching a baby cry when it can't tell you what's the matter, and there ain't no way for you to tell it to quit. He thought of one thing or another he might say. That he'd had to take a gambler's chance. That a poor risk was better than no hope at all. But he was worn out from swimming and struggling, too tired to feel like talking much. Bantry kept on crying, not letting up, and Peter Jackson got himself on his feet and went limping up to the house with the dogs.

That was what did it for Bantry, though, or so it seemed. Anyway, he was a lot different after that. He acted nicer with the dogs, feeding them treats, stroking them and loving them up, when he had never as much as touched one before, if he had a way around it. He began to volunteer to do extra things, helping more around the house and garden when his chores in the kennel were done. He put on pads and learned to help Jackson train dogs for K-9. He followed Jackson around, trying to strike up conversation, like, for a change, he was hungry for company. He was especially nice with Bronwen and Caesar, and Caesar seemed to take a shine to him right back. Bantry had turned the corner, is what it looked like. In about two more weeks Peter Jackson called the courthouse and said they could send somebody out to pick him up.

As it turned out, it was me they sent. I was still a part-time deputy then, and the call came on a Saturday when I was on duty. Bantry was packed and all ready to go when I got there. Soon as I had parked the car, he came walking over, carrying his grip. Caesar was walking alongside of him, and every couple of steps they took, Bantry would reach down and give him a pat on the head.

"Hello, Mr. Trimble," he said. He put out his hand and we shook.

"You look bright-eyed and bushy-tailed," I said. "I'd scarce have known you, Bantry."

"You can call me Don," he said, and smiled.

I told him to go on and get in the front while I went down to take a message to Jackson. It surprised me just a touch he hadn't already come out himself. He was sitting out on his back stoop when I found him, staring out across the lake. Bronwen was sitting there next to him. Every so often she'd slap her paw up on his knee, like she was begging him for something. Jackson didn't appear to be paying her much mind.

"Well, sir, you're a miracle worker," I said. "I wouldn't have believed it if I'd just been told, but it looks like you done it again."

"Hello, Trimble," Jackson said, flicking his eyes over me and then back away. He'd known I was there right along, just hadn't shown it. Bronwen slapped her paw back up on his knee.

"Maynard said tell you he'll have another one ready to send out here shortly," I said. Jackson looked off across the lake.

"I ain't going to have no more of'm," he said.

"Why not?" I said. Bronwen pawed at him another time, and Jackson reached over and started rubbing her ears.

"Well, I figured something out," Jackson said, still staring down there at the water. "It ain't any different than breaking an animal, what I been doing to them boys."

I stepped up beside him and looked where he was looking, curious to see what might be so interesting down there on the lake. There wasn't so much as a fish jumping. Nothing there but that blue, blue water, cold-looking and still as if it was ice.

"What if you're right?" I said. "More'n likely it's the very thing they need."

"Yes, but a man is not an animal," he said. He waited a minute and clicked his tongue. "Anyhow, I'm getting too old," he said.

"You?" I said. "Ain't nobody would call *you* old." It was a true fact I never had thought of him that way myself, though he might have been near seventy by that time. He'd been a right smart older than his wife.

Jackson raised up his left hand and shook it under my nose. I could see how his fingers were getting skinny, the way an old man's will, and how loose his wedding band was rattling. Then he laid his hand back down on Bronwen's head.

"I'm old," he said. "I can feel it now, sure enough. The days run right by me and I can't get a hold on them. And you want to know what?"

"What?" I said. Walked right into it like the sharp edge of a door.

"It's a relief," Peter Jackson told me. "That's what."

PINCKNEY BENEDICT

Dog

Eldridge heard the noise before Broom did. Broom was watching cartoons on the little black-and-white tv on the floor in the living room and he had the sound up pretty high so he missed it.

The noise that Eldridge heard was a squeak, a high squeak and a scratching sound. He was coming out of the bathroom when he heard it, walking in his bare feet, just a towel wrapped around his waist. He figured at first it was the floor of the trailer—it was an old trailer that he and Broom lived in and beginning to rust out a little, starting to settle down uneven on the cinderblock foundations. Then he heard it again when he was a little ways down the hall toward the biggest bedroom and he knew this time that it was something that was alive.

"Yo Broom," he yelled down the hall into the living room. He could hear the tv in there, knew Broom probably wouldn't call back to him even if he heard. He and Broom had lived together in the trailer a couple years. He had got to know Broom pretty well. "Broom," he called again. "We got rats, Broom." He walked on down the hall into his bedroom.

Broom came in after him a second later. He had a can of beer in his hand. Starting earlier and earlier in the day, Eldridge thought. It was a bad habit to get into. Eldridge never touched the stuff before lunch, couldn't even hardly stomach a Coca-Cola before lunch. "What's that," Broom said. The tv roared away in the living room.

"I say we got rats," Eldridge said. "Or somethen." He stomped on the floor hard, trying to get the rats or whatever to make the noise again. The one window in the bedroom rattled in its frame. "Jesus," Broom said. "You like

85

to knock the whole place down." He was a skinny kid was Broom, twenty-one or two, Eldridge wasn't sure which. He looked young though, always got carded in bars. It was pretty funny to watch his face when a bartender would say, "I gotta see some ID." It really pissed Broom off and his face would work and crease while he dug in the pocket of his jeans for his wallet. He was still having a bad time with acne and his face was ugly to see when he got mad, all red and mottled and looking like a goddam map of Mars.

He stood still for a second, tilted his head toward the floor like a rabbit dog. Eldridge was quiet, listening too. The only sound was music from the tv. "I don' hear nothen," Broom said. "No rats."

"Jest listen a while," Eldridge said. He pulled on a tee shirt. He wore a lot of tee shirts, muscle-shirts he called them, about a size too small with the sleeves cut off at the shoulder. Some girl one time or another had told him she liked that "sculpted" look. He had never forgot that, would say it from time to time to Broom or whoever, "I got that sculpted look." Pretty much whoever he said it to thought he was a jerk about his looks. He was average, except for the muscles, the washboard stomach and the thick arms. He never told anybody about the girl who had told him she thought he looked "grotesque." Never said a word about that.

"I heard it," Eldridge said. "Scratchen against the floor."

"Huh," Broom said. He started to head back to his tv show. Then the sound came again, seemed like it came from right under Eldridge's room this time. Broom heard it: a scratch and a whine. "There you go," Eldridge said. "There it is." He was pleased that Broom had heard it.

"Ain' rats," Broom said.

"What do you mean," Eldridge said. "If it ain' rats what is it?"

"I don' know but it ain' rats," Broom said. He paused a second like he was thinking. "Sound to me like a dog. Sound to me like we got a dog under the trailer."

"How you think it got there?" Eldridge said. Now that he thought about it the noise had seemed a lot like a dog to him too.

"Crawled under I guess. Maybe looken for some place jest to lay down and die. Maybe it's sick, maybe shot, I ain' got the least idee."

"I guess we got to go see then don' we?" Eldridge said. He leaned into his closet, shoved some clothes that were on the floor in there to one side, moved a couple boxes. He looked up on the shelf in the closet too. "Where's that flashlight," he said, "the big hunten lamp. What'd you do with the damn flashlight."

"Hell if I know," Broom said. "Last time I had it was last fall, last November. We were out spotlighten some deer, you 'member, with Fat Ed and that whole gang. Got us a couple too didn' we? Yeah, we sure ate all right after that for a while. Old Fat Ed's deer meat chili. Goddam."

"Yeah," Eldridge said. He had gone under the bed now, looking for the light. "But then what'd we do with it? Jesus," he said. He came back out from under the bed holding the lamp. It was a big Black and Decker that you could either run off its six-volt battery or plug into your cigarette lighter like a police light. It had deer blood on the handle and on the green plastic shockproof case. Eldridge flicked at the blood with his fingertips and some of it flaked off onto the floor.

"That was under your bed?" Broom said. "It must of smelled like hell. How did you live with that thing in here?"

"You ain' no garden yourse'f, Broom," Eldridge said. "You should take a smell of what your room is like sometime." Broom's face creased up like he was going to lose his temper. Then the sound came again and this time it was definitely a dog, kind of a half bark. Sounded like a dog barking in a coffee can. Pretty good-sized dog too, from the noise.

The dog growled and Eldridge felt the hair on the back of his neck rise. He could feel the vibrations from the growl rising up through the metal floor. It was like he was standing on the dog's rib cage. It was just under their feet and Eldridge caught himself looking down even though there was nothing there to see but old brown carpet. "Shoot," Broom said. "Did you hear that?"

Eldridge flicked the switch on the hunting lamp and the light came on. The beam was yellow. "Look kind of weak," Broom said. "Under there all the time the batt'ry probably gone bad."

"Jest cause it's so light up here," Eldridge said. "It'll be a lot brighter under the trailer."

"Huh," Broom said. "I expect that's so. I expect it's jest the day."

Eldridge kept flicking the switch on the light, testing it to see if it would get brighter or dimmer maybe. The yellow beam stayed the same. He went out to the living room, turned the tv off.

"You gonna take somethen under there with you?" Broom said. "I sure as hell wouldn' go under there without nothen to take the dog on."

"Take what," Eldridge said.

"I don' know. Sharp stick maybe."

"I'm jest gonna chase the dog out from under there. I ain' want to get in a fight with it."

"Well," Broom said. "But you wouldn' catch me under there without nothen. Never know what that dog could be like under there."

It was probably one of the strays that were always getting in the garbage or some dog that people from town had dumped off in the bushes Eldridge decided. Jest sick or strayed or something. Nothing to worry about.

He opened the door, stepped out onto the cinder block that was their front porch step. It shifted in the soft earth and he almost fell. "Son bitch," he said. It was a bright hot day and Eldridge had to shield his eyes from the sun.

"Wonder whose dog it might could be," Broom said. "People round here ought to take better care of their animals than let them run loose like that. Ought to be laws about that."

"Nobody's dog," Eldridge said. "It jest come here to die. That's when a dog goes in a dark place alone, when it wants to die."

He got down on his knees, peered into the crawl space. There was only one place to get under, right near the trailer door. The rest of the crawl space was closed off with tin. It looked like a pretty tight squeeze through the hole to Eldridge.

"I bet it's Seldomridge's dog," Broom said. "You know that big black bastard of a hound he got that's all the time getten in people's sheep. Somebody probably poisoned the son of a gun."

"Could be," Eldridge said.

The dirt under the trailer was black and damp, looked like dirt that would have worms up on the surface. There was no grass, just a lot of leaves piled up around the foundations of the place and around the pipes. Eldridge didn't think he'd ever seen so many pipes in a place before, couldn't think of what they would all be for. Septic tank he knew, for one. He felt his chest start to get tight.

"I hope it ain' got the rabies," Broom said. "I seen a dog that had the rabies once and it was an awful thing."

"It ain' got the rabies, Broom," Eldridge said.

"Got bit by a coon or a skunk and that sucker was plain crazy. Slobbers all over his mouth and blood runnen out his snout and down his chin. Walked all stiff-legged and hunchback and snapped at everthen that come too near. Like to bit some kids that was thowen stones at it."

Eldridge edged to the entrance into the crawl space. He tried to ignore Broom.

"Ended up by finally tearen his own guts out, he was that out of his head. Nothen else to bite on so he ripped out his own belly and bleeden and howlen while he buried his nose. Jesus was that somethen." He sounded excited.

"Was it," Eldridge said. He couldn't see anything under the trailer. The dog was way in the back.

"You bet," Broom said. "The county sheriff even come out to the trailer park where it was after a while but it was already dead by that time. Pulled out its own innards and the kids was hitten at it with rocks and sticks too. Big fat deputy put a round into it jest to make sure but it was dead as hell, flies crawlen on its tongue and all."

Broom paused to get his breath. Eldridge was glad of the quiet.

"You see it?" Broom said after a minute. "I'd hate for that to be Seldom-ridge's big old dog under there and stinken with the rabies. He'd bite on you sure as hell and then you'd have it too." He was standing on the cinder block by the door, rocking it back and forth in its place. It made a sucking sound in the dirt as he moved it.

Eldridge dropped to his stomach, belly-crawled a little ways in. He got his head under the trailer; his shoulders struck the tin on either side. He hunkered down, drew his shoulders in, got a little further. It was hard to raise the light in the narrow space. He couldn't get it up high enough to shine where he thought the dog should be. A leaf caught against his face and he could smell the rot on it. It smelled like it had been lying under the trailer for years.

"You see it yet?" Broom called from outside. His voice was muffled. Eldridge looked back, craned his head around as far as he could. He saw Broom's head, upside-down. All that Eldridge could see of the head was an outline, dark against the bright sunlight. He had never noticed before how odd-shaped Broom's head was, not like an egg or round but pressed in at the temples: rounded above and rounded below like a badly poured pancake. Broom's hair was hanging down and touching the ground.

"It ain' where I can see it," Eldridge said. "I'm gonna have to go in a little ways more."

"What?" Broom said. Eldridge didn't bother to say it again. He hauled himself forward with his elbows, throwing the Black and Decker's beam ahead of him. Even in the dark under the trailer the beam was yellow. It looked like Broom had been right in the first place about the battery. Outside, out from under the trailer, he could hear Broom yelling to him. He didn't try to catch the words.

The ground under him was cool and slick like he had thought it would feel. His knees were damp, and his forearms; the mud soaked through his pants, got into the creases of skin at his elbows. It was a tight place to be in and it made him nervous. He wasn't even thinking about the dog. He was all the way under the trailer. He pushed with his toes, tried to get some purchase to help him along but there wasn't enough grip there.

Eldridge couldn't believe the amount of stuff that there was under the trailer. Something that looked like the differential off an old four-wheel-drive was near him on his left half-covered in leaves. He figured the people that had owned the trailer before him and Broom moved in had tossed it under there, why he had no idea. Next to that was a denim work glove looking like a dead man's hand sticking up out of the ground. Near the entrance was a little doll of a man that some kid had lost a long time before, what they called a Talking GI Joe. Eldridge knew if he pulled the string in its back the tiny record inside wouldn't make anything but gibberish.

A spiderweb that had stretched from one pipe to another touched his face, attached itself to him under his nose. He batted at it. "Son bitch," he said. The spiderweb floated up, got in his eyes. He kept his mouth tight shut for fear that it might get in there too. The thought of the cobweb in his mouth made him feel sick to his stomach. He shook his head, couldn't get rid of the thing. It seemed like it was floating in the air, more strands of it sticking to him all the time. He started to crawl back out toward the light to get the spiderweb out of his eyes. He needed both hands free from crawling for that.

As he moved back his tee shirt pulled up under his arms, left his belly bare to the cool dirt. He gritted his teeth. He couldn't believe how much he wanted to make a noise. Broom wasn't saying anything anymore and Eldridge wished that he was, wished that he had left the TV on in the living room so that he could hear its noise through the floor. He figured he was about under the living room now.

When he twisted his head around he couldn't even see Broom's feet anymore. "Broom," he yelled. "Broom, where the hell you go?" His voice sounded loud bounced back to him from the pipes and the floor of the place, filled the crawl space. He shoved himself back some more, could feel the heat of the sun on the backs of his legs. Backwards was slow going but he only had a couple of more feet to be outside where he could stand up again. He blinked, trying to get rid of the spiderweb. There were bits of leaf or something caught in the strands and he could feel them against his face. His elbows dug into the ground as he pushed himself backwards.

Something moved at the far end of the trailer. He swung the light around as best he could, played it over the gray thing that he thought was the dog. No eyes, he couldn't see any eyes, couldn't tell if it was fur or not, no legs or tail.

He saw the dog. Like those trick pictures where at first you can't see what it is, just a bunch of light and dark places, and then you can, you can see the head of Jesus or the sea gull or whatever is there—that's the way that Eldridge saw the dog. It had risen up but there wasn't even enough room for it to stand straight-legged in the crawl space. It stood with its back against the floor of the trailer, legs bent, weaving a little. Its eyes were almost closed, swelled and full of pus; they shone half-moons of red light from the beam of Eldridge's flashlight.

It had the mange and not just a little mange either but the kind that can kill a dog. In places the thing looked like it had been peeled, the hair and skin taken off with a dull knife. Its chest was wide and deep but it was so starved, its stomach curved up almost to its backbone like a racing dog's belly. It wasn't a racing dog though; it looked like one of those big German guard dogs. It growled, its wet lips peeled back from the gums and fluttering. The sound was deadened by the distance and by the bare dirt but it filled Eldridge's head.

He shoved himself back out from under the trailer. He kept the flashlight on the dog as he backed out. It didn't come any closer to him. It growled and growled and the growl swelled until it filled the whole crawl space like the sound of an organ. The dog was drooling and the drool was flecked white with pus.

Eldridge nicked his shoulder on the sharp edge of the tin at the entrance. He rolled over and stood up, dropping the flashlight. He rubbed at his eyes, got most of the spiderweb off his face. It stuck to his hands instead. "Broom," he called. He looked behind him, half expecting to see the mangy dog hauling itself out from under the trailer after him.

"Did you see it?" Broom said. He was sitting in the door, his feet on the cinder block. "You seen it under there didn' you?"

Eldridge nodded.

"Thought so," Broom said. "Was it Seldomridge's mutt like I said? You gonna go under there again so you can kill the sucker?"

"Ain' goen under there again," Eldridge said.

"Don' you worry, Eldridge," Broom said. "You'll get him next time. You jest got rattled a little is all. You'll be okay."

"You don' get it," Eldridge said. "That bastard can have it. I ain' goen in there after him again. You want to, you can get him out. I ain'." He thought about that dog with its lips pulled back. He wanted to get inside but he couldn't get past Broom sitting there in the doorway.

"Maybe he'll come out of there after a while on his own," Broom said.

"Maybe he'll get hungry and jest come on out of there and we won' have to fool with him at all."

Eldridge pushed past Broom on into the trailer. "Shut that door," he said. He tried to get Broom out of the way so he could pull the door closed.

"He scared you that bad did he?" Broom said. He brushed Eldridge's hands off him. "Jesus Christ," he said, "what's wrong with you. Let me go."

Eldridge let go of him and he came on inside. "You don' want to pull on me like that," he said. "Man that's scared of a dog."

"You didn' see him," Eldridge said.

"Wouldn' of scared me if I did," Broom said.

"You didn' see him," Eldridge said again. "You go under there if you want. You shoot him if you want. But I'm tellen you I ain' goen in after that dog."

"Ain' nobody asken you to," Broom said. "We'll wait a while, see if he comes out by himse'f."

"If he don' then what?" Eldridge said.

"Then I'll figure a way to get him out," Broom said.

"With what?" Eldridge said. "A sharp stick?"

"Maybe so," Broom said. "Maybe that's how I'll do it." Eldridge laughed at him and Broom's face got red and angry.

Eldridge couldn't get to sleep that night for thinking about the dog. It hadn't come out that day at all and Broom hadn't gone in after it either. Eldridge was glad about that in a way. Still it meant he couldn't get to sleep for knowing the dog was probably not more than three or four feet from him, through the floor.

Once or twice he heard it moving around under the trailer, shifting so he could picture its mangy back brushing up against the floor and the pipes, see it pushing leaves around to make for a better bed. Always when he was about to get to sleep the dog would move around and moan and he would get to thinking about it again with its ugly animal-shine eyes and the pus in its drool. After a while he was afraid that he could smell the dog through the floor, smell it in the bed it was making for itself.

"Broom," he said, lying there. He knew Broom would hear him if he was awake. The walls in the trailer weren't much. He could hear Broom sometimes when he snored. He'd had to pound on the wall more than once to get Broom to roll over and shut up. "Broom," he said again.

He shifted over to his stomach, put his nose down in the pillow. He thought that if he could see down through the pillow and the mattress, straight through the floor, he would be looking right at the dog, at where the dog was asleep.

He wondered if the dog had dreams. He had seen dogs whine in their sleep, twitch their legs. "Chasen rabbits," was what he always thought to himself when he saw a dog twitch in its sleep. But this didn't sound like that when the dog under the trailer would move. This was bigger, shifting and bumping, and different. Eldridge didn't know what a sick dog would dream about when it had found the dark place where it wanted to die.

The dog whined and at first the whine was a high sound like a mosquito that is close to your ear. Then it was louder, a wail like some ghost, and Eldridge sat up in bed. "Goddam," he said. He listened to the dog howling. He would have sworn it was in the room with him it was so loud. He tossed his pillow away from him and it bounced on his dresser, landed on the floor. "I can' do this," he said. He got out of bed.

He crossed the room, walking softly. The noise the dog was making started to die away some but he kept walking, up on the balls of his feet. The padding under the carpet was going bad and it had broken up into lumps that moved when he stepped on them. Eldridge went into the bathroom that was down the hall from the smaller bedroom, took a leak. While he was in there he looked at himself in the mirror. He looked the same but tired. He wondered what time it was.

He flushed the toilet, thought about the dog lying near the pipe to the septic tank. The water rushing through would probably wake the dog up. Then it would really take to moving around down there. Eldridge didn't want to think about that.

On the way back to his room he opened Broom's door. He couldn't see Broom very well in the dark but he could hear him breathing. "You been hearen that dog, Broom?" he said. "Moven around under there."

"What the hell," Broom said, sitting up on his elbows in the bed. "What you doen, Eldridge?"

"Jest talken," Eldridge said. "I heard the dog still under there, it's keepen me awake. I thought you might of heard it."

"I was asleep till you woke me up," Broom said. He sounded angry. Eldridge didn't know if he had really been asleep or not. He reached up, grabbed the top of the doorway over his head, swung his weight on his arms. It felt good to stretch the muscles out.

"Well, I jest thought you might be up," Eldridge said. "We got to get that dog out from under there." Broom didn't say anything back. He was pretending to be asleep again. It made Eldridge mad that Broom wouldn't talk to him.

"I ain' goen to sleep in there anymore for a time," Eldridge said. "I want you to trade me rooms." Broom was still pretending to be asleep. "It's a bigger room," Eldridge said. "You know you always wanted it, Broom." He was tired standing there begging with Broom but he knew he wasn't going to be able to sleep in the other bedroom.

"Christ, Broom," he said. He didn't like the smell of Broom's place and it was too hot from having the window closed all the time. He hated to ask for it. Broom turned over, put his back to Eldridge. With both his hands he was holding tight to the pillow.

After a while more of standing there looking at Broom's back, Eldridge went and got the blanket off his bed. He had to look a little while in the dark to find where he had thrown the pillow. He took his stuff and spent the night on the floor in the living room.

"Hey, Ed," Eldridge called. He and Broom stood out in the hot dust in front of Fat Ed Venner's house. There was an old Scout with no wheels sitting out in the yard. It had been up on jacks but one of them had collapsed so it was canted at an angle. Eldridge pointed at it. "You 'member when Ed used to have that thing out on the road?"

Broom shook his head. "Nope," he said. He had been quiet the whole morning.

It was a Sunday so they figured Fat Ed would probably be at home.

Eldridge's back hurt. He had slept on it wrong on the hard floor. Broom kicked at the ground and the dry red clay scattered.

The screen door of Fat Ed's house swung open and a woman stepped out onto the porch. She was thin, about forty years old, wiping her hands on a towel. Probably making Sunday supper, Eldridge thought. She wore an old dress that the color had washed out of years before. Her figure made the dress look like it was filled with sticks. She stood on the porch, looking out at Broom and Eldridge. She had to squint against the sun to see them.

"Ed here?" Eldridge asked. The woman still didn't say anything. Broom kicked at the dirt again and Eldridge moved away from him to keep from getting the legs of his jeans dirty. Broom's boots were covered with dust.

"Around back," the woman said. Eldridge didn't move. "In the shed," she said. "You find him back there. You can always find him back there." She looked them up and down. "I want that you should ask him what it is he wants to work on them old useless junk for anyway." Broom didn't say anything. Eldridge cleared his throat.

"He all the time back there and putten together his worthless stuff and his daddy and me we got to walk into town if we want to go, ain' got a car between us that run. Now what kind of a son is that I want you should ask him."

"We jest come to borry somethen from him," Eldridge said.

"His uncle got him a job he could take anytime down to the garage at Organ Cave and he could easy do the work but he don' want it. He'd ruther hang around out back there and do nothen."

"I expect we'll go around and see him now," Eldridge said. The woman made him nervous. She was muttering to herself, lips moving but no sound coming out. She turned on him.

"And tell him not to be haven his yahoo friends comen round here on a Sunday."

"Biddy," Broom said, but not loud enough that she could hear him. Eldridge started around toward the back of the house. It wasn't so much, just a little frame house. One of the windows on the side had gotten busted out; it was patched up with cardboard and duct tape. The skinny woman stayed on the porch watching them go. Her eyes were hard and bright. Eldridge couldn't figure what made her so mad.

Fat Ed was standing outside the shed. There was a small motorcycle carburetor at his feet in a half-full bucket of gasoline. He didn't smile when he saw Broom and Eldridge. He was cleaning his nails with a jackknife, running the blade in deep under each nail trying to get at the grease and dirt there. "Yo Ed," Eldridge said.

Fat Ed nodded at them and his soft cheeks jiggled. He was sweating in the heat. He stood a hair under six feet tall, weighed maybe three hundred pounds. Eldridge couldn't figure a person letting himself get like that. Fat Ed moved like a Hereford steer, real slow and deliberate. He folded up the jackknife, stowed it in the pocket of his coveralls.

"Ain' seen you fellers in a while," he said.

"Hey Ed," Eldridge said. "What is it you worken on these days?" He pointed down at the carb in the bucket.

Ed grunted. " 'Nother chopper," he said. "Boy was sellen a Vincent Black Shadow down to Heflin and didn' have the least idee what he had. I got it off him for next to nothen." Past Ed's wide body Eldridge could see that there were at least three motorcycles in the shed, one hanging by the wheels from a rack in the rafters, and parts for others, fenders and tires and throttle cable.

"We come to see could we borry a pistol, Fat Ed," Broom said like he was tired of waiting for Ed to finish talking. Ed's face turned red at the name and he pressed his lips together.

"Jesus, Broom," Eldridge said.

"What," Broom said. "He knows he's fat, don' he. What does he care if we know it."

"What is it you need it for?" Fat Ed said. He stood there and looked at them for a minute. They knew he had a bunch of pistols in his place, Colts and Mausers and Smith & Wessons. He even had a nickel-plated Llama revolver he'd shown to them one time. Fat Ed liked guns. They generally borrowed their rifles from him when they went deer hunting.

"We got to kill a dog," Eldridge said. "It's got in up under the trailer to die."

Fat Ed started for the back of the house and Eldridge had to walk fast to keep up with him. "Why'nt you jest let it die then?" Fat Ed said. "Then you won' have to borry nothen."

" 'Cause who the hell knows when it's goen to die?" Broom said. He stood where he was, nearly shouting at Ed.

"We got to kill it today, Ed," Eldridge said. He figured Fat Ed wasn't going to lend them the pistol and that Broom had messed it up for them. "We figure it might have the rabies."

"Huh," Fat Ed said. "I guess I can see that. I guess maybe you better had kill the thing. What kind of pistol is it you want?"

"A big one," Broom said.

Eldridge looked at him and he shut up. "Pretty good-sized dog," Eldridge said. "Don' want to get in under there with some twenny-two and jest make the sucker mad."

"Yeah," Fat Ed said. "You gonna be the one to use it?"

"He ain'," Broom called out. "He ain' goen back in under there he says. Come out from under yesterday like to piss in his pants he's so scared."

"You shut up," Eldridge said, " 'fore I come over there and smack you one."

Broom spat. "Shoot," he said. He said something else under his breath.

"What's that," Eldridge said. Broom didn't say anything, stared at Eldridge and Fat Ed. His lips were moving.

"You can have it if it's you gonna use it," Fat Ed said. He looked at Broom. "I don' want that bastard to be the one."

"Shoot," Broom said again.

Eldridge nodded. "You bet, Ed," he said. "I'm gonna be the one."

Ed opened the door into the house. "That's all right then," he said. "You best not to come in the house. My ma don' like company on Sundays too much." He went inside and pulled the door to behind him.

Eldridge turned to Broom. "We about didn' get the gun 'cause of you," he said. "What do you want to talk like that for when we're asken to borry somethen?"

"Fat son bitch," Broom said. He put his hands in his pockets. "I don' know what we ever want to bother with him for anyhow."

"Hush up," Eldridge said.

"Don' you tell me. I'm tired of you tellen me all the time what to do, how to act. You and him, that fat hog, with all them motorcycles. What's he want with a motorcycle?"

"You want that dog there under our place till it decides to die?" Eldridge said.

"Who cares? You the one that's scared of it."

Fat Ed came back out of the house. He carried a flat black pistol in his right hand, a big one with checkered wooden grips. "Here you go," he said.

"Ho yeah," Broom said. "That'll do her." Fat Ed shot him a look, handed the pistol to Eldridge. It was heavy in his hand.

"That there's a Colt forty-five," he said. "You give that one a try. It's got a clip already in it."

"You bet," Eldridge said. "We'll see you after a while."

"Don' worry about it," Ed said. "I got to get back to work on that Vincent." He headed back into the shed, hunched next to a big bike that was heeled over on its kickstand in the middle of the shed. Eldridge watched Ed's hands working at the motor like small trained animals, tightening a bolt, cleaning a valve.

"Let's go," Eldridge said. He started back around the house toward the road. It was a couple of miles walk back to the trailer and the sun was hot.

"Fat bastard," Broom said. He trotted to keep up with Eldridge as they rounded the house. Broom kept his eyes on the pistol. Eldridge could tell he liked the way it looked. Around the other side of the house Fat Ed's mother was standing on the porch, her hand shading her eyes.

"You figure she been up there the whole time waiten on us?" Broom asked Eldridge. Eldridge shrugged.

"Did you tell him?" the woman called out to them. "He ain' got an ounce of sense, all the time tinkeren with them crazy bikes. I never did see nothen like it."

Broom puffed his lips out, made a shooting sound, laughed to himself. They kept walking. When they rounded the bend in the road about a quarter mile away, the woman was still out on the porch watching them.

* * *

When they got back to the trailer neither one of them went inside. They were both hot and sat down in the dirt of the yard. They looked at the trailer and at the entrance to the crawl space next to the door.

"You figure it's still under there?" Broom asked.

"I figure," Eldridge said. "Where would it go?"

They sat like that for a few minutes. A horsefly buzzed around Broom's head but he batted at it and it went away without biting him. Eldridge weighed the Colt in his hand, tipped it back and forth to test the balance. He worked the slide, saw the first oily brass round slip into the chamber. Fat Ed took good care of his guns.

"Get me the lamp, Broom," Eldridge said. Broom sat there.

"I ain' gonna get nothen," Broom said. "You such a big man you go get it."

Eldridge got up, went into the trailer. Fat Ed's gun swung heavy at his side. It was hot in the trailer, hotter than it was outside, and smelled bad. He wondered if the dog had died or something.

The lamp was in the living room and he got it, switched it on. The light was still pale and yellow. He walked outside again, kneeled down to go into the crawl space.

"Why don' you let me go," Broom said. "You been under and it scared you."

Eldridge didn't say anything back to him. He crawled in past the truck differential and the GI Joe. He looked at where the dog was, pointed the gun ahead of him. He wanted to get close so he could make sure to put it away with one shot. He shoved himself forward. The sweat from his palm slicked the wooden grip. He thumbed the hammer of the .45 back.

"Dog," he said. He couldn't figure why he was talking but the sound of his voice made him feel better. "I got to put you down," he said. The dog stirred in its bed of leaves and he shined the light down there on it.

The dog was off its feet, tried to struggle up but couldn't. It thrashed in the leaves, heaved its weight. It whined. Eldridge pulled himself forward. He sighted down the blued barrel on the dog.

It managed to get on its feet but the hind legs were shaky. The dog wheeled to face Eldridge, showed its teeth at him. A loop of saliva hung from its long snout. It presented its chest like it wasn't afraid, like it wanted the bullet. Most animals could smell guns Eldridge knew.

Eldridge squeezed the trigger. The sound of the gun was deafening in the crawl space. Eldridge knew the shot went wild as soon as he let it go. The empty brass spanged off the bottom of the trailer and pattered across Eldridge's back. It felt warm through his shirt. He brought the pistol down again.

The dog hauled itself forward, scrabbling with its front paws. Its back legs were stiff, trailed out behind it. Through the ringing in his ears Eldridge could hear that it was growling, the same growl that he had heard in his bedroom up above.

He centered the sights of the pistol on the deep chest of the dog. The hair was missing there in whorls and patches; the skin was flaked and sore-looking. There was an old red leather collar around the dog's neck with a metal tag attached. The dog was only about a dozen feet from him.

He fired and the heavy round tore into the dog, ripped out from down around its hip. The slug snapped the dog's head around, knocked it off its feet and back about a yard. The dog raised its snout and tried to howl. It couldn't make anything but a noise like air rushing through a pipe. There was blood on its nose and teeth. It moved its front paws in the dirt, lying on its side.

"Got you," Eldridge said. He moved up to where the dog lay on its side in the dirt, panting like almost any dog might on a hot day trying to pull some cool out of the hot still air. The skinny rib cage went in and out, in and out. The bullet had caved in the chest cavity and the dog was about dead.

Eldridge looked at the dog's eyes and they were flat and lifeless as mud puddles. There was mucus caked in the corners of its eyes and the dog blinked, trying to clear them. It opened its jaws wide and puked blood onto the cool dark floor of the crawl space.

Eldridge held the light close to the dog's head. He looked at the tag on the red leather collar but the metal was tarnished and he couldn't read what was written there. The collar was old and the leather was cracked. While he was trying to make out what was engraved on the collar the dog flopped once. It closed its eyes and he couldn't hear the breath pumping into its shattered lungs anymore.

* * *

Eldridge watched a big black digger beetle, big as the first joint of his thumb, crawl across clumps of rotted leaves and dirt toward the dog. He figured the dog's blood had brought it. The smell of the blood was strong, like sulfur, there under the trailer.

The beetle's shell was shiny and polished-looking, like the finish on a new car. The bug went past the toes of Eldridge's boots and he thought about squashing it. When he pointed the flashlight at it, the beetle hurried in under the dog's body. "Christ Amighty," Eldridge said.

The dog was in a strange position, half on its back, one front leg sticking up in the air. Its thick gray tongue was pushed out of its mouth, looked dry. Eldridge put the pistol on the damp ground next to him. He felt tired.

He clicked the flashlight off. In the dark the dog was just a hump. He closed his eyes. "Didn' have nobody in the world to take up for you, did you," he said. If they left the dog under the trailer, he knew the digger beetles would come and bury it, lots more than just the one he had seen.

He could hear Broom shouting his name out from under the trailer. After a while of shouting he stuck his head into the crawl space. His face was a dark patch, hard to see framed against the bright sunlight. "Yo Eldridge," he shouted. He squinted his eyes but Eldridge figured he couldn't see anything without the hunting lamp. Eldridge liked it that Broom couldn't see him.

"Crazy son bitch," Broom said when Eldridge didn't answer. He disappeared back outside and Eldridge heard him go into the trailer. Broom stomped on the floor not far above Eldridge's head. Eldridge closed his eyes. After a minute, he heard the tv in the living room come on. It sounded like Broom had turned it up very loud. Eldridge sighed and shook his head, listening to Broom's footsteps cross and recross the living room of the trailer.

LEE K. ABBOTT

Where Is Garland Steeples Now?

Every time Garland told the story, which, according to his sister, Darlene Neff, was so farfetched and shifty an item that it couldn't be true, he gave its hero, the dog, a new name. Garland's first week back after discharge, those medals of his—the Army Commendation Medal, the Good Conduct Medal, the NDS medal, and that unit citation for valor from the Republic of Vietnam—still untattered, the dog was called Chester Sims, supposedly after a spec four known to Garland up in the MR3 with the 18th ARVN. In April, however, a month after Garland had begun working at that 7-Eleven, which was practically in sight of Arlington Stadium, the dog was known as Mr. Eddie and had only three legs, the absent one reportedly blown off clean in a place identified as the Crescent of Fertile Minds. In June, before Garland started the bank robbing he became famous for, the dog was Spike or Marvin, and its story—from the time it was met and loved and then murdered by Garland—took nearly thirty minutes of telling. Ivy Parks, Darlene Neff's neighbor, heard that the dog was named Nick Carter, after Garland's favorite reading matter, and was supposed to be as big as the enemy itself and, what with toothsome grin and mange, probably rabid. In July, on the day he brought home the gleaming roadmaster, its engine a masterpiece of brightwork, Garland told his boss, Mr. Hemsley, that his dog was named Tiger and that, like all stories, Tiger's was part joy and part trouble, the whole of it unhappy as Xmas in Russia—not a word of which Hemsley believed on account of Garland's goofy grin and the way his eyes turned dark whenever he reached the passages about being able to speak canine, a fact he illustrated by going "Aarrff" and "Woof" and "Grrrr" until the story was not English at all but only bark, ardent growl and gesture that looked like four-legged distress.

After a time, though, everybody, from Darlene's husband, Virgil, to Ike Fooley who lived down the street, to Bonnie Suggs, the First Federal teller to whom he told it while pointing a big old cannonlike gun—everybody knew it as Garland H. Steeples's story, "The Dog of Vietnam," a narrative he told a thousand times in 1971, always mentioning how he was on loan to the 1/26, Hotel Company, in particular a fivesome of ethnic savages who billed themselves as the Detroit Pistons (because of their affection for basketball and place of national origin), who high-stepped around Firebase Maggie dressed up in these abso-fucking-lutely outrageous tailored outfits they'd gotten on Nathan Road in Hong Kong (black leaf-patterned camouflage suits so tight they were skin itself, with matching boonie hats). "I was truly happy," he told Darcel Worthy, a man who'd come into the store one night looking for ginger ale and Cheez Whiz. "I had me a mission in this life," Garland said, "and folks around to help me do it. Plus, I was eighteen, which means I was permanently optimistic." He had his mind right, he said; he was not terribly aggravated by peace-creeps nor otherwise upset about the downscale living and dying that took place when Victor Charles sought his destiny and Uncle Sugar aimed to resist. Truth to tell, he was some excited by all that NVA bang-bang and the hardware by which, including CAR-15 and beautimous Claymore mine, he endeavored to hush it. "I was gonna do my two years, get loose of that place and go back to the world an adult."

Anyway, Garland would say, having established time, place and central character, into Firebase Maggie one day walked this dog—here G's eyes would get all misty and quite unfocused from the memory of it all—with mussed hair like a twenty-dollar streetwalker and an expression that said, "I could be forty thousand years old, but screw you anyway, GI." That animal, someone said, brought to mind such words as *scourge* and *mishap*. "It was a Vietnam dog, all right," Garland told his brother-in-law. "It had floppy ears, one practically chewed right to the bone, and you could tell it just loved being around the smells and wealth of us. I knew right then I had to have me that animal." It took nearly twenty minutes for the beast to take the pressed meat Garland offered, what with its disposition being more wary than trusting; then the two of them went back to G's hooch and shared a cornflake bar while the human one introduced the animal to the CO and an E-8 master sergeant named Krebs; Garland pointed out that beyond the bangalores and perimeter wire and artful maze of land mines lay an almost impenetrable jungle in which lurked a shitload of high-principled cutthroats who rode bicycles and who would like nothing more than, given their usual diet of rat and rice, to feast upon haunch of dog or backbone filet. "So what do you say, Vietnam dog, how 'bout you and me becoming pals?" While the animal appeared to debate the question, Garland cast about for more convincing arguments. "The way I look at it," Garland said, "you are alone and I'm alone, which means that we ought to be together having fun. Loneliness ain't for the kind we are." Whereupon that critter, so the story went, lay its muzzle on its forepaws and seemed to ponder for a time; then, with an affirmative noise, it leaped aboard our boy, leaving sloppy lick marks all over his cheeks.

It was, according to Darlene Neff's recollection, the sort of love as was had between Pancho and Cisco, Tonto and the Lone Ranger—Garland and his grungy sidekick as inseparable as white on chalk. They went everywhere together—latrine, commo tent, even on a dark-of-night extraction near Hill 199 when a Chinook warrant officer, trying to evade heavy ground fire, almost pitched them into outer space. "I told that dog everything about me," Garland confessed to Billy Pickering, the boy who delivered the *Times-Herald*. "I showed him pictures, too: me at Disneyland, me at high-school graduation, me pissing into the Grand Canyon." He even read to that dog, its favorite passages being those when Marc Bolan, the Executioner, blasted the bejesus out of the lowdown evil other guy. He taught that dog how to sit up, how to roll over like a drunk, and how to cross its front legs like a Frenchman named René. He taught him how to beg like you were being done a favor; and once, after some three-star action in Recon Zone Hood, he got that furry creature high on Cambodian weed and they staggered off to eyeball the stars and make up miracles to astound the in-country gangsters they had occasion to deal with.

"Oh, that was some smart animal," Garland used to tell the other clerk, a wide-hipped Big Springs woman named Colette. Why, he took that dog one time into the big airbase at Da Nang, made it walk right up to Mr. Bob Hope and shake his Hollywood hand, Garland later coming up on stage to take a bow for having such an intelligent and well-mannered companion. Yet that dog could be plumb feisty too. One time, so the story went, it bit the rear end of a larcenous Friendly, which prompted a blizzard of directives up and down the chain of command—which resulted, so rumor had it, in MACV itself, in the estimable person of General William Westmoreland, saying it favored and did encourage man-pet love as a morale booster, as essential to a given hombre's welfare as letters from home or exotic R & R.

The trouble started, Garland told the ticket-taker at Six Flags, when his dog—then called Buster or, if female, Sally—chewed through its leash and somehow found its way to Garland's side, forty klicks into the murk-filled hinterlands. The TL, a Philly deliveryman who liked to be called Bigfoot, was all for shooting Buster. He said "Shit" and "Goddam" and "Ain't this a crock?" and twice flicked the safety off his Sixteen with the full intent of vaporizing the entire hair and teeth and scrawny, pest-ridden hindquarters of him who was one man's best friend. Garland was outraged: "You don't touch my dog," he yelled. "Touching my dog will get you killed many times!" A COM/SIT report which surfaced after the war said an hour's discussion followed, during which it was reported that because LURPs in II Corps were supposedly bringing along skivvy bar girlfriends (not to mention those Highway 14 Rangers who'd taken a Saigon rock 'n' roll band named Teenage Wasteland into the Ir Drang Valley), it seemed okay to bring along old Shep or whatever the hell his name was. "He's got to watch his ass," the TL said. "I don't want to hear no squealing or nothing."

According to EYES ONLY paperwork out of the GVN, the murder and Garland's subsequent ill-will began the night he went into the bush with the Detroit Pistons to bury several Black Boxes on a so-called high-speed trail down which Charlie and his ilk were conveying ordnance so sophisticated it was feared that Uncle Ho himself would soon be following in an AirStream house trailer with Bar-B-Que and Magnavox color TV. Garland said the night was pure Alfred Hitchcock: pale moon, inhospitable flora, fauna such as might have been invented by Dr. Frankenstein, not to mention an E & E route they all believed led right past the open door of the Hanoi Politburo. Buster was there, too, half dipped in lampblack to give him that dangerous hell-I-don't-care evil look it took humans only twenty minutes to acquire over there. Everything was fine for a time, the good guys being sneaky and expert, the six of them, men and dog, stopping for a while to eat and catnap, then there was a crackling noise in the woods, a six-sided shiver of recognition, and the TL tumbled over in a heap, a big hole where his chest used to be, which was followed by scrambling, jumping and diving. According to the governor of Texas, who'd heard it from the TBI, who'd gotten their information from the Tarrant County sheriff whose deputies had interviewed the guard and two tellers at the Citizens' Bank on Cedar Street, the ATL took it in the neck, and one by one, in a storm of tears and rendered hearts, all the other Detroit Pistons fouled out, there being now in the whole wide world only two creatures to worry about: a dog that could have been named Butch and a Van Nuys (CA) PFC named Garland H. Steeples whose insides and sense of self were all scrambled on account of fear and a handful of U.S. Army methamphetamine.

"I didn't move for an hour," Garland said in the holdup note he gave to the girl at the Quik-Mart in Richardson. It was a seven-page document in which, his handwriting cramped with hysteria, Garland said he and his mutt huddled in a hidey-hole while all about them flocked deadly sons-of-bitches got up in gray pith helmets and regular greens. "That dog and I were doing some heavy communicating," he wrote. "I was saying *Scoot down, scrunch up, pull that branch over you;* and that dog was saying in body language *Stop leaning on me, let go of my neck, watch your elbow.*" The man at the Texaco station, which Garland stuck up the last time he was in the state, said that Steeples and his dog had a real primary thing going in that hole: they were one breath, one heartbeat, one desire. They could see little, smell nothing but their own stinks and hear nothing but Haiphong gobbledygook. "I could sing to you," Garland said. That dog gave him one dark eyeball and the chin tilt a rich man uses to convey impatience and distaste. "How about this?" Garland wondered, doing several lines of—almost inconceivable in this situation—"Soul Xmas in Bethlehem." His voice, a whisper really, had all the charm of dirt. "I know some others," he said. Around them, they could hear crackling undergrowth and native chitty-chat. "Dog," Garland began, "I believe we're gonna die." He felt the animal looking at him with intense concentration, its eyes like tiny wet marbles; it was then, Garland swore, that he plainly heard that dog talk. It said,

"Steeples, why don't you just shut up for about five minutes and let me think."
If they had been somewhere else, Garland proposed, that canine would have
been smoking a Havana cigar and wearing La Dolce Vita sunshades. Old
Bowzer then said, "How'd I get myself into this pickle?"

(This was Darlene Neff's favorite part, wherein her brother and this
humanoidlike dog crouched face to muzzle in a jungle mud pit, exchanging
opinions. "Garland said that dog sounded like Walter Cronkite," she told her
neighbor one day. "Said that dog was smarter than some teachers he'd known.
Said he had no problem seeing that dog driving a Buick or opening a Sears
account." Even after he was long gone, Darlene liked to describe Garland's
face every time he came to this spot in his adventure: it was a miserable,
fraught-filled expression, what it was, as if he were again in that distant world,
a place of darkness and terror and heat in which it was entirely possible that
persons much influenced by loneliness and imminent doom might indeed
strike up a relationship with rotted tree stump or far-off fleecy cloud.)

Here it was, then, Garland remembered, that his amigo, Old Yeller,
actually barked—a sound so loud and alien in this place it was like a spotlight
shining in his eyes—and he found his hands clamped immediately around that
dog's snout. "You're trying to get me killed," Garland said. Through the leaf
growth, our boy could see the enemy frozen with curiosity. "Steeples," that
dog said, "what the hell are you doing to my neck?" Garland brought the dog's
face to his own. "If I let you go," he whispered, "don't yell no more, okay?"
The animal seemed to take a long time to consider. "Boy," the dog said, "you
ain't learned much about me, have you?" Yet as soon as he was released the
dog started to take off, the racket he was making loud enough to be heard on
the moon. Garland grabbed him by the throat. "What're you doing?" The dog
eyed him suspiciously: "I am leaving here and you, 'bye." Garland clamped
his hands over the jaws again. It was a moment, he remembered, as still as
death itself: two creatures, one with a big brain and no hope, the other with
eons of instinct and four legs for running. "Honest," Garland said once, "I
was inside his brain. I knew where he came from, which was Long Binh, and
that its old momma was the dog equivalent of a three-dollar business suit."
It was thinking dog thoughts: bone and hank, piss on bush and fly on out of
there. Garland could almost see himself through the animal's eyes: a skinny

work of American manhood, some pimpled, its cheeks completely tear-ravaged. "You're about to do something mean, ain't you?" that dog said. "Dog, you are some first-rate animal, you know." The dog affected the aspect, yes, of supreme disinterest: "I could've been a lot of things in this world." Garland could see the bad guys pressing in from nearabouts, all of them evidently waiting for the next peep or telltale howl. He tried explaining that there was nothing else he could do—life was a pisser, it seemed, ignorant of him and his desires. "I'd like to live, plus you're an orphan—and a dog besides." Whereupon that dog, Garland had to admit, tried to talk him out of it, tried appealing to our boy's sense of fair play, of loyalty; said it aimed to go on down to My Khe, heard there was a whole pack of poodles down there, all named Fifi or Babette, with painted toenails and French-cut hair; said it was scraggly, sure, but in the long view offered by such as Monsieur Descartes just as valuable as Lassie or Rin Tin Tin himself. Garland shook his head; he was truly sorry. "Well, then," the dog said, "go ahead and do it, you old son-of-a-bitch." Whereupon that dog composed himself into a sterling example of insouciance and turned on in its eyes a light such as might emanate from that vast afterworld they both knew about.

"So I started squeezing," Garland wrote in a letter to the Dallas *Morning News*. He threw his whole weight, all 176 pounds, into his grip, one arm around the head in a Kung Fu–inspired move the Army had guaranteed to incapacitate utterly. That dog, Garland reported, was thinking airy thoughts the whole time—about getting a bath with GI soap, about having commissary chopped steak in the Philippines, about having maybe even a Washington, D.C., backyard to cavort in. It didn't squirm or struggle or shiver a bit. Though it was still dark, Garland could sense the NVA folks milling about like customers at a circus; and he could feel, as old Buster got short of breath and his eyes rolled up partways, things giving loose inside himself as well—his heart thudding, his stomach doing a flip, his lungs filling up with some awful liquid he assumed was related to having to do unfortunate deeds for the best of reasons in the worst of times. "I don't know how long it took," Garland wrote, " 'cause the next thing I knew it was morning, the enemy had melted away like mist, and I was holding this limp, crushed friend to my chest."

* * *

After he was gone for about four months, you heard this story often and with considerable conviction, it now having entered the popular imagination. It was told by a KINT DJ and appeared in the CB cross-talk on I-10 or up around Odessa. Darrell Royal, then coaching the Longhorns and in Houston for a cookout, told a high-school running back named Scooter that it, the story, was pure-D invention—wish and whine from those of mashed spirit. You heard it in Goree, at the VFW hall in Heron, at Mildred's Diner. It was heard at the Flying R dude ranch in Big Bend country once, all its grit removed, the story itself as slick and unfelt as glass. You heard it gussied up or nude as an oyster. Were it woman, a legislator from Huntington County once said, it would be named Sheree or Debbi-do, a being that looked good with a cocktail or a water bed. Once, Cappy Eads, a one hundred percent look-alike for Santa Claus himself, heard it from the My Sin saleswoman at Neiman-Marcus who'd heard it from her neighbor who'd heard it from her nephew who'd gotten it from a wild-haired East Dallas youth. Cappy said that old Tramp's story was only cheek and shinbone, the bulk and organ of it removed, the murder itself taking place in a thousand middle-class bedrooms, Garland no more than a shade or Vincent Price ghoul from the netherworlds. Sometimes, in fact, Garland wasn't in the story at all, his place taken by an equally unfulfilled round-eyed youth; and sometimes it wasn't a dog which died, but a crawly-grimy piece of work which looked like a vision drunks weep over; and sometimes the story itself took a whole day and much whiskey to tell, its moments from getting to losing spirited, mean and epic enough for silver screen or drive-in movie.

After a year or so, it left Texas for the rest of North America. In Florida, you heard it as "Another Story of Fate and Circumstance," the human no longer a boy but an adult named Dalrhymple or Poot, the dog a specter called forth from the lower waters by tribulation and shared failure. In South Carolina, it had a dozen episodes, including one in which that *canus familiaris* took up a Parker Bros. ballpoint and, after some cogitation, wrote its name and several sentences of the complex-compound variety. At Frank J. Wiley Junior High School in Chaney, Nebraska, it produced a dozen essays, foremost of which was written by Oogie Pringle, Jr., who, at the honors assembly, recited the whole thing, devoting particular attention to those sections in which the dog, some cleaned up for this telling, and on the verge of everlasting darkness, was saying "Okay" at the very instant the protagonist, Garland H. Steeples, was crumbling to dust in his frozen, desperate and wracked heart.

The story was told last, it appears, by the famous West Coast psychic Charlene Dibbs, in the studios of KNET Phoenix, who informed an audience of St. Vincent Gray Ladies that she, at this precise instant, was in mental contact with the notorious felon and veteran, Garland Steeples. It was a moment of dire expectation. She could visualize him now, she said, as if he were sitting across from her, his face darkened by three days of bristly beard, his clothes shabby and loose. "I see him as a hobo," she said, there being in her voice a lilt such as used by those fetched up by UFOs or victims of out-of-body travel. It was Garland H. Steeples, she said, who was living in reduced circumstances, most probably in a trailer park, him the uneasy guest of a woman named Rae Nell. "At this time," she announced, "I will try to invade his mind." There were many oooohhhs and aaahhhs as Charlene Dibbs set herself to this task, her eyes squinty with concentration. "May I have quiet, please?" she said, "I am getting interference." You could see she was doubtlessly picking up the troublesome thoughts of several naughty people, among them those in pain or about to be. "He is miles away," she said. There were mountains in his distance, she said, but mainly he lived in a flat, barren place—a place of winds and wild climates. "My, that boy is unhappy." It was here, everybody would one day remember, that Ms. Dibbs's face suddenly took on a strained, unlived-in look and she pitched forward in her chair until she had arranged herself in a crouch, alert and suspicious. She made sounds, too, throaty and wet, as if what was to be said was best put in grunts and groans. And then, in what came to be known as the climax to this story of man and dog, it came to pass that an army of viewers from Yuma to North Tucson saw Charlene Dibbs, as if by magic, transformed into one Garland H. Steeples, and you could see that he was out there—anywhere, everywhere—long of tooth and gleeless, as if he had centuries to wait, as if he again were in a deprived venue and again faced with the impossible choice between life and love.

MARY HOOD

How Far She Went

They had quarreled all morning, squalled all summer about the incidentals: how tight the girl's cut-off jeans were, the "Every Inch a Woman" T-shirt, her choice of music and how loud she played it, her practiced inattention, her sullen look. Her granny wrung out the last boiled dish cloth, pinched it to the line, giving the basin a sling and a slap, the water flying out in a scalding arc onto the Queen Anne's lace by the path, never mind if it bloomed, that didn't make it worth anything except to chiggers, but the girl would cut it by the everlasting armload and cherish it in the old churn, going to that much trouble for a weed but not bending once—unbegged—to pick the nearest bean; she was sulking now. Bored. Displaced.

"And what do you think happens to a chigger if nobody ever walks by his weed?" her granny asked, heading for the house with that sidelong uneager unanswered glance, hoping for what? The surprise gift of a smile? Nothing. The woman shook her head and said it. "Nothing." The door slammed behind her. Let it.

"I hate it here!" the girl yelled then. She picked up a stick and broke it and threw the pieces—one from each hand—at the laundry drying in the noon. Missed. Missed.

Then she turned on her bare, haughty heel and set off high-shouldered into the heat, quick but not far, not far enough—no road was *that* long—only as far as she dared. At the gate, a rusty chain swinging between two lichened posts, she stopped, then backed up the raw drive to make a run at the barrier,

112

lofting, clearing it clean, her long hair wild in the sun. Triumphant, she looked back at the house where she caught at the dark window her granny's face in its perpetual eclipse of disappointment, old at fifty. She stepped back, but the girl saw her.

"You don't know me!" the girl shouted, chin high, and ran till her ribs ached.

As she rested in the rattling shade of the willows, the little dog found her. He could be counted on. He barked all the way, and squealed when she pulled the burr from his ear. They started back to the house for lunch. By then the mailman had long come and gone in the old ruts, leaving the one letter folded now to fit the woman's apron pocket.

If bad news darkened her granny's face, the girl ignored it. Didn't talk at all, another of her distancings, her defiances. So it was as they ate that the woman summarized, "Your daddy wants you to cash in the plane ticket and buy you something. School clothes. For here."

Pale, the girl stared, defenseless only an instant before blurting out, "You're lying."

The woman had to stretch across the table to leave her handprint on that blank cheek. She said, not caring if it stung or not, "He's been planning it since he sent you here."

"I could turn this whole house over, dump it! Leave you slobbering over that stinking jealous dog in the dust!" The girl trembled with the vision, with the strength it gave her. It made her laugh. "Scatter the Holy Bible like confetti and ravel the crochet into miles of stupid string! I could! I will! I won't stay here!" But she didn't move, not until her tears rose to meet her color, and then to escape the shame of minding so much she fled. Just headed away, blind. It didn't matter, this time, how far she went.

The woman set her thoughts against fretting over their bickering, just went on unalarmed with chores, clearing off after the uneaten meal, bringing in the laundry, scattering corn for the chickens, ladling manure tea onto the porch flowers. She listened though. She always had been a listener. It gave her a cocked look. She forgot why she had gone into the girl's empty room, that ungirlish, tenuous lodging place with its bleak order, its ready suitcases never unpacked, the narrow bed, the contested radio on the windowsill. The woman drew the cracked shade down between the radio and the August sun. There wasn't anything else to do.

It was after six when she tied on her rough oxfords and walked down the drive and dropped the gate chain and headed back to the creosoted shed where she kept her tools. She took a hoe for snakes, a rake, shears to trim the grass where it grew, and seed in her pocket to scatter where it never had grown at all. She put the tools and her gloves and the bucket in the trunk of the old Chevy, its prime and rust like an Appaloosa's spots through the chalky white finish. She left the trunk open and the tool handles sticking out. She wasn't going far.

The heat of the day had broken, but the air was thick, sultry, weighted with honeysuckle in second bloom and the Nu-Grape scent of kudzu. The maple and poplar leaves turned over, quaking, silver. There wouldn't be any rain. She told the dog to stay, but he knew a trick. He stowed away when she turned her back, leaped right into the trunk with the tools, then gave himself away with exultant barks. Hearing him, her court jester, she stopped the car and welcomed him into the front seat beside her. Then they went on. Not a mile from her gate she turned onto the blue gravel of the cemetery lane, hauled the gearshift into reverse to whoa them, and got out to take the idle walk down to her buried hopes, bending all along to rout out a handful of weeds from between the markers of old acquaintance. She stood there and read, slow. The dog whined at her hem; she picked him up and rested her chin on his head, then he wriggled and whined to run free, contrary and restless as a child.

The crows called strong and bold MOM! MOM! A trick of the ear to hear it like that. She knew it was the crows, but still she looked around. No one called her that now. She was done with that. And what was it worth anyway? It all came to this: solitary weeding. The sinful fumble of flesh, the fear, the listening for a return that never came, the shamed waiting, the unanswered prayers, the perjury on the certificate—hadn't she lain there weary of the whole lie and it only beginning? And a voice telling her, "Here's your baby, here's your girl," and the swaddled package meaning no more to her than an extra anything, something store-bought, something she could take back for a refund.

"Tie her to the fence and give her a bale of hay," she had murmured, drugged, and they teased her, excused her for such a welcoming, blaming the anesthesia, but it went deeper than that; *she* knew, and the *baby* knew: there was no love in the begetting. That was the secret, unforgivable, that not another good thing could ever make up for, where all the bad had come from, like a visitation, a punishment. She knew that was why Sylvie had been wild, had gone to earth so early, and before dying had made this child in sudden wedlock, a child who would be just like her, would carry the hurting on into another generation. A matter of time. No use raising her hand. But she *had* raised her hand. Still wore on its palm the memory of the sting of the collision with the girl's cheek; had she broken her jaw? Her heart? Of course not. She said it aloud: "Takes more than that."

She went to work then, doing what she could with her old tools. She pecked the clay on Sylvie's grave, new-looking, unhealed after years. She tried again, scattering seeds from her pocket, every last possible one of them. Off in the west she could hear the pulpwood cutters sawing through another acre across the lake. Nearer, there was the racket of motorcycles laboring cross-country, insectlike, distracting.

She took her bucket to the well and hung it on the pump. She had half filled it when the bikers roared up, right down the blue gravel, straight at her. She let the bucket overflow, staring. On the back of one of the machines was the girl. Sylvie's girl! Her bare arms wrapped around the shirtless man riding between her thighs. They were first. The second biker rode alone. She studied their strangers' faces as they circled her. They were the enemy, all of them. Laughing. The girl was laughing too, laughing like her mama did. Out in the middle of nowhere the girl had found these two men, some moth-musk about her drawing them (too soon!) to what? She shouted it: "What in God's—" They roared off without answering her, and the bucket of water tipped over, spilling its stain blood-dark on the red dust.

The dog went wild barking, leaping after them, snapping at the tires, and there was no calling him down. The bikers made a wide circuit of the church-yard, then roared straight across the graves, leaping the ditch and landing upright on the road again, heading off toward the reservoir.

Furious, she ran to her car, past the barking dog, this time leaving him behind, driving after them, horn blowing nonstop, to get back what was not theirs. She drove after them knowing what they did not know, that all the roads beyond that point dead-ended. She surprised them, swinging the Impala across their path, cutting them off; let them hit it! They stopped. She got out, breathing hard, and said, when she could, "She's underage." Just that. And put out her claiming hand with an authority that made the girl's arms drop from the man's insolent waist and her legs tremble.

"I was just riding," the girl said, not looking up.

Behind them the sun was heading on toward down. The long shadows of the pines drifted back and forth in the same breeze that puffed the distant sails on the lake. Dead limbs creaked and clashed overhead like the antlers of locked and furious beasts.

"Sheeeut," the lone rider said. "I told you." He braced with his muddy boot and leaned out from his machine to spit. The man the girl had been riding with had the invading sort of eyes the woman had spent her lifetime bolting doors against. She met him now, face-to-face.

"Right there, missy," her granny said, pointing behind her to the car.

The girl slid off the motorcycle and stood halfway between her choices. She started slightly at the *poosh!* as he popped another top and chugged the beer in one uptilting of his head. His eyes never left the woman's. When he was through, he tossed the can high, flipping it end over end. Before it hit the ground he had his pistol out and, firing once, winged it into the lake.

"Freaking lucky shot," the other one grudged.

"I don't need luck," he said. He sighted down the barrel of the gun at the woman's head. *"Pow!"* he yelled, and when she recoiled, he laughed. He swung around to the girl; he kept aiming the gun, here, there, high, low, all around. "Y'all settle it," he said with a shrug.

The girl had to understand him then, had to know him, had to know better. But still she hesitated. He kept looking at her, then away.

"She's fifteen," her granny said. "You can go to jail."

"You can go to hell," he said.

"Probably will," her granny told him. "I'll save you a seat by the fire." She took the girl by the arm and drew her to the car; she backed up, swung around, and headed out the road toward the churchyard for her tools and dog. The whole way the girl said nothing, just hunched against the far door, staring hard-eyed out at the pines going past.

The woman finished watering the seed in, and collected her tools. As she worked, she muttered, "It's your own kin buried here, you might have the decency to glance this way one time . . ." The girl was finger-tweezing her eyebrows in the side mirror. She didn't look around as the dog and the woman got in. Her granny shifted hard, sending the tools clattering in the trunk.

When they came to the main road, there were the men. Watching for them. Waiting for them. They kicked their machines into life and followed, close, bumping them, slapping the old fenders, yelling. The girl gave a wild glance around at the one by her door and said, "Gran'ma?" and as he drew his pistol, "Gran'ma!" just as the gun nosed into the open window. She frantically cranked the glass up between her and the weapon, and her granny, seeing, spat, "Fool!" She never had been one to pray for peace or rain. She stamped the accelerator right to the floor.

The motorcycles caught up. Now she braked, hard, and swerved off the road into an alley between the pines, not even wide enough for the school bus, just a fire scrape that came out a quarter mile from her own house, if she could get that far. She slewed on the pine straw, then righted, tearing along the dark tunnel through the woods. She had for the time being bested them; they were left behind. She was winning. Then she hit the wallow where the tadpoles were already five weeks old. The Chevy plowed in and stalled. When she got it cranked again, they were stuck. The tires spattered mud three feet up the near trunks as she tried to spin them out, to rock them out. Useless. "Get out and run!" she cried, but the trees were too close on the passenger side. The girl couldn't open her door. She wasted precious time having to crawl out under the steering wheel. The woman waited but the dog ran on.

They struggled through the dusky woods, their pace slowed by the thick straw and vines. Overhead, in the last light, the martins were reeling free and sure after their prey.

"Why? Why?" the girl gasped as they lunged down the old deer trail. Behind them they could hear shots, and glass breaking as the men came to the bogged car. The woman kept on running, swatting their way clear through the shoulder-high weeds. They could see the Greer cottage, and made for it. But it was ivied-over, padlocked, the woodpile dry-rotting under its tarp, the electric meter box empty on the pole. No help there.

The dog, excited, trotted on, yelping, his lips white-flecked. He scented the lake and headed that way, urging them on with thirsty yips. On the clay shore, treeless, deserted, at the utter limit of land, they stood defenseless, listening to the men coming on, between them and home. The woman pressed her hands to her mouth, stifling her cough. She was exhausted. She couldn't think.

"We can get under!" the girl cried suddenly, and pointed toward the Greers' dock, gap-planked, its walkway grounded on the mud. They splashed out to it, wading in, the woman grabbing up the telltale, tattletale dog in her arms. They waded out to the far end and ducked under. There was room between the foam floats for them to crouch neck-deep.

The dog wouldn't hush, even then; never had yet, and there wasn't time to teach him. When the woman realized that, she did what she had to do. She grabbed him whimpering; held him; held him under till the struggle ceased and the bubbles rose silver from his fur. They crouched there then, the two of them, submerged to the shoulders, feet unsteady on the slimed lake bed. They listened. The sky went from rose to ocher to violet in the cracks over their heads. The motorcycles had stopped now. In the silence there was the glissando of locusts, the dry crunch of boots on the flinty beach, their low man-talk drifting as they prowled back and forth. One of them struck a match.

"—they in these woods we could burn 'em out."

The wind carried their voices away into the pines. Some few words eddied back.

"—lippy old smartass do a little work on her knees besides praying—"

Laughter. It echoed off the deserted house. They were getting closer.

One of them strode directly out to the dock, walked on the planks over their heads. They could look up and see his boot soles. He was the one with the gun. He slapped a mosquito on his bare back and cursed. The carp, roused by the troubling of the waters, came nosing around the dock, guzzling and snorting. The girl and her granny held still, so still. The man fired his pistol into the shadows, and a wounded fish thrashed, dying. The man knelt and reached for it, chuffing out his beery breath. He belched. He pawed the lake for the dead fish, cursing as it floated out of reach. He shot it again, firing at it till it sank and the gun was empty. Cursed that too. He stood then and unzipped and relieved himself of some of the beer. They had to listen to that. To know that about him. To endure that, unprotesting.

Back and forth on shore the other one ranged, restless. He lit another cigarette. He coughed. He called, "Hey! They got away, man, that's all. Don't get your shorts in a wad. Let's go."

"Yeah." He finished. He zipped. He stumped back across the planks and leaped to shore, leaving the dock tilting amid widening ripples. Underneath, they waited.

The bike cranked. The other ratcheted, ratcheted, then coughed, caught, roared. They circled, cut deep ruts, slung gravel, and went. Their roaring died away and away. Crickets resumed and a near frog bic-bic-bicked.

Under the dock, they waited a little longer to be sure. Then they ducked below the water, scraped out from under the pontoon, and came up into free air, slogging toward shore. It had seemed warm enough in the water. Now they shivered. It was almost night. One streak of light still stood reflected on the darkening lake, drew itself thinner, narrowing into a final cancellation of day. A plane winked its way west.

The girl was trembling. She ran her hands down her arms and legs, shedding water like a garment. She sighed, almost a sob. The woman held the dog in her arms; she dropped to her knees upon the random stones and murmured, private, haggard, "Oh, honey," three times, maybe all three times for the dog, maybe once for each of them. The girl waited, watching. Her granny rocked the dog like a baby, like a dead child, rocked slower and slower and was still.

"I'm sorry," the girl said then, avoiding the dog's inert, empty eye.

"It was him or you," her granny said, finally, looking up. Looking her over. "Did they mess with you? With your britches? Did they?"

"No!" Then, quieter, "No, ma'am."

When the woman tried to stand up she staggered, lightheaded, clumsy with the freight of the dog. "No, ma'am," she echoed, fending off the girl's "Let me." And she said again, "It was him or you. I know that. I'm not going to rub your face in it." They saw each other as well as they could in that failing light, in any light.

The woman started toward home, saying, "Around here, we bear our own burdens." She led the way along the weedy shortcuts. The twilight bleached the dead limbs of the pines to bone. Insects sang in the thickets, silencing at their oncoming.

"We'll see about the car in the morning," the woman said. She bore her armful toward her own moth-ridden dusk-to-dawn security light with that country grace she had always had when the earth was reliably progressing underfoot. The girl walked close behind her, exactly where *she* walked, matching her pace, matching her stride, close enough to put her hand forth (if the need arose) and touch her granny's back where the faded voile was clinging damp, the merest gauze between their wounds.

STEPHANIE VAUGHN

Dog Heaven

Every so often that dead dog dreams me up again.

It's twenty-five years later. I'm walking along Forty-second Street in Manhattan, the sounds of the city crashing beside me—horns and gearshifts, insults—somebody's chewing gum holding my foot to the pavement, when that dog wakes from his long sleep and imagines me.

I'm sweet again. I'm sweet-breathed and flat-limbed. Our family is stationed at Fort Niagara, and the dog swims his red heavy fur into the black Niagara River. Across the street from the officers' quarters, down the steep shady bank, the river, even this far downstream, has been clocked at nine miles per hour. The dog swims after a stick I have thrown.

"Are you crazy?" my grandmother says, even though she is not fond of dog hair in the house, the way it sneaks into the refrigerator every time you open the door. "There's a current out there! It'll take that dog all the way to Toronto!"

"The dog knows where the backwater ends and the current begins," I say, because it is true. He comes down to the river all the time with my father, my brother MacArthur, or me. You never have to yell the dog away from the place where the river water moves like a whip.

Sparky Smith and I had a game we played called Knockout. It involved a certain way of breathing and standing up fast that caused the blood to leave the brain as if a plug had been jerked from the skull. You came to again just as soon as you were on the ground, the blood sloshing back, but it always seemed as if you had left the planet, had a vacation on Mars, and maybe stopped back at Fort Niagara half a lifetime later.

There weren't many kids my age on the post, because it was a small command. Most of its real work went on at the missile batteries flung like shale along the American-Canadian border. Sparky Smith and I hadn't been at Lewiston-Porter Central School long enough to get to know many people, so we entertained ourselves by meeting in a hollow of trees and shrubs at the far edge of the parade ground and telling each other seventh-grade sex jokes that usually had to do with keyholes and doorknobs, hot dogs and hot-dog buns, nuns, priests, preachers, schoolteachers, and people in blindfolds.

When we ran out of sex jokes, we went to Knockout and took turns catching each other as we fell like a cut tree toward the ground. Whenever I knocked out, I came to on the grass with the dog barking, yelping, crouching, crying for help. "Wake up! Wake up!" he seemed to say. "Do you know your name? Do you know your name? My name is Duke! My name is Duke!" I'd wake to the sky with the urgent call of the dog in the air, and I'd think, Well, here I am, back in my life again.

Sparky Smith and I spent our school time smiling too much and running for office. We wore mittens instead of gloves, because everyone else did. We made our mothers buy us ugly knit caps with balls on top—caps that in our previous schools would have identified us as weird but were part of the winter uniform in upstate New York. We wobbled onto the ice of the post rink, practicing in secret, banged our knees, scraped the palms of our hands, so that we would be invited to skating parties by civilian children.

"You skate?" With each other we practiced the cool look.

"Oh, yeah. I mean like I do it some—I'm not a racer or anything."

Every school morning, we boarded the Army-green bus—the slime-green, dead-swamp-algae-green bus—and rode it to the post gate, past the concrete island where the MPs stood in their bulletproof booth. Across from the gate, we got off at a street corner and waited with the other Army kids, the junior-high and high-school kids, for the real bus, the yellow one with the civilian kids on it. Just as we began to board, the civilian kids—there were only six of them but eighteen of us—would begin to sing the Artillery Song with obscene variations one of them had invented. Instead of "Over hill, over dale," they sang things like "Over boob, over tit." For a few weeks, we sat in silence watching the heavy oak trees of the town give way to apple orchards and potato farms, and we pretended not to hear. Then one day Sparky Smith began to sing the real Artillery Song, the booming song with caissons rolling along in it, and we all joined in and took over the bus with our voices.

When we ran out of verses, one of the civilian kids, a football player in high school, yelled, "Sparky is a *dog's* name. Here, Sparky, Sparky, Sparky." Sparky rose from his seat with a wounded look, then dropped to the aisle on his hands and knees and bit the football player in the calf. We all laughed, even the football player, and Sparky returned to his seat.

"That guy's just lucky I didn't pee on his leg," Sparky said.

Somehow Sparky got himself elected homeroom president and me home-room vice-president in January. He liked to say, "In actual percentages—I mean in actual per capita terms—we are doing much better than the civilian kids." He kept track of how many athletes we had, how many band members, who among the older girls might become a cheerleader. Listening to him even then, I couldn't figure out how he got anyone to vote for us. When he was campaigning, he sounded dull and serious, and anyway he had a large head and looked funny in his knit cap. He put up a homemade sign in the lunch-room, went from table to table to find students from 7-B to shake hands with, and said to me repeatedly, as I walked along a step behind him and nodded, "Just don't tell them that you're leaving in March. Under no circumstances let them know that you will not be able to finish out your term."

In January, therefore, I was elected homeroom vice-president by people I still didn't know (nobody in 7-B rode our bus—that gave us an edge), and in March my family moved to Fort Sill, in Oklahoma. I surrendered my vice-presidency to a civilian girl, and that was the end for all time of my career in public office.

Two days before we left Fort Niagara, we took the dog, Duke, to Charlie Battery, fourteen miles from the post, and left him with the mess sergeant. We were leaving him for only six weeks, until we could settle in Oklahoma and send for him. He had stayed at Charlie Battery before, when we visited our relatives in Ohio at Christmastime. He knew there were big meaty bones at Charlie Battery, and scraps of chicken, steak, turkey, slices of cheese, special big-dog bowls of ice cream. The mess at Charlie Battery was Dog Heaven, so he gave us a soft, forgiving look as we walked with him from the car to the back of the mess hall.

My mother said, as she always did at times like that, "I wish he knew more English." My father gave him a fierce manly scratch behind the ears. My brother and I scraped along behind with our pinched faces.

"Don't you worry," the sergeant said. "He'll be fine here. We like this dog, and he likes us. He'll run that fence perimeter all day long. He'll be his own early-warning defense system. Then we'll give this dog everything he ever dreamed of eating." The sergeant looked quickly at my father to see if the lighthearted reference to the defense system had been all right. My father was in command of the missile batteries. In my father's presence, no one spoke lightly of the defense of the United States of America—of the missiles that would rise from the earth like a wind and knock out (knock out!) the Soviet planes flying over the North Pole with their nuclear bombs. But Duke was my father's dog, too, and I think that my father had the same wish we all had—to tell him that we were going to send for him, this was just going to be a wonderful dog vacation.

"Sergeant Carter has the best mess within five hundred miles," my father said to me and MacArthur.

We looked around. We had been there for Thanksgiving dinner when the grass was still green. Now, in late winter, it was a dreary place, a collection of rain-streaked metal buildings standing near huge dark mounds of earth. In summer, the mounds looked something like the large grassy mounds in southern Ohio, the famous Indian mounds, softly rounded and benignly mysterious. In March, they were black with old snow. Inside the mounds were the Nike missiles, I supposed, although I didn't know for sure where the missiles were. Perhaps they were hidden in the depressions behind the mounds.

* * *

124

Once during "Fact Monday" in Homeroom 7-B, our teacher, Miss Bintz, had given a lecture on nuclear weapons. First she put a slide on the wall depicting an atom and its spinning electrons.

"Do you know what this is?" she said, and everyone in the room said, "An atom," in one voice, as if we were reciting a poem. We liked "Fact Monday" sessions because we didn't have to do any work for them. We sat happily in the dim light of her slides through lectures called "Nine Chapters in the Life of a Cheese" ("First the milk is warmed, then it is soured with rennet"), "The Morning Star of English Poetry" ("As springtime suggests the beginning of new life, so Chaucer stands at the beginning of English poetry"), and "Who's Who Among the Butterflies" ("The Monarch—*Anosia plexippus*—is king"). Sparky liked to say that Miss Bintz was trying to make us into third-graders again, but I liked Miss Bintz. She had high cheekbones and a passionate voice. She believed, like the adults in my family, that a fact was something solid and useful, like a penknife you could put in your pocket in case of emergency.

That day's lecture was "What Happens to the Atom When It's Smashed." Miss Bintz put on the wall a black-and-white slide of four women who had been horribly disfigured by the atomic blast at Hiroshima. The room was half darkened for the slide show. When she surprised us with the four faces of the women, you could feel the darkness grow, the silence in the bellies of the students.

"And do you know what this is?" Miss Bintz said. No one spoke. What answer could she have wanted from us, anyway? She clicked the slide machine through ten more pictures—close-ups of blistered hands, scarred heads, flattened buildings, burned trees, maimed and naked children staggering toward the camera as if the camera were food, a house, a mother, a father, a friendly dog.

"Do you know what this is?" Miss Bintz said again. Our desks were arranged around the edge of the room, creating an arena in the center. Miss Bintz entered that space and began to move along the front of our desks, looking to see who would answer her incomprehensible question.

"Do you know?" She stopped in front of my desk.

"No," I said.

"Do you know?" She stopped next at Sparky's desk.

Sparky looked down and finally said, "It's something horrible."

"That's right," she said. "It's something very horrible. This is the effect of an atom smashing. This is the effect of nuclear power." She turned to gesture at the slide, but she had stepped in front of the projector, and the smear of children's faces fell across her back. "Now let's think about how nuclear power got from the laboratory to the people of Japan." She had begun to pace again. "Let's think about where all this devastation and wreckage actually comes from. You tell me," she said to a large, crouching boy named Donald Anderson. He was hunched over his desk, and his arms lay before him like tree limbs.

"I don't know," Donald Anderson said.

"Of course you do," Miss Bintz said. "Where did all of this come from?"

None of us had realized yet that Miss Bintz's message was political. I looked beyond Donald Anderson at the drawn window shades. Behind them were plate-glass windows, a view of stiff red-oak leaves, the smell of wood smoke in the air. Across the road from the school was an orchard, beyond that a pasture, another orchard, and then the town of Lewiston, standing on the Niagara River seven miles upstream from the long row of redbrick Colonial houses that were the officers' quarters at Fort Niagara. Duke was down by the river, probably, sniffing at the reedy edge, his head lifting when ducks flew low over the water. Once the dog had come back to our house with a live fish in his mouth, a carp. Nobody ever believed that story except those of us who saw it: me, my mother and father and brother, my grandmother.

Miss Bintz had clicked to a picture of a mushroom cloud and was now saying, "And where did the bomb come from?" We were all tired of "Fact Monday" by then. Miss Bintz walked back to where Sparky and I were sitting. "You military children," she said. "You know where the bomb comes from. Why don't you tell us?" she said to me.

Maybe because I was tired, or bored, or frightened—I don't know—I said to Miss Bintz, looking her in the eye, "The bomb comes from the mother bomb."

Everyone laughed. We laughed because we needed to laugh, and because Miss Bintz had all the answers and all the questions and she was pointing them at us like guns.

"Stand up," she said. She made me enter the arena in front of the desks, and then she clicked the machine back to the picture of the Japanese women. "Look at this picture and make a joke," she said. What came next was the lecture she had been aiming for all along. The bomb came from the United States of America. We in the United States were worried about whether another country might use the bomb, but in the whole history of the human species only one country had ever used the worst weapon ever invented. On she went, bombs and airplanes and bomb tests, and then she got to the missiles. They were right here, she said, not more than ten miles away. Didn't we all know that? "You know that, don't you?" she said to me. If the missiles weren't hidden among our orchards, the planes from the Soviet Union would not have any reason to drop bombs on top of Lewiston-Porter Central Junior High School.

I had stopped listening by then and realized that the pencil I still held in my hand was drumming a song against my thigh. Over hill, over dale. I looked back at the wall again, where the mushroom cloud had reappeared, and my own silhouette stood wildly in the middle of it. I looked at Sparky and dropped the pencil on the floor, stooped down to get it, looked at Sparky once more, stood up, and knocked out.

Later, people told me that I didn't fall like lumber, I fell like something soft collapsing, a fan folding in on itself, a balloon rumpling to the floor. Sparky saw what I was up to and tried to get out from behind his desk to catch me, but it was Miss Bintz I fell against, and she went down, too. When I woke up, the lights were on, the mushroom cloud was a pale ghost against the wall, voices in the room sounded like insect wings, and I was back in my life again.

"I'm so sorry," Miss Bintz said. "I didn't know you were an epileptic."

At Charlie Battery, it was drizzling as my parents stood and talked with the sergeant, rain running in dark tiny ravines along the slopes of the mounds.

MacArthur and I had M&M's in our pockets, which we were allowed to give to the dog for his farewell. When we extended our hands, though, the dog lowered himself to the gravel and looked up at us from under his tender red eyebrows. He seemed to say that if he took the candy he knew we would go, but if he didn't perhaps we would stay here at the missile battery and eat scraps with him.

We rode back to the post in silence, through the gray apple orchards, through small upstate towns, the fog rising out of the rain like a wish. MacArthur and I sat against opposite doors in the backseat, thinking of the loneliness of the dog.

We entered the kitchen, where my grandmother had already begun to clean the refrigerator. She looked at us, at our grim children's faces—the dog had been sent away a day earlier than was really necessary—and she said, "Well, God knows you can't clean the dog hair out of the house with the dog still in it."

Whenever I think of an Army post, I think of a place the weather cannot touch for long. The precise rectangles of the parade grounds, the precisely pruned trees and shrubs, the living quarters, the administration buildings, the PX and commissary, the nondenominational church, the teen club, the snack bar, the movie house, the skeet-and-trap field, the swimming pools, the runway, warehouses, the Officers' Club, the NCO Club. Men marching, women marching, saluting, standing at attention, at ease. The bugle will trumpet reveille, mess call, assembly, retreat, taps through a hurricane, a tornado, flood, blizzard. Whenever I think of the clean, squared look of a military post, I think that if one were blown down today in a fierce wind, it would be standing again tomorrow in time for reveille.

The night before our last full day at Fort Niagara, an Arctic wind slipped across the lake and froze the rain where it fell, on streets, trees, power lines, rooftops. We awoke to a fabulation of ice, the sun shining like a weapon, light rocketing off every surface except the surfaces of the Army's clean streets and walks.

MacArthur and I stood on the dry, scraped walk in front of our house and watched a jeep pass by on the way to the gate. On the post, everything was operational, but in the civilian world beyond the gate, power lines were down, hanging like daggers in the sun, roads were glazed with ice, cars were in ditches, highways were impassable. No yellow school buses were going to be on the roads that morning.

"This means we miss our very last day in school," MacArthur said. "No good-byes for us."

We looked up at the high, bare branches of the hard maples, where drops of ice glimmered.

"I just want to shake your hand and say so long," Sparky said. He had come out of his house to stand with us. "I guess you know this means you'll miss the surprise party."

"There was going to be a party?" I said.

"Just cupcakes," Sparky said. "I sure wish you could stay the school year and keep your office."

"Oh, who cares!" I said, suddenly irritated with Sparky, although he was my best friend. "Jesus," I said, sounding to myself like an adult—like Miss Bintz, maybe, when she was off duty.

"Jesus," I said again. "What kind of office is home goddam room vice-president in a crummy country school?"

MacArthur said to Sparky, "What kind of cupcakes were they having?"

I looked down at MacArthur and said, "Do you know how totally ridiculous you look in that knit cap? I can't wait until we get out of this place."

"Excuse me," MacArthur said. "Excuse me for wearing the hat you gave me for my birthday."

It was then that the dog came back. We heard him calling out before we saw him, his huge woof-woof "My name is Duke! My name is Duke! I'm your dog! I'm your dog!" Then we saw him streaking through the trees, through the park space of oaks and maples between our house and the post gate. Later the MPs would say that he stopped and wagged his tail at them before he passed through the gate, as if he understood that he should be stopping to show his ID card. He ran to us, bounding across the crusted, glass-slick snow—ran into the history of our family, all the stories we would tell about him after he was dead. Years and years later, whenever we came back together at the family table, we would start the dog stories. He was the dog who caught the live fish with his mouth, the one who stole a pound of butter off the commissary loading dock and brought it to us in his soft bird dog's mouth without a tooth mark on the package. He was the dog who broke out of Charlie Battery the morning of an ice storm, traveled fourteen miles across the needled grasses of frozen pastures, through the prickly frozen mud of orchards, across backyard fences in small towns, and found the lost family.

The day was good again. When we looked back at the ice we saw a fairyland. The redbrick houses looked like ice castles. The ice-coated trees, with their million dreams of light, seemed to cast a spell over us.

"This is for you," Sparky said, and handed me a gold-foiled box. Inside were chocolate candies and a note that said, "I have enjoyed knowing you this year. I hope you have a good life." Then it said, "P.S. Remember this name. Someday I'm probably going to be famous."

"Famous as what?" MacArthur said.

"I haven't decided yet," Sparky said.

We had a party. We sat on the front steps of our quarters, Sparky, MacArthur, the dog, and I, and we ate all the chocolates at eight o'clock in the morning. We sat shoulder to shoulder, the four of us, and looked across the street through the trees at the river, and we talked about what we might be doing a year from then. Finally, we finished the chocolates and stopped talking and allowed the brilliant light of that morning to enter us.

Miss Bintz is the one who sent me the news about Sparky four months later. BOY DROWNS IN SWIFT CURRENT. In the newspaper story, Sparky takes the bus to Niagara Falls with two friends from Lewiston-Porter. It's a searing July day, a hundred degrees in the city, so the boys climb down the gorge into the river and swim in a place where it's illegal to swim, two miles downstream from the Falls. The boys Sparky is visiting—they're both student-council members as well as football players, just the kind of boys Sparky himself wants to be—have sneaked down to this swimming place many times: a cove in the bank of the river, where the water is still and glassy on a hot July day, not like the water raging in the middle of the river. But the current is a wild invisible thing, unreliable, whipping out with a looping arm to pull you in. "He was only three feet in front of me," one of the boys said. "He took one more stroke and then he was gone."

We were living in civilian housing not far from the post. When we had the windows open, we could hear the bugle calls and the sound of the cannon firing retreat at sunset. A month after I got the newspaper clipping about Sparky, the dog died. He was killed, along with every other dog on our block, when a stranger drove down our street one evening and threw poisoned hamburger into our front yards.

All that week I had trouble getting to sleep at night. One night I was still awake when the recorded bugle sounded taps, the sound drifting across the Army fences and into our bedrooms. Day is done, gone the sun. It was the sound of my childhood in sleep. The bugler played it beautifully, mournfully, holding fast to the long, high notes. That night I listened to the cadence of it, to the yearning of it. I thought of the dog again, only this time I suddenly saw him rising like a missile into the air, the red glory of his fur flying, his nose pointed heavenward. I remembered the dog leaping high, prancing on his hind legs the day he came back from Charlie Battery, the dog rocking back and forth, from front legs to hind legs, dancing, sliding across the ice of the post rink later that day, as Sparky, MacArthur, and I played crack-the-whip, holding tight to each other, our skates careening and singing. "You're AWOL! You're AWOL!" we cried at the dog. "No school!" the dog barked back. "No school!" We skated across the darkening ice into the sunset, skated faster and faster, until we seemed to rise together into the cold, bright air. It was a good day, it was a good day, it was a good day.

TOBIAS WOLFF

Passengers

Glen left Depoe Bay a couple of hours before sunup to beat the traffic and found himself in a heavy fog; he had to lean forward and keep the windshield wipers going to see the road at all. Before long the constant effort and the lulling rhythm of the wipers made him drowsy, and he pulled into a gas station to throw some water in his face and buy coffee.

He was topping off the tank, listening to the invisible waves growl on the beach across the road, when a girl came out of the station and began to wash the windshield. She had streaked hair and wore knee-length, high-heeled boots over her blue jeans. Glen could not see her face clearly.

"Lousy morning for a drive," she said, leaning over the hood. Her blue jeans had studs poking through in different patterns and when she moved they blinked in the light of the sputtering yellow tubes overhead. She threw the squeegee into a bucket and asked Glen what kind of mileage he got.

He tried to remember what Martin had told him. "Around twenty-five per," he said.

She whistled and looked the car up and down as if she were thinking of buying it from him.

Glen held out Martin's credit card but the girl laughed and said she didn't work there.

"Actually," she said, "I was kind of wondering which way you were headed."

"North," Glen said. "Seattle."

"Hey," she said. "What a coincidence. I mean that's where I'm going, too."

Glen nodded but he didn't say anything. He had promised not to pick up any hitchhikers; Martin said it was dangerous and socially irresponsible, like feeding stray cats. Also Glen was a little browned off about the way the girl had come up to him all buddy-buddy, when really she just wanted something.

"Forget it," she said. "Drive alone if you want. It's your car, right?" She smiled and went back into the station office.

After Glen paid the attendant he thought things over. The girl was not dangerous—he could tell by how tight her jeans were that she wasn't carrying a gun. And if he had someone to talk to there wouldn't be any chance of dozing off.

The girl did not seem particularly surprised or particularly happy that Glen had changed his mind. "Okay," she said, "just a sec." She stowed her bags in the trunk, a guitar case and a laundry sack tied at the neck like a balloon, then cupped her hands around her mouth and yelled, "Sunshine! Sunshine!" A big hairy dog ran out of nowhere and jumped up on the girl, leaving spots of mud all over the front of her white shirt. She clouted him on the head until he got down and then pushed him into the car. "In back!" she said. He jumped onto the backseat and sat there with his tongue hanging out.

"I'm Bonnie," the girl said when they were on the road. She took a brush out of her purse and pulled it through her hair with a soft ripping noise.

Glen handed her one of his business cards. "I'm Glen," he said.

She held it close to her face and read it out loud. "Rayburn Marine Supply. Are you Rayburn?"

"No. Rayburn is my employer." Glen did not mention that Martin Rayburn was also his roommate and the owner of the car.

"Oh," she said, "I see, here's your name in the corner. Marine Supply," she repeated. "What are you, some kind of defense contractors?"

"No," Glen said. "We sell boating supplies."

"That's good to hear," Bonnie said. "I don't accept rides from defense contractors."

"Well, I'm not one," Glen said. "Mostly we deal in life jackets, caps, and deck furniture." He named the towns along the coast where he did business, and when he mentioned Eureka, Bonnie slapped her knee.

"All right!" she said. She said that California was her old stomping grounds. Bolinas and San Francisco.

When she said San Francisco Glen thought of a high-ceilinged room with sunlight coming in through stained glass windows, and a lot of naked people on the floor flopping all over each other like seals. "We don't go that far south," he said. "Mendocino is as far as we go." He cracked the window a couple of inches; the dog smelled like a sweater just out of mothballs.

"I'm really beat," Bonnie said. "I don't think I slept five straight minutes last night. This truck driver gave me a ride up from Port Orford and I think he must have been a foreigner. Roman fingers and Russian hands, ha ha." She yawned. "What the hell, at least he wasn't out napalming babies."

The fog kept rolling in across the road. Headlights from passing cars and trucks were yellow and flat as buttons until they were close; then the beams swept across them and lit up their faces. The dog hung his head over the back of the seat and sighed heavily. Then he put his paws up alongside his ears. The next time Glen looked over at him the dog was hanging by its belly, half in front and half in back. Glen told Bonnie that he liked dogs but considered it unsafe to have one in the front seat. He told her that he'd read a story in the paper where a dog jumped onto an accelerator and ran a whole family off a cliff.

She put her hand over the dog's muzzle and shoved hard. He tumbled into the backseat and began noisily to clean himself. "If everybody got killed," Bonnie said, "how did they find out what happened?"

"I forget," Glen said.

"Maybe the dog confessed," Bonnie said. "No kidding, I've seen worse evidence than that hold up in court. This girlfriend of mine, the one I'm going to stay with in Seattle, she got a year's probation for soliciting and you know what for? For smiling at a guy in a grocery store. It's a hell of a life, Glen. What's that thing you're squeezing, anyway?"

"A tennis ball."

"What do you do that for?"

"Just a habit," Glen said, thinking that it would not be productive to discuss with Bonnie his performance at golf. Being left-handed, he had a tendency to pull his swing and Martin had suggested using the tennis ball to build up his right forearm.

"This is the first time I've ever seen anyone squeeze a tennis ball," Bonnie said. "It beats me how you ever picked up a habit like that."

The dog was still cleaning himself. It sounded awful. Glen switched on the tape deck and turned it up loud.

"Some station!" Bonnie said. "That's the first time I've heard 101 Strings playing '76 Trombones.' "

Glen told her that it was a tape, not the radio, and that the song was "Oklahoma!" All of Martin's tapes were instrumental—he hated vocals—but it just so happened that Glen had a tape of his own in the glove compartment, a Peter, Paul and Mary. He said nothing to Bonnie about it because he didn't like her tone.

"I'm going to catch some zees," she said after a time. "If Sunshine acts cute just smack him in the face. It's the only thing he understands. I got him from a cop." She rolled up her denim jacket and propped it under her head. "Wake me up," she said, "if you see anything interesting or unusual."

The sun came up, a milky presence at Glen's right shoulder, whitening the fog but not breaking through it. Glen began to notice a rushing sound like water falling hard on pavement and realized that the road had filled up with cars. Their headlights were bleached and wan. All the drivers, including Glen, changed lanes constantly.

Glen put on "Exodus" by Ferrante and Teicher, Martin's favorite. Martin had seen the movie four times. He thought it was the greatest movie ever made because it showed what you could do if you had the will. Once in a while Martin would sit in the living room by himself with a bottle of whiskey and get falling-down drunk. When he was halfway there he would yell Glen's name until Glen came downstairs and sat with him. Then Martin would lecture him on various subjects. He often repeated himself, and one of his favorite topics was the Jewish people, which was what he called the Jews who died in the camps. He made a distinction between them and the Israelis. This was part of his theory.

According to Martin the Jewish people had done the Israelis a favor by dying out; if they had lived they would have weakened the gene pool and the Israelis would not have had the strength or the will to take all that land away from the Arabs and keep it.

One night he asked whether Glen had noticed anything that he, Martin, had in common with the Israelis. Glen admitted that he had missed the connection. The Israelis had been in exile for a long time, Martin said; he, himself, while in the Navy, had visited over thirty ports of call and lived at different times in seven of the United States before coming home to Seattle. The Israelis had taken a barren land and made it fruitful; Martin had taken over a failing company and made it turn a profit again. The Israelis defeated all their enemies and Martin was annihilating his competition. The key, Martin said, was in the corporate gene pool. You had to keep cleaning out the deadwood and bringing in new blood. Martin named the deadwood who would soon be cleaned out, and Glen was surprised; he had supposed a few of the people to be, like himself, new blood.

The fog held. The ocean spray gave it a sheen, a pearly color. Big drops of water rolled up the windshield, speckling the gray light inside the car. Glen saw that Bonnie was not a girl but a woman. She had wrinkles across her brow and in the corners of her mouth and eyes, and the streaks in her hair were real-streaks—not one of these fashions as he'd first thought. In the light her skin showed its age like a coat of dust. She was old, not *old* old, but old: older than him. Glen felt himself relax, and realized that for a moment there he had been interested in her. He squinted into the fog and drove on with the sensation of falling through a cloud. Behind Glen the dog stirred and yelped in his dreams.

Bonnie woke up outside Olympia. "I'm hungry," she said, "let's score some pancakes."

Glen stopped at a Denny's. While the waitress went for their food Bonnie told Glen about a girlfriend of hers, not the one in Seattle but another one, who had known the original Denny. Denny, according to her girlfriend, was *muy* weird. He had made a proposition. He would set Bonnie's girlfriend up with a place of her own, a car, clothes, the works; he wanted only one thing in return. "Guess what," Bonnie said.

"I give up," Glen said.

"All right," Bonnie said, "you'd never guess it anyway." The proposition, she explained, had this price tag: her girlfriend had to invite different men over for dinner, one man at a time, at least three days a week. The restaurateur didn't care what happened after the meal, had no interest in this respect either as participant or observer. All he wanted was to sit under the table while they ate, concealed by a floor-length tablecloth.

Glen said that there had to be more to it than that.

"No sir," Bonnie said. "That was the whole proposition."

"Did she do it?" Glen asked.

Bonnie shook her head. "She already had a boyfriend, she didn't need some old fart living under her table."

"I still don't get it," Glen said, "him wanting to do that. What's the point?"

"The point?" Bonnie looked at Glen as if he had said something comical. "Search me," she said. "I guess he's just into food. Some people can't leave their work at the office. This other girlfriend of mine knew a mechanic and before, you know, he used to smear himself all over with grease. Can you feature that?" Bonnie went at her food—a steak, an order of pancakes, a salad and two wedges of lemon meringue pie—and did not speak again until she had eaten everything but the steak, which she wrapped in a place mat and stuck in her purse. "I have to admit," she said, "that was the worst meal I ever ate."

Glen went to the men's room and when he came out again the table was empty. Bonnie waved him over to the door. "I already paid," she said, stepping outside.

Glen followed her across the parking lot. "I was going to have some more coffee," he said.

"Well," she said, "I'll tell you straight. That wouldn't be a good idea right now."

"In other words you didn't pay."

"Not exactly."

"What do you mean, 'not exactly'?"

"I left a tip," she said. "I'm all for the working girl but I can't see paying for garbage like that. They ought to pay us for eating it. It's got cardboard in it, for one thing, not to mention about ten million chemicals."

"What's got cardboard in it?"

"The batter. Uh-oh, Sunshine's had a little accident."

Glen looked into the backseat. There was a big stain on the cover. "Godalmighty," Glen said. The dog looked at him and wagged his tail. Glen turned the car back on to the road; it was too late to go back to the restaurant, he'd never be able to explain. "I noticed," he said, "you didn't leave anything on your plate, considering it was garbage."

"If I hadn't eaten it, they would have thrown it out. They throw out pieces of butter because they're not square. You know how much food they dump every day?"

"They're running a business," Glen said. "They take a risk and they're entitled to the profits."

"I'll tell you," Bonnie said. "Enough to feed the population of San Diego. Here, Sunshine." The dog stood with his paws on the back of the seat while Bonnie shredded the steak and put the pieces in his mouth. When the steak was gone she hit the dog in the face and he sat back down.

Glen was going to ask Bonnie why she wasn't afraid of poisoning Sunshine but he was too angry to do anything but steer the car and squeeze the tennis ball. They could have been arrested back there. He could just see himself calling Martin and saying that he wouldn't be home for dinner because he was in jail for walking a check in East Jesus. Unless he could get that seat cleaned up he was going to have to tell Martin about Bonnie, and that wasn't going to be any picnic, either. So much for trying to do favors for people.

"This fog is getting to me," Bonnie said. "It's really boring." She started to say something else, then fell silent again. There was a truck just ahead of them; as they climbed a gentle rise the fog thinned and Glen could make out the logo on the back—WE MOVE FAMILIES NOT JUST FURNITURE—then they descended into the fog again and the truck vanished. "I was in a sandstorm once," Bonnie said, "in Arizona. It was really dangerous but at least it wasn't boring." She pulled a strand of hair in front of her eyes and began picking at the ends. "So," she said, "tell me about yourself."

Glen said there wasn't much to tell.

"What's your wife's name?"

"I'm not married."

"Oh yeah? Somebody like you, I thought for sure you'd be married."

"I'm engaged," Glen said. He often told strangers that. If he met them again he could always say it hadn't worked out. He'd once known a girl who probably would have married him but like Martin said, it didn't make sense to take on freight when you were traveling for speed.

Bonnie said that she had been married for the last two years to a man in Santa Barbara. "I don't mean married in the legal sense," she said. Bonnie said that when you knew someone else's head and they knew yours, that was being married. She had ceased to know his head when he left her for someone else. "He wanted to have kids," Bonnie said, "but he was afraid to with me, because I had dropped acid. He was afraid we would have a werewolf or something because of my chromosomes. I shouldn't have told him."

Glen knew that the man's reason for leaving her had nothing to do with chromosomes. He had left her because she was too old.

"I never should have told him," Bonnie said again. "I only dropped acid one time and it wasn't even fun." She made a rattling sound in her throat and put her hands up to her face. First her shoulders and then her whole body began jerking from side to side.

"All right," Glen said, "all right." He dropped the tennis ball and began patting her on the back as if she had hiccups.

Sunshine uncoiled from the backseat and came scrambling over Glen's shoulder. He knocked Glen's hand off the steering wheel as he jumped onto his lap, rooting for the ball. The car went into a broadside skid. The road was slick and the tires did not scream. Bonnie stopped jerking and stared out the window. So did Glen. They watched the fog whipping along the windshield as if they were at a movie. Then the car began to spin. When they came out of it Glen watched the yellow lines shoot away from the hood and realized that they were sliding backward in the wrong lane of traffic. The car went on this way for a time, then it went into another spin and when it came out it was pointing in the right direction though still in the wrong lane. Not far off, Glen could see weak yellow lights approaching, bobbing gently like the running lights of a ship. He took the wheel again and eased the car off the road. Moments later a convoy of logging trucks roared out of the fog, airhorns bawling; the car rocked in the turbulence of their wake.

Sunshine jumped into the backseat and lay there, whimpering. Glen and Bonnie moved into each other's arms. They just held on, saying nothing. Holding Bonnie, and being held by her, was necessary to Glen.

"I thought we were goners," Bonnie said.

"They wouldn't even have found us," Glen said. "Not even our shoes."

"I'm going to change my ways," Bonnie said.

"Me too," Glen said, and though he wasn't sure just what was wrong with his ways, he meant it.

"I feel like I've been given another chance," Bonnie said. "I'm going to pay back the money I owe, and write my mother a letter, even if she is a complete bitch. I'll be nicer to Sunshine. No more shoplifting. No more—" Just then another convoy of trucks went by and though Bonnie kept on talking Glen could not hear a word. He was thinking they should get started again.

Later, when they were back on the road, Bonnie said that she had a special feeling about Glen because of what they had just gone through. "I don't mean boy-girl feelings," she said. "I mean—do you know what I mean?"

"I know what you mean," Glen said.

"Like there's a bond," she said.

"I know," Glen said. And as a kind of celebration he got out his Peter, Paul and Mary and stuck it in the tape deck.

"I don't believe it," Bonnie said. "Is that who I think it is?"

"Peter, Paul and Mary," Glen said.

"That's who I thought it was," Bonnie said. "You like that stuff?"

Glen nodded. "Do you?"

"I guess they're all right. When I'm in the mood. What else have you got?"

Glen named the rest of the tapes.

"Jesus," Bonnie said. She decided that what she was really in the mood for was some peace and quiet.

* * *

By the time Glen found the address where Bonnie's girlfriend lived, a transients' hotel near Pioneer Square, it had begun to rain. He waited in the car while Bonnie rang the bell. Through the window of the door behind her he saw a narrow ladder of stairs; the rain sliding down the windshield made them appear to be moving upward. A woman stuck her head out the door; she nodded constantly as she talked. When Bonnie came back her hair had separated into ropes. Her ears, large and pink, poked out between strands. She said that her girlfriend was out, that she came and went at all hours.

"Where does she work?" Glen asked. "I could take you there."

"Around," Bonnie said. "You know, here and there." She looked at Glen and then out the window. "I don't want to stay with her," she said, "not really. I don't want to get caught up in all this again."

Bonnie went on talking like that, personal stuff, and Glen listened to the raindrops plunking off the roof of the car. He thought he should help Bonnie, and he wanted to. Then he imagined bringing Bonnie home to Martin and introducing them; Sunshine having accidents all over the new carpets; the three of them eating dinner while Bonnie talked, interrupting Martin, saying the kinds of things she said. Martin would die. Glen savored the thought, but he couldn't, he just couldn't.

When Bonnie finished talking, Glen explained to her that he really wanted to help out but that it wasn't possible.

"Sure," Bonnie said, and leaned back against the seat with her eyes closed.

It seemed to Glen that she did not believe him. That was ungrateful of her and he became angry. "It's true," he said.

"Hey," Bonnie said, and touched his arm.

"My roommate is allergic to dogs."

"Hey," Bonnie said again. "No problem." She got her bags out of the trunk and tied Sunshine's leash to the guitar case, then came around the car to the driver's window. "Well," she said, "I guess this is it."

"Here," Glen said, "in case you want to stay somewhere else." He put a twenty-dollar bill in her hand.

She shook her head and tried to give it back.

"Keep it," he said. "Please."

She stared at him. "Jesus," she said. "Okay, why not? The price is right." She looked up and down the street, then put the bill in her pocket. "I owe you one," she said. "You know where to find me."

"I didn't mean—" Glen said.

"Wait," Bonnie said. "Sunshine! Sunshine!"

Glen looked behind him. Sunshine was running up the street after another dog, pulling Bonnie's guitar case behind him. "Nuts," Bonnie said, and began sprinting up the sidewalk in the rain, cursing loudly. People stopped to watch, and a police car slowed down. Glen hoped that the officers hadn't noticed them together. He turned the corner and looked back. No one was following him.

A few blocks from home Glen stopped at a gas station and tried without success to clean the stain off the seat cover. On the floor of the car he found a lipstick and a clear plastic bag with two marijuana cigarettes inside, which he decided had fallen out of Bonnie's purse during the accident.

Glen knew that the cigarettes were marijuana because the ends were crimped. The two engineers he'd roomed with before moving in with Martin had smoked it every Friday night. They would pass cigarettes back and forth and comment on the quality, then turn the stereo on full blast and listen with their eyes closed, nodding in time to the music and now and then smiling and saying "Get down!" and "Go for it!" Later on they would strip the refrigerator, giggling as if the food belonged to someone else, then watch TV with the sound off and make up stupid dialogue. Glen suspected they were putting it on; he had taken puffs a couple of times and it didn't do anything for him. He almost threw the marijuana away but finally decided to hang on to it. He thought it might be valuable.

Glen could barely eat his dinner that night; he was nervous about the confession he had planned, and almost overcome by the smell of Martin's after-shave. Glen had sniffed the bottle once and the lotion was fine by itself, but for some reason it smelled like rotten eggs when Martin put it on. He didn't just use a drop or two, either; he drenched himself, slapping it all over his face and neck with the sound of applause. Finally Glen got his courage up and confessed to Martin over coffee. He had hoped that the offense of giving Bonnie a ride would be canceled out by his honesty in telling about it, but when he was finished Martin hit the roof.

For several minutes Martin spoke very abusively to Glen. It had happened before and Glen knew how to listen without hearing. When Martin ran out of abuse he began to lecture.

"Why didn't she have her own car?" he asked. "Because she's used to going places free. Someday she's going to find out that nothing's free. You could have done anything to her. *Anything.* And it would have been her fault, because she put herself in your power. When you put yourself in someone else's power you're nothing, nobody. You just have to accept what happens."

After he did the dishes Glen unpacked and sat at the window in his room. Horns were blowing across the sound. The fog was all around the house, thickening the air; the breath in his lungs made him feel slow and heavy.

He wondered what it really felt like, being high. Once Glen had gone hunting with his stepfather outside Wenatchee and while they were watching the sun come up a flight of geese skimmed the orchard behind them and passed overhead in a rush. As the geese wheeled south and crossed in front of the sunrise they called back and forth to each other with a sound like laughter, and their wings were outlined in gold. Glen had felt so good that he had forgotten his gun. Maybe it would be like that, like starting all over again.

He decided to try it; this time, instead of just a few puffs, he had two whole marijuana cigarettes all to himself. But not in his room—Martin came in all the time to get things out of the closet, plant food and stationery and so on, and he might smell it. Glen didn't want to go outside, either. There was always the chance of running into the police.

In the basement, just off the laundry room, was another smaller room where Martin kept wood for the fireplace. He wouldn't be going in there for another two or three months, when the weather turned cold. Probably the smell would wear off by that time; then again, maybe it wouldn't. What the hell, thought Glen.

He put on his windbreaker and went into the living room where Martin was building a model airplane. "I'm going out for a while," he said. "See you later." He walked down the hall and opened the front door. "So long!" he yelled, then slammed the door shut so Martin would hear, and went down the stairs into the basement.

Glen couldn't turn on the lights because then the fan would go on in the laundry room; the fan had a loud squeak and Martin might hear it. Glen felt his way along the wall and stumbled into something. He lit a match and saw an enormous pile of Martin's shirts, all of them white, waiting to be ironed. Martin only wore cotton because wash 'n' wear gave him hives. Glen stepped over them into the wood room and closed the door. He sat on a log and smoked both of the marijuana cigarettes all the way down, holding in the smoke the way he'd been told. Then he waited for it to do something for him but it didn't. He was not happy. Glen stood up to leave, but at that moment the fan went on in the room outside so he sat down again.

He heard Martin set up the ironing board. Then the radio came on. Whenever the announcer said something Martin would talk back. "First the good news," the announcer said. "We're going to get a break tomorrow, fair all day with highs in the seventies." "Who cares?" Martin said. The announcer said that peace-seeking efforts had failed somewhere and Martin said, "Big deal." A planeload of athletes had been lost in a storm over the Rockies. "Tough tittie," said Martin. When the announcer said that a drug used in the treatment of cancer had been shown to cause demented behavior in laboratory rats, Martin laughed.

There was music. The first piece was a show tune, the second a blues number sung by a woman. Martin turned it off after a couple of verses. "I can sing better than that," he said. Substituting *da-da-dum* for the words, he brought his voice to a controlled scream, not singing the melody but cutting across the line of it, making fun of the blues.

Glen had never heard a worse noise. It became part of the absolute darkness in which he sat, along with the bubbling sigh of the iron and the sulfurous odor of Martin's after-shave and the pall of smoke that filled his little room. He tried to reckon how many shirts might be in that pile. Twenty, thirty. Maybe more. It would take forever.

AMY HEMPEL

Nashville Gone to Ashes

After the dog's cremation, I lie in my husband's bed and watch the Academy Awards for animals. That is not the name of the show, but they give prizes to animals for Outstanding Performance in a movie, on television, or in a commercial. Last year the Schlitz Malt Liquor bull won. The time before that, it was Fred the Cockatoo. Fred won for draining a tinky bottle of "liquor" and then reeling and falling over drunk. It is the best thing on television is what my husband Flea said.

With Flea gone, I watch out of habit.

On top of the warm set is big white Chuck, catching a portion of his four million winks. His tail hangs down and bisects the screen. On top of the dresser, and next to the phone, is the miniature pine crate that holds Nashville's gritty ashes.

Neil the Lion cops the year's top honors. The host says Neil is on location in Africa, but accepting for Neil is his grandson Winston. A woman approaches the stage with a ten-week cub in her arms, and the audience all goes *Awwww*. The home audience, too, I bet. After the cub, they bring the winners on stage together. I figure they must have been sedated—because none of them are biting each other.

I have my own to tend to. Chuck needs tomato juice for his urological problem. Boris and Kirby need brewer's yeast for their nits. Also, I left the vacuum out and the mynah bird is shrieking. Birds think a vacuum-cleaner hose is a snake.

Flea sold his practice after the stroke, so these are the only ones I look after now. These are the ones that always shared the house.

My husband, by the way, was F. Lee Forest, D.V.M.

The hospital is right next door to the house.

It was my side that originally bought him the practice. I bought it for him with the applesauce money. My father made an applesauce fortune because *his* way did not use lye to take off the skins. Enough of it was left to me that I had the things I wanted. I bought Flea the practice because I could.

Will Rogers called vets the noblest of doctors because their patients can't tell them what's wrong. The doctor has to reach, and he reaches with his heart.

I think it was that love that I loved. That kind of involvement was reassuring; I felt it would extend to me, as well. That it did not or that it did, but only as much and no more, was confusing at first. I thought, My love is so good, why isn't it calling the same thing back?

Things might have collapsed right there. But the furious care he gave the animals gave me hope and kept me waiting.

I did not take naturally to my husband's work. For instance, I am allergic to cats. For the past twenty years, I have had to receive immunotherapy. These are not pills; they are injections.

Until I was seventeen, I thought a ham was an animal. But I was not above testing a stool sample next door.

I go to the mynah first and put the vacuum cleaner away. This bird, when it isn't shrieking, says only one thing. Flea taught it what to say. He put a sign on its cage that reads TELL ME I'M STUPID. So you say to the bird, "Okay, you're stupid," and the bird says, real sarcastic, "I can talk—can you *fly?*"

Flea could have opened in Vegas with that. But there is no cozying up to a bird.

It will be the first to go, the mynah. The second if you count Nashville.

I promised Flea I would take care of them, and I am. I screened the new owners myself.

*　*　*

146

Nashville was his favorite. She was a grizzle-colored saluki with lightly feathered legs and Nile-green eyes. You know those skinny dogs on Egyptian pots? Those are salukis, and people worshiped them back then.

Flea acted like he did, too.

He fed that dog dates.

I used to watch her carefully spit out the pit before eating the next one. She sat like a sphinx while he reached inside her mouth to massage her licorice gums. She let him nick tartar from her teeth with his nail.

This is the last time I will have to explain that name. The pick of the litter was named Memphis. They are supposed to have Egyptian names. Flea misunderstood and named his Nashville. A woman back East owns Boston.

At the end of every summer, Flea took Nashville to the Central Valley. They hunted some of the rabbits out of the vineyards. It's called coursing when you use a sight hound. With her keen vision, Nashville would spot a rabbit and point it for Flea to come after. One time she sighted straight up at the sky—and he said he followed her gaze to a plane crossing the sun.

Sometimes I went along, and one time we let Boris hunt, too.

Boris is a Russian wolfhound. He is the size of a float in the Rose Bowl Parade.

He's a real teenager of a dog—if Boris didn't have whiskers, he'd have pimples. He goes through two Nylabones a week, and once he ate a box of nails.

That's right, a box.

The day we loosed Boris on the rabbits he had drunk a cup of coffee. Flea let him have it, with half-and-half, because caffeine improves a dog's trailing. But Boris was so excited, he didn't distinguish his prey from anyone else. He even charged *me*—him, a whole hundred pounds of wolfhound, cranked up on Maxwell House. A sight like that will put a hem in your dress. Now I confine his hunting to the park, let him chase park squab and bald-tailed squirrel.

The first thing F. Lee said after his stroke, and it was three weeks after, was "hanky-panky." I believe these words were intended for Boris. Yet Boris was the one who pushed the wheelchair for him. On a flat pave of sidewalk, he took a running start. When he jumped, his front paws pushed at the back of the chair, rolling Flea yards ahead with surprising grace.

I asked how he'd trained Boris to do that, and Flea's answer was "I didn't."

I could love a dog like that, if he hadn't loved him first.

Here's a trick I found for how to finally get some sleep. I sleep in my husband's bed. That way the empty bed I look at is my own.

Cold nights I pull his socks on over my hands. I read in his bed. People still write from when Flea had the column. He did a pet Q and A for the newspaper. The new doctor sends along letters for my amusement. Here's one I liked—a man thinks his cat is homosexual.

The letter begins, "My cat Frank (not his real name) . . ."

In addition to Flea's socks, I also wear his watch.

A lot of us wear our late husband's watch.

It's the way we tell each other.

At bedtime, I think how Nashville slept with Flea. She must have felt to him like a sack of antlers. I read about a marriage breaking up because the man let his Afghan sleep in the marriage bed.

I had my own bed. I slept in it alone, except for those times when we needed—not sex—but sex was how we got there.

In the mornings, I am not alone. With Nashville gone, Chuck comes around.

Chuck is a white-haired, blue-eyed cat, one of the few that aren't deaf— not that he comes when he hears you call. His fur is thick as a beaver's; it will hold the tracing of your finger.

Chuck, behaving, is the Nashville of cats. But the most fun he knows is pulling every tissue from a pop-up box of Kleenex. When he gets too rowdy, I slow him down with a comb. Flea showed me how. Scratching the teeth of a comb will make a cat yawn. Then you have him where you want him—any cat, however cool.

Animals are pure, Flea used to say. There is nothing deceptive about them. I would argue: think about cats. They stumble and fall, then quickly begin to wash—I *meant* to do that. Pretense is deception, and cats pretend: Who me? They move in next door where the food is better and meet you in the street and don't know your name, or *their* name.

But in the morning Chuck purrs against my throat, and it feels like prayer.

In the morning is when I pray.

The mailman changed his mind about the bird, and when Mrs. Kaiser came for Kirby and Chuck, I could not find either one. I had packed their supplies in a bag by the door—Chuck's tomato juice and catnip mouse, Kirby's milk of magnesia tablets to clean her teeth.

You would expect this from Chuck. But Kirby is responsible. She's been around the longest, a delicate smallish golden retriever trained by professionals for television work. She was going to get a series, but she didn't grow to size. Still, she can do a number of useless tricks. The one that wowed them in the waiting room next door was Flea putting Kirby under arrest.

"Kirby," he'd say, "I'm afraid you are under arrest." And the dog would back up flush to the wall. "I am going to have to frisk you, Kirb," and she'd slap her paws against the wall, standing still while Flea patted her sides.

Mrs. Kaiser came to visit after her own dog died.

When Kirby laid a paw in her lap, Mrs. Kaiser burst into tears.

I thought, God love a dog that hustles.

It is really just that Kirby is head-shy and offers a paw instead of her head to pat. But Mrs. Kaiser remembered the gesture. She agreed to take Chuck, too, when I said he needed a childless home. He gets jealous of kids and has asthma attacks. Myself, I was thinking, with Chuck gone I could have poinsettias and mistletoe in the house at Christmas.

When they weren't out back, I told Mrs. Kaiser I would bring them myself as soon as they showed. She was standing in the front hall talking to Boris. Rather, she was talking *for* Boris.

" 'Oh,' he says, he says, 'what a nice bone,' he says, he says, 'can *I* have a nice bone?' "

Boris walked away and collapsed on a braided rug.

" 'Boy,' he says, he says, 'boy, am I bushed.' "

Mrs. Kaiser has worn her husband's watch for years.

When she was good and gone, the animals wandered in. Chuck carried a half-eaten chipmunk in his mouth. He dropped it on the kitchen floor, a reminder of the cruelty of a world that lives by food.

After F. Lee's death, someone asked me how I was. I said that I finally had enough hangers in the closet. I don't think that that is what I meant to say. Or maybe it is.

Nashville *died* of *her* broken heart. She refused her food and simply called it quits.

An infection set in.

At the end, I myself injected the sodium pentobarbital.

I felt upstaged by the dog, will you just listen to me!

But the fact is, I think all of us were loved just the same. The love Flea gave to me was the same love he gave them. He did not say to the dogs, I will love you if you keep off the rug. He would love them no matter what they did.

It's what I got, too.

I wanted conditions.

God, how's that for an admission!

My husband said an animal can't disappoint you. I argued this, too. I said, Of course it can. What about the dog who goes on the rug? How does it feel when your efforts to alter behavior come to nothing?

I *know* how it feels.

I would like to think bigger thoughts. But it looks like I don't have a memory of our life that does not include one of the animals.

Kirby still carries in his paper Sunday mornings.

She used to watch while Flea did the crossword puzzle. He pretended to consult her: "I can see why you'd say *dog,* but don't you see—*cat* fits just as well?"

Boris and Kirby still scrap over his slippers. But as Flea used to say, the trouble seldom exceeds their lifespan.

Here we all still are. Boris, Kirby, Chuck—Nashville gone to ashes. Before going to bed I tell the mynah bird she may not be dumb but she's stupid.

Flowers were delivered on our anniversary. The card said the roses were sent by F. Lee. When I called the florist, he said Flea had "love insurance." It's a service they provide for people who forget. You tell the florist the date, and automatically he sends flowers.

Getting the flowers that way had me spooked. I thought I would walk it off, the long way, into town.

Before I left the house, I gave Laxatone to Chuck. With the weather warming up, he needs to get the jump on furballs. Then I set his bowl of Kibbles in a shallow dish of water. I added to the water a spoonful of liquid dish soap. Chuck eats throughout the day; the soapy moat keeps bugs off his plate.

On the walk into town I snapped back into myself.

Two things happened that I give the credit to.

The first thing was the beggar. He squatted on the walk with a dog at his side. He had with him an aged sleeping collie with granular runny eyes. Under its nose was a red plastic dish with a sign that said FOOD FOR DOG—DONATION PLEASE.

The dog was as quiet as any Flea had healed and then rocked in his arms while the anesthesia wore off.

Blocks later, I bought a pound of ground beef.

I nearly ran the distance back.

The two were still there, and a couple of quarters were in the dish. I felt pretty good about handing over the food. I felt good until I turned around and saw the man who was watching me. He leaned against the grate of a closed shoe-repair with an empty tin cup at his feet. He had seen. And I was giving *him—nothing.*

How far do you take a thing like this? I think you take it all the way to heart. We give what we can—that's as far as the heart can go.

This was the first thing that turned me back around to home. The second was just plain rain.

BOBBIE ANN MASON

Lying Doggo

Grover Cleveland is growing feeble. His eyes are cloudy, and his muzzle is specked with white hairs. When he scoots along on the hardwood floors, he makes a sound like brushes on drums. He sleeps in front of the wood stove, and when he gets too hot he creeps across the floor.

When Nancy Culpepper married Jack Cleveland, she felt, in a way, that she was marrying a divorced man with a child. Grover was a young dog then. Jack had gotten him at the Humane Society shelter. He had picked the shyest, most endearing puppy in a boisterous litter. Later, he told Nancy that someone said he should have chosen an energetic one, because quiet puppies often have something wrong with them. That chance remark bothered Nancy; it could have applied to her as well. But that was years ago. Nancy and Jack are still married, and Grover has lived to be old. Now his arthritis stiffens his legs so that on some days he cannot get up. Jack has been talking of having Grover put to sleep.

"Why do you say 'put to sleep'?" their son, Robert, asks. "I know what you mean." Robert is nine. He is a serious boy, quiet, like Nancy.

"No reason. It's just the way people say it."

"They don't say they put *people* to sleep."

"It doesn't usually happen to people," Jack says.

"Don't you dare take him to the vet unless you let me go along. I don't want any funny stuff behind my back."

"Don't worry, Robert," Nancy says.

Later, in Jack's studio, while developing photographs of broken snow fences on hillsides, Jack says to Nancy, "There's a first time for everything, I guess."

"What?"

"Death. I never really knew anybody who died."

"You're forgetting my grandmother."

"I didn't really know your grandmother." Jack looks down at Grover's face in the developing fluid. Grover looks like a wolf in the snow on the hill. Jack says, "The only people I ever cared about who died were rock heroes."

Jack has been buying special foods for the dog—pork chops and liver, vitamin supplements. All the arthritis literature he has been able to find concerns people, but he says the same rules must apply to all mammals. Until Grover's hind legs gave way, Jack and Robert took Grover out for long, slow walks through the woods. Recently, a neighbor who keeps Alaskan malamutes stopped Nancy in the Super Duper and inquired about Grover. The neighbor wanted to know which kind of arthritis Grover had—osteo- or rheumatoid? The neighbor said he had rheumatoid and held out knobbed fingers. The doctor told him to avoid zucchini and to drink lots of water. Grover doesn't like zucchini, Nancy said.

Jack and Nancy and Robert all deal with Grover outside. It doesn't help that the temperature is dropping below twenty degrees. It feels even colder because they are conscious of the dog's difficulty. Nancy holds his head and shoulders while Jack supports his hind legs. Robert holds up Grover's tail.

Robert says, "I have an idea."

"What, sweetheart?" asks Nancy. In her arms, Grover lurches. Nancy squeezes against him and he whimpers.

"We could put a diaper on him."

"How would we clean him up?"

"They do that with chimpanzees," says Jack, "but it must be messy."

"You mean I didn't have an original idea?" Robert cries. "Curses, foiled again!" Robert has been reading comic books about masked villains.

"There aren't many original ideas," Jack says, letting go of Grover. "They just look original when you're young." Jack lifts Grover's hind legs again and grasps him under the stomach. "Let's try one more time, boy."

Grover looks at Nancy, pleading.

Nancy has been feeling that the dying of Grover marks a milestone in her marriage to Jack, a marriage that has somehow lasted almost fifteen years. She is seized with an irrational dread—that when the dog is gone, Jack will be gone too. Whenever Nancy and Jack are apart—during Nancy's frequent trips to see her family in Kentucky, or when Jack has gone away "to think"—Grover remains with Jack. Actually, Nancy knew Grover before she knew Jack. When Jack and Nancy were students, in Massachusetts, the dog was a familiar figure around campus. Nancy was drawn to the dog long before she noticed the shaggy-haired student in the sheepskin-lined corduroy jacket who was usually with him. Once, in a seminar on the Federalist period that Nancy was auditing, Grover had walked in, circled the room, and then walked out, as if performing some routine investigation, like the man who sprayed Nancy's apartment building for silverfish. Grover was a beautiful dog, a German shepherd, gray, dusted with a sooty topcoat. After the seminar, Nancy followed the dog out of the building, and she met Jack then. Eventually, when Nancy and Jack made love in his apartment in Amherst, Grover lay sprawled by the bed, both protective and quietly participatory. Later, they moved into a house in the country, and Nancy felt that she had an instant family. Once, for almost three months, Jack and Grover were gone. Jack left Nancy in California, pregnant and terrified, and went to stay at an Indian reservation in New Mexico. Nancy lived in a room on a street with palm trees. It was winter. It felt like a Kentucky October. She went to a park every day and watched people with their dogs, their children, and tried to comprehend that she was there, alone, a mile from the San Andreas fault, reluctant to return to Kentucky. "We need to decide where we stand with each other," Jack had said when he left. "Just when I start to think I know where you're at, you seem to disappear." Jack always seemed to stand back and watch her, as though he expected her to do something excitingly original. He expected her to be herself, not someone she thought people wanted her to be. That was a twist: he expected the unexpected. While Jack was away, Nancy indulged in crafts projects. At the Free University, she learned batik and macramé. On her own, she learned to crochet. She had never done anything like that before. She threw away her file folders of history notes for the article she had wanted to write. Suddenly, making things with her hands was the only endeavor that made sense. She crocheted a bulky, shapeless sweater in a shell stitch for Jack. She made baby things, using large hooks. She did not realize that such heavy blankets were unsuitable for a baby until she saw Robert—a tiny, warped-looking creature, like one of her clumsily made crafts. When Jack returned, she was in a sprawling adobe hospital, nursing a baby the color of scalded skin. The old song "In My Adobe Hacienda" was going through her head. Jack stood over her behind an unfamiliar beard, grinning in disbelief, stroking the baby as though he were a new pet. Nancy felt she had fooled Jack into thinking she had done something original at last.

"Grover's dying to see you," he said to her. "They wouldn't let him in here."

"I'll be glad to see Grover," said Nancy. "I missed him."

She had missed, she realized then, his various expressions: the staccato barks of joy, the forceful, menacing barks at strangers, the eerie howls when he heard cat fights at night.

Those early years together were confused and dislocated. After leaving graduate school, at the beginning of the seventies, they lived in a number of places—sometimes on the road, with Grover, in a van—but after Robert was born they settled in Pennsylvania. Their life is orderly. Jack is a free-lance photographer, with his own studio at home. Nancy, unable to find a use for her degree in history, returned to school, taking education and administration courses. Now she is assistant principal of a small private elementary school, which Robert attends. Now and then Jack frets about becoming too middle-class. He has become semipolitical about energy, sometimes attending antinuclear power rallies. He has been building a sun space for his studio and has been insulating the house. "Retrofitting" is the term he uses for making the house energy-efficient.

"Insulation is his hobby," Nancy told an old friend from graduate school,

Tom Green, who telephoned unexpectedly one day recently. "He insulates on weekends."

"Maybe he'll turn into a butterfly—he could insulate himself into a cocoon," said Tom, who Nancy always thought was funny. She had not seen him in ten years. He called to say he was sending a novel he had written— "about all the crazy stuff we did back then."

The dog is forcing Nancy to think of how Jack has changed in the years since then. He is losing his hair, but he doesn't seem concerned. Jack was always fanatical about being honest. He used to be insensitive about his directness. "I'm just being honest," he would say pleasantly, boyishly, when he hurt people's feelings. He told Nancy she was uptight, that no one ever knew what she thought, that she should be more expressive. He said she "played games" with people, hiding her feelings behind her coy Southern smile. He is more tolerant now, less judgmental. He used to criticize her for drinking Cokes and eating pastries. He didn't like her lipstick, and she stopped wearing it. But Nancy has changed too. She is too sophisticated now to eat fried foods and rich pies and cakes, indulging in them only when she goes to Kentucky. She uses makeup now—so sparingly that Jack does not notice. Her cool reserve, her shyness, has changed to cool assurance, with only the slightest shift. Inwardly, she has reorganized. "It's like retrofitting," she said to Jack once, but he didn't notice any irony.

It wasn't until two years ago that Nancy learned that he had lied to her when he told her he had been at the Beatles' Shea Stadium concert in 1966, just as she had, only two months before they met. When he confessed his lie, he claimed he had wanted to identify with her and impress her because he thought of her as someone so mysterious and aloof that he could not hold her attention. Nancy, who had in fact been intimidated by Jack's directness, was troubled to learn about his peculiar deception. It was out of character. She felt a part of her past had been ripped away. More recently, when John Lennon died, Nancy and Jack watched the silent vigil from Central Park on TV and cried in each other's arms. Everybody that week was saying that they had lost their youth.

Jack was right. That was the only sort of death they had known.

* * *

Grover lies on his side, stretched out near the fire, his head flat on one ear. His eyes are open, expressionless, and when Nancy speaks to him he doesn't respond.

"Come on, Grover!" cries Robert, tugging the dog's leg. "Are you dead?"

"Don't pull at him," Nancy says.

"He's lying doggo," says Jack.

"That's funny," says Robert. "What does that mean?"

"Dogs do that in the heat," Jack explains. "They save energy that way."

"But it's winter," says Robert. "I'm freezing." He is wearing a wool pullover and a goose-down vest. Jack has the thermostat set on fifty-five, relying mainly on the wood stove to warm the house.

"I'm cold too," says Nancy. "I've been freezing since 1965, when I came North."

Jack crouches down beside the dog. "Grover, old boy. Please. Just give a little sign."

"If you don't get up, I won't give you your treat tonight," says Robert, wagging his finger at Grover.

"Let him rest," says Jack, who is twiddling some of Grover's fur between his fingers.

"Are you sure he's not dead?" Robert asks. He runs the zipper of his vest up and down.

"He's just pretending," says Nancy.

The tip of Grover's tail twitches, and Jack catches it, the way he might grab at a fluff of milkweed in the air.

Later, in the kitchen, Jack and Nancy are preparing for a dinner party. Jack is sipping whiskey. The wood stove has been burning all day, and the house is comfortably warm now. In the next room, Robert is lying on the rug in front of the stove with Grover. He is playing with a computer football game and watching *Mork and Mindy* at the same time. Robert likes to do several things at once, and lately he has included Grover in his multiple activities.

Jack says, "I think the only thing to do is just feed Grover pork chops and steaks and pet him a lot, and then when we can stand it, take him to the vet and get it over with."

"When can we stand it?"

157

"If I were in Grover's shape, I'd just want to be put out of my misery."

"Even if you were still conscious and could use your mind?"

"I guess so."

"I couldn't pull the plug on you," says Nancy, pointing a carrot at Jack. "You'd have to be screaming in agony."

"Would you want me to do it to you?"

"No. I can see right now that I'd be the type to hang on. I'd be just like my Granny. I think she just clung to life, long after her body was ready to die."

"Would you really be like that?"

"You said once I was just like her—repressed, uptight."

"I didn't mean that."

"You've been right about me before," Nancy says, reaching across Jack for a paring knife. "Look, all I mean is that it shouldn't be a matter of *our* convenience. If Grover needs assistance, then it's our problem. We're responsible."

"I'd want to be put out of my misery," Jack says.

During that evening, Nancy has the impression that Jack is talking more than usual. He does not notice the food. She has made chicken Marengo and is startled to realize how much it resembles chicken cacciatore, which she served the last time she had the same people over. The recipes are side by side in the cookbook, gradations on a theme. The dinner is for Stewart and Jan, who are going to Italy on a teaching exchange.

"Maybe I shouldn't even have made Italian," Nancy tells them apologetically. "You'll get enough of that in Italy. And it will be real."

Both Stewart and Jan say the chicken Marengo is wonderful. The olives are the right touch, Jan says. Ted and Laurie nod agreement. Jack pours more wine. The sound of a log falling in the wood stove reminds Nancy of the dog in the other room by the stove, and in her mind she stages a scene: finding the dog dead in the middle of the dinner party.

Afterward, they sit in the living room, with Grover lying there like a log too large for the stove. The guests talk idly. Ted has been sandblasting old paint off a brick fireplace, and Laurie complains about the gritty dust. Jack stokes the fire. The stove, hooked up through the fireplace, looks like a robot from an old science-fiction movie. Nancy and Jack used to sit by the fireplace in Massachusetts, stoned, watching the blue frills of the flames, imagining that they were musical notes, visual textures of sounds on the stereo. Nobody they know smokes grass anymore. Now people sit around and talk about investments and proper flue linings. When Jack passes around the Grand Marnier, Nancy says, "In my grandparents' house years ago, we used to sit by their fireplace. They burned coal. They didn't call it a fireplace, though. They called it a grate."

"Coal burns more efficiently than wood," Jack says.

"Coal's a lot cheaper in this area," says Ted. "I wish I could switch."

"My grandparents had big stone fireplaces in their country house," says Jan, who comes from Connecticut. "They were so pleasant. I always looked forward to going there. Sometimes in the summer the evenings were cool and we'd have a fire. It was lovely."

"I remember being cold," says Nancy. "It was always very cold, even in the South."

"The heat just goes up the chimney in a fireplace," says Jack.

Nancy stares at Jack. She says, "I would stand in front of the fire until I was roasted. Then I would turn and roast the other side. In the evenings, my grandparents sat on the hearth and read the Bible. There wasn't anything *lovely* about it. They were trying to keep warm. Of course, nobody had heard of insulation."

"There goes Nancy, talking about her deprived childhood," Jack says with a laugh.

Nancy says, "Jack is so concerned about wasting energy. But when he goes out he never wears a hat." She looks at Jack. "Don't you know your body heat just flies out the top of your head? It's a chimney."

Surprised by her tone, she almost breaks into tears.

It is the following evening, and Jack is flipping through some contact sheets of a series on solar hot-water heaters he is doing for a magazine. Robert sheds his goose-down vest, and he and Grover, on the floor, simultaneously inch away from the fire. Nancy is trying to read the novel written by the friend from Amherst, but the book is boring. She would not have recognized her witty friend from the past in the turgid prose she is reading.

"It's a dump on the sixties," she tells Jack when he asks. "A really cynical look. All the characters are types."

"Are we in it?"

"No. I hope not. I think it's based on that Phil Baxter, who cracked up at that party."

Grover raises his head, his eyes alert, and Robert jumps up, saying, "It's time for Grover's treat."

He shakes a Pet-Tab from a plastic bottle and holds it before Grover's nose. Grover bangs his tail against the rug as he crunches the pill.

Jack turns on the porch light and steps outside for a moment, returning with a shroud of cold air. "It's starting to snow," he says. "Come on out, Grover."

Grover struggles to stand, and Jack heaves the dog's hind legs over the threshold.

Later, in bed, Jack turns on his side and watches Nancy, reading her book, until she looks up at him.

"You read so much," he says. "You're always reading."

"Hmm."

"We used to have more fun. We used to be silly together."

"What do you want to do?"

"Just something silly."

"I can't think of anything silly." Nancy flips the page back, rereading. "God, this guy can't write. I used to think he was so clever."

In the dark, touching Jack tentatively, she says, "We've changed. We used to lie awake all night, thrilled just to touch each other."

"We've been busy. That's what happens. People get busy."

"That scares me," says Nancy. "Do you want to have another baby?"

"No. I want a dog." Jack rolls away from her, and Nancy can hear him breathing into his pillow. She waits to hear if he will cry. She recalls Jack returning to her in California after Robert was born. He brought a God's-eye, which he hung from the ceiling above Robert's crib, to protect him. Jack never wore the sweater Nancy made for him. Instead, Grover slept on it. Nancy gave the dog her granny-square afghan, too, and eventually, when they moved back East, she got rid of the pathetic evidence of her creative period—the crochet hooks, the piles of yarn, some splotchy batik tapestries. Now most of the objects in the house are Jack's. He made the oak counters and the dining room table; he remodeled the studio; he chose the draperies; he photographed the pictures on the wall. If Jack were to leave again, there would be no way to remove his presence, the way the dog can disappear completely, with his sounds. Nancy revises the scene in her mind. The house is still there, but Nancy is not in it.

In the morning, there is a four-inch snow, with a drift blowing up the back-porch steps. From the kitchen window, Nancy watches her son float silently down the hill behind the house. At the end, he tumbles off his sled deliberately, wallowing in the snow, before standing up to wave, trying to catch her attention.

On the back porch, Nancy and Jack hold Grover over newspapers. Grover performs unselfconsciously now. Nancy says, "Maybe he can hang on, as long as we can do this."

"But look at him, Nancy," Jack says. "He's in misery."

Jack holds Grover's collar and helps him slide over the threshold. Grover aims for his place by the fire.

After the snowplow passes, late in the morning, Nancy drives Robert to the school on slushy roads, all the while lecturing him on the absurdity of raising money to buy official Boy Scout equipment, especially on a snowy Saturday. The Boy Scouts are selling water-savers for toilet tanks in order to earn money for camping gear.

"I thought Boy Scouts spent their time earning badges," says Nancy. "I thought you were supposed to learn about nature, instead of spending money on official Boy Scout pots and pans."

"This is nature," Robert says solemnly. "It's ecology. Saving water when you flush is ecology."

Later, Nancy and Jack walk in the woods together. Nancy walks behind

Jack, stepping in his boot tracks. He shields her from the wind. Her hair is blowing. They walk briskly up a hill and emerge on a ridge that overlooks a valley. In the distance they can see a housing development, a radio tower, a winding road. House trailers dot the hillsides. A snowplow is going up a road, like a zipper in the landscape.

Jack says, "I'm going to call the vet Monday."

Nancy gasps in cold air. She says, "Robert made us promise you won't do anything without letting him in on it. That goes for me too." When Jack doesn't respond, she says, "I'd want to hang on, even if I was in a coma. There must be some spark, in the deep recesses of the mind, some twitch, a flicker of a dream—"

"A twitch that could make life worth living?" Jack laughs bitterly.

"Yes." She points to the brilliantly colored sparkles the sun is making on the snow. "Those are the sparks I mean," she says. "In the brain somewhere, something like that. That would be beautiful."

"You're weird, Nancy."

"I learned it from you. I never would have noticed anything like that if I hadn't known you, if you hadn't got me stoned and made me look at your photographs." She stomps her feet in the snow. Her toes are cold. "You educated me. I was so out of it when I met you. One day I was listening to Hank Williams and shelling corn for the chickens and the next day I was expected to know what wines went with what. Talk about weird."

"You're exaggerating. That was years ago. You always exaggerate your background." He adds in a teasing tone, "Your humble origins."

"We've been together fifteen years," says Nancy. She stops him, holding his arm. Jack is squinting, looking at something in the distance. She goes on. "You said we didn't do anything silly anymore. What should we do, Jack? Should we make angels in the snow?"

Jack touches his rough glove to her face. "We shouldn't unless we really feel like it."

It was the same as Jack chiding her to be honest, to be expressive. The same old Jack, she thought, relieved.

* * *

162

"Come and look," Robert cries, bursting in the back door. He and Jack have been outside making a snowman. Nancy is rolling dough for a quiche. Jack will eat a quiche but not a custard pie, although they are virtually the same. She wipes her hands and goes to the door of the porch. She sees Grover swinging from the lower branch of the maple tree. Jack has rigged up a sling, so that the dog is supported in a harness, with the canvas from the back of a deck chair holding his stomach. His legs dangle free.

"Oh, Jack," Nancy calls. "The poor thing."

"I thought this might work," Jack explains. "A support for his hind legs." His arms cradle the dog's head. "I did it for you," he adds, looking at Nancy. "Don't push him, Robert. I don't think he wants to swing."

Grover looks amazingly patient, like a cat in a doll bonnet.

"He hates it," says Jack, unbuckling the harness.

"He can learn to like it," Robert says, his voice rising shrilly.

On the day that Jack has planned to take Grover to the veterinarian, Nancy runs into a crisis at work. One of the children has been exposed to hepatitis, and it is necessary to vaccinate all of them. Nancy has to arrange the details, which means staying late. She telephones Jack to ask him to pick up Robert after school.

"I don't know when I'll be home," she says. "This is an administrative nightmare. I have to call all the parents, get permissions, make arrangements with family doctors."

"What will we do about Grover?"

"Please postpone it. I want to be with you then."

"I want to get it over with," says Jack impatiently. "I hate to put Robert through another day of this."

"Robert will be glad of the extra time," Nancy insists. "So will I."

"I just want to face things," Jack says. "Don't you understand? I don't want to cling to the past like you're doing."

"Please wait for us," Nancy says, her voice calm and controlled.

On the telephone, Nancy is authoritative, a quick decision-maker. The problem at work is a reprieve. She feels free, on her own. During the afternoon, she works rapidly and efficiently, filing reports, consulting health authorities, notifying parents. She talks with the disease-control center in Atlanta, inquiring about guidelines. She checks on supplies of gamma globulin. She is so preoccupied that in the middle of the afternoon, when Robert suddenly appears in her office, she is startled, for a fleeting instant not recognizing him.

He says, "Kevin has a sore throat. Is that hepatitis?"

"It's probably just a cold. I'll talk to his mother." Nancy is holding Robert's arm, partly to keep him still, partly to steady herself.

"When do I have to get a shot?" Robert asks.

"Tomorrow."

"Do I have to?"

"Yes. It won't hurt, though."

"I guess it's a good thing this happened," Robert says bravely. "Now we get to have Grover another day." Robert spills his books on the floor and bends to pick them up. When he looks up, he says, "Daddy doesn't care about him. He just wants to get rid of him. He wants to kill him."

"Oh, Robert, that's not true," says Nancy. "He just doesn't want Grover to suffer."

"But Grover still has half a bottle of Pet-Tabs," Robert says. "What will we do with them?"

"I don't know," Nancy says. She hands Robert his numbers workbook. Like a tape loop, the face of her child as a stranger replays in her mind. Robert has her plain brown hair, her coloring, but his eyes are Jack's—demanding and eerily penetrating, eyes that could pin her to the wall.

After Robert leaves, Nancy lowers the venetian blinds. Her office is brilliantly lighted by the sun, through south-facing windows. The design was accidental, nothing to do with solar energy. It is an old building. Bars of light slant across her desk, like a formidable scene in a forties movie. Nancy's secretary goes home, but Nancy works on, contacting all the parents she couldn't get during working hours. One parent anxiously reports that her child has a swollen lymph node on his neck.

"No," Nancy says firmly. "That is *not* a symptom of hepatitis. But you should ask the doctor about that when you go in for the gamma globulin."

Gamma globulin. The phrase rolls off her tongue. She tries to remember an odd title of a movie about gamma rays. It comes to her as she is dialing the telephone: *The Effect of Gamma Rays on Man-in-the-Moon Marigolds.* She has never known what that title meant.

The office grows dim, and Nancy turns on the lights. The school is quiet, as though the threat of an infectious disease has emptied the corridors, leaving her in charge. She recalls another movie, *The Andromeda Strain.* Her work is like the thrill of watching drama, a threat held safely at a distance. Historians have to be detached, Nancy once said, defensively, to Jack, when he accused her of being unfriendly to shopkeepers and waiters. Where was all that Southern hospitality he had heard so much about? he wanted to know. It hits her now that historians are detached about the past, not the present. Jack has learned some of this detachment: he wants to let Grover go. Nancy thinks of the stark images in his recent photographs—snow, icicles, fences, the long shot of Grover on the hill like a stray wolf. Nancy had always liked Jack's pictures simply for what they were, but Jack didn't see the people or the objects in them. He saw illusions. The vulnerability of the image, he once said, was what he was after. The image was meant to evoke its own death, he told her.

By the time Nancy finishes the scheduling, the night maintenance crew has arrived, and the coffeepot they keep in a closet is perking. Nancy removes her contact lenses and changes into her fleece-lined boots. In the parking lot, she maneuvers cautiously along a path past a mountain of black-stained snow. It is so cold that she makes sparks on the vinyl car seat. The engine is cold, slow to turn over.

At home, Nancy is surprised to see balloons in the living room. The stove is blazing and Robert's face is red from the heat.

"We're having a party," he says. "For Grover."

"There's a surprise for you in the oven," says Jack, handing Nancy a glass of sherry. "Because you worked so hard."

"Grover had ice cream," Robert says. "We got Häagen-Dazs."

"He looks cheerful," Nancy says, sinking onto the couch next to Jack. Her glasses are fogged up. She removes them and wipes them with a Kleenex. When she puts them back on, she sees Grover looking at her, his head on his paws. His tail thumps. For the first time, Nancy feels ready to let the dog die.

When Nancy tells about the gamma globulin, the phrase has stopped rolling off her tongue so trippingly. She laughs. She is so tired, she throbs with relief. She drinks the sherry too fast. Suddenly, she sits up straight and announces, "I've got a clue. I'm thinking of a parking lot."

"East or West?" Jack says. This is a game they used to play.

"West."

"Aha, I've got you," says Jack. "You're thinking of the parking lot at that hospital in Tucson."

"Hey, that's not fair going too fast," cries Robert. "I didn't get a chance to play."

"This was before you were born," Nancy says, running her fingers through Robert's hair. He is on the floor, leaning against her knees. "We were lying in the van for a week, thinking we were going to die. Oh, God!" Nancy laughs and covers her mouth with her hands.

"Why were you going to die?" Robert asks.

"We weren't really going to die." Both Nancy and Jack are laughing now at the memory, and Jack is pulling off his sweater. The hospital in Tucson wouldn't accept them because they weren't sick enough to hospitalize, but they were too sick to travel. They had nowhere to go. They had been on a month's trip through the West, then had stopped in Tucson and gotten jobs at a restaurant to make enough money to get home.

"Do you remember that doctor?" Jack says.

"I remember the look he gave us, like he didn't want us to pollute his hospital." Nancy laughs harder. She feels silly and relieved. Her hand, on Jack's knee, feels the fold of the long johns beneath his jeans. She cries, "I'll never forget how we stayed around that parking lot, thinking we were going to die."

"I couldn't have driven a block, I was so weak," Jack gasps.

"You were yellow. *I* didn't get yellow."

"All we could do was pee and drink orange juice."

"And throw the pee out the window."

"Grover was so bored with us!"

Nancy says, "It's a good thing we couldn't eat. We would have spent all our money."

"Then we would have had to work at that filthy restaurant again. And get hepatitis again."

"And on and on, forever. We would still be there, like Charley on the MTA. Oh, Jack, do you *remember* that crazy restaurant? You had to wear a ten-gallon hat—"

Abruptly, Robert jerks away from Nancy and crawls on his knees across the room to examine Grover, who is stretched out on his side, his legs sticking out stiffly. Robert, his straight hair falling, bends his head to the dog's heart.

"He's not dead," Robert says, looking up at Nancy. "He's lying doggo."

"Passed out at his own party," Jack says, raising his glass. "Way to go, Grover!"

VERONICA GENG

Canine Château

(A DOCUMENT FROM THE PENTAGON'S ONGOING PROBE INTO A DEFENSE CONTRAC-
TOR'S $87.25 BILL FOR DOG BOARDING)

Dear Secretary Weinberger:

I have received your request for particulars about the "nauseating" and
"preposterous" bill run up at this establishment by Tuffy. I would be more
than happy to supply details—I would be *delighted.* As someone who devotes
his life to the humane treatment of animals, I welcome this opportunity to
enlighten the Department of Defense and the Congress, neither of which
seems to have the faintest idea what a dog requires.

Before I get into that, however, may I point out that Canine Château is
far from being some little fly-by-night dog dorm with a few bunk beds, a Small
Business Administration loan, and a penchant for padding its bills to make
ends meet. We have been a major and highly profitable concern since 1981.
Up until that time, I had been a tool designer at Low-Bid Tool & Die (in Van
Nuys), running a private specialty shop called Jeff's Claw Clipper out of my
office. (And I suppose I'm going to get in trouble for *that* now with the IRS.)
They phased out my job in favor of a computer when Low-Bid won the
contract to produce the "manicure kits" (I think you know what I'm talking
about) that President Reagan sent as gifts to Saudi Arabia. But I wanted to
remain within the industry, and I realized the potential for expanding Jeff's
Claw Clipper into a full-service kennel targeted specifically to the defense-
contract segment of the pet-boarding market.

I had heard of a lovely old Spanish Colonial mansion for sale up on
Mulholland Drive, and as soon as I saw it I knew it was absolutely right. At

first I ran into all kinds of opposition—zoning boards, mortgage officers, you name it—but these people very quickly came around when they found out who our clientele would be. We are now the largest (and, to my knowledge, the only) kennel in California catering exclusively to the special needs of defense-contractor pets. These animals, as you may know, are extremely high-strung, and are vulnerable to kidnap by agents of foreign powers who might wish to extort from defense contractors certain classified information (such as details about the offensive capability of purported "tie clasps" regularly shipped by the U.S. to El Salvador). This is a particular danger during sensitive arms-negotiation talks. No kennels could be more relaxing and safe than ours: Canine Château, nestled on a sunny, grass-carpeted five-acre site behind bougainvillea-twined fencing of 33-mm. molybdenum-reinforced warhead-quality steel with FX-14 radial vidicon sensors and zinc-carbon detonators; and, farther south on Mulholland in a newly renovated Art Deco villa, Maison Meow, similarly secured. (Birds, goldfish, and so on may guest at either location, depending on space availability.) We are constantly upgrading these facilities, thanks to the many satisfied pet owners who generously donate not only their technological expertise but also a good deal of materials and equipment that would otherwise just be thrown away at the end of the defense-contracting workday and carted off to a garbage dump or landfill site (at government expense), where it would serve no conceivable purpose except to pollute the environment.

All things considered, then, perhaps I may be forgiven if I preen myself somewhat on our success and our high standards—aesthetic, hygienic, techno-logical, *and* financial. Canine Château operates under my close personal super-vision, and I have something of a reputation among the staff as a strict taskmaster. I wear the key to the pantry around my neck on a platinum chain; and not only is the level in the kibble bin measured twice a day but the bin itself is equipped with a state-of-the-art laser lock, which cannot be opened without a microcoded propylene wafer issued to select personnel only after the most rigorous security check of their backgrounds and habits. Waste of any kind is simply not tolerated—let alone fraud.

Now, as to Tuffy's bill. Tuffy's one-week stay at Canine Château was booked under our "No Frills" Plan. We are hardly a dog pound, of course, but I suspect that even you, Secretary Weinberger, with your military-barracks frame of reference, would find Tuffy's accommodations Spartan. We have had dogs in here—and I'm not going to say *whose* dogs they were, but I think you know the ones I mean—who have run up astronomical bills on shopping sprees at our accessories bar. I'm not criticizing them; most of these dogs are accustomed to a California standard of living, and we can't just suddenly alter a dog's life-style, because the dog won't understand and will become morose. Nor am I suggesting that you, Secretary Weinberger, would seek favorable publicity at the expense of innocent animals whose taste for luxuries was created by profits in the very same industries that you depend upon for the perpetuation of your own livelihood and the good of the country. However, I question the Pentagon's decision to pay without a peep such previous bills as $3,000 for one golden retriever's ion-drive–propulsion duck decoy with optional remote aerial-guidance system and quartz-fiber splashdown shield, and then to quibble over Tuffy's, which was relatively modest.

But enough. As you requested, I am enclosing an annotated itemization of Tuffy's bill, which I trust will carry my point.

Very truly yours,
Jeff Chateau
President, Canine Château

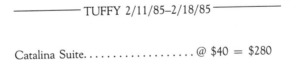

——————— TUFFY 2/11/85–2/18/85 ———————

Catalina Suite. . . . .@ $40 = $280

[All "No Frills" accommodations are suites, and this is our cheapest rate. If it seems a bit steep, consider that each suite is actually an individual bunker, deployed with gyroscopic mounts on an elliptical underground track and activated to a speed of 35 m.p.h. by random changes in the earth's magnetic field. This is a security precaution, and, we feel, an essential one.]

Variety Menu (Mature Dog Cycle), plus tips. . $340

[I suppose that you, Secretary Weinberger, when *your* family goes away, would be just thrilled to have a neighbor shove a bowl of something through the door once a day. Well, an animal is no different. Our gracious waiters and waitresses are trained to make each animal's regular mealtimes as relaxed, enjoyable, and *safe* as possible. They carry conventional Geiger counters at all times, and constantly monitor food, water, and serving utensils with a combat-type bacterial scanner.]

Valet. $15

[Dry-cleaning of hand-knitted dog sweater. This was February, remember, and winter in the Hollywood Hills can be cruel.]

3 Cases of Marinated Mouse Knuckles. $156

[Obviously a computer billing error, as this item is served only at Maison Meow. We will be pleased to delete the charge from the original invoice.]

Contribution. $100

[A tax-deductible voluntary charge to support our lobbying efforts in Congress for continuation of the tax-deductible status for this charge.]

Insurance. $10

[Indemnifies us against layoffs, work stoppages, and rises in the wholesale-price index.]

Cost Overrun. $245
SUBTOTAL: $1,146.00

Discounts

[We then applied our discount schedule, which allows us to maintain a high volume of business while welcoming guests from a wide range of economic brackets: not just executive animals but those at entry level in the defense-contracting and subcontracting industries, whose owners may be privy to compromising information about seemingly innocuous items manufactured for the U.S. government. The discounts were offered at our discretion and may be revoked at any time (for instance, if government-required paperwork increases our operating costs).]

Discount for booking 30 days in advance . . . $400

Special discount for off-peak arrival and departure. $275

Reduction for booking through a state-certified pet-kennel reservations agent . . . $149.75

Quantity refund for four or more stays per annum when the prime interest rate is at or below 15% $200.00

Rebate for using Teamsters-approved pet-carrier $34

DISCOUNTS: $1,058.75

SUBTOTAL: $1,146.00
LESS DISCOUNTS: $1,058.75

TOTAL: $87.25

[Our billing is calculated by the same model of computer used to regulate the range finder on a Polaris submarine. We have every confidence in its conclusion that $87.25 is neither too low nor too high a price to pay for peace of mind.]

RAYMOND CARVER

Jerry and Molly and Sam

As Al saw it, there was only one solution. He had to get rid of the dog without Betty or the kids finding out about it. At night. It would have to be done at night. He would simply drive Suzy—well, someplace, later he'd decide where—open the door, push her out, drive away. The sooner the better. He felt relieved making the decision. Any action was better than no action at all, he was becoming convinced.

It was Sunday. He got up from the kitchen table where he had been eating a late breakfast by himself and stood by the sink, hands in his pockets. Nothing was going right lately. He had enough to contend with without having to worry about a stinking dog. They were laying off at Aerojet when they should be hiring. The middle of the summer, defense contracts let all over the country and Aerojet was talking of cutting back. *Was* cutting back, in fact, a little more every day. He was no safer than anyone else even though he'd been there two years going on three. He got along with the right people, all right, but seniority or friendship, either one, didn't mean a damn these days. If your number was up, that was that—and there was nothing anybody could do. They got ready to lay off, they laid off. Fifty, a hundred men at a time.

No one was safe, from the foreman and supers right on down to the man on the line. And three months ago, just before all the layoffs began, he'd let Betty talk him into moving into this cushy two-hundred-a-month place. Lease, with an option to buy. Shit!

Al hadn't really wanted to leave the other place. He had been comfortable enough. Who could know that two weeks after he'd move they'd start laying off? But who could know anything these days? For example, there was Jill. Jill worked in bookkeeping at Weinstock's. She was a nice girl, said she loved Al. She was just lonely, that's what she told him the first night. She didn't make it a habit, letting herself be picked up by married men, she also told him the first night. He'd met Jill about three months ago, when he was feeling depressed and jittery with all the talk of layoffs just beginning. He met her at the Town and Country, a bar not too far from his new place. They danced a little and he drove her home and they necked in the car in front of her apartment. He had not gone upstairs with her that night, though he was sure he could have. He went upstairs with her the next night.

Now he was having an *affair,* for Christ's sake, and he didn't know what to do about it. He did not want it to go on, and he did not want to break it off: you don't throw everything overboard in a storm. Al was drifting, and he knew he was drifting, and where it was all going to end he could not guess at. But he was beginning to feel he was losing control over everything. Everything. Recently, too, he had caught himself thinking about old age after he'd been constipated a few days—an affliction he had always associated with the elderly. Then there was the matter of the tiny bald spot and of his having just begun to wonder how he would comb his hair a different way. What was he going to do with his life? he wanted to know.

He was thirty-one.

All these things to contend with and then *Sandy,* his wife's younger sister, giving the kids, Alex and Mary, that mongrel dog about four months ago. He wished he'd never seen that dog. Or Sandy, either, for that matter. That bitch! She was always turning up with some shit or other that wound up costing him money, some little flimflam that went haywire after a day or two and *had* to be repaired, something the kids could scream over and fight over and beat the shit out of each other about. God! And then turning right around to touch him, through *Betty,* for twenty-five bucks. The mere thought of all the twenty-five- or fifty-buck checks, and the one just a few months ago for eighty-five to make her car payment—her *car* payment, for God's sake, when he didn't even know if he was going to have a roof over his head—made him want to *kill* the goddamn dog.

Sandy! Betty and Alex and Mary! Jill! And Suzy the goddamn dog! This was Al.

He had to start someplace—setting things in order, sorting all this out. It was time to *do* something, time for some straight thinking for a change. And he intended to start tonight.

He would coax the dog into the car undetected and, on some pretext or another, go out. Yet he hated to think of the way Betty would lower her eyes as she watched him dress, and then, later, just before he went out the door, ask him where, how long, etc., in a resigned voice that made him feel all the worse. He could never get used to the lying. Besides, he hated to use what little reserve he might have left with Betty by telling her a lie for something different from what she suspected. A wasted lie, so to speak. But he could not tell her the truth, could not say he was *not* going drinking, was *not* going calling on somebody, was instead going to do away with the goddamn dog and thus take the first step toward setting his house in order.

He ran his hand over his face, tried to put it all out of his mind for a minute. He took out a cold half quart of Lucky from the fridge and popped the aluminum top. His life had become a maze, one lie overlaid upon another until he was not sure he could untangle them if he had to.

"The goddamn dog," he said out loud.

"She doesn't have good sense!" was how Al put it. She was a sneak, besides. The moment the back door was left open and everyone gone, she'd pry open the screen, come through to the living room, and urinate on the carpet. There were at least a half dozen map-shaped stains on it right now. But her favorite place was the utility room, where she could root in the dirty clothes, so that all of the shorts and panties now had crotch or seat chewed away. And she chewed through the antenna wires on the outside of the house, and once Al pulled into the drive and found her lying in the front yard with one of his Florsheims in her mouth.

"She's crazy," he'd say. "And she's driving me crazy. I can't make it fast enough to replace it. The sonofabitch, I'm going to kill her one of these days!"

Betty tolerated the dog at greater durations, would go along apparently unruffled for a time, but suddenly she would come upon it, with fists clenched, call it a bastard, a bitch, shriek at the kids about keeping it out of their room, the living room, etc. Betty was that way with the children, too. She could go along with them just so far, let them get away with just so much, and then she would turn on them savagely and slap their faces, screaming, "Stop it! Stop it! I can't stand any more of it!"

But then Betty would say, "It's their first dog. You remember how fond you must have been of your first dog."

"My dog had brains," he would say. "It was an Irish setter!"

The afternoon passed. Betty and the kids returned from someplace or another in the car, and they all had sandwiches and potato chips on the patio. He fell asleep on the grass, and when he woke it was nearly evening.

He showered, shaved, put on slacks and a clean shirt. He felt rested but sluggish. He dressed and he thought of Jill. He thought of Betty and Alex and Mary and Sandy and Suzy. He felt drugged.

"We'll have supper pretty soon," Betty said, coming to the bathroom door and staring at him.

"That's all right. I'm not hungry. Too hot to eat," he said, fiddling with his shirt collar. "I might drive over to Carl's, shoot a few games of pool, have a couple of beers."

She said, "I see."

He said, "Jesus!"

She said, "Go ahead, I don't care."

He said, "I won't be gone long."

She said, "Go ahead, I said. I said I don't care."

In the garage, he said, "Goddamn you all!" and kicked the rake across the cement floor. Then he lit a cigarette and tried to get hold of himself. He picked up the rake and put it away where it belonged. He was muttering to himself, saying, "Order, order," when the dog came up to the garage, sniffed around the door, and looked in.

"Here. Come here, Suzy. Here, girl," he called.

The dog wagged her tail but stayed where she was.

176

He went over to the cupboard above the lawn mower and took down one, then two, and finally three cans of food.

"All you want tonight, Suzy, old girl. All you can eat," he coaxed, opening up both ends of the first can and sliding the mess into the dog's dish.

He drove around for nearly an hour, not able to decide on a place. If he dropped her off in just any neighborhood and the pound were called, the dog would be back at the house in a day or two. The county pound was the first place Betty would call. He remembered reading stories about lost dogs finding their way hundreds of miles back home again. He remembered crime programs where someone saw a license number, and the thought made his heart jump. Held up to public view, without all the facts being in, it'd be a shameful thing to be caught abandoning a dog. He would have to find the right place.

He drove over near the American River. The dog needed to get out more anyway, get the feel of the wind on its back, be able to swim and wade in the river when it wanted; it was a pity to keep a dog fenced in all the time. But the fields near the levee seemed too desolate, no houses around at all. After all, he did want the dog to be found and cared for. A large old two-story house was what he had in mind, with happy, well-behaved reasonable children who needed a dog, who desperately needed a dog. But there were no old two-story houses here, not a one.

He drove back onto the highway. He had not been able to look at the dog since he'd managed to get her into the car. She lay quietly on the backseat now. But when he pulled off the road and stopped the car, she sat up and whined, looking around.

He stopped at a bar, rolled all the car windows down before he went inside. He stayed nearly an hour, drinking beer and playing the shuffleboard. He kept wondering if he should have left all the doors ajar too. When he went back outside, Suzy sat up in the seat and rolled her lips back, showing her teeth.

He got in and started off again.

* * *

Then he thought of the place. The neighborhood where they used to live, swarming with kids and just across the line in Yolo County, that would be just the right place. If the dog were picked up, it would be taken to the Woodland Pound, not the pound in Sacramento. Just drive onto one of the streets in the old neighborhood, stop, throw out a handful of the shit she ate, open the door, a little assistance in the way of a push, and out she'd go while he took off. Done! It would be done.

He stepped on it getting out there.

There were porch lights on and at three or four houses he saw men and women sitting on the front steps as he drove by. He cruised along, and when he came to his old house he slowed down almost to a stop and stared at the front door, the porch, the lighted windows. He felt even more insubstantial, looking at the house. He had lived there—how long? A year, sixteen months? Before that, Chico, Red Bluff, Tacoma, Portland—where he'd met Betty— Yakima . . . Toppenish, where he was born and went to high school. Not since he was a kid, it seemed to him, had he known what it was to be free from worry and worse. He thought of summers fishing and camping in the Cascades, autumns when he'd hunt pheasants behind Sam, the setter's flashing red coat a beacon through cornfields and alfalfa meadows where the boy that he was and the dog that he had would both run like mad. He wished he could keep driving and driving tonight until he was driving onto the old bricked main street of Toppenish, turning left at the first light, then left again, stopping when he came to where his mother lived, and never, never, for any reason ever, ever leave again.

He came to the darkened end of the street. There was a large empty field straight ahead and the street turned to the right, skirting it. For almost a block there were no houses on the side nearer the field and only one house, completely dark, on the other side. He stopped the car and, without thinking any longer about what he was doing, scooped a handful of dog food up, leaned over the seat, opened the back door nearer the field, threw the stuff out, and said, "Go on, Suzy." He pushed her until she jumped down reluctantly. He leaned over farther, pulled the door shut, and drove off, slowly. Then he drove faster and faster.

* * *

He stopped at Dupee's, the first bar he came to on the way back to Sacramento. He was jumpy and perspiring. He didn't feel exactly unburdened or relieved, as he had thought he would feel. But he kept assuring himself it was a step in the right direction, that the good feeling would settle on him tomorrow. The thing to do was to wait it out.

After four beers a girl in a turtleneck sweater and sandals and carrying a suitcase sat down beside him. She set the suitcase between the stools. She seemed to know the bartender, and the bartender had something to say to her whenever he came by, once or twice stopping briefly to talk. She told Al her name was Molly, but she wouldn't let him buy her a beer. Instead, she offered to eat half a pizza.

He smiled at her, and she smiled back. He took out his cigarettes and his lighter and put them on the bar.

"Pizza it is!" he said.

Later, he said, "Can I give you a lift somewhere?"

"No, thanks. I'm waiting for someone," she said.

He said, "Where you heading for?"

She said, "No place. Oh," she said, touching the suitcase with her toe, "you mean that?" Laughing. "I live here in West Sac. I'm not going anyplace. It's just a washing-machine motor inside belongs to my mother. Jerry—that's the bartender—he's good at fixing things. Jerry said he'd fix it for nothing."

Al got up. He weaved a little as he leaned over her. He said, "Well, good-bye, honey. I'll see you around."

"You bet!" she said. "And thanks for the pizza. Hadn't eaten since lunch. Been trying to take some of this off." She raised her sweater, gathered a handful of flesh at the waist.

"Sure I can't give you a lift someplace?" he said.

The woman shook her head.

In the car again, driving, he reached for his cigarettes and then, frantically, for his lighter, remembering leaving everything on the bar. The hell with it, he thought, let her have it. Let her put the lighter and the cigarettes in the suitcase along with the washing machine. He chalked it up against the dog, one more expense. But the last, by God! It angered him now, now that he was getting things in order, that the girl hadn't been more friendly. If he'd been in a different frame of mind, he could have picked her up. But when you're depressed, it shows all over you, even the way you light a cigarette.

He decided to go see Jill. He stopped at a liquor store and bought a pint of whiskey and climbed the stairs to her apartment and he stopped at the landing to catch his breath and to clean his teeth with his tongue. He could still taste the mushrooms from the pizza, and his mouth and throat were seared from the whiskey. He realized that what he wanted to do was to go right to Jill's bathroom and use her toothbrush.

He knocked. "It's me, Al," he whispered. "Al," he said louder. He heard her feet hit the floor. She threw the lock and then tried to undo the chain as he leaned heavily against the door.

"Just a minute, honey. Al, you'll have to quit pushing—I can't unhook it. There," she said, and opened the door, scanning his face as she took him by the hand.

They embraced clumsily, and he kissed her on the cheek.

"Sit down, honey. Here." She switched on a lamp and helped him to the couch. Then she touched her fingers to her curlers and said, "I'll put on some lipstick. What would you like in the meantime? Coffee? Juice? A beer? I think I have some beer. What do you have there . . . whiskey? What would you like, honey?" She stroked his hair with one hand and leaned over him, gazing into his eyes. "Poor baby, what would you like?" she said.

"Just want you hold me," he said. "Here. Sit down. No lipstick," he said, pulling her onto his lap. "Hold. I'm falling," he said.

She put an arm around his shoulders. She said, "You come on over to the bed, baby, I'll give you what you like."

"Tell you, Jill," he said, "skating on thin ice. Crash through any minute . . . I don't know." He stared at her with a fixed, puffy expression that he could feel but not correct. "Serious," he said.

She nodded. "Don't think about anything, baby. Just relax," she said. She pulled his face to hers and kissed him on the forehead and then the lips. She turned slightly on his lap and said, "No, don't move, Al," the fingers of

180

both hands suddenly slipping around the back of his neck and gripping his face at the same time. His eyes wobbled around the room an instant, then tried to focus on what she was doing. She held his head in place in her strong fingers. With her thumbnails she was squeezing out a blackhead to the side of his nose.

"Sit still!" she said.

"No," he said. "Don't! Stop! Not in the mood for that."

"I almost have it. Sit still, I said! . . . There, look at that. What do you think of that? Didn't know that was there, did you? Now just one more, a big one, baby. The last one," she said.

"Bathroom," he said, forcing her off, freeing his way.

At home it was all tears, confusion. Mary ran out to the car, crying, before he could get parked.

"Suzy's gone," she sobbed. "Suzy's gone. She's never coming back, Daddy, I know it. She's gone!"

My God, heart lurching. *What have I done?*

"Now don't worry, sweetheart. She's probably just off running around somewhere. She'll be back," he said.

"She isn't, Daddy, I know she isn't. Mama said we may have to get another dog."

"Wouldn't that be all right, honey?" he said. "Another dog, if Suzy doesn't come back? We'll go to the pet store—"

"I don't want another dog!" the child cried, holding on to his leg.

"Can we have a monkey, Daddy, instead of a dog?" Alex asked. "If we go to the pet store to look for a dog, can we have a monkey instead?"

"I don't want a monkey!" Mary cried. "I want Suzy."

"Everybody let go now, let Daddy in the house. Daddy has a terrible, terrible headache," he said.

Betty lifted a casserole dish from the oven. She looked tired, irritable . . . older. She didn't look at him. "The kids tell you? Suzy's gone? I've combed the neighborhood. Everywhere, I swear."

"That dog'll turn up," he said. "Probably just running around somewhere. That dog'll come back," he said.

"Seriously," she said, turning to him with her hands on her hips, "I think it's something else. I think she might have got hit by a car. I want you to drive around. The kids called her last night, and she was gone then. That's the last's been seen of her. I called the pound and described her to them, but they said all their trucks aren't in yet. I'm supposed to call again in the morning."

He went into the bathroom and could hear her still going on. He began to run the water in the sink, wondering, with a fluttery sensation in his stomach, how grave exactly was his mistake. When he turned off the faucets, he could still hear her. He kept staring at the sink.

"Did you hear me?" she called. "I want you to drive around and look for her after supper. The kids can go with you and look, too . . . Al?"

"Yes, yes," he answered.

"What?" she said. "What'd you say?"

"I said yes. Yes! All right. Anything! Just let me wash up first, will you?"

She looked through from the kitchen. "Well, what in the hell is eating you? I didn't ask you to get drunk last night, did I? I've had enough of it, I can tell you! I've had a hell of a day, if you want to know. Alex waking me up at five this morning getting in with me, telling me his daddy was snoring so loud that . . . that you *scared* him! *I* saw you out there with your clothes on passed out and the room smelling to high heaven. I tell you, I've had enough of it!" She looked around the kitchen quickly, as if to seize something.

He kicked the door shut. Everything was going to hell. While he was shaving, he stopped once and held the razor in his hand and looked at himself in the mirror: his face doughy, characterless—*immoral,* that was the word. He laid the razor down. *I believe I have made the gravest mistake this time. I believe I have made the gravest mistake of all.* He brought the razor up to his throat and finished.

He did not shower, did not change clothes. "Put my supper in the oven for me," he said. "Or in the refrigerator. I'm going out. Right now," he said.

"You can wait till after supper. The kids can go with you."

"No, the hell with that. Let the kids eat supper, look around here if they want. I'm not hungry, and it'll be dark soon."

"Is everybody going crazy?" she said. "I don't know what's going to

182

happen to us. I'm ready for a nervous breakdown. I'm ready to lose my mind. What's going to happen to the kids if I lose my mind?" She slumped against the draining board, her face crumpled, tears rolling off her cheeks. "You don't love them, anyway! You never have. It isn't the dog I'm worried about. It's us! It's us! I know you don't love me anymore—goddamn you!—but you don't even love the kids!"

"Betty, Betty!" he said. "My God!" he said. "Everything's going to be all right. I promise you," he said. "Don't worry," he said. "I promise you, things'll be all right. I'll find the dog and then things will be all right," he said.

He bounded out of the house, ducked into the bushes as he heard his children coming: the girl crying, saying, "Suzy, Suzy"; the boy saying maybe a train ran over her. When they were inside the house, he made a break for the car.

He fretted at all the lights he had to wait for, bitterly resented the time lost when he stopped for gas. The sun was low and heavy, just over the squat range of hills at the far end of the valley. At best, he had an hour of daylight.

He saw his whole life a ruin from here on in. If he lived another fifty years—hardly likely—he felt he'd never get over it, abandoning the dog. He felt he was finished if he didn't find the dog. A man who would get rid of a little dog wasn't worth a damn. That kind of man would do anything, would stop at nothing.

He squirmed in the seat, kept staring into the swollen face of the sun as it moved lower into the hills. He knew the situation was all out of proportion now, but he couldn't help it. He knew he must somehow retrieve the dog, as the night before he had known he must lose it.

"I'm the one going crazy," he said, and then nodded his head in agreement.

He came in the other way this time, by the field where he had let her off, alert for any sign of movement.

"Let her be there," he said.

He stopped the car and searched the field. Then he drove on, slowly. A station wagon with the motor idling was parked in the drive of the lone house, and he saw a well-dressed woman in heels come out the front door with a little girl. They stared at him as he passed. Farther on he turned left, his eyes taking in the street and the yards on each side as far down as he could see. Nothing. Two kids with bicycles a block away stood beside a parked car.

"Hi," he said to the two boys as he pulled up alongside. "You fellows see anything of a little white dog around today? A kind of white shaggy dog? I lost one."

One boy just gazed at him. The other said, "I saw a lot of little kids playing with a dog over there this afternoon. The street the other side of this one. I don't know what kind of dog it was. It was white maybe. There was a lot of kids."

"Okay, good. Thanks," Al said. "Thank you very, very much," he said.

He turned right at the end of the street. He concentrated on the street ahead. The sun had gone down now. It was nearly dark. Houses pitched side by side, trees, lawns, telephone poles, parked cars, it struck him as serene, untroubled. He could hear a man calling his children; he saw a woman in an apron step to the lighted door of her house.

"Is there still a chance for me?" Al said. He felt tears spring to his eyes. He was amazed. He couldn't help but grin at himself and shake his head as he got out his handkerchief. Then he saw a group of children coming down the street. He waved to get their attention.

"You kids see anything of a little white dog?" Al said to them.

"Oh sure," one boy said. "Is it your dog?"

Al nodded.

"We were just playing with him about a minute ago, down the street. In Terry's yard." The boy pointed. "Down the street."

"You got kids?" one of the little girls spoke up.

"I do," Al said.

"Terry said he's going to keep him. He don't have a dog," the boy said.

"I don't know," Al said. "I don't think my kids would like that. It belongs to them. It's just lost," Al said.

He drove on down the street. It was dark now, hard to see, and he began to panic again, cursing silently. He swore at what a weathervane he was, changing this way and that, one moment this, the next moment that.

He saw the dog then. He understood he had been looking at it for a time. The dog moved slowly, nosing the grass along a fence. Al got out of the car, started across the lawn, crouching forward as he walked, calling, "Suzy, Suzy, Suzy."

The dog stopped when she saw him. She raised her head. He sat down on his heels, reached out his arm, waiting. They looked at each other. She moved her tail in greeting. She lay down with her head between her front legs and regarded him. He waited. She got up. She went around the fence and out of sight.

He sat there. He thought he didn't feel so bad, all things considered. The world was full of dogs. There were dogs and there were dogs. Some dogs you just couldn't do anything with.

ALICE ADAMS

Molly's Dog

Accustomed to extremes of mood, which she experienced less as "swings" than as plunges, or more rarely as soarings, Molly Harper, a newly retired screenwriter, was nevertheless quite overwhelmed by the blackness—the horror, really, with which, one dark predawn hour, she viewed a minor trip, a jaunt from San Francisco to Carmel, to which she had very much looked forward. It was to be a weekend, simply, at an inn where in fact she had often stayed before, with various lovers (Molly's emotional past had been strenuous). This time she was to travel with Sandy Norris, an old non-lover friend, who owned a bookstore. (Sandy usually had at least a part-time lover of his own, one in a series of nice young men.)

Before her film job, and her move to Los Angeles, Molly had been a poet, a good one—even, one year, a Yale Younger Poet. But she was living, then, from hand to mouth, from one idiot job to another. (Sandy was a friend from that era; they began as neighbors in a shabby North Beach apartment building, now long since demolished.) As she had approached middle age, though, being broke all the time seemed undignified, if not downright scary. It wore her down, and she grabbed at the film work and moved down to L.A. Some years of that life were wearing in another way, she found, and she moved from Malibu back up to San Francisco, with a little saved money, and her three beautiful, cross old cats. And hopes for a new and calmer life. She meant to start seriously writing again.

In her pre-trip waking nightmare, though, which was convincing in the way that such an hour's imaginings always are (one sees the truth, and sees

186

that any sunnier ideas are chimerical, delusions) at three or four A.M., Molly pictured the two of them, as they would be in tawdry, ridiculous Carmel: herself, a scrawny sun-dried older woman, and Sandy, her wheezing, chain-smoking fat queer friend. There would be some silly awkwardness about sleeping arrangements, and instead of making love they would drink too much.

And, fatally, she thought of another weekend, in that same inn, years back: she remembered entering one of the cabins with a lover, and as soon as he, the lover, had closed the door they had turned to each other and kissed, had laughed and hurried off to bed. Contrast enough to make her nearly weep—and she knew, too, at four in the morning, that her cherished view of a meadow, and the river, the sea, would now be blocked by condominiums, or something.

This trip, she realized too late, at dawn, was to represent a serious error in judgment, one more in a lifetime of dark mistakes. It would weigh down and quite possibly sink her friendship with Sandy, and she put a high value on friendship. Their one previous lapse, hers and Sandy's, which occurred when she stopped smoking and he did not (according to Sandy she had been most unpleasant about it, and perhaps she had been), had made Molly extremely unhappy.

But, good friends as she and Sandy were, why on earth a weekend together? The very frivolousness with which this plan had been hit upon seemed ominous; simply, Sandy had said that funnily enough he had never been to Carmel, and Molly had said that she knew a nifty place to stay. And so, why not? they said. A long time ago, when they both were poor, either of them would have given anything for such a weekend (though not with each other) and perhaps that was how things should be, Molly judged, at almost five. And she thought of all the poor lovers, who could never go anywhere at all, who quarrel from sheer claustrophobia.

Not surprisingly, the next morning Molly felt considerably better, although imperfectly rested. But with almost her accustomed daytime energy she set about getting ready for the trip, doing several things simultaneously, as was her tendency: packing clothes and breakfast food (the cabins were equipped with little kitchens, she remembered), straightening up her flat and arranging the cats' quarters on her porch.

By two in the afternoon, the hour established for their departure, Molly was ready to go, if a little sleepy; fatigue had begun to cut into her energy. Well, she was not twenty anymore, or thirty or forty, even, she told herself, tolerantly.

Sandy telephoned at two-fifteen. In his raspy voice he apologized; his assistant had been late getting in, he still had a couple of things to do. He would pick her up at three, three-thirty at the latest.

Irritating: Molly had sometimes thought that Sandy's habitual lateness was his way of establishing control; at other times she thought that he was simply tardy, as she herself was punctual (but why?). However, wanting a good start to their weekend, she told him that that was really okay; it did not matter what time they got to Carmel, did it?

She had begun a rereading of *Howards End*, which she planned to take along, and now she found that the book was even better than she remembered it as being, from the wonderful assurance of the first sentence, "One may as well begin with Helen's letters to her sister—" Sitting in her sunny window, with her sleeping cats, Molly managed to be wholly absorbed in her reading—not in waiting for Sandy, nor in thinking, especially, of Carmel.

Just past four he arrived at her door: Sandy, in his pressed blue blazer, thin hair combed flat, his reddish face bright. Letting him in, brushing cheeks in the kiss of friends, Molly thought how nice he looked, after all: his kind blue eyes, sad witty mouth.

He apologized for lateness. "I absolutely had to take a shower," he said, with his just-crooked smile.

"Well, it's really all right. I'd begun *Howards End* again. I'd forgotten how wonderful it is."

"Oh well. *Forster.*"

Thus began one of the rambling conversations, more bookish gossip than "literary," which formed, perhaps, the core of their friendship, its reliable staple. In a scattered way they ran about, conversationally, among favorite old novels, discussing characters not quite as intimates but certainly as contemporaries, as alive. *Was* Margaret Schlegel somewhat prudish? Sandy felt that she was; Molly took a more sympathetic view of her shyness. Such talk, highly pleasurable and reassuring to them both, carried Molly and Sandy, in his small green car, past the dull first half of their trip: down the Bayshore Highway, past San Jose and Gilroy, and took them to where (Molly well remembered) it all became beautiful. Broad stretches of bright green early summer fields; distant hills, grayish-blue; and then islands of sweeping dark live oaks.

At the outskirts of Carmel itself a little of her predawn apprehension came back to Molly, as they drove past those imitation Cotswold cottages, fake-Spanish haciendas, or bright little gingerbread houses. And the main drag, Ocean Avenue, with its shops, shops—all that tweed and pewter, "imported" jams and tea. More tourists than ever before, of course, in their bright synthetic tourist clothes, their bulging shopping bags—Japanese, French, German, English tourists, taking home their awful wares.

"You turn left next, on Dolores," Molly instructed, and then heard herself begin nervously to babble. "Of course if the place has really been wrecked we don't have to stay for two nights, do we. We could go on down to Big Sur, or just go home, for heaven's sake."

"In any case, sweetie, if they've wrecked it, it won't be your fault." Sandy laughed, and wheezed, and coughed. He had been smoking all the way down, which Molly had succeeded in not mentioning.

Before them, then, was their destination: the inn, with its clump of white cottages. And the meadow. So far, nothing that Molly could see had changed. No condominiums. Everything as remembered.

They were given the cabin farthest from the central office, the one nearest the meadow, and the river and the sea. A small bedroom, smaller kitchen, and in the living room a studio couch. Big windows, and that view.

"Obviously, the bedroom is yours," Sandy magnanimously declared, plunking down his bag on the studio couch.

"Well" was all for the moment that Molly could say, as she put her small bag down in the bedroom, and went into the kitchen with the sack of breakfast things. From the little window she looked out to the meadow, saw that it was pink now with wildflowers, in the early June dusk. Three large brown cows

were grazing out there, near where the river must be. Farther out she could see the wide, gray-white strip of beach, and the dark blue, turbulent sea. On the other side of the meadow were soft green hills, on which—yes, one might have known—new houses had arisen. But somehow inoffensively; they blended. And beyond the beach was the sharp, rocky silhouette of Point Lobos, crashing waves, leaping foam. All blindingly undiminished: a miraculous gift.

Sandy came into the kitchen, bearing bottles. Beaming Sandy saying, "Mol, this is the most divine place. We must celebrate your choice. Immediately."

They settled in the living room with their drinks, with that view before them: the almost imperceptibly graying sky, the meadow, band of sand, the sea.

And, as she found that she often did, with Sandy, Molly began to say what had just come into her mind. "You wouldn't believe how stupid I was, as a very young woman," she prefaced, laughing a little. "Once I came down here with a lawyer, from San Francisco, terribly rich. Quite famous, actually." (The same man with whom she had so quickly rushed off to bed, on their arrival—as she did not tell Sandy.) "Married, of course. The first part of my foolishness. And I was really broke at the time—*broke*, I was poor as hell, being a typist to support my poetry habit. You remember. But I absolutely insisted on bringing all the food for that stolen, illicit weekend, can you imagine? What on earth was I trying to prove? Casseroles of crabmeat, endive for salads. Honestly, how crazy I was!"

Sandy laughed agreeably, and remarked a little plaintively that for him she had only brought breakfast food. But he was not especially interested in that old, nutty view of her, Molly saw—and resolved that that would be her last "past" story. Customarily they did not discuss their love affairs.

She asked, "Shall we walk out on the beach tomorrow?"

"But of course."

Later they drove to a good French restaurant, where they drank a little too much wine, but they did not get drunk. And their two reflections, seen in a big mirror across the tiny room, looked perfectly all right: Molly, gray-haired, dark-eyed and thin, in her nice flowered silk dress; and Sandy, tidy and alert, a small plump man, in a neat navy blazer.

After dinner they drove along the beach, the cold white sand ghostly in the moonlight. Past enormous millionaire houses, and blackened wind-bent cypresses. Past the broad sloping river beach, and then back to their cabin, with its huge view of stars.

In her narrow bed, in the very small but private bedroom, Molly thought again, for a little while, of that very silly early self of hers: how eagerly self-defeating she had been—how foolish, in love. But she felt a certain tolerance now for that young person, herself, and she even smiled as she thought of all that intensity, that driven waste of emotion. In many ways middle age is preferable, she thought.

In the morning, they met the dog.

After breakfast they had decided to walk on the river beach, partly since Molly remembered that beach as being far less populated than the main beach was. Local families brought their children there. Or their dogs, or both.

Despite its visibility from their cabin, the river beach was actually a fair distance off, and so instead of walking there they drove, for maybe three or four miles. They parked and got out, and were pleased to see that no one else was there. Just a couple of dogs, who seemed not to be there together: a plumy, oversize friendly Irish setter, who ran right over to Molly and Sandy; and a smaller, long-legged, thin-tailed dark gray dog, with very tall ears—a shy young dog, who kept her distance, running a wide circle around them, after the setter had ambled off somewhere else. As they neared the water, the gray dog sidled over to sniff at them, her ears flattened, seeming to indicate a lowering of suspicion. She allowed herself to be patted, briefly; she seemed to smile.

Molly and Sandy walked near the edge of the water; the dog ran ahead of them.

The day was glorious, windy, bright blue, and perfectly clear; they could see the small pines and cypresses that struggled to grow from the steep sharp rocks of Point Lobos, could see fishing boats far out on the deep azure ocean.

From time to time the dog would run back in their direction, and then she would rush toward a receding wave, chasing it backward in a seeming happy frenzy. Assuming her (then) to live nearby, Molly almost enviously wondered at her sheer delight in what must be familiar. The dog barked at each wave, and ran after every one as though it were something new and marvelous.

Sandy picked up a stick and threw it forward. The dog ran after the stick, picked it up and shook it several times, and then, in a tentative way, she carried it back toward Sandy and Molly—not dropping it, though. Sandy had to take it from her mouth. He threw it again, and the dog ran off in that direction.

The wind from the sea was strong, and fairly chilling. Molly wished she had a warmer sweater, and she chided herself: she could have remembered that Carmel was cold, along with her less practical memories. She noted that Sandy's ears were red, and saw him rub his hands together. But she thought, I hope he won't want to leave soon, it's so beautiful. And such a nice dog. (Just that, at that moment: a very nice dog.)

The dog, seeming for the moment to have abandoned the stick game, rushed at a just-alighted flock of sea gulls, who then rose from the wet waves' edge and with what must have been (to a dog) a most gratifying flapping of wings, with cluckings of alarm.

Molly and Sandy were now close to the mouth of the river, the gorge cut into the beach, as water emptied into the sea. Impossible to cross—although Molly could remember when one could, when she and whatever companion had jumped easily over some water, and had then walked much farther down the beach. Now she and Sandy simply stopped there, and regarded the newish houses that were built up on the nearby hills. And they said to each other:

"What a view those people must have!"

"Actually the houses aren't too bad."

"There must be some sort of design control."

"I'm sure."

"Shall we buy a couple? A few million should take care of it."

"Oh sure, let's."

They laughed.

They turned around to find the dog waiting for them, in a dog's classic pose of readiness: her forelegs outstretched in the sand, rump and tail up in the air. Her eyes brown and intelligent, appraising, perhaps affectionate.

"Sandy, throw her another stick."

"You do it this time."

"Well, I don't throw awfully well."

"Honestly, Mol, she won't mind."

Molly poked through a brown tangle of seaweed and small broken sticks, somewhat back from the waves. The only stick that would do was too long, but she picked it up and threw it anyway. It was true that she did not throw very well, and the wind made a poor throw worse: the stick landed only a few feet away. But the dog ran after it, and then ran about with the stick in her mouth, shaking it, holding it high up as she ran, like a trophy.

Sandy and Molly walked more slowly now, against the wind. To their right was the meadow, across which they could just make out the cottages where they were staying. Ahead was a cluster of large, many-windowed ocean-front houses—in one of which, presumably, their dog lived.

Once their walk was over, they had planned to go into Carmel and buy some wine and picnic things, and to drive out into the valley for lunch. They began to talk about this now, and then Sandy said that first he would like to go by the Mission. "I've never seen it," he explained.

"Oh well, sure."

From time to time on that return walk one or the other of them would pick up a stick and throw it for the dog, who sometimes lost a stick and then looked back to them for another, who stayed fairly near them but maintained, still, a certain shy independence.

She was wearing a collar (Molly and Sandy were later to reassure each other as to this) but at that time, on the beach, neither of them saw any reason to examine it. Besides, the dog never came quite that close. It would have somehow seemed presumptuous to grab her and read her collar's inscription.

In a grateful way Molly was thinking, again, how reliable the beauty of that place had turned out to be: their meadow view, and now the river beach.

They neared the parking lot, and Sandy's small green car.

An older woman, heavy and rather bent, was just coming into the lot, walking her toy poodle, on a leash. *Their* dog ran over for a restrained sniff, and then ambled back to where Molly and Sandy were getting into the car.

"Pretty dog!" the woman called out to them. "I never saw one with such long ears!"

"Yes—she's not ours."

"She isn't lost, is she?"

"Oh no, she has a collar."

Sandy started up the car; he backed up and out of the parking lot, slowly. Glancing back, Molly saw that the dog seemed to be leaving too, heading home, probably.

But a few blocks later—by then Sandy was driving somewhat faster—for some reason Molly looked back again, and there was the dog. Still. Racing. Following them.

She looked over to Sandy and saw that he, too, had seen the dog, in the rearview mirror.

Feeling her glance, apparently, he frowned. "She'll go home in a minute," he said.

Molly closed her eyes, aware of violent feelings within herself, somewhere: anguish? dread? She could no more name them than she could locate the emotion.

She looked back again, and there was the dog, although she was now much farther—hopelessly far—behind them. A small gray dot. Racing. Still.

Sandy turned right in the direction of the Mission, as they had planned. They drove past placid houses with their beds of too-bright, unnatural flowers, too yellow or too pink. Clean glass windows, neat shingles. Trim lawns. Many houses, all much alike, and roads, and turns in roads.

As they reached the Mission, its parking area was crowded with tour buses, campers, vans, and ordinary cars.

There was no dog behind them.

"You go on in," Molly said. "I've seen it pretty often. I'll wait out here in the sun."

She seated herself on a stone bench near the edge of the parking area—in the sun, beside a bright clump of bougainvillea, and she told herself that by now, surely, the dog had turned around and gone on home, or back to the beach. And that even if she and Sandy had turned and gone back to her, or stopped and waited for her, eventually they would have had to leave her, somewhere.

Sandy came out, unenthusiastic about the church, and they drove into town to buy sandwiches and wine.

In the grocery store, where everything took a very long time, it occurred to Molly that probably they should have checked back along the river beach road, just to make sure that the dog was no longer there. But by then it was too late.

They drove out into the valley; they found a nice sunny place for a picnic, next to the river, the river that ran on to their beach, and the sea. After a glass of wine Molly was able to ask, "You don't really think she was lost, do you?"

But why would Sandy know, any more than she herself did? At that moment Molly hated her habit of dependence on men for knowledge—any knowledge, any man. But at least, for the moment, he was kind. "Oh, I really don't think so," he said. "She's probably home by now." And he mentioned the collar.

Late that afternoon, in the deepening, cooling June dusk, the river beach was diminishingly visible from their cabin, where Molly and Sandy sat with their pre-dinner drinks. At first, from time to time, it was possible to see people walking out there: small stick figures, against a mild pink sunset sky. Once, Molly was sure that one of the walkers had a dog along. But it was impossible, at that distance, and in the receding light, to identify an animal's markings, or the shape of its ears.

They had dinner in the inn's long dining room, from which it was by then too dark to see the beach. They drank too much, and they had a silly outworn argument about Sandy's smoking, during which he accused her of being bossy; she said that he was inconsiderate.

Waking at some time in the night, from a shallow, winey sleep, Molly thought of the dog out there on the beach, how cold it must be, by now—the hard chilled sand and stinging waves. From her bed she could hear the sea's relentless crash.

The pain that she experienced then was as familiar as it was acute.

They had said that they would leave fairly early on Sunday morning and go home by way of Santa Cruz: a look at the town, maybe lunch, and a brief tour of the university there. And so, after breakfast, Molly and Sandy began to pull their belongings together.

Tentatively (but was there a shade of mischief, of teasing in his voice? Could he sense what she was feeling?) Sandy asked, "I guess we won't go by the river beach?"

"No."

They drove out from the inn, up and onto the highway; they left Carmel. But as soon as they were passing Monterey, Pacific Grove, it began to seem intolerable to Molly that they had not gone back to the beach. Although she realized that either seeing or *not* seeing the dog would have been terrible.

If she now demanded that Sandy turn around and go back, would he do it? Probably not, she concluded; his face had a set, stubborn look. But Molly wondered about that, off and on, all the way to Santa Cruz.

For lunch they had sandwiches in a rather scruffy, open-air place; they drove up to and in and around the handsome, almost deserted university; and then, anxious not to return to the freeway, they took off on a road whose sign listed, among other destinations, San Francisco.

Wild Country: thickly wooded, steeply mountainous. Occasionally through an opening in the trees they could glimpse some sheer cliff, gray sharp rocks; once a distant small green secret meadow. A proper habitat for mountain lions, Molly thought, or deer, at least, and huge black birds. "It reminds me of something," she told Sandy disconsolately. "Maybe even someplace I've only read about."

"Or a movie," he agreed. "God knows it's melodramatic."

Then Molly remembered: it was indeed a movie that this savage scenery made her think of, and a movie that she herself had done the screenplay for. About a quarreling, alcoholic couple, Americans, who were lost in wild Mexican mountains. As she had originally written it, they remained lost, presumably to die there. Only, the producer saw fit to change all that, and he had them romantically rescued by some good-natured Mexican bandits.

They had reached a crossroads, where there were no signs at all. The narrow, white roads all led off into the woods. To Molly, the one on the right looked most logical, as a choice, and she said so, but Sandy took the middle one. "You really like to be in charge, don't you," he rather unpleasantly remarked, lighting a cigarette.

There had been a lot of news in the local papers about a murderer who attacked and then horribly killed hikers and campers, in those very Santa Cruz mountains, Molly suddenly thought. She rolled up her window and locked the door, and she thought again of the ending of her movie. She tended to believe that one's fate, or doom, had a certain logic to it; even, that it was probably written out somewhere, even if by one's self. Most lives, including their endings, made a certain sort of sense, she thought.

The gray dog then came back powerfully, vividly to her mind: the small heart pounding in that thin, narrow rib cage, as she ran after their car. Unbearable: Molly's own heart hurt, as she closed her eyes and tightened her hands into fists.

"Well, Christ," exploded Sandy at that moment. "We've come to a dead end. Look!"

They had; the road ended abruptly, it simply stopped, in a heavy grove of cypresses and redwoods. There was barely space to turn around.

Not saying, "Why didn't you take the other road?" Molly instead cried out, uncontrollably, "But why didn't we go back for the dog?"

"Jesus, Molly." Red-faced with the effort he was making, Sandy glared. "That's what we most need right now. Some stray bitch in the car with us."

"What do you mean, stray bitch? She chose us—she wanted to come with us."

"How stupid you are! I had no idea."

"You're so selfish!" she shouted.

Totally silent, then, in the finally righted but possibly still lost car, they stared at each other: a moment of pure dislike.

And then, "Three mangy cats, and now you want a dog," Sandy muttered. He started off, too fast, in the direction of the crossroads. At which they made another turn.

Silently they traveled through more woods, past more steep gorges and ravines, on the road that Molly had thought they should have taken in the first place.

She had been right; they soon came to a group of signs which said that they were heading toward Saratoga. They were neither to die in the woods nor to be rescued by bandits. Nor murdered. And, some miles past Saratoga, Molly apologized. "Actually I have a sort of a headache," she lied.

"I'm sorry, too, Mol. And you know I like your cats." Which was quite possibly also a lie.

They got home safely, of course.

But somehow, after that trip, their friendship, Molly and Sandy's, either "lapsed" again, or perhaps it was permanently diminished; Molly was not sure. One or the other of them would forget to call, until days or weeks had gone by, and then their conversation would be guilty, apologetic.

And at first, back in town, despite the familiar and comforting presences of her cats, Molly continued to think with a painful obsessiveness of that beach dog, especially in early hours of sleeplessness. She imagined going back to Carmel alone to look for her; of advertising in the Carmel paper, describing a young female with gray markings. Tall ears.

However, she did none of those things. She simply went on with her calm new life, as before, with her cats. She wrote some poems.

But, although she had ceased to be plagued by her vision of the dog (running, endlessly running, growing smaller in the distance) she did not forget her.

And she thought of Carmel, now, in a vaguely painful way, as a place where she had lost, or left something of infinite value. A place to which she would not go back.

E. S. GOLDMAN

Dog People

Sometimes when Allan Stonnier drove out and the dogs were there, he revved up and aimed. He had an agreement with them that no matter how disdainfully they stood their ground, they would at the last moment lurch out of range if he went no more than a certain speed. The time he brushed McCoors's brown dog he felt bad about it, but the dog hadn't cooperated. The dog was too cocky. Stonnier had nothing against it. How could a man have anything against a dog? After that, when he revved up he was ready to brake, fast.

McCoors was coming through his woodlot and saw Stonnier drive at the dogs. He said, "If you ever hit one of my dogs, I'll break your fucking head."

"I wouldn't hit your dogs. I just want to scare them. Keep your dogs off my property. You have land."

"I'll break your fucking head."

"I'll be where you can find me."

That was a long time ago, when you could still talk to people about their dogs.

This morning Stonnier was out early, and running. It was a typical Cape Cod spring, more evident on calendars from the hardware store than on the land. A dry northeaster thrashed the roadside picket of unleafed oak, cherry, and locust. A patch of melting snow, sprawled like a dirty old sheepdog on the lee side of a downed pine, drained toward the dozer cut that had made Stonnier's lane forty years ago. Stonnier's running shoes threw wet sand from the runnels. He took in all the air his chest would hold; he had been a runner since making the mile relay team at Nauset Regional, and had known ever since that even when the air was foul you had to fill up.

The air held the thaw of dog shit banked over the winter by neighbor dogs on his paths and driveway lane, in his mown field and kitchen garden—butts and drools and knobs, clumped grains and hamburgers, indistinguishable except in shape from their previous incarnation in bags and cans. Stonnier couldn't see how a dog took any nourishment from such food. It looked the same coming as going. No wonder they used so much. From time to time deposits were withdrawn on Stonnier's rakes and shoes, were wheeled into the garage on the tires of his Ford hatchback. Verna's gloves gathered the stuff in the seagrass mulch on the asparagus. He would have been better off to have set out a little later, when the sun was high enough to define the footing better.

He looked as if he had seventy or so disciplined years on him; he was a man of medium height, bony, with a cleaving profile—a fisherman before he had the stake to buy The Fish & Chips. He loped along the lane evasively, like a football player training on a course of automobile tires.

When it still was possible to speak to people about their dogs, Verna had said, "You could talk to him. He probably doesn't realize what his dogs do when he isn't looking."

But why not? He knew the dogs ran all day while he and his wife were away in their store. What did he think the dogs did with what had been put in them when they were turned out in the morning?

McCoors said, "I don't think my dogs did it." He said he would keep an eye on them. He tied them. They barked. They barked from eight o'clock, when he left, to six, when he came home and let them run until dark. Stonnier skipped a stone at them a couple of times, to let them know he didn't want them near his house. They stayed beyond the turn in the driveway so he wouldn't see them.

Stonnier encountered McCoors one day when they both were looking for their property bounds. Stonnier mentioned that the dogs barked all day and McCoors might not know it because he was away.

McCoors said, "If you tie up dogs, they bark." He tied them up to please

Stonnier. Now Stonnier was complaining again. McCoors broke off the conversation and walked away. McCoors had a tough body, and eyes that quickly turned mean.

Stonnier told Verna that the man reminded him of a prison guard. "I guess there are all-kinds-of-looking prison guards, but McCoors is what I think of. That's nothing against prison guards." Stonnier always tried to be fair.

Deakler, another two-dog man, bought the place on the other side of the hill. His dogs came over to find out about McCoors's dogs at the same time McCoors's dogs came over to investigate the new neighbors. They met on Stonnier's driveway where it joined the Association lane, smelled each other, peed on the young azaleas Stonnier had raised from cuttings in tin cans, and agreed to meet there each day when their food was sufficiently digested. Wahlerson's half chow and Paul's black Newfie heard about the club and came up the Association lane to join.

Stonnier spoke to Deakler.

Deakler was an affable man who had been the sales vice-president of a generator-reconditioning company and knew how to get along while not giving in. "Well, you know how it is with dogs. You don't want to keep a dog tied up all the time. That's why we moved out here."

"I shouldn't have to take care of other people's dog dirt."

"Shoo them off if they bother you. Do them good."

"They scare my granddaughter when she visits. They charge."

"They never bit anybody. People have dogs. She should get used to them."

"That's up to her, if she wants to get used to dogs charging and growling at her. I had dogs. I like dogs. I have nothing against your dogs. They should stay on their own property. Is that a communist idea?"

Deakler looked at him speculatively, as if it might be.

"I don't like to quarrel with neighbors," Stonnier said. "We'll have to see. There's a leash law. I don't like to be talking law."

Stonnier already knew from the small-animal officer that if you couldn't keep a dog off your property, you had to catch it before you called for somebody to take it away.

"You don't have to catch your own bank robbers," Stonnier had said.
The SAO had cut him down. "That's how the town wants it—don't talk to me."

"Laws are one thing," Deakler said. "This is all Association property. Private property. You don't have to leash your dog if it's on private property."

Deakler told him something he hadn't thought about. The leash law didn't even apply to members of the Association, because the Association was made up of private properties, including the beach and the roads that all the private-property owners owned in common.

"That's why I came out here," Deakler said. "It isn't all closed in, like it is in town."

Stonnier brought it up at the Association meeting in July. Oh, that was twenty-four years ago—how time flies. He remembered getting up to speak to the others on Giusti's patio. He had not in his lifetime before—or later—often spoken in meetings of that size. He thought he could remember every time. Three times at town meeting—about the algae on the pond and the proposed parking ordinance and the newspaper not printing what the Otter River Bank was doing on mortgages—and at the Board of Trade, about extending town water to the new subdivisions. Subjects that affected him. His house. His business. That's how the world worked. You spoke for yourself, and if you made sense, others voted with you even when that went a little against their own interests. That's how he always voted. He didn't sign petitions for things like the new children's park, but he voted for the park. The Taxpayers' Association said the park would put points on the tax bill. That was all right—it still made sense that the kids have a place with a fence around it, where dogs couldn't get in. That was what he would want for his own grand-children if they lived in town. A few years back he would have asked, "Why don't they fence in the dogs, and let the kids run?" but you couldn't ask anything like that anymore.

Mostly he jogged these days. He paced an easy 120, waiting for his body to tell him how hard he could run. It wasn't his heart, it was his back: were the tendons and nerves lined up so that the jolt passed through like smoke and went off into the air, or would it jam somewhere on his hip or fourth vertebra? He told Verna, "He says it's in the vertebra, but that's not where I feel it." They knew all about hearts, but they didn't know anything about backs except to rest them. They told his father and his grandfather the same thing. He felt secure, and let out to 130.

He had thought his statement—that he had nothing against dogs but that the town leash law ought to prevail in the Association—would appeal to reasonable people. The dogs tramped down the lettuce, shat so that you couldn't trust where to walk after dark, chased cars, growled at strangers. He didn't say "shat," he said "did their business." Somebody said, "They doo-doo on your Brooks Brothers shoes," a reference to a man who at that time was running for president of the U.S.A., and everybody laughed except Morrison and Dannels, who were large contributors to the candidate's committee. Half-way along into the laughter Stonnier caught on and joined to show his fellowship, although he sensed that the joke took the edge off the seriousness of his argument.

He had expected David Haseley would say something. Haseley had several times mentioned to him—or agreed with him—that the dogs were out of hand. As a retired high officer of a very large business in Cleveland, Haseley was usually taken seriously, but he chose not to speak to the motion. Only Larry Henry's widow, Marcia, spoke for it. Verna had been good to Marcia, shopped for her, looked in on her when she was laid up.

Sensing the anger of their neighbors, who spoke of liberties being taken from people everywhere, and now this, the summer people kept quiet or voted with the dog people. The ayes lacked the assertive spine of the nays. Stonnier thought that most members hadn't voted and that a written ballot might have turned out better. But that didn't seem to be the way to press an issue among neighbors.

In a spirit of goodwill members unanimously supported a resolution that people were responsible for their own dogs. It did not specify how the responsibility should be manifested.

After the meeting Stonnier said to Haseley that he had thought more people would support the leash law. Haseley nodded in the meditative, prudential manner that had earned him his good name and said, "Yes, that's so." He might have meant "I agree with you, that's what you thought." People didn't use words like they used to. "Speak up and say as best you can what you mean, so people know what's in your mind," Stonnier's mother had said to him. Now you had to be sure you asked the right question, or you might not find out what they really thought.

Stonnier hadn't pressed Haseley, toward whom he felt diffident not only because of his bearing but also because the older man was of the management class—as were all the others in the Association but himself. They were vice-presidents, deans, professors, accountants, lawyers; immigrants from Providence, Amherst, Ohio, Pennsylvania; taxed, many of them, in Florida, which the Stonniers had visited in their camper but had not been taken by sufficiently to give it six months and a day every year. The others had all gone beyond high school.

"I still don't know how he voted," he said to Verna.

Allan and Verna Stonnier were second-generation Cape Cod, the only native-born in the West Bay Association, the first to raise children there and see them bused to school in Orleans and then go out on their own. Allan had done well with The Fish & Chips—better than such a modest-looking enterprise had implied—but he remained somewhat apart from the others. His three-acre parcel on the waterfront had cost under three thousand dollars, but that was when you had to bounce a half mile in a rut to get out there. After the fire at The Fish & Chips, ten years ago, a real-estate woman who called about buying the lot asked about the house, too. She had a customer she thought would pay more than a million dollars for it if Allan would consider selling. They thought he would sell his house and get out, but nothing could make him move after the fire. He was so set that Verna had to make it half a joke when she said that with a million dollars and the insurance from the fire they could live anywhere they wanted. By now the house might be worth two million, the way prices were. He knew it as well as she did, and if he wanted to talk about it, he would say so. "It's the whole country," he said. "Everywhere. You might as well deal with it where you are." A million dollars after tax wasn't all that much anymore anyhow.

McCoors's two dogs came out to yap at him. He said, *"Yah,"* and raised his elbow, and they shut up and backed off while he padded on toward the wider, graveled lane that looped through the fifty-three properties in the West Bay Association and carried their owners' cars to the blacktop and town.

Shoeman's black-and-white sort-of spitz bitch met him there and trotted with him companionably. Stonnier considered her a friend. Some mornings she stayed with him past three or four properties, but this morning the collie next door came out and growled and she stopped at the line. *"Yah,"* Stonnier growled back at the collie; he raised his elbow and jogged on.

After one spring thaw Stonnier dug a pit near the line close to McCoors's driveway. McCoors was quick to defend the integrity of his property. He had taken his neighbor on the other side to court in a right-of-way dispute. McCoors asked Stonnier what he was doing. He was going to bury dog shit.

"You don't have to do that here," McCoors said.

"It's your dogs'," Stonnier said.

That afternoon a man from the Board of Health drove up to the house. Allan was down at The Fish & Chips, watching some workmen shingle a new roof. The man told Verna that burying garbage was against the law. He told her about the hazard to the groundwater supply. He said the fine could be fifty dollars a day as long as the nuisance continued unabated. He left a red notice. This unsettled Verna, because she had always thought ways could be found to work things out.

Allan went to the board and said they were off base. A human being had to get a porcelain bowl and running water and an expensive piping system to get rid of his waste, but a dog could leave it anywhere. Their ruling was off base. The health officer said he didn't write the laws, he enforced them, and Allan better close the pit and not open another one. The newspaper carried a story under the headline PRIVATE DUMP OWNER THREATENED WITH FINE. Stonnier thought it gave the idea that he was trying to get away with something.

He wrote a letter to the editor. Melvin Brate didn't print it. Stonnier thought that Brate was still peeved about a letter he had written earlier, saying that the Otter River Bank was using small type to sneak foreclosures over on people, trying to get out of old, low interest rates into the new crazy rates. Stonnier knew about that because they had done it to his cousin. In his letter to the editor Stonnier gave the names of the man who ran the bank and the men who were on its investment committee and said that was no way for neighbors to act when they had signed their names to a contract. The bank was the biggest advertiser in the paper, so naturally Melvin Brate didn't print the letter. Allan got up at town meeting in non-agenda time and read his bank letter to the voters to let them know what was going on. This was the first time he had ever gotten to his feet to talk to more than a thousand people, and it was no harder than holding your hand in a fire.

Melvin Brate sat with his arms folded and looked hard at the floor while Allan spoke about his newspaper's not saying anything about what the bank was doing. Just that day Brate had published an editorial titled "Your Free Press: Bastion of Liberty," which he counted on for an award from the League of Weekly Publishers, and here was this fried-clam peddler carrying on. It wasn't surprising that Brate didn't print the dog-shit letter either, even though Stonnier called the stuff "scat."

Verna was secretly glad that the letter wasn't published. She thought a way could be found to deal with the problem so that dog owners wouldn't get upset and people wouldn't look at her sideways and stop going to The Fish & Chips. She knew that speaking to Allan was useless unless she could say it in another way, and she couldn't think of any. He had been such a usual man when she married him, and people were getting the idea he was an oddball. She couldn't clearly see why that was, because he had a right to complain about the dogs; nevertheless, he ought to do it a different way for his own sake, and not write to the paper or take it up at town meeting. It irritated people.

One day Stonnier counted eighteen dogs at the juncture of his land and the Association lane.

The Association lane went into the blacktop that wound and rolled toward the town. The houses on either side were on the required acreage and fully suited to their purposes. Once home to cranberry farmers, fuel dealers, printers, boat builders, lobstermen—Stonnier knew the names that went with the oldest properties—they had been bid away in the sixties and seventies by retirement and stock-market bankrolls at stiff prices. The new owners had the means to dormer up and lay on wings and garages. On some properties two and three houses stood where before there had been a single low shingled house, a big garden, and woods. The newcomers followed the traditional styles of the Chatham Road, rendered for art shows on the high school green— saltboxes, houses-and-a-half, Greek revival, all well shrubbed and fenced. One ghost of gnawed and mossy shingles had withstood all tenders to purchase and a siege of trumpet vines, rampant lilacs, and fattening cedars intent on taking it down.

Only the jolly French house looked as though it ought to have been in the old town, along with other houses of the style built by managers of the company that had laid the telephone cable to France; indeed, it had been trucked from town in the deal with the architectural commission that had licensed the Cable Station Motel to be built. To Stonnier, the French house's journey down the Chatham Road at two miles an hour, with outriders from the telephone company and the electric company and the police, was the most memorable event since the passage of the great glacier, which he had not witnessed. Had he not come into money so late, this would have been the house Stonnier built for his family. The French house sat square on the ground and knew how to shed water off its hat. It looked like a toby jug; it was gold and blue, its cornice was striped with purple, and the door was gunpowder red.

"It's different," he said to Verna, who thought it was a rather queer house that would fit in better if it were white. "You just like things one way or another," he said. He liked the moment of coming out on the blacktop around the corner from West Bay and finding himself two weeks further into spring, jogging by the French house with the long hedge of breaking forsythia skirted with daffodils and crocuses. The air here stank too. Some of it was spring rot coming out of the ground. Most of it was dog.

Ahead on the long straight stretch Gordon's basset (that dog must be a hundred years old), carrying his skin like a soaked blanket, turned and turned in the middle of the road, trying to find a way to let his rear end down and create the right precedent for the rest of him. He slept there every morning for an hour or two, unless the snow was a foot deep. Regular drivers knew to watch for him, and the Lord protected Sam the basset against everybody else. That dog was going to get it one day. The driver who did it better have a good head start and not ask around whose dog it was so that he could tell them he was sorry but he had passed another car and there the dog was, in the middle of the road, and he had done his best to avoid him, he was sorry, he knew what it was to lose a dog, he had two himself, don't shoot, please don't shoot. You couldn't know anymore what to expect if there was a dog in it. Juries looked at those dog people out there. If you ran for sheriff, you took questions at public meetings and the dog people heard your answers. Senators wanted some of that dog-PAC money, especially because the dog-PAC people said that what they were really interested in wasn't dogs but good government. If a dog question was coming up at town meeting, you saw people voting you never saw anywhere else. They went home after voting on dogs, and left the rest to find a quorum for the payroll and potholes.

Allan Stonnier was the only human being afoot on the Chatham Road. His red sweatshirt was well known at this hour. Most of the sparse traffic was pickups, with elbows crooked out the windows, wheels crunching and kicking up cans, wrappers, cups, laid down by the pickups that had gone that way earlier, tools and dogs riding behind. He saw Dexter Reddick's green pickup, with the sunburst on the radiator. Without being too obvious, Stonnier adjusted course to the edge of the road. He couldn't be absolutely sure Reddick wouldn't take a swerve at him for the hell of it. He prepared to break from the shoulder for the grass slope. Reddick went by with angry eyes, threw up a finger. Reflexively, Stonnier gave it back. He heard the pickup brake hard behind him and push hard in reverse as it came back. He kept going. Reddick passed, got twenty feet beyond, and put his head out the window.

"What did I see you do?"

"The same as you." By then he was past the truck, and Reddick had to grind back again to talk to him.

"Let me see you do that again, you fuckhead. You old fart. You can't get it up. You firebug. I'll burn your ass." Stonnier kept going. Barricaded behind shovels, rakes, and lawnmowers, Reddick's Labs yammered and spittled at him. Reddick jack-started a groove in the blacktop and went on his way. Stonnier decided to take the side road that went toward the dump.

Pilliard's pack of huskies, brought back from Alaska last year, saw him coming and started their manic racket. Pilliard had one-upped everybody at the Landing Bar with that one. Jesus, twelve huskies, did you ever see such dogs? You could hide your arm in the fur. The strut and drive of those legs. They had Chinese faces as if they were people. Those people fucked their dogs. Pilliard had them in the cyclone-fenced stockade he had put up to hold his cords when he was in the stovewood business. Ten feet high, and ground area about as big as any factory you would find in a place like Cape Cod—lots of room even for twelve huskies.

Pilliard's idea was to take them to fairs and show them, for a good price, pulling a sled he'd fitted with siliconed nylon runners that slipped over turf. Take your picture with a real team of Eskimo huskies. Children's birthday parties. Beats ponies all hollow. Fourth of July parades. He brought Santa Claus to the mall. Altogether, the bookings amounted to only a dozen brief outings all year. The dogs were used to doing miles of work in cold weather. In the stockade they hung around. At night they could be heard barking for hours for their own reasons, and the sound carried to West Bay.

Verna thought Allan must be running on the dump road, because he would be there about now, and there went Pilliard's huskies. They didn't often see people go by on foot. They acknowledged pedestrians and slow drivers by lunging at the fence, climbing, piling on, snarling, yelping powerfully. Allan had driven her by, and slowed the car so she could hear it up close. It scared her. It was more like mad screaming than barking, all of them exciting each other. Some things Verna wished Allan wouldn't do, and one of them was to run past Pilliard's huskies.

"Run someplace else," Pilliard said. "You don't like dogs and they know it, and they don't like you, so why don't you run someplace else."

What was the use explaining to a man who already knew it that Stonnier was running on a public road, and he was there before the dogs anyhow. And even if he wasn't . . .

Stonnier left them yelping, went over the crest of the rise and around the next corner, running, feeling good, well sweated as he went toward halfway. It was the dumb part of the route, the mall and the file of flat-roofed taxpayers and show-windowed front porches of old downtown; service stations, eating places, clothes shops, music stores, cleaners, laundries, drugstores elbowing to be seen along the old bypassed highway number.

He could have gone around by the marsh road and avoided town, but one thing could be said for Main Street. It smelled better than anywhere else. Better than West Bay behind the dunes, where the ocean lost its innocence; better than the Chatham Road and all the lived-on lanes and roads from the bridge to Province Lands. He had never thought he'd live to see the day when downtown smelled better than the countryside. If a stray wandered into the mall, the small-animal officer showed up fast and snared him into the cage mounted on his police wagon. The merchants saw to it. You couldn't let a leashed dog step onto one of those neat rectangles of shrubbery if you didn't want a ticket. If a dog hunched to empty out, you had to drag him to the library lawn. Even the dog people understood the deal. You left the merchants alone, they left you alone.

Soon after dawn old downtown could have been a movie set in storage. The cars and service trucks of early risers were parked in front of Annie O, who opened first, for the fishermen. The overnight lights in the stores and the streetlights watched him go by. Stanchions of sulfur light guarded the plaza of Canine City, with its eleven veterinarians, four cosmetologists, several outfitters; the portrait studio featured the work of fifteen internationally known dog artists; an architect displayed model residences: cape, half-cape, Federal, Victorian, Bauwowhaus, duplex, ranch.

The stoplight turned irrationally against him, as if programmed to recognize a man of ordinary size in a red sweatshirt running in from the west. The wind batted through the open cross street and went back again behind the solid buffer of storefronts until it came to the empty lot on the cove where The Fish & Chips had been. He faced into it, running in place, when he got there.

The real-estate people never stopped bringing him offers. He was going to leave that up to his daughter to decide. The land was money in the bank.

"That's what everybody needs, Verna—something in back of him so no matter how hard he's pushed he doesn't have to give in to others. That's what it's all about. More people could be like that if they didn't want too much."

The Conservation Commission asked, If he wasn't going to use it, would he consider deeding it to them for the honor of his name in Melvin Brate's paper and the tax deduction? They thought a price might be worked out if he met them halfway. He thought about it. He got as far as thinking about what kind of sign he would require them to put up if he sold them the land, but he could never get the wording right. He knew if he got it right they wouldn't do it. He neatened up the section of burned-out foundation the building inspector allowed, and let the lot sit there with the sign.

SITE OF THE FISH & CHIPS RESTAURANT
BURNED DOWN BY VANDALS A.D. 2002 IN HONOR OF
THEIR DOGS

Someone stole the sign the first night. He wasn't going to fool with them; he went right to a concrete monument, anchored with bent iron rods into a six-foot-square concrete pad. They tried to jump it out with a chain but they would have needed a dozer and they never got that far. They hit it with a hammer now and then. They painted out the inscription. He used to go back a few times a year to put it in shape, but he hadn't had to touch it for two years now. The old generations had lost interest, and not even the young Reddicks cared much unless something happened to stir them up.

Coming on their first glimpse of salt water in twenty miles, visitors swung onto the apron and reached for their cameras. Alert to station their wives at the photo opportunity where George Washington watered his horse and the salt water beckoned, they walked over to read the legend about the restaurant and the vandals and the dogs. They would throw up their hands. What's that all about? Stonnier himself wasn't satisfied with the statement, but after so many years the story was boring to anybody but himself anyhow.

He had kept a dozen clipped mallards for his own table in a chicken-wire pen half in and half out of the water, the way you penned ducks if you had a waterfront. He had heard a terrible squawking, and when he looked out from the kitchen door the two dogs that patroled Reddick's garage at night were running wild in the pen, breaking wings and necks, tossing every duck they could get their jaws on. He hollered at them, but you couldn't call a dog off anything like that. He got his shotgun and drove a charge into the side of one; the other ran off, and Reddick came over from his garage, goddamning him.

The paper said that Reddick was there to get his dogs, and Stonnier threatened him with the gun to keep him off, and he shot the dog.

A week later a southerly breeze pulled an early-morning fire out of the rubbish trailer onto the shingle. Flame was all through The Fish & Chips by the time the pumper got there. His was the fourth restaurant that went up that fall, and the arson investigator from the state asked him how his business had been. They went over his records at the bank. The insurance company took two years to pay up.

He ran where he stood while he looked around and checked out the site. It was as usual. The fresh northeaster gusted at him out of a mist that lay up to the land at the water's edge. A gull stalked the tidal drain looking for garbage. Another, unseen, cried as if lost. On the scrim of fog his memory raised the shed of The Fish & Chips, with the huge lobster standing guard, and then the new Fish & Chips with the Cape Cod roof and the kitchen wing. He was looking out the back window and saw Reddick's dogs in the pen and went after them. A charred beam leaned on a course of cement block that had been the foundation. Ravined and grainy, the blacktop was being worked by frost and roots. Spindly cedars had found footing. He remembered when they had poured the blacktop: four inches, and four of gravel under it, and then sand, and the cedars had found enough to grow on down there. He felt himself already cooling out, and took off at a 120 jog back through town, wiping sweat from his forehead with the flat of his hand.

The last thing he discussed with himself as he went up the rise at the mall and turned again toward Pilliard's was how his daughter and her children could be made to keep their minds on being positioned not to give in to others. All he could do was leave them the land; they had to understand what it was for. If they sold it, they would have the money, and if you had money, you had all kinds of duties to it. You had to see that you didn't lose any of it, and you had to get the best interest for it, and you bought things you didn't need that brought you new duties, like a place in Florida. The land would stay there to back you up. He didn't stop thinking about that until he got into range of Pilliard's huskies and they started in on him again. Pilliard was carrying an armful of pipe, fence posts maybe, and spat a word he couldn't hear. He kept going.

The wind off the bay blew some of the sound away, but Verna heard the pack distinctly again. She threw a last handful of cracked corn for the quail and jays and listened. She wore untied walking shoes for slippers and a nubby white robe over her nightgown. She had brushed her hair but not in detail, and its style was a simple black-speckled gray flare cut off at her earlobe. She took her wristwatch out of the robe pocket but couldn't read it. Her glasses were still inside, on the table. If that was Allan, he would be nine or ten minutes. Then he would shower and she would be dressed and have breakfast on. It wasn't an egg day. He might want tuna on toast.

The dogs went on. She wasn't dressed to stay out, but the dogs kept barking. She picked up a dead branch, carefully positioned it, and flicked a dog divot into the rough. All the deposits over which oak leaves had settled stirred and gave off a tribal odor, as if they were a single living thing giving warning. She threw another handful of corn without noticing exactly what she was doing. Pilliard's dogs sounded louder, but that couldn't be. They were where they were. In the tops of the scratch pines the wind had not changed. Individual voices could be distinguished rising out of the wild yammer of the pack.

Were Pilliard's dogs out? He leashed and ran them sometimes in the back of the dump, but that was farther, not nearer, and never this early. She felt nervous and wished to know something. She started toward the house to look up Pilliard's name and telephone him but knew immediately that was not the thing to do. The thing to do was to get in the car and drive over there.

She was not constrained now by any civilized notion that she should not be seen, even by herself, to overreact. She suddenly wished to act as quickly and as arbitrarily as she knew how and to get over to the dump road. The Ford spurted back out of the garage, skidded while she pulled on the wheel to get it around, and went out the lane faster than McCoors's dogs had ever seen it come at them. They couldn't believe it was going that fast until it kicked the big kind-of Airedale into the ditch. She had no time for regret or succor and pushed the gas harder. The wheels jumped out of potholes and ruts, clawing air, and jolted down. She was frightened by her speed. She held on as if she were a passenger. Coming to the fork at the blacktop she judged—willed, rather—that she could beat the blue car and cut it off. Its horn lectured her past Sam the basset, sitting on the stripe with his back to her, knowing she wouldn't dare, until she lost the sound at the turn beyond the straight-away.

A quarter mile up toward Pilliard's she saw them on the road. She looked for a human figure but could see only the pack and whatever it was they were larking around on the road. She kept her hand on the horn and drove at them, not thinking any longer that he could possibly have gone another way, or got up a tree, or even gone into Pilliard's house. She put the pedal on the floor. She was angry at Allan for getting himself into anything like this. He could have lived his life like other people. But he hadn't, and that's how it was, and, enraged, she owed him as many of them as she could get her wheels into.

DAVID UPDIKE

Out on the Marsh

I turned twenty-one a month or two ago, and I have been rather surprised lately to find myself suddenly conscious of my age. Twenty-one: that sounds very different from twenty right now, though I don't think I would have thought so a year ago. Against my better judgment, I now think of myself as standing at the edge of what presents itself as "the rest of my life," the previous twenty years being some sort of vague and distant warm-up. I am suddenly aware, I suppose, that my present actions are an indicator, a preview, of what's to come. I feel old.

At night, sitting under the dim yellow light of my desk lamp, I take from my wallet two photographs, from expired driver's licenses, of me at sixteen and at twenty. My hair has grown, my cheeks have broadened. Do I look older? Have I lost the question in my eye? I am handsome, I am told; I smile and look away. This picture of me at sixteen was on my first license, and I have always liked it. At the registry of motor vehicles, when it came time to turn my license in for a new one, I told the woman at the desk that I wanted to keep the picture, and she took a pair of large scissors, snipped it brusquely from the rest, and tossed it onto her desk with a flip of her chubby wrist. I have kept it with me since.

Have I become more sedate lately? I am home from college for spring vacation and spend my days puttering around the house and taking long solitary walks on the marsh with Mtoti, my dog. He has recently become my best friend, and I must admit I find his company entirely sufficient. A large red-haired golden retriever, he walks with a sway that suggests he should not

215

eat so much. The other day we found a deer carcass, completely decomposed except for the fur and a foot, which he tried to sneak away from me to eat in the woods. I went after him and got the foot and threw it into the creek, only to have him grunt and grovel and wheeze in a vain and pathetic search through the mud. He walked right over it twice, but could not see or smell it through the water, so I pointed it out to him with a long stick, and he stole away with it back to the house and finished it under a tree on the lawn.

It is on these recent wanderings that I have become acquainted with Mr. Birch, not so much in conversation as by seeing him, a familiar, waving figure on the marsh—a mobile landmark—at all hours of the day, collecting old scraps of wood, gazing toward the horizon. He lives here on the marsh with his wife, along the road that runs from town to the ocean, in a small white house on a knoll hidden in the trees. They are both in their eighties, and in the winter, when the tide is high and the wind blows from the northeast, the neighbors worry for them, knowing that the road to their house is covered with water and the knoll the house sits on has become an island. But when the tide subsides, and we hurry over to see if everything is all right, we find them, invariably, fine, surprised and amazed by our concern.

Now and then the paths of our wanderings intersect, and Mr. Birch and I stand together briefly, looking out over the marsh, trying to think of things to say. I ask him questions mostly, about the weather or the birds, and he returns short, soft-spoken answers, and we set off on our different ways, glad to have had someone to talk to, relieved to be again alone. It is his distant presence I cherish most—the sight of his ancient and erect form gliding across the marsh in his aluminum motorboat, his arm raised in a wave, his collar flapping in the wind—and the sense that all I see and hear and love here is shared.

Mr. Birch spends much of his time working in the small yard next to his house. The other day, after watching him and Mrs. Birch climb into their tired green Rambler and drive over the bridge toward town, I walked up to the house and stood in the yard. I was struck there by the wonderful haphazard order of the objects he has collected and saved and arranged in a randomness I knew not to be random—a disorder I thought to be the highest form of order, a personal one, which only Mr. Birch understands. A buoy hangs by a rope from a lilac bush. The wheelbarrow is concealed, covered by a heavy piece of gray canvas, faded by the sun. Stumps double as stools, clothespins cling like birds to the line, a mattress dries in the sun. The grass is full but matted, padded by his step, and a beaten path bends through a gap in the bushes, marking his daily route between the house and the yard, between the yard and the marsh. I wonder if it has ever occurred to him that he alone has made this track—years of work, three decades of soft steps. Or at his age do you take these things for granted?

I met him recently on the road in front of his house and he pointed out two pine trees, forty feet high, that he and his wife planted from pots when they first moved here. We stood there marveling at their height, and I—and Mr. Birch, too, perhaps, as he leaned over to pet the dog—thought of what these trees implied about his age. It was a beautiful spring day, with a high, cool wind blowing through the tops of the trees. We said good-bye and I walked slowly over the bridge back toward my house. I had been out on the marsh for several hours that day, and Mtoti was tired and followed a few feet behind me. I turned to him and ran backward, urging him on, clapping my hands, calling his name, and he worked himself into a run. On the lawn we stopped, and I bent down to hug him. In the afternoon light, I could see that the gray flecks of his muzzle had gone to white, and I realized that he had drifted into old age without my having noticed. I have thought of him all these years as my peer, but it is only now, in the blue light of spring, that I realize he has grown old without me.

JOHN UPDIKE

Deaths of Distant Friends

Though I was between marriages for several years, in a disarray that preoccupied me completely, other people continued to live and to die. Len, an old golf partner, overnight in the hospital for what they said was a routine examination, dropped dead in the lavatory, having just placed a telephone call to his hardware store saying he would be back behind the counter in the morning. He owned the store and could leave a clerk in charge on sunny afternoons. His swing was too quick, and he kept his weight back on his right foot, and the ball often squirted off to the left without getting into the air at all; but he sank some gorgeous putts in his day, and he always dressed with a nattiness that seemed to betoken high hopes for his game. In buttercup-yellow slacks, sky-blue turtleneck, and tangerine cashmere cardigan he would wave from the practice green as, having driven out from Boston through clouds of grief and sleeplessness and moral confusion, I would drag my cart across the asphalt parking lot, my cleats scraping, like a monster's claws, at every step.

Though Len had known and liked Julia, the wife I had left, he never spoke of my personal condition or of the fact that I drove an hour out from Boston to meet him instead of, as formerly, ten minutes down the road. Golf in that interim was a haven; as soon as I stepped off the first tee in pursuit of my drive, I felt enclosed in a luminous wide sanctuary, safe from women, stricken children, solemn lawyers, disapproving old acquaintances—the entire offended social order. Golf had its own order, and its own love, as the three or four of us staggered and shouted our way toward each hole, laughing at misfortune and applauding the rare strokes of relative brilliance. Sometimes the summer sky would darken and a storm arise, and we would cluster in an abandoned equipment shed or beneath a tree that seemed less tall and vulnerable to lightning than its brothers. Our natural nervousness and our impatience at having the excitements of golf interrupted would in this space of shelter focus into an almost amorous heat—the breaths and sweats of middle-aged men packed together in the pattering rain like cattle in a boxcar. Len's face bore a number of spots of actinic keratosis; he was going to have them surgically removed before they turned into skin cancer. Who would have thought that the lightning bolt of a coronary would fall across his plans and clean remove him from my tangled life? Never again (no two snowflakes or fingerprints, no two heartbeats traced on the oscilloscope, and no two golf swings are exactly alike) would I see his so hopefully addressed drive ("Hello dere, ball," he would joke, going into his waggle and squat) squirt off low to the left in that unique way of his, and hear him exclaim in angry frustration (he was a born-again Baptist, and had developed a personal language of avoided curses), "Ya dirty ricka-fric!"

I drove out to Len's funeral and tried to tell his son, "Your father was a great guy," but the words fell flat in that cold, bare Baptist church. Len's gaudy colors, his Christian effervescence, his hopeful and futile swing, our crowing back and forth, our fellowship within the artificial universe composed of variously resistant lengths and types of grass were all tints of life too delicate to capture, and had flown.

A time later, I read in the paper that Miss Amy Merrymount, ninety-one, had at last passed away, as a dry leaf passes into leaf mold. She had always seemed ancient; she was one of those New Englanders, one of the last, who spoke of Henry James as if he had just left the room. She possessed letters, folded and unfolded almost into pieces, from James to her parents, in which she was mentioned, not only as a little girl but as a young lady "coming into her 'own,' into a liveliness fully rounded." She lived in a few rooms, crowded with antiques, of a great inherited country house of which she was constrained to rent out the larger portion. Why she had never married was a mystery that sat upon her lightly in old age; the slender smooth beauty that sepia photographs remembered, the breeding and intelligence and (in a spiritual sense) ardor she still possessed must have intimidated as many suitors as these virtues attracted and must have given her, in her own eyes, in an age when the word *inviolate* still had force and renunciation a certain prestige, a value whose winged moment of squandering never quite arose. Also, she had a sardonic dryness to her voice and something restless and dismissive in her manner. She was a keen self-educator; she kept up with new developments in art and science, took up organic foods and political outrage when they became fashionable, and liked to have young people about her. When Julia and I moved to town with our babies and fresh faces, we became part of her tea circle, and in an atmosphere of tepid but mutual enchantment maintained acquaintance for twenty years.

Perhaps not so tepid: now I think Miss Merrymount loved us, or at least loved Julia, who always took on a courteous brightness, a soft daughterly shine, in those underheated and window-lit rooms crowded with spindly, feathery heirlooms once spread through the four floors of a Back Bay town house. In memory the glow of my former wife's firm chin and exposed throat and shoulders merges with the ghostly smoothness of those old framed studio photos of the Merrymount sisters—there were three, of whom two died sadly young, as if bequeathing their allotment of years to the third, the survivor sitting with us in her gold-brocaded wing chair. Her face had become unforeseeably brown with age, and totally wrinkled, like an Indian's, with something in her dark eyes of glittering Indian cruelty. "I found her rather disappointing," she might dryly say of an absent mutual acquaintance, or, of one who had been quite dropped from her circle, "She wasn't absolutely first-rate."

The search for the first-rate had been a pastime of her generation. I cannot think, now, of whom she utterly approved, except Father Daniel Berrigan and Sir Kenneth Clark. She saw them both on television. Her eyes with their opaque glitter were failing, and for her cherished afternoons of reading (while the light died outside her windows and a little fire of birch logs danced in the brass-skirted fireplace) were substituted scheduled hours tuned in to educational radio and television. In those last years, Julia would go and read to her—Austen, *Middlemarch*, Joan Didion, some Proust and Mauriac in French, when Miss Merrymount decided that Julia's accent passed muster. Julia would practice a little on me, and, watching her lips push forward and go small and tense around the French sounds like the lips of an African mask of ivory, I almost fell in love with her again. Affection between women is a touching, painful, exciting thing for a man, and in my vision of it—tea yielding to sherry in those cluttered rooms where twilight thickened until the white pages being slowly turned and the patient melody of Julia's voice were the sole signs of life—love was what was happening between this gradually dying old lady and my wife, who had gradually become middle-aged, our children grown into absent adults, her voice nowhere else hearkened to as it was here. No doubt there were confidences, too, between the pages. Julia always returned from Miss Merrymount's, to make my late dinner, looking younger and even blithe, somehow emboldened.

In that awkward postmarital phase when old friends still feel obliged to extend invitations one doesn't yet have the presence of mind to decline, I found myself at a large gathering at which Miss Merrymount was present. She was now quite blind and invariably accompanied by a young person, a round-faced girl hired as companion and guide. The fragile old lady, displayed like peacock feathers under a glass bell, had been established in a wing chair in a corner of the room beyond the punch bowl. At my approach, she sensed a body coming near and held out her withered hand, but when she heard my voice her hand dropped. "You have done a dreadful thing," she said, all on one long intake of breath. Her face turned away, showing her hawk-nosed profile, as though I had offended her sight. The face of her young companion, round as a radar dish, registered slight shock; but I smiled, in truth not displeased. There is a relief at judgment, even adverse. It is good to think that somewhere a seismograph records our quakes and slippages. I imagine Miss Merrymount's death, not too many months after this, as a final, serenely flat line on the hospital monitor attached to her. Something sardonic in that flat line, too—of unviolated rectitude, of magnificent patience with a world that for over ninety years failed to prove itself other than disappointing. By this time, Julia and I were at last divorced.

* * *

Everything of the abandoned home is lost, of course—the paintings on the walls, the way shadows and light contend in this or that corner, the gracious burst of evening warmth from the radiators. The pets. Canute was a male golden retriever we had acquired as a puppy when the children were still a tumbling, preteen pack. Endlessly amiable, as his breed tends to be, he suffered all, including castration, as if life were a steady hail of blessings. Curiously, not long before he died, my youngest child, who sings in a female punk group that has just started up, brought Canute to the house where now I live with Lisa as my wife. He sniffed around politely and expressed with only a worried angle of his ears the wonder of his old master reconstituted in this strange-smelling home; then he collapsed with a heavy sigh onto the kitchen floor. He looked fat and seemed lethargic. My daughter, whose hair is cut short and dyed mauve in patches, said that the dog roamed at night and got into the neighbors' garbage, and even into one neighbor's horse feed. This sounded like mismanagement to me. Julia's new boyfriend is a middle-aged former Dartmouth quarterback, a golf and tennis and backpack freak, and she is hardly ever home, so busy is she keeping up with him and trying to learn new games. The house and lawn are neglected; the children drift in and out with their friends and once in a while clean out the rotten food in the refrigerator. Lisa, sensing my suppressed emotions, said something tactful and bent down to scratch Canute behind one ear. Since the ear was infected and sensitive, he feebly snapped at her, then thumped the kitchen floor with his tail, in apology.

Like me when snubbed by Miss Merrymount, my wife seemed more pleased than not, encountering a touch of resistance, her position in the world as it were confirmed. She discussed dog antibiotics with my daughter, and at a glance one could not have been sure who was the older, though it was clear who had the odder hair. It is true, as the cliché runs, that Lisa is young enough to be my daughter. But now that I am fifty, every female under thirty-five is young enough to be my daughter. Most of the people in the world are young enough to be my daughter.

A few days after his visit, Canute disappeared, and a few days later he was found far out on the marshes near my old house, his body bloated. The dog officer's diagnosis was a heart attack. Can that happen, I wondered, to four-footed creatures? The thunderbolt had hit my former pet by moonlight, his heart full of marshy joy and his stomach fat with garbage, and he had lain for days with ruffling fur while the tides went in and out. The image makes me happy, like the sight of a sail popping full of wind and tugging its boat swiftly out from shore. In truth—how terrible to acknowledge—all three of these deaths make me happy, in a way. Witnesses to my disgrace are being removed. The world is growing lighter. Eventually there will be none to remember me as I was in those embarrassing, disarrayed years when I scuttled without a shell, between houses and wives, a snake between skins, a monster of selfishness, my grotesque needs naked and pink, my social presence beggarly and vulnerable. The deaths of others carry us off bit by bit, until there will be nothing left; and this, too, will be, in a way, a mercy.

MARY LA CHAPELLE

The Understanding

"I'm a poodle."

That's what he would like to tell someone. Not that they didn't know that already. But he would like to tell them so they would know that *he* knew. Just once as the mailman came up the walk, instead of yelping and running from window to door to window again, he would like to wait patiently, even serenely, until the man had come to the first step. He would stand on his hind legs then, push the screen door ajar to show his face, and say, "Boo. I'm a poodle."

That would make an impression. If only there were a way he could express to someone that he was special—a poodle, but more than a poodle. The truth was that he'd changed in the last few years, though he continued to behave in much the same way he always had—pouting, running in circles, and being manipulative. Like the time he had defecated in the pocket of their neighbor's pool table. This had been his way of protesting being left there while the rest of the family went on vacation. That was years ago, but he'd do it again, given the same circumstances. Not because it was his nature, but because those were the means available to someone who had no hands and who couldn't talk. And yet, if someone could get inside his head, they would see that he understood much more than it appeared. They would see all the many things he had learned from living with Gretta.

Shortly, however, he was to be taken away from her, and a doubt had been growing in him about whether he really knew anything at all. He was afraid he might only know what Gretta knew, and once separated from her, the meanings he had come to recognize might just fade out, like radio music driving away in a car.

It was a slow, sunny day on the screen porch. Gretta held him in her lap, picking through his fur with one old hand and clipping it with the other. She didn't actually look at him as she did this, but felt out his long hairs, pulled them between the scissors and snipped them off, letting them float to the floor. There was comfort in her touch and in the quiet, and even in the snipping sound. Yet he was dismayed. He would be gone soon, perhaps even before the mailman arrived. He squirmed in Gretta's lap. She turned him over and began to clip the hair under his chin. Since she was nearly blind, he recognized this as a critical task and lay motionless, looking up into her face.

Gretta Ormson was 101 years old. She wore her hearing aid only a few hours during the day. The rest of the day she was stone deaf, and she sat with the stillness of a stone, like a Buddha, with her long, waxy earlobes, and her cataractous eyes. Her hands were particularly remarkable, hugely out of proportion as they curved over the ends of her chair arms. At rest there was still a kind of vibration under their loose skin, which, depending on the day or hour, changed in color from gray to a rough red to a purple cast. He loved Gretta's hands.

They shimmered with something a painter would ache to capture and never could. Except, perhaps, Rembrandt. Once there was a program about his paintings on public television; he couldn't tell if Gretta was able to hear what it was about, but she had fallen asleep anyway, and the sound of the narrator's voice mixed in with the sound of her breathing, which was the sound of old leaves blowing in the yard. "There is a light," the narrator had said, "in each of his paintings, like a beacon, that draws one into them." And when Binky had looked over at Gretta's hands resting on the arms of her chair, he already knew how this could be true.

Two weeks ago, the day he had first heard the news, had been the same warm kind of day on the sun porch. A flyswatter lay forgotten across Gretta's lap. Her hearing aid remained in the box on the kitchen table, and she barely stirred at all. An airplane roared above. A fly was buzzing behind her head, then around it in a circle, landing, lost for a moment in her hair. It dropped down onto her hand, took a walk along the blue, cordlike vein. Binky perked up, protective, and watched it take a pinch of her skin in its little chopsticks. Then he stood up to make it fly away. These were the kind of daily activities they shared together.

After the fly left and boredom had set in again, Binky had crawled over to the chair next to Gretta's and found the spot under the springs that he had been digging at for the past few days. He'd finally reached the stuffing; it was coming away in clumps, making him giddy as it sprinkled down onto his chest and head.

Whack! the flyswatter came down on his belly. Whack, whack, on each of his feet. "No! Binky!" she had scolded him. She prodded him from under the chair with her swatter, pushed him across the floorboards until he was lying at the toes of her shoes, his paws drooping in the air like the heads of remorseful ducks.

Later, she had reached behind her chair and raised the window shade to put a patch of sun on the floor where he lay. And forgiven, he fell asleep, dreaming he was a young dog running after a scent, and the grass was bending around him, and he had no words or thoughts, just the scent and his running.

He had been brought out of his nap by the rumble of Barb's Oldsmobile pulling up to the house. Barb was Gretta's youngest daughter. All of her other children were in their seventies or, some of them, dead, but Barb was a latecomer and only in her fifties. There was always something breathless and earnest about her, as if she would never get over being the baby of the family. On his hind legs, he leaned against the porch door while his breath created a little circle of fog on the window. Gretta's chair was creaking a little, which meant she was watching her come, too. When Barb finally opened the door, he fell out through the crack, and she had to catch him with her knee.

"Ouch! Binky!" she said, because she had arthritis in her knees. She pushed him back into the porch. He jumped around her and yelped once before he jumped onto the footstool by the door so she could pet him. Then he whined. Then he jumped down and ran around her legs. Then he jumped onto the stool again. This was how he was with Barb.

She rubbed him all over with her long fingernails and said, "Oh, Binky!

Goo'boy!" Finally, she had gathered him up and sat down in the chair across from Gretta. "Mom?"

Gretta raised the lids of her eyes a fraction and looked at Barb as if deciding whether she wanted to see her or not. "Hi," she said finally. "Are you already finished from work?" Barb worked part-time as a secretary. She visited Gretta every day.

"No, Mother, it's Friday." (Friday, Binky knew, Barb never worked.)

"Did you work hard today?"

"No, Mother, it's Friday. I'm always off on Friday." Barb leaned over to look in Gretta's ear.

"No, I don't have my hearing aid in. I can't hear a word you're saying. Is that a new blouse?"

"I got it today."

"What?"

"I got it . . . Mom, don't ask me questions if you can't hear me. I'll go get your hearing aid. I brought you a shake from Burger King," Barb shouted in Gretta's ear. Binky dropped to the floor when Barb stood up. She pulled a paper cup with a plastic top and a straw out of a bag. Gretta took it in both hands and immediately put the straw in her mouth. When Gretta drank a shake she looked like a Buddha drinking a shake.

"What happened to the chair?" Barb came back onto the porch pushing some of the stuffing into the corner with her foot. Binky had his paws tucked under and was avoiding her gaze. She handed Gretta the Indian bead box that always held her hearing aid. Gretta went through the ritual—opening the box, putting the battery in place, adjusting the dial, which caused a painful whistling. Eventually she placed it in the great hole in her ear and adjusted the dial until the whistling stopped.

"*What . . . happened . . . to . . . the . . . chair?*" Barb said loudly, each word a separate enunciation.

"He." Gretta motioned listlessly toward him with her big hand.

"Binky!" Barb leaned over and shook her finger at him. "Don't do that!"

Binky tried to look as dumb as he could.

"He needs a trim," Barb said. "Why don't you let me call the Poodle Patrol?"

· The Poodle Patrol made house calls. Dogs were carried to someone waiting at the back door of their van. Inside they were clipped and shaved and powdered. Binky was usually given a number sixteen, which meant he got a hairpiece, resembling a shaving brush, molded on the top of his head. The rest of his body was shaved down to pink skin, except for his legs which were trimmed and left fluffy. Then he was returned with a ribbon around his shaving brush that said, "Poodle Perfect."

The whole tone of his day had changed when Barb mentioned the Poodle Patrol. He began to feel anxious and miserable. Just when he had achieved a plain comfortable scruffiness, he would be transformed into a fluff.

It was a great frustration. And he wondered as he did every time, if Gretta would bother with this, had her daughter Leslie not insisted upon it every month until the time of her death. In her lifetime, Leslie had succeeded in forming him into a parody of what one might find most ridiculous in people. Even now, when he was being finicky about his food, rigid in his routine, and generally snotty, he blamed Leslie.

When Barb suggested Monday, Gretta had said, "No. Costs too much."

"Mom, it costs as much as anyone else, and I hate taking him in the car."

"I'll trim him on my own," she said. "Then I'm giving him away."

Barb had plopped down in her chair, as if a little dumbstruck. She looked at Binky, and then back again at Gretta. "Well, okay, I guess," she said. "Okay then."

It seemed that Gretta had been trimming him for hours. He watched the little curls of his white fur make a larger and larger pile on the floor. He couldn't say he hadn't seen it coming. His bladder had lost its discipline over the years, and he couldn't hold out much past three in the morning. Last winter she had told Barb that it would be his last. It was too much taking him out on dark, icy mornings. Now it was September, and he supposed she had no reason to change her mind.

For days he had expected he'd get the news that they'd found him an owner. Barb left flyers with the Poodle Patrol, of all people, so they could circulate them to their customers. And though he'd heard no specific talk about it, he believed today would be the day. Perhaps Gretta would trim him badly enough that no one else would want him.

Sometimes he'd tried to imagine an owner other than Gretta, but the task made his head reel as much as trying to picture a color never seen before, or eternity, or being dead. He had to find her then, curl beside her in her chair, and tuck his muzzle beneath her hip. If someone were to ask her, she'd say she didn't own him at all. That it was always Leslie and Steiner that had owned him. And that he was just a living thing left behind.

There were even owners before them. He wasn't sure what he remembered: a lot of tumbling and disorder and then a stretch of being alone and hungry outside. Then he was inside again, which must have been this house. Leslie and her husband, Steiner, lived here then. They said that he was a stray—that Steiner brought him in to show Leslie and that she oohed and cooed. She was in love with him (or the idea of him) from that moment on. But Binky had never felt her love. He didn't feel anything like that in the world until near the time of her death. By that time she was just a dim remainder of a person. And so it wasn't her that had the love anymore but something persistent and steady in the air around her.

No, Binky didn't know what he could exactly remember of Leslie or what it was that he'd reconstructed from her artifacts. There were little coats she had made for him, crocheted in bright colors with matching hats. There was a raincoat, a rainhat, and a rayon sailor suit for formal occasions. There were her ashtrays and lamps, some rococo, the rest French Provincial. There were filigreed napkin holders, and goblets etched with palm trees, and, more than anything, there was a canopy bed. It was completely out of proportion to the small room that she and Steiner had shared in Gretta's house. In fact, the ceiling pressed against the canopy so that it drooped instead of arched.

The house filled up and overflowed with these things, and Gretta still kept many of them, as if maintaining her daughter's desires. But every once in a while she'd find something like a pineapple platter from Hawaii and dump it without a flinch, as if it had suddenly come loose of Leslie's pleasure, and

229

without that turned instantly useless. And in his more anxious times, Binky wondered if he hadn't grown useless in the same way.

Gretta pushed Binky in her no-nonsense way off her lap. And he landed with a poof of dog curls around him. She began to rock forward in her chair, one, two, three, and four, until she had gained enough momentum to pull herself up on her feet. Binky waltzed backward, made little starts with his shoulders, as if he might jump into her arms. He wagged his tail incessantly—hoping for what? To be let outside? To be fed? To be petted fondly? This he didn't know. The sudden desire for her to do something with him just came over him at times, and it always took him a while to guess what it was.

He circled around her legs as she hobbled away until she pushed him aside with her cane. He imagined suddenly that they could go on a vacation together before he had to leave. He had never gone along when the family went on vacation, and she hadn't traveled for years. Maybe it would be a good thing for both of them. They could go to Florida for the winter, and she could find a room with a balcony. He imagined the sun she would like and the sea gulls flying over the beach.

He followed her with his small steps to the bathroom. But for the first time, he didn't follow her in. He just waited in the hallway and felt forlorn. He knew, after all, that they wouldn't ever go away together. And here he was in the hallway.

When Leslie was sick, he had been left there too. And it was those last days of her cancer when things had begun to have names and meanings for him. He didn't know what cancer was then, or even sickness, really. He only knew that he was no longer welcome in her bedroom and that he was treated roughly by Steiner, Barb, and Gretta, too, if he tried to enter. So he had slept on the rug that lay between Gretta's and Leslie's rooms. A small light burned in the hallway and a small light near Leslie's bed. There was an endless procession by the others night after night from one light to the other. Their weight as they passed him on the floorboards was heavy and kept him awake. But still he never wanted another place for himself to sleep. It was as close as he could be without being inside.

Something happened. He began to distinguish between them better than he had before. He noticed that Barb would take her shoes off before entering the room, and the shoes had high spikes, and that sometimes, after she had left them, one of them would tip over and lie next to him. He noticed that Steiner would often stand in Leslie's doorway without going in, his hand just dangling there. And later Binky would look at the others and see that Steiner's hand didn't move as much as theirs did, but hung at his side as if heavy.

He began to know extraordinary things for a dog—not just the feeling of weight or the look of size, but how one thing could be like another, and how they could be different. Gretta's step was the steadiest in those days. And it was for her mother that Leslie would call the latest into the night. Binky would hear the two of them talking in low tones. Their voices were the same as winter trees groaning together in the wind, and Binky, not knowing that it was a painful sound, was comforted by it and let the sound lull him to sleep.

One afternoon the family all gathered in Leslie's room. They went in and out. Barb came out with Leslie's purse and set it on the dining room table. Steiner made trips to the car. Finally Gretta came out with Leslie. She was wrapped in blankets. She walked slowly past Binky. He couldn't see her face, and it seemed that she couldn't see him either. Gretta, who was a stout woman then, held her from behind and by the elbow as they left the house.

They were gone for days, one of them returning only occasionally to put food in his dish and to let him out. And when they finally came home to stay, Leslie wasn't with them. But he remembered Barb coming in, and how she had again set Leslie's purse on the dining room table.

This must have been late summer, because the air was thick like a blanket over him. Many people visited during the rest of the day and into the night, some of them leaving later than the first bird calls. And he was overwhelmed with the density of them in that little house, their smells, altogether, like an invasion upon a peace that by this time he had become comfortable with. Little children had grabbed him up in their boredom, handled his parts, as if identifying them to each other, his paws, his legs, his pink belly. One of them would blow into his ear to make him shudder, then they'd laugh when he finally broke away to hide under the sofa.

When the house was finally quiet, Binky was the only one left awake. Barb had gone home with her husband and children. He had found Steiner stretched on the parlor davenport dead asleep. He climbed onto Steiner's chest, sniffed around his open mouth, and found the familiar sweet smell that Steiner had held in his glass all day.

He had traveled along the living room furniture, finding cake crumbs and the remainders of casseroles on paper plates. There were filled ashtrays, sweating glasses, coffee cups with red lip marks on their rims.

In the kitchen there was a drip from the faucet, a faint sound of something incomplete and not right in the house. The first light had only come up to the window, but not in—it stood there waiting like a stranger. And the whole house was gray with this strangeness. He was afraid of the quiet—the quiet left in Leslie's room; the quiet in the bathroom. And when he went looking for Gretta, he had found her door closed for the first time in months. But he could hear the rumble of her old air conditioner. He pushed against the door, and when it finally clicked open, he fell in through the crack.

It was cool and dry inside. Gretta was asleep on the single bed with her hand laid over her eyes. There were beads of water gathering on the underbody of the air conditioner, the dripping silenced by the drone of the fan. Light was slowly leaking into the room. An airplane vaguely roared overhead. He watched her sleeping. A bus shook the windows from two streets away. Light was creeping up the bottom of the bed, actually laying itself across her feet. The fingers of her hand fluttered, then slid away from her face. Her eyes were already open. There was nothing in them but the same languid feeling of the morning that had so far filled the room. And when she turned her eyes in his direction, he had stood up.

She looked past him as though someone had entered the room at the same time. And she looked as if, in the next moment, she would be either very terrified or very calm. But she was calm. He saw something in her gaze that he'd never understood before. It was memory. It reminded him of a full bottle poised on the edge of a table. She turned her eyes up, and he looked up, and the bottle trembled between them, then tipped over, silently; Leslie's black hair, how she looked while she laughed, and her perfume didn't spill out, but slowly dripped into Gretta's eyes and remained there.

Binky had stood transfixed, motionless as a hunting dog that has sighted something moving in the trees, excited and fearful too, that he might see it again and he might not. There was nothing he could do to see more. This was how he felt about his understanding: he was only on the edge of it. Looking at Gretta, he realized she wasn't seeing him now. Her eyes were closed as if she had fallen back to sleep, as if nothing had just happened in that room. And that's when he noticed her hands for the first time. They were gripping the sheets around her chest, as if they had somehow remained awake to keep her covered.

Today, Binky felt a similar tension—not simply about the fact that he had to leave. It was that he felt his chance to know things was ending. Gretta sat in her overstuffed chair, a few yards away from where he lay on the carpet. She was doing what she called her "handwork." Lately, she spent her time making pastel-colored pom-poms out of mesh. They were used to scrub dishes. She called them "chore girls" and gave them to all her visitors. "They are miraculous," she would tell them.

Every time she finished one she tossed it in Binky's direction, sometimes hitting him on the top of the head, sometimes not coming close at all. She could be playful in her own way. But it was that dull time of late morning, and he could smell chicken in the oven, reminding him of all the times he had smelled it before, and this made him sad.

Since Leslie's death, Steiner had died too. "Of drinking," Barb would say. And Gretta's son Darrel of a heart attack in North Dakota, and her brother Inver, finally, of just being old. All of her last friends were gone—Mrs. Burdon, Mrs. Matthews, Mrs. Johnson with the scent of schnauzer on her skirt hem that invariably gave Binky an erection, until Gretta would say, "Put that pink thing away."

All were gone except their neighbor, Mrs. Wood, who would do better to die. But "Meanness kept her alive," Barb said, a confusing concept to Binky since it didn't apply to Gretta.

Wood, they called her. Ninety-six years old and gnarled into the shape of an umbrella handle, she would creep, every few days, down the sidewalk to their house. Binky dreaded her since she was given to generally poking and swatting him with her cane. Her hearing was barely keener than Gretta's, so much of their visit consisted of misunderstanding each other.

Wood would say, "My gas bill was terrible this month."

"Oh! I don't blame you," Gretta would say. "It's been over fifty years, and I miss my husband as if it'd only been a year."

"Mine's not over a hundred and fifty, but it's still a crime. We're old women. They'd let us freeze if it came to it."

"I was forty-nine, standing on the window ledge, washing the windows, and Orrin came in the front door. 'Gretta, I don't know what's wrong with me,' he said." Whether or not Wood had heard, Gretta had told her this story many times.

"It's a scheme." Wood would pound her cane into the floor. "Don't believe them. They call me all the time telling me they should insulate my house, fix the doors and the windows. To save me money. Ha!"

Gretta would be quiet for a minute, resting. Wood would gurgle and rattle deep down in her throat, trying to settle something disagreeable in herself. They talked. "He was on the bed," Gretta would say, never without holding herself across the ribs and rocking the way he had. "He said, 'It hurts so much,' and he was such a big man who never complained."

Binky knew the script of their visits. Wood had many complaints, and Gretta would stare out the window. Sometimes she had the look of a young woman, as if none of her children had died yet, as if they hadn't even been born. Binky could see her as a girl on the Dakota farm, the miles of flatland stretching around her and her blue eyes full of the sky, which she always said was the thing she had loved most about the plains. Eventually she would look over at Wood, remember her, and ask her a question which she already knew the answer to.

She would always put the water on to boil when Wood arrived and, toward the middle of the visit, make tea for Wood and decaf for herself. For years she had offered coffee, but Wood couldn't "abide" it.

Sometimes when she set the cup on the table before her guest, she'd say in a normal voice, not loud enough to hear, "Here's your tea, instead of good coffee, goddamn you."

And always there was this, loudly: "I came over yesterday, and the door wasn't open."

"I've told you before," Gretta would shout. "I can't just leave the door open. We've been burglarized. You know that man walked right in while I was hanging clothes on the line. Call me before you leave, and I'll let you in."

But Wood rarely called. She had high expectations, Gretta said. There was a time when Binky would bark and jump on the arm of Gretta's chair to let her know Wood was there. But he had stopped.

One day she had come to the porch door and knocked with her cane. Gretta was taking her nap on the couch, her hand curled over her eyes, deaf. And Binky went to the porch where Wood stood behind the locked screen door. Rap! Rap! She banged the frame. "I'm here." But he didn't move. Maybe because her walk had been painful or because the sun was glaring through her thin white hair, she looked defenseless. "Tell her, dog," she said. But he didn't want her in the house.

Wood turned away and descended each step like it was a day. She came around the side windows, which were over her head. Binky watched the rubber tip of her cane bounce against the panes. She banged on the back door, and finally she was gone.

It was dinnertime. Gretta opened the oven door and the chicken spattering sounded like applause. "Grease is a great thing," the chicken almost seemed to say. Binky loved Gretta's food. Years of it had left a lacquerlike film on the enamel of the stove and the yellow wallpaper. He could smell it everywhere in the house. If she did nothing else in a day, she still cooked. It wasn't Monday or Tuesday or Thursday; it was meat loaf or pork chops or roast. It was the substance of her day, her inspiration and her pleasure.

Some mornings, after dressing in the same knit pants and sweater she'd worn for days, before she'd even put her shoes on, she'd announce her menu plan, as if the whole family still lived in the house. "*Mashed rutabagas* and *potatoes*. Yes! Lord God, it's been a long time. It sure has." She'd go into the kitchen, dig two rutabagas and potatoes out, and thump them down on the counter with conviction. "I'll do that later for dinner," she'd promise.

Barb arrived as Gretta was setting a plate for her on the table. "Mother! What did you do to Binky?"

Binky stood up, alarmed.

"Doesn't he look better?"

"You missed trimming one of his legs. It looks like he's wearing a cast. Oh, Mother, can you see the bald spots? Poor thing." Barb picked Binky up, and he felt like crying.

"Worse things have happened," Gretta grumbled. "Sit down now—we have chicken, creamed carrots, and rolls."

"Just coffee." Barb looked over at Binky laying on the rug. "My God," she said, shaking her head.

Sitting beside Gretta at the table, she opened the drawstring on the plastic bag that she had brought with her. "I washed some of his things," she said. And Binky, watching her pull out his vests and his small wool leggings, felt nostalgic for those sillier days.

"Good." Gretta fingered the material. "He'll be ready then. Have you talked to the man?"

"He said he'd call tonight."

What man? Binky's heart stopped and waited.

"What?" Gretta asked.

Barb leaned closer. *"He said he'd call me tonight about picking him up,"* she said louder and more clearly, exacerbating Binky's misery.

Gretta continued eating quietly. "Have some food," she said after a minute.

"Mother, I said no."

When Gretta had finally picked a drumstick nearly clean she tossed it on the rug next to Binky. He took it in his mouth listlessly.

Gretta dipped a biscuit in her coffee. "They say you shouldn't give chicken bones to a dog." Then she went back to eating. "I suppose one day he'll choke and die."

She stopped eating. "I'll miss him," she said. "I'll miss sitting with him."

"Yes, I know." Barb leaned forward. "But it's right. It's the right time."

Then Gretta looked up distractedly. "I'm calling Wood for dinner." She labored to get up.

"Mother!"

"She should be here; it's been a long time." She was finally on her feet; her napkin clung to her knee, then fell to the floor. "Dial her number," she told Barb. "Dial her number."

"Mom, I am."

"Hello," Gretta said as soon as she had the phone to her ear.

"Mom, she hasn't answered."

"Hello." Binky could hear Wood's voice sounding like an insect's over the line.

"I'm inviting you for dinner," Gretta said.

"I can't hear you. Who is this?"

And Gretta, who had her hearing aid in this time, said, "She can't hear me. Come to dinner!" she shouted one more time.

"Here, let me try." Barb took the phone. "Mrs. Wood. . . . *Can . . . you . . . come . . . for . . . dinner?*" But there was only confusion on the other end.

Then they were both shouting into the phone different things at the same time: "We've got food" and "You're invited." The way fans hopelessly cheer a losing team to win.

Then a click. And all three of them, including Binky, watched in their minds as Wood walked from the phone to stand bewildered in the middle of her living room.

"You go see about her, Barb," Gretta said, "and Binky and I will stay here."

Early evenings, Gretta had to tend her garden. This was something she would do every day until the first frost. It was her constitutional. Tonight she looked over the narrow plot along the south side of the house that bordered the driveway and Binky stood on the concrete beside her. The mums were still healthy, and the bees were kicking their hind legs into them in that frantic way they have at summer's end.

It had been years since she had been able to kneel on the ground and ever hope to get back up again. But Binky still remembered those days. Now she managed by putting one hand on the house for support and reaching down with the other. She folded the wilted petal of a pansy back, as if to look at its face. "Almost gone, aren't you?" she commiserated. "Pop your head off, I'm afraid." And she did, because the rule of thumb with pansies was to keep them thinned.

The pavement was still warm from the day, and Binky lay down. Gretta inched her way along the garden, pulling up weeds and dead plants and tossing them onto the driveway to be swept together later. Every few feet that she progressed, Binky would slide his body along to follow her.

The sun's angle had changed, and it seemed to lie like an arm around Gretta's shoulders as she leaned over her work. Her hearing aid had gone back into its box after dinner. And this time of day, when she was deaf, Binky felt deaf, too. The world took on a stillness in early evening, as if the two of them were together in a painting.

Binky rolled on his back. The sky was blue, and a plane passed silently, high over the treetops. He felt deeply peaceful. Dreaming, he had the sensation that the plane's shadow was covering him, and he suddenly felt very cold. No, it was a man's shadow. There was a man somewhere? Instinctively he rolled and found himself in a tense crouch. He was growling with that rumbling growl deep within his body that signified to him there was a danger even before he knew what that danger was.

Was the man really there? It was so strange. He stood, hands in his coat pockets, on the driveway not eight feet away from Gretta and said nothing. Was he the man who had come to take him home with him? No, Binky somehow felt this wasn't true.

The stranger watched Gretta as she continued to reach into the garden, searching out and grasping the roots of dead plants. And Binky watched her, too, with a great protectiveness. He loved the independence of her hands as they worked, as if through a century of sheer use they had come to possess a soul of their own. She moved quietly along the garden, the man standing behind her. Her face was smooth, and she seemed unaware she was being watched. As if to change this, the man stepped toward her. Binky crouched. He had never felt so protective of her in his life. His heart became huge in his chest; his lips drew back over his teeth; and he poised for an attack, growling louder and louder, finally leaping at the stranger. But the man disappeared, leaving Binky to attack thin air.

Binky, naturally, felt foolish, like the times in his youth he had zealously leaped at the mailman only to crash into the door between them. He knew he was whimpering as he went back to Gretta. And the fact that she couldn't hear him and didn't know what had happened made him feel utterly alone. He thought of Wood walking along this garden, trying to beat on the windows, and the loneliness of it. Gretta was slowly sweeping the weeds together in the driveway, and the light brushing sound was no more comforting than the sound of time passing. Why was she giving him away? What was going to happen to him?

Binky howled. He stood in the middle of Gretta's pile of sweepings and continued to howl. She tried to push him aside with her broom, but he wouldn't budge, and he knew that, eventually, if she looked at him, she couldn't help but see that he was calling out to her. She did finally, and she picked him up, held his head in her hand, looked into his face. He was trembling. "You're a troublesome little thing," she said. "Even so, I can't give you away today. I will though, Binky." She took his paw firmly in her large hand. "It won't be long before we'll just have to find another place for you."

"Now," she said, walking to the corner of the house, "there are just a few more things we should do tonight. We need to check the rain bucket." It was full, and somehow she managed to pour it into her watering can, still holding Binky. She set it back under the drainpipe. "It's bound to rain again," she said. "You can feel it, can't you?" And he put his nose up to the air as if to show her he was listening. And sure enough there was rain in the air, coming from the west. Suddenly the fact that it was coming felt very immediate, as if he could see it beating against the western plains, like an army's march in their direction.

The rain was an oddly comforting thought. Somehow that Gretta was so sure of it made him feel safe again. He'd almost forgotten about the visitor in the driveway, but the thought of him came back again, quite simply. He understood. It wasn't earth-shattering. It didn't even change anything. Gretta had known the man was there the whole time. He was Death, wasn't he? And he had visited for years—he was in her windows and in her yard and in her morning cup of coffee. He would make no huge claim on her. She was peaceful with this, and Binky loved her for her strength, and for the moment he had the feeling they could live forever.

She walked slowly, carrying him back to the porch, occasionally stopping to knock a dirt clod back into the garden with her shoe, and he knew they would sit in her porch chair watching the sky darken in the west. She would have no inclination to go in until her expectations were met, until the thunder was in their neighborhood and the rain started washing across the street onto their yard and up against their windows.

BARBARA NODINE

Dog Stories

Since we arrived in Banaras, I've become very sick. David is not sick, not yet; but he's also in danger of dying. We don't know yet.

Many Indians believe they will go directly to Nirvana if they die in Banaras. They want to get out of this world and never come back. We're Americans, and it's hard for me to think this way. I do not want to die here or anywhere.

Less than a year ago, we finished school, married, and came here. Since then, we've killed dogs, many of them. David and I threw them in the Ganga. Perhaps the dogs will have their revenge.

Twice a week, David rows a small boat to the opposite shore of the Ganga where the silent burial dunes lie in gentle green curves against the horizon. He goes there to search the sand and water for relics to use in his art pieces. He has collected vertebra in the shape of a gigantic flying insect; crinkled cow hooves; a skull of some large aquatic creature with moveable fin bones.

"I can't believe what I can find," he says. But when David goes to the dunes, he must wade in the Ganga which is filled with excrement and the partially burned bodies of Indians who have died from diseases more horrible than I had ever known. He tells me, "I think you have to take some risks. Once I know that material is over there, I have to use it."

In the mornings when the sun rises fiery orange in the gold mists over the Ganga, I miss Duchess, who was my first dog, my true dog. Duchess was my birthday present when I was nine, a German shepherd puppy and my best friend until I met David. The mists on the Ganga are so heavy in the early hours that I can only see the shadows of bathers and often a sudden flash from a burning bier on the *ghats,* the steps leading into the sacred river where the bodies of the dead are burned. I wake and think for a moment I am back home and hear Duchess cry for me. But it is only the call of a water buffalo along the shore, or the chant of a holy man sitting cross-legged on the riverbank facing the glowing sun.

At home I ran with Duchess in empty streets, past large homes with wide lots. She ran ahead of me, a black silhouette against the grays of early morning. In India, the streets are Technicolor and never empty. I can see Duchess look back over one shoulder then the other to check that I'm still there, her hind end out of alignment like a car that's been in an accident. When I think of her, I want to hold her in my arms. Perhaps I killed her too. Can you again and again in your life kill something you love and suffer no consequences? In India the rules are different. Many times death is preferred to life.

Here we live on the shore of the Ganga in a former palace of the king of Banaras. The stone building is old and in disrepair now, but from our balcony we can see the shoreline of Banaras stretching along the Ganga: the *ghats,* the ancient temples and palaces, the bathers and cattle crowding the shallow river's edge, the boats pushing their way through to the deeper waters.

The floor of our one large room is concrete, and tilts slightly toward a drain to the outside. Our bed sits in the middle of the room like a low wood table. The red handmade Indian mattress on top is no thicker than a quilt. Our mosquito net hangs from strings tied to hooks in the ceiling and forms a light green canopy.

Our bathroom contains a faucet and a squat toilet which we flush with a pail of water. Our pet lizard, which David painted red, clings to the bathroom wall at night.

There are two shelves in our kitchen, a window, our plug-in electric hot plate, and a large basket of fruits and vegetables. If we leave the door open, even a crack, a monkey may dash in and grab a banana. When I cook, three or four children peer in the window to see what I'm making, and they tell me when I'm not rolling the *chapatis* correctly, or should add more hot chiles. When I practice my cello, the children gather around the door to hear their Indian music on a strange instrument. When David is sculpting, they believe he is creating the likeness of the Goddess Sarasvati.

We arrived in Banaras in October before the three-day Festival of Lights. Indian families lined their houses and windowsills with strands of red, blue, and yellow electric bulbs. In the evenings the Ganga glowed with thousands of single-wick oil lamps set in small clay dishes and floated out into the current. We thought India was a land of enchantment.

An Indian family with five small children lived a short distance from our palace across a small mustard field and the narrow sewage-filled Asi River. For several days after the Festival of Lights, we heard from their house a puppy's tortured barking. Then we watched as the children twisted the puppy's legs, threw him off the roof, tied him with a noose and swung him around. Their mother pretended not to notice.

When we could stand it no longer, David crossed the mustard field and motioned to the mother that he wanted the puppy. She grabbed the dog by his tail, and hurled him into the Asi. David waded to where the puppy struggled in the water, lifted it in his arms, and carried it back into our house.

We set it on the concrete floor and washed it off with the hose. The puppy, a male, was blinded in one eye and his belly was bloated. After we bathed him, his fur was pure white and his belly a light pink. David gave him a red *tika*—the third eye and the mark of a Brahmin. When I played my cello, our baby puppy dozed under my music stand. He pooped under David's sculpture table. We named him Ashirvad, which means "blessing" in Hindi.

We had come to Banaras so I could study an ancient oral tradition of northern Indian music taught in the graduate program at the Banaras Hindu University. Each lesson lasts several hours. My teacher tunes his *tampura*, a stringed drone instrument made from a gourd, which he strums while he sings. Then I tune the cello. The sound of the *tampura* and open cello strings calms the mind and moves us into the mood of the particular *raga*, or scale, we've chosen to play. There is a *raga* for each time of day: *Bhairavi,* for the freshness of morning; *Bhim Palasi,* for the calmness of the slowly sinking afternoon sun; *Malkauns,* for the evening tranquillity when darkness encloses all things; and *Bihag,* for after-midnight stillness. In India, the music is everything, the performer is not important. I don't ever want to go back to Western music.

I bought a used bicycle and went everywhere on it, my sari flying in the wind. I made a special backpack for my cello, and it towered over me like another body as I pedaled to the university.

One day on the way home from my music lessons, I found a little dog huddled at the base of a small temple on a road not far from here. When I picked her up to put her in the bike basket, her only movement was a slight shiver. I laid my finger gently on her nose and called her Bonine, because she was like a little bare bone.

Duchess was never this small or this humbled. Duchess was a fat puppy and carried her head high.

When I got home, Ashirvad accepted the new dog warmly and jumped around her, but Bonine only attempted to sit—a slow lowering of her butt like she was about to poop. I gave her rice, which she didn't eat, and yogurt, which she lapped up without joy. When she squatted again, she passed two drops of blood.

David and I knew she had no chance to get well. We were afraid she would contaminate Ashirvad or ourselves. We couldn't put her back on the streets because Indians treat dogs like rats.

Bonine slept in my arms as David and I walked south along the Ganga shore past the university to where the crowds were thinner. David lit a stick of incense and stuck it in the sand. Against a stone he placed a portrait he had drawn of a beautiful Indian woman with the words, "This is our puppy's next reincarnation; may it be a better life." I set Bonine on the sand and poured goat's milk from a jar into three small cups. Our cheeks were wet as David and I sipped the milk in silence and watched Bonine lap a few drops. With a wax crayon, David marked the Indian peace symbol on a heavy rock, wrapped the drawing around it, and tied a string from the rock to the puppy's neck.

I stood on the shore while David waded out into the Ganga and threw our puppy in. There was a splash, then a string of bubbles, then nothing. We stood apart that way, waiting; then David waded back. I reached up to put my arms around his neck. He nuzzled his head down between my neck and shoulder. His arms around my waist drew me to him. We pressed our bodies together, hard.

Later I passed the same corner to find a familiar old bag-of-bones woman in a potato sack, asleep, surrounded by three mangy dogs. I realized Bonine had been one of her dogs. I had never seen the woman awake; she may have been very sick. I had the thought that we could do her a favor by throwing her in the Ganga as well. In India, life and death do not seem to be separate states, but rather a continuum. Many are on the borderline—lepers with disintegrating feet and faces; starving animals; deformed beggars; daily corpses burning on the *ghats*.

Banaras celebrates the winter solstice in January when the sun moves into Capricorn in the Zodiac. Bright tissue paper kites fill the markets, and the sky above the city dances with color. David made kites for both of us. Mine was orange and red with big painted eyes, and his was purple with three rippling green tails. We ran along the Ganga riverbank, Ashirvad dashing between us, while the kites dove down toward the water and then up again to join hundreds of others in the clear blue sky.

The weather is cool that time of year and the sun always shines. David and I were walking back from the market with a dozen mangoes in our cloth grocery bags. We saw in the shadow between two buildings a crippled puppy with enormous brown eyes, dragging its hindquarters through garbage in search of food. I had seen the same puppy a few days before on the same garbage heap and thought it amazing it had survived. David emptied his mangoes into my bag and carefully lifted the puppy out of the garbage and into his bag.

At home I gave the puppy a flea bath and picked ten spider leeches from his ears. He learned his name in three days. We'd call "Crip" and he'd quickly drag his crippled body to us. Whenever we came home, his beautiful brown eyes would light up even though his tail couldn't wag.

When we took Crip outside, he fell into the polluted gutters that ran beside the roads. In the house, we couldn't keep him clean because he had no control over his bowels. One day I noticed tapeworms in his stool.

Crip loved to take a swift slide down the bluff to the Asi River when we weren't looking, getting his dead legs tangled in the bushes. After dark he would whimper to let us know where he was, and David would have to climb down with a flashlight to get him. David came back one night carrying Crip at arm's length because he was covered with filth again. "We shouldn't be doing this," he said. I knew he was right.

That evening Crip ate cheese and whey. Then David wrapped him in a cloth, and I gathered the incense, a large brick, and some heavy string. Ashirvad jumped playfully at our heels as we again walked down to the Ganga. At the riverbank, I lit the incense. David put the noose around Crip's neck and set him on the brick. After David waded into the river, he stretched out his arms and held the brick high so that the dog was silhouetted against the darkening blue sky. Then I heard Crip drop into the deep waters.

Instead of silence, I heard thrashing. In the beam of the flashlight, we saw Crip swimming with only his front legs. His nose was pointed toward the surface, pushing up from under the water.

I screamed. David cried, "The string's too long," reached for the dog and raised him skyward. He forgot about the attached hanging brick which pulled the noose tight. Crip choked, barked, and coughed. Ashirvad barked and ran in circles. I grabbed Ashirvad and knelt with my arm around him to hold him still. David laid Crip on the shore and frantically tugged at the noose to let the puppy cross back into the world of the living. Then David stopped and looked at me. I couldn't move. After a moment, he looked down again. He took his knife out of his pocket and shortened the string.

During July and August, the monsoon season, David and I traveled to Nepal, and left Ashirvad with a fellow student. While we were away, our building and that part of Banaras closest to the Ganga were flooded with ten feet of water. We slept on the floor of a friend's house for two nights while we chased away the snakes, cleaned and whitewashed our muddy walls. When we moved back in, the water still came to the edge of our balcony.

We'd put off getting back Ashirvad until we were settled. Ashirvad had been passed from person to person three times while we were in Nepal, and the last keeper said he planned to turn him out the next day. When we went inside to see Ashirvad, he ran to us and stayed very close. He barked at the other people in the room.

He followed closely as we walked back toward our building, but before we had gone twenty meters, he was attacked by a pack of dogs. Ashirvad ran between our legs, and we tripped over him as we yelled and shouted. We knew Crip had been paralyzed by other dogs. These dogs darted in closer and snapped at our legs and Ashirvad, until David took off his sandal and threw it at them. Finally they ran away.

Back in our room, Ashirvad whined as soon as one of us left him even though he hadn't been hurt. We wondered what would happen when we both left. What would we do when we went on vacations, or to music festivals in other cities?

I lay awake that night, and I could tell by David's breathing he lay awake too. I think we were afraid to talk to each other. We knew we'd have to leave Ashirvad sometime; no one here wanted a dog; it's better that he die healthy than diseased, starved, or eaten by other dogs. We knew drowning was painless and quick.

I turned over on my stomach and put my nose against David's cheek. "We can use three bricks and a short string," I said.

At four in the morning, Ashirvad trotted with us to the water's edge. He sat erect and licked David's hands as he tied the bricks by a short rope to his neck. Then, without a pause, David lifted Ashirvad and waded out to where the waters of the Ganga were deep. We sat on the riverbank until the first orange light emerged over the green opposite shore. May Ashirvad be a Brahmin in his next life.

A few months ago, David and I began to take early-morning walks down a road we called "cow alley." We often took along unrisen bread to feed four newborn puppies who lived there with their bony big-eyed mama. The weather was too cool for bread to rise on our balcony during this season, but we baked it anyway.

A couple of weeks ago, we found one of the puppies dead in the road, but the other three were healthy and spunky. David put a piece of bread in front of the nose of the dead pup. An Indian girl saw him and said with a puzzled look on her face, "But he's dead." David acted surprised and said, "But he died because he didn't get enough to eat." Because she was an Indian the little girl believed the puppy's spirit had already taken another form. But to us it would be as unusual for the puppy to be born again into another incarnation as to come back to life in this one.

One day last week, I couldn't find my favorite pup, a little runty female. David heard that the pup was ill, and that the potbellied cowherd who lives there had tied it up nearby. When we found the cowherd, he told us the pup had gone crazy and bitten the children. The puppy didn't act crazy when we saw her. She was lying down and looked sleepy. But she moved her head as though the piece of rope still around her neck kept her from swallowing. I asked David to cut the rope and he took out his knife. Then he held his hand in front of the pup's nose to make friends. The dog snapped at his hand, and punctured David's finger with a single puppy tooth.

David immediately thought of rabies, so we ran home and fetched a big bucket and burlap bag. The puppy howled and ran away from us, hiding under a falling-down shed. We shooed her out, finally cornered her in the bend of a stone wall, and flung the bag over her. David held and petted her through the burlap until she stopped whimpering. Then we loaded the bucket with the dog in the bag on the handlebars of David's bike and rode to a nearby veterinarian.

Of course, he wasn't there. In India, nothing gets done the first time, so David rode back with the pup later that evening. The veterinarian said she was probably okay, but that we should keep her with us for ten days, and if she doesn't die before then, she doesn't have rabies. We put her on the balcony, fed her our best food—eggs, milk, rice—and hoped she would live.

The next day, the puppy snapped constantly. She twisted her head as if to stretch out her neck. Later she would go to the water tin, dip in her nose, then jump away and shake off the water as though it were boiling hot. The veterinarian had explained that a rabid dog cannot drink water. Its throat contracts as if it's being choked.

In the morning the puppy was dead. I walked to the riverbank with David, who carried the little twisted dead body. I couldn't smell the burning incense; I was breathing through my mouth because my nose was stopped up with fear. "Remember, we didn't kill this dog," David said. I couldn't speak. I couldn't tell him my fear was for him. He waded out and added her to the other dead puppies in the Ganga.

We heard that in Delhi, David could get four or five injections in the arm rather than fourteen daily shots in the stomach, the only treatment available here. We tried to call the best hospital in Delhi, but we couldn't even find the number. No one has a phone book here, and there's no directory assistance. David started the two weeks of daily shots in Banaras.

David asked the doctors if I could catch rabies from him. First they told him that I wouldn't unless his spit came in contact with an open wound of mine. But one doctor thought that if the puppy's saliva had reached my eyes or mouth, there was a slight chance I could get rabies. He said the incubation period is ten days to eighteen months, that the shots David was taking are seventy-five percent effective.

I felt well until last night. David and I walked along the Ganga south of the Asi *ghat.* Little Indian boys were driving herds of black water buffalo into the water by tapping them on their behinds with short slender sticks. Farther out in the water, two boys with turbans and loincloths poled a flat boat as they shouted and pointed in the water. We thought they had bumped into one of the decaying human bodies that float in the Ganga. Bodies of Yogi, children under ten, and smallpox victims, all considered holier than ordinary people, are taken out in small gondolalike boats and dropped into the river without burning. But no Indian would disturb these bodies; it's against their religion. David called to them in Hindi, to ask what was in the water. They answered back, "Hairy monster."

"Bring it over," David called. We met them at the shore. They pushed their "hairy monster" with their poles, jumping back from it in the boat as if it were a demon that would grab them. Whatever they had was dead, because it didn't splash in the water, or swim away from their poles.

At first all we could see was a big black-and-brown furry bulk. It didn't look like anything Indian. It had too much fur for a pig. It wasn't a goat or a calf, nor a monkey with a skinny tail. We didn't think it could be a dog because it was huge. There are no large dogs in India. David helped the boys pull the carcass into shallow water, and spread it out a little.

Then I saw it was Duchess. I saw the scar on her left ear where a black Labrador bit her before she was full-grown. Her tongue hung out the color of yellow dahl. I ran down the riverbank crying.

I didn't sleep last night. I thought I might be getting malaria and took a double dose of the malaria prevention pills we brought with us to India.

First thing this morning, David brought an Ayurvedic medicine doctor to see me. One of our friends, a Norwegian who is in our Hindi class, knows him and thinks he is good, especially at curing malaria. This doctor said he couldn't cure rabies. Everyone who gets rabies dies, he said. He gave me a bitter powder to boil in water for twenty minutes, and told me to take it every four hours until I feel better. I try to force it down, but my throat closes up and my jaws clench like I'm being strangled.

David says that dog from the river was a mongrel and the cut in its ear was fresh, but I don't believe him. I know Duchess is dead.

My head hurts, I'm cold, and my body is shaking. When I close my eyes, I see the waters of the Ganga rising higher and higher, swirling around me.

PAMELA PAINTER

Confusing the Dog

M_y wife and I, we have this game we play called "Confusing the Dog." My wife, she plays the game, knows all the rules, but she doesn't know I named it. I named it about the time I realized we were hooked—us and the dog.

The game goes like this: I go to bed or my wife goes to bed. One of us changes sides. Then the other one comes in. We don't have a plan or pattern, every few weeks it just happens.

"Well, now, it's been a while," my wife might say when she sees me in bed on her side.

"Just get in bed," I'll say.

Or it might go like this:

"So, tonight's the night," I might say. Now, see, she's changed to my side.

"Just get in bed," she'll say.

The other one can tell immediately because whoever made the trade has already moved the pillows and magazines. We read at night or watch TV. Sometimes my wife tears out recipes or coupons and sorts them into bright piles between us on the bed. I catch up on Magic Johnson or Kareem Abdul-Jabbar. Maybe check out the swimsuit issue of *Sports Illustrated*. On "Confusing the Dog" nights we don't read or anything, we turn out the lights and wait.

Pretty soon the dog realizes the rest of the house is empty and all activity, what little there is, has moved to the bedroom. So the dog trots in, his nails clicking on the bare floor, and he looks for his place on the bed. He cocks his head at us and sniffs a little, wagging his tail. Then he begins to travel back and forth and back and forth around the bed. The tip of his long tail moves just above the horizon line of the bedspread like a shark's fin in dangerous waters. Without even touching her, I can feel my wife lying quiet and tense beside me like she's praying or something.

The dog's this shaggy cross between a golden retriever and a Lab. A light molasses color. We got the dog about two years ago at the pound. "Someone must have dropped him off at the interstate," they said. "No tags on him or nothing." They thought he was about ten or eleven. My wife, she took to him the minute they let him out of his cage. He wagged that long bushy tail of his and nuzzled her hand. "He's so good, sometimes we let him out just for company," they said. "Look at those eyes," she said. "He looks like he was here waiting for us." "Not many people want an older dog," they said. So that was it. He went home with us that very day.

We got an older dog because we'd just found out that we couldn't have kids and my wife didn't want a puppy right then. I can understand that. We got him in the summer before my wife returned to work. She cooks mornings at the high school. Afternoons she's mostly home with the dog.

"Confusing the Dog" started when I twisted my ankle at a Saturday basketball game. I've been away from organized ball almost fifteen years now, but I still go down to the gym on Saturdays for pickup games with the guys from the plant. Maybe a few tips for the St. Francis kids. I was the best point guard our high school ever had. I kept the ball low and moving. Still do. I dribble it off the tips of my fingers, never touching my palms. Either hand. For me, the real power is keeping it in play. Points only make it more real.

Well, one weekend I sprained my ankle going in for a lay-up. I came down hard and there went the old ankle. The guys took me to the doctor's and then brought me home with crutches and two six-packs. My wife held the door and we all shuffled past while the dog barked and ran around sniffing at my bandaged ankle and the crutches. "What happened to you?" she said.

That night I suggested we trade places because the doc said to keep my ankle elevated and quiet. Ever since we got married, I've been sleeping between my wife and the bedroom door—sleeping that way through two apartments and one house. It's as if I'll be on hand to protect her from a burglar or something. I imagine all guys sleep this way, waiting for a crash in the night, for a big shape to fill up the doorway. I imagine women sleep tuned in to smaller sounds. Raccoons in the garbage cans or babies crying to be changed and fed. I think my wife still sleeps this way even though we won't be having any kids—unless a baby comes along for adoption before that agency decides we're too old. My wife, she got the room all ready—painted it, made curtains—but nothing's happened yet.

So, we switched places that night for the first time, me with my foot bandaged and stiff, propped up on pillows like a beacon. My wife put my magazines beside me on her table and the remote for the TV, then she got into bed real careful.

In the dim light of our bed lamps the dog went crazy. He traveled back and forth and back and forth. He sleeps in the crook of my wife's knees, between her and the wall. But that night he couldn't find his place. He kept seeing me, probably smelling my fear that he'd pounce on my ankle.

"Maybe we should keep the dog out tonight," I said.

"Good idea," she said. She started getting out of bed real careful-like again, then suddenly the dog got smart. He let out a bark and jumped up and got himself settled in between us, this big dog, although it took a while for him to adjust to the warmer wall—me. We slept that way for almost a month. Ankles take a while to heal, like everything else. Then one night my wife said, "Let's change back," and the same thing happened. Back and forth, back and forth.

Tonight, again, I'm feeling restless. When my wife comes in, she notices immediately.

"It's been a while," I say from her side of the bed. I am sitting up, sheets tucked tight beneath my arms.

She laughs. "He loves it." My wife is game. She puts on one of my old T-shirts and climbs in. I turn off the light. As we begin to listen, I grope for her hand beneath the sheet. I scratch her palm a little like I used to do. It's been a long time for other things too. She gives my hand a squeeze, then pats it. Then she lets it go. We wait for the dog.

Sure enough, pretty soon the dog comes along and back and forth, and back and forth. We are both tense, listening. The dog is getting older now and he's been showing signs of arthritis in his joints. So my wife begins to give him hints. She whispers his name. She pats the bed between us down behind her knees. I feel the bedspread flatten and puff, flatten and puff. Soon the dog heaves himself up with a bark and flops down in the space between us. Hair flies everywhere. He scratches. He slobbers and smells bad. He snores. He sleeps long after we get up, get dressed. Sometimes he whimpers in his sleep. I worry about the dog. I worry about us.

PETER CAMERON

The Secret Dog

When my wife, Miranda, finally falls asleep, I get out of bed and stand for a moment in the darkness, making sure she won't wake up.

Then I go downstairs to the closet where I keep my dog. On the door is a sign that says, MIRANDA: KEEP OUT. Miranda is allergic to dogs and will not allow them in the house. So I have a secret dog.

I open the door to the closet without turning on any lights. Dog is sleeping and wakes up when she hears me. I have trained her to sleep all day and never to bark. She is very smart. She is remarkable. I kneel in the hall. Dog walks over and presses her head into my stomach and I hold it gently. I can hear her wagging her tail, but even though it is a very quiet sound, I know it will wake Miranda.

Dog and I go out to the car. I purposely park down the street so Miranda won't hear the car start. I tell her I can never find a space in front of the house. She suspects nothing. Once Dog and I are in the car, I feed her. I keep her food (Gainesburgers) in the glove compartment. I keep the glove compartment locked. Dog stands on the front seat next to me and eats her dinner. I stroke her back while she is eating. Every few bites she turns around—looks over her shoulder—and smiles at me.

When she is done I start the car. I drive about a mile to an A&P that is open all night. As I drive, Dog stands with her nose out the window. I open the window only a crack. I am afraid she might jump out. Since Dog sleeps all day, she is very excited to be awake at last. When we stop at red lights I reach over and pat her. She wags her tail.

At the A&P we get out. First I take her behind the store to a grassy bank beside the railroad tracks where she relieves herself. Every few days she does this in the closet, but usually she is very good about waiting till we get out. She hops about the tracks, sniffing and wagging her tail. She is a joy to watch. She squats, and I look the other way.

Then we go back to the parking lot, which is usually empty. Every now and then a car pulls in, and someone jumps out and runs into the A&P. We have plenty of room. This is when I train her. I have a book, which I also keep locked in the glove compartment, called *How to Train Your Schnauzer.* Dog is not a schnauzer, but it seems to be working well. Already she can heel, sit, lie down and stand on command. I open the book on the hood of the car. I always park under a light so I can read. We are on week nine, although we've only been working for four weeks. That is how smart Dog is.

I have to give Dog plenty of exercise so she will sleep all day. We begin running. Dog runs right beside me. We run a mile or two and then walk back to the car. Dog trots beside me, panting. Her long, pink tongue hangs out the side of her mouth. She stops and sniffs at discarded papers that flutter on the sidewalk.

We do this every night.

One night when I come in, there is a light on in the kitchen. This has never happened before. I put Dog in her closet and quietly close the door. I walk slowly up to the kitchen. Miranda is standing by the table in her bathrobe. She is slicing a banana into a bowl of cereal. She won't look at me. Her hair is loose and hangs down over her face, which is bowed over the banana. I cannot see her face. I sit down, and still she will not look at me. Miranda, I often think, looks more beautiful when woke from sleep than during the day. Her face is slack and warm, and her body is tired and soft. She looks very beautiful to me, head bowed, slicing the banana.

Suddenly the knife slits her finger. Miranda does not acknowledge this wound. She continues to slice the banana. I realize she is crying.

"You cut yourself," I say quietly. I think I can hear Dog plopping down on the floor in the closet.

Miranda raises her cut finger to her mouth. She sucks on it, then wraps it in a napkin. She tucks her hair behind her ears and sits down. Then she looks up at me. "Where have you been?" she whispers. There are two pink spots, high on her white cheeks. There is also a little blood on her lips. She has stopped crying. "Where have you been?" she repeats.

I watch the napkin she wrapped her finger in turn red, slowly. I cannot speak. Miranda stands up. She runs her finger under the faucet and looks at it. She wraps it in a clean napkin. She is facing away from me, toward the sink. "Who are you seeing?" she says. "Do I know her?"

It has never occurred to me that Miranda might think I am having an affair. This is a great relief, for if she believes this she must not suspect Dog. "I'm not having an affair," I say. "I haven't seen anyone."

Miranda looks over at me. "Really?" she says.

"Yes," I say. "Really."

"Where have you been?" asks Miranda.

I think for a moment. "I can't tell you."

Miranda looks down at her injured finger. "Why can't you tell me?"

"It's a secret," I say. "I can't tell you because it's a secret. But I'm not having an affair. Do you understand?"

For a few seconds Miranda says nothing. She glances above my head at her reflection in the window. I, too, turn and watch her in the window. She looks very beautiful. I see her mouth move in the window, against the night. "Yes," she says, "I understand."

The next day at work I find I am very tired. I have been sleeping very little since I got Dog. Suddenly I wake up. Joyce, my boss, is standing in front of my desk. She smiles at me. "You've been sleeping," she says. "That isn't allowed."

I sit up straight and open my top desk drawer as if I'm looking for something. Then I close it. I look up at Joyce. She just stands there. "Why are you sleeping?" she asks. "Are you that tired?"

"I'm very tired," I say.

"Why?" asks Joyce.

257

"My wife just had a baby," I lie. "It's been very sick, and I have to stay up all night with it. That's why I'm tired." This is a very bad lie. Miranda and I can't have a baby. We've been trying for years to have one.

"When did Miranda have a baby?" Joyce smiles. She sits down in my customer chair. "I didn't even know she was pregnant."

"A month ago," I say. "I thought I told you. I guess I've been too tired."

"How wonderful!" says Joyce. "Lucky you! What is it?"

"What do you mean?" I say. "It's a baby."

"A boy or a girl?" asks Joyce. She is so nice.

"It's a girl."

"What's her name?"

I think for a second. "Dorothy," I say.

"Well," says Joyce, "congratulations." She stands up and winks at me. "Just try to stay awake," she says. "But I understand."

The next night when I get home there is a big bouquet on the kitchen table. Miranda is sitting at the table smoking. Before she says anything, she points to the flowers with her cigarette. Then she hands me a little card. A stork flies across the top, carrying a baby wrapped in a diaper. Pink ribbons hang from the words CONGRATULATIONS ON THE NEW ARRIVAL! and underneath that is written WELCOME DOROTHY! LOVE, JOYCE. The o in Joyce contains two little eyes and a big smile.

Miranda stubs her cigarette in the ashtray. "Who," she says, "is Dorothy?"

"I don't know," I say.

"If this is Joyce's idea of a joke," cries Miranda, "I think she must be pretty sick." She stands up and looks at the flowers. They are irises and tulips. "She must be pretty sick," Miranda repeats. "Since when do we have a baby? Did you tell Joyce we had a baby?" Miranda looks at me. "Did you?"

I don't know what to say. I never thought Joyce would send us flowers. I didn't think she was that nice. "Yes," I say finally.

"You did?" Miranda is screaming, and it occurs to me that she is probably hysterical. "How could you? Why?"

"I fell asleep at work," I say. "It was just an excuse. I told Joyce I had to stay up nights with our baby. With Dorothy. I said Dorothy was very sick and I had to stay up nights with her."

"You jerk," says Miranda. "You moron. I don't understand you anymore. I bet you are having an affair."

"Calm down," I say. "That's not true. You know that's not true. You said you understood. Remember?"

"But I don't understand," says Miranda. "I don't understand anymore. Where do you go at night?"

"It's a secret," I say. "I told you it was a secret."

"I don't know what to say." Miranda stands up. "I don't feel well. I'm going to bed." She walks to the door. Then she turns around. She is trembling. "Get rid of the flowers," she says.

That night I wait a long time before I go down to Dog. I want to make sure Miranda is sleeping. Finally I am satisfied. Miranda's face is turned away from mine on the pillow and her arm is thrown back above her head. She is hardly moving. Her cheeks move in and out a little and the blankets rise and fall across her breasts, but besides that she is perfectly still. The lights from passing cars move across her face, and she almost looks dead, she is so still.

I go down to get Dog. It is wonderful to see her. She comes out of the closet and whines a little, very quietly. Then she rubs her head against my chest. I am very sad tonight, and even Dog cannot cheer me up. Patting her, kissing her between her eyes, only makes me sadder. Dog senses this and lies down close to me on the car seat.

At the A&P I almost lose Dog. She runs between two huge trucks that are parked behind the store, and I can't find her. It is dark back there and quiet. I can hear Dog's tags and collar jingling, but it sounds very far away, on the other side of the tracks. I am almost afraid to call her, it is so quiet. The moon is out, and the broken glass glints on the pavement. I whistle softly, and Dog comes. I can hear her coming across the tracks and back between the trucks. She runs across the parking lot, in and out of the shadows, like a ghost. I put out my hand to touch her, and she is there.

I go in the A&P to buy dog food. Dog is afraid of the electric door and hesitates when it swings open of its own accord. I pick her up.

"You can't bring the dog in here," says the checkout girl, "unless he's a Seeing-Eye dog. Are you blind?"

Since I am carrying Dog, I can hardly claim I am blind. "No," I say. I put Dog down.

"Well, then he can't come in. Sorry."

I pick up Dog and go out. Dog is tired; her body is limp and warm in my arms. I carry her like a baby, her head against my shoulder. I put her in the car, lock the door, and go back in the store.

I walk up and down the aisles enjoying myself. Pet food is always in the middle aisle, regardless of the store. This fascinates me. The only other customer in the store is in pet food. She has on a long green dress, sandals, and a pink scarf. Her hair sticks out of the scarf in all directions. It is red. She stares at me as I walk down the aisle. She is waiting to tell me something. I can tell.

"I read palms," she whispers as I reach out for the Gainesburgers. "I tell fortunes."

I say nothing. I read the box. "Complete as a meal in a can," it says, "without any of the mess."

"Do me a favor," the woman says. She touches my arm.

"What?" I say.

"Escort me up and down the aisles," she says. "I'll read your palm when we're done."

"Why?" I say.

"Why what?" Before I can answer she says, "Why not? I'm lonely. Please."

"Okay," I say. I hope this won't take too long.

We walk toward the front of the store. The woman consults her shopping list. "My name is Jane," she says, as if this is written on her list. "Just Jane. Soda. Will you do me another favor?" She looks up at me.

"What?" I say.

She touches my arm again. "Pretend you're my husband," she says. "Pretend we're married and we're shopping. Will you do that?"

"Why?" I ask.

Once again she looks at her list, as if the answer is there. "Soda," she mumbles. "What kind of soda do you like?" She hesitates. "Dear."

We are in the beverage aisle, and all the bottles gleam around us. "I like 7-Up," I say, because that is the first kind I see.

"The un-cola," says Jane. "I don't like it. I like Coke. But we'll get 7-Up for you." She puts a large plastic bottle of 7-Up in the cart. We proceed.

"Please don't get that for me." I feel very foolish. "If you like Coke, get Coke. I like Coke fine."

She stops. "Do you?" she says. "Do you like Coke fine?"

"Yes."

"But which do you like better?"

"Please get whatever you want," I say. "This is silly."

Jane puts the 7-Up back on the wrong shelf. "Do you like birch beer?" she asks.

"Yes," I say.

"Fine, then." Jane reaches for some birch beer. "We'll get that."

We continue through the store like this. We disagree about yogurt, deodorant, bread, juice, and ice cream. The checkout girl rings up my dog food first. Then she does Jane's groceries. I help her carry them out to her car. It is the only other one in the parking lot. I can see Dog, with her front paws on the dashboard, watching me. "Good night," I say to Jane. I'm very glad this is over.

"Wait," says Jane. "I promised to tell your fortune. Give me your palm."

I hold out my hand, and Jane takes it. Her hand is warm and wet. "Move." She pushes me toward my car, under the light. She opens my palm and holds it flattened. The light makes it look very white. For a long time she says nothing. I can hear Dog whine in the car.

When Jane speaks, she addresses my palm, not me. "I see blue lights. I see swimmers. I see rhododendrons. You will live a long time." She pauses. "You will always feel like this." She slowly rolls my fingers toward my palm, making a fist. She looks up at me.

"Like what?" I ask. "Always feel like what?"

Jane lets go of my hand and makes a vague gesture with her own, indicating the A&P, the parking lot, my car with Dog in it. "Like this," she repeats softly. "You will always feel like this."

Joyce is there, standing above me. "Perhaps you should take a vacation," she says. "You can't keep falling asleep at work."

I feel very tired. I just want to go back to sleep. I don't know what to say.

"Do you have vacation time coming?" says Joyce. "Perhaps you should take it now."

"I'm tired," I say. Joyce is a little out of focus, because I just woke up.

"I know you're tired," says Joyce. She seems to be talking very loudly. Joyce sent us flowers. She is very nice. "You look very tired. That's why I think you should take a vacation. Do you think that would be a good idea? Do you understand?"

"I guess so," I say.

"Well, think about it," says Joyce. "Think about it, and let me know. Things can't go on like this."

"I know," I say.

"Good," says Joyce. Then she leaves.

When I get home that night things are fine. Miranda suggests we go out to dinner, and we do. It is very nice. We drink a lot of wine and eat and eat, and then we go home. We watch the news on TV. It is terrible news; even the local news is terrible. Miranda yawns and goes into the bathroom. I can hear her in there: the water flowing, the toilet flushing. It sounds so lovely, so safe. It is windy and cold outside, and the trees rattle against the windows. I can hear Miranda setting the alarm in the bedroom and the radio playing softly.

"Are you coming?" she calls down the hall. "Come to bed."

I get in bed with Miranda and pretend to go to sleep. It is hard to stay awake. My head is spinning with all the wine I drank, and I am so tired. But I stay awake until Miranda falls asleep. Her breathing softens, and she grows beautiful in sleep. I get up and go down to Dog.

When I open the closet, Dog is not there. It is empty. I call her softly, thinking she has got out somehow. I call and call, in whispers, but she doesn't come.

I stand in the hall for a long while thinking I must have fallen asleep. I do not understand what is happening, and I begin to cry a little. I go back upstairs and into the bathroom and close the door. When I stop crying, I come out and stand in the bedroom. The moonlight falls through the window and onto the bed, onto the part where I am not sleeping. Miranda sleeps against the wall, in shadows. The first time I saw Miranda was in a hotel in Florida. She was coming out of her room with a folding chair. She asked me to hold it while she answered the phone, which was ringing in her room. I stood in the corridor and held the chair for what seemed a very long time. I could hear Miranda talking, but I couldn't make out what she was saying.

Miranda wakes up. She turns over, into the moonlight, and looks up at me. "What are you doing?" she says sleepily. "Why aren't you in bed? Are you crying?"

I realize I am still crying a little. Miranda sits up in bed, very beautiful, the pale light on her face. "Why are you crying?" she whispers.

I don't know what to say. The wind blows, and the bedroom seems to shake. I can hardly speak. "Where is Dog?" I say. "What did you do with Dog?"

"Dog?" says Miranda, "what dog?" She leans forward, across the bed, toward me. "There never was any dog."

MARK STRAND

Dog Life

Glover Barlett and his wife, Tracy, lay in their king-size bed under a light blue cambric comforter stuffed with down. They stared into the velvety, perfumed dark. Then Glover turned on his side to look at his wife. Her golden hair surrounded her face, making it seem smaller. Her lips were slightly parted. He wanted to tell her something. But what he had to say was so charged that he hesitated. He had mulled it over in private; now he felt he must bring it into the open, regardless of the risks. "Darling," he said, "there's something I've been meaning to tell you."

Tracy's eyes widened with apprehension. "Glover, please, if it's going to upset me, I'd rather not hear. . . ."

"It's just that I was different before I met you."

"What do you mean 'different'?" Tracy asked, looking at him.

"I mean, darling, that I used to be a dog."

"You're putting me on," said Tracy.

"No, I'm not," said Glover.

Tracy stared at her husband with mute astonishment. A silence weighted with solitude filled the room. The time was ripe for intimacy; Tracy's gaze softened into a look of concern.

"A dog?"

"Yes, a collie," said Glover reassuringly. "The people who owned me lived in Connecticut in a big house with lots of lawn, and there were woods out back. All the neighbors had dogs, too. It was a happy time."

Tracy's eyes narrowed. "What do you mean 'a happy time'? How could it have been 'a happy time'?"

"It was. Especially in autumn. We bounded about in the yellow twilight, excited by the clicking of branches and the parade of odors making each circuit of air an occasion for reverie. Burning leaves, chestnuts roasting, pies baking, the last exhalations of earth before freezing, drove us practically mad. But the autumn nights were even better: the blue luster of stones under the moon, the spectral bushes, the gleaming grass. Our eyes shone with a new depth. We barked, bayed, and babbled, trying again and again to find the right note, a note that would reach back thousands of years into our origins. It was a note that if properly sustained would be the distilled wail of our species and would carry within it the triumph of our collective destiny. With our tails poised in the stunned atmosphere, we sang for our lost ancestors, our wild selves. Darling, there was something about those nights that I miss."

"Are you telling me that something is wrong with our marriage?"

"Not at all. I'm only saying that there was a tragic dimension to my life in those days. You have to imagine me with a friend or two on the top of a windswept knoll, crying for the buried fragments of our cunning, for the pride we lost during the period of our captivity, our exile in civilization, our fateful domestication. There were times when I could detect within the coarsest bark a futility I have not known since. I think of my friend Spot; her head high, her neck extended. Her voice was operatic and filled with a sadness that was thrilling as she released, howl by howl, the darkness of her being into the night."

"Did you love her?" Tracy asked.

"No, not really. I admired her more than anything."

"But there were dogs you did love?"

"It's hard to say that dogs actually love," said Glover.

"You know what I mean," said Tracy.

Glover turned on his back and stared at the ceiling. "Well, there was Flora, who had a lovely puff of hair on her head, inherited from her Dandie Dinmont mother. She was teeny, of course, and I felt foolish, but still . . . And there was Muriel, a melancholic Irish setter. And Cheryl, whose mother was a long-coated Chihuahua and whose father was a cross between a fox terrier and a shelty. She was intelligent, but her owners made her wear a little tartan jacket which humiliated her. She ran off with a clever mutt—part puli, part

265

dachshund. After that I saw her with a black-and-white papillon. Then she moved, and I never saw her again."

"Were there others?" said Tracy.

"There was Peggy Sue, a German short-haired pointer whose owners would play Buddy Holly on their stereo. The excitement we experienced when we heard her name is indescribable. We would immediately go to the door and whimper to be let out. How proudly we trotted under the gaudy scattering of stars! How immodest we were under the moon's opalescence! We pranced and pranced in the exuberant light."

"You make it sound so hunky-dory. There must've been bad times."

"The worst times were when my owners laughed. Suddenly they became strangers. The soft cadences of their conversation, the sharpness of their commands, gave way to howls, gurgles, and yelps. It was as if something were released in them, something absolute and demonic. Once they started it was hard for them to stop. You can't imagine how frightening and confusing it was to see my protectors out of control. The sounds they made seemed neither expressive or communicative, nor did they indicate pleasure or pain, but rather a weird mixture of both. It was a limbo of utterance from which I felt completely excluded. But why go on, those days are past."

"How do you know?"

"I just do. I feel it."

"But if you were a dog once, why not a dog twice?"

"Because there are no signs of that happening again. When I was a dog, there were indications that I would end up as I am now. I never liked exposing myself and was pained by having to perform private acts in public. I was embarrassed by the pomp of bitches in heat—their preening and wagging, by the panting lust of my brothers. I became withdrawn; I brooded; I actually suffered a kind of canine *terribilità*. It all pointed to one thing."

When Glover had finished, he waited for Tracy to speak. He was sorry he had told her so much. He felt ashamed. He hoped she would understand his having been a dog was not his choice, that such aberrations are born of necessity and are not lamentable. At times, the fury of a man's humanity will find its finest manifestation in amazing alterations of expectedness. For people are only marginally themselves. Glover, who earlier in the night had begun to slide into an agony of contrition, now felt righteous pride. He saw that Tracy's eyes were closed. She had fallen asleep. The truth had been endurable, had been overshadowed by a need that led her safely into the doom of another night. They would wake in the early morning and look at each other as always. What he had told her would be something they would never mention again, not out of politeness, or sensitivity for the other, but because such achievements of frailty, such lyrical lapses, are unavoidable in every life.

ROD KESSLER

Another Thursday with the Meyerhoffs

Meyerhoff perched on his porcelain throne upstairs waiting for the phone to ring and bring in some business. He had the morning paper spread out over his knees. Downstairs the door slammed shut, and a moment later he heard the life jump into the engine of his wife's car, a wide-axled Pontiac the color of martini olives. She was leaving for her Thursday therapy appointment. Meyerhoff's wife had been diagnosed as infertile. The diagnosis had been reconfirmed. They never talked about it now, but she blamed him. She didn't say it in so many words, but he could tell. Meyerhoff couldn't remember whether she had just come up the stairs to say good-bye. She had come up for something—probably to tell him to walk the dog.

His wife was a woman of intense moods. Her therapy hours stirred her so that, when she came back to the house, she invariably retreated into the bedroom to cry. Later she would be ready to face Meyerhoff and the world again, but she never discussed her therapy sessions. She was often resentful of Meyerhoff, though, and even openly hostile. She brought up remarks Meyerhoff had made in all innocence during the previous week and then showed him how insensitive and uncaring he had been all along. On occasion, she returned filled with love for Meyerhoff. Or if not with love, then with sympathy, which Meyerhoff was willing to settle for. Meyerhoff never knew what to expect when his wife came home from therapy, except that she would close the bedroom door and cry.

Meyerhoff's dog was six months old and had developed into a car chaser.

Actually, he was Meyerhoff's wife's dog, but Meyerhoff exercised him as frequently as his wife did. More frequently. The dog had some shepherd in him and was shaped like a bullet. When Meyerhoff took him over to the baseball fields behind Catalina High School, the dog invariably squatted and did his business. But Meyerhoff's wife, who loved the dog, had many dry runs. Sometimes she would return from a dismal half hour of it, her blouse dripping with perspiration from the midday Arizona sun, and she would shrug. Then Meyerhoff would get up from his pile of real estate clippings and take the dog out again. The dog's name was Sunshine, something Meyerhoff's wife had come up with. Meyerhoff made the effort not to call him Sunny.

The Meyerhoffs lived blocks away from Speedway and Grant Boulevard, the heavily trafficked streets. Their neighborhood with its tall palm trees was quiet, and they didn't put Sunshine on a leash. Sunshine wasn't used to a leash and wouldn't squat with one on.

Meyerhoff folded his paper and stood up, once again disappointed. There was nothing to see, and he didn't bother to flush. He washed his hands out of habit. He looked at himself in the mirror and worked up the smile he used on his clients. The wrinkles fanning away from his eyes were cut deep into his face. It was the climate. It was the sun. It was the smile itself. He worked it up again and saw that he looked ferocious, feral, maniacal. It was depressing. He had expected to see a younger man's face when he looked in the mirror. His life was . . . what? Not even half over. Meyerhoff noticed that once again his wife had left the toothpaste uncapped.

Meyerhoff padded down the stairs to collect the dog. He eased his feet into running sneakers that still looked new after six months, and the two of them headed through the heat toward the high school.

The first car that came along, the dog went for it, barking with delight, his claws scratching the hot, graveled surface of the street. Meyerhoff was too old to chase after the dog. He might have done it five years ago, but not now, not in public. Besides, he had a bum leg from a fall while skiing down Mount Lemmon a few years back. He bellowed at the dog, but the dog ignored him.

Meyerhoff wished he could deliver a long-range shock to the dog. He wished he had an electrical device attached to the dog's collar. Sunshine pranced back to Meyerhoff after the car got away, but he stayed far enough out of range to escape easily should Meyerhoff make a sudden lunge for him. The dog and Meyerhoff had been through this before.

Sunshine wouldn't sniff up to Meyerhoff's hand even though he held out a dog cookie and made his voice sound friendly. Sunshine knew better. He was a big puppy, and his ears flopped. The ears didn't stand up like a shepherd's ears. Meyerhoff wished he had a little button in his hand that would give Sunshine a handsome surprise.

The dog was no better at home. Sunshine woke Meyerhoff at daybreak with his pathetic whimpering and cold nose. Meyerhoff's wife seemed to encourage the dog in this. His wife was always happy to see the dog in the morning.

Meyerhoff was sure that the dog was jumping on the furniture when he was out. He hadn't caught him at it, but he had found hairs on the blue-and-coffee-colored serape they had bought down in Nogales. Meyerhoff had plans to sneak up to the house some afternoon and peek through the living room windows. He also suspected that his wife let Sunshine sit on the big, leather lounge chair.

Meyerhoff had spent hours training the dog to sit still and to lie down on command, but the dog would do nothing unless bribed with dog cookies. Sometimes not even dog cookies availed. When Meyerhoff's clients—young marrieds, retired couples—came over to look at listings, the dog was incorrigible, barking and snapping. On quiet evenings, the dog liked to visit Meyerhoff's lap the moment he opened his magazine. Sunshine also stationed himself in front of the screen when the television news came on.

Sometimes Meyerhoff got down on the rug to roughhouse with the puppy. Actually, he would pinch the dog with vengeance and hope that his wife didn't notice. He would take up the loose skin on the dog's back and give it a quick bite. Or he would clamp his fist around the dog's snout and hold it until the dog squealed. Meyerhoff would pretend that the puppy had squealed with delight.

Following the dog through the gate into the grounds of the high school, Meyerhoff wished he had the dog's snout in his fist right then. The dog trotted ahead, hurrying to try to spray his latest news on two ornamental mesquite trees and the base of the drinking fountain. But he quickly got down to it on the clay track just in front of the home team's stands.

The dog strutted over to Meyerhoff, grinning, and Meyerhoff scratched behind his ears. He wanted to walk over and inspect the dog's stool but thought better of it. A chubby man jogging the track was eyeing him, and he would have felt silly. At least the dog hadn't started chasing joggers. Meyerhoff's running shoes still looked new because he didn't jog. The chubby man, who was at least Meyerhoff's age, waved to Meyerhoff, but Meyerhoff pretended that he hadn't seen. Meyerhoff didn't like chubby people. He didn't like messy things. He was pleased that he had managed to keep his own weight down without jogging. But then, maybe jogging would be the thing to loosen up his system?

The dog's system didn't need loosening up, Meyerhoff reflected, as he walked homeward past the front yards of his neighbors, yards decorated with saguaros and prickly pear cactus gardens or with bushy oleanders, their pastel flowers scenting the air. It intrigued Meyerhoff that he could always get the dog to squat, but his wife couldn't. The dog just took him more seriously. The dog knew that he, Meyerhoff, could really let him have it, back home on the rug. The dog probably regarded him as the leader of the pack.

They made it home without encountering another car.

Later, Meyerhoff's wife came out of the bedroom, dabbing a wad of pink tissue paper inside the corner of her eyeglasses. She wanted to know if he had taken the dog out.

"Sure," he told her, a little wary. "And he was right on the money."

Meyerhoff's wife moved into the kitchen and started to mix herself a drink. Meyerhoff went into the kitchen, too, and leaned against the counter. The dog was in the corner underneath the vent from the swamp cooler. The fan was running at top speed, and they had to raise their voices to hear each other.

"It's no wonder," said Meyerhoff's wife. "He saves it for you."

"What do you mean?" said Meyerhoff. It annoyed him that his wife never offered to mix a drink for him too. Years ago she had served in a cocktail lounge, and she knew how. It wasn't exactly a cocktail lounge, but what else could you call it? She had worked there, and he had been a regular. He had even played softball on a team the place sponsored. It could happen to anyone.

"Don't you ever wonder why the dog holds it for you?" she asked. She had her drink in her hand and was leaning against the counter too. "Don't you ever wonder?"

"So what?" said Meyerhoff.

"I'd say it was pretty obvious," she said. She held up her glass and stared into it, just as if she were analyzing a urine specimen. "It's the only thing he ever does that pleases you. It's the only thing that either of us does."

The remark took Meyerhoff aback. What if she's right? he wondered. The dog's regularity gave rhythm to the day. It gave the day shape. It did please him. He realized that it did please him. He could admit that. He turned to her and told her that it did please him. And then he worked up one of his smiles.

JIM SHEPARD

Reach for the Sky

Guy comes into the shelter this last Thursday, a kid, really, maybe doing it for his dad, with a female golden/ Labrador cross, two or three years old. He's embarrassed, not ready for forms and questions, but we get dogs like this all the time, and I'm not letting him off the hook, not letting him out of here before I know he knows that we have to kill a lot of these dogs, dogs like his. Her name is Rita and he says, "Rita, sit!" like being here is part of her ongoing training. Rita sits halfway and then stands again, and looks at him in that tuned-in way goldens have.

"So . . ." The kid looks at the forms I've got on the counter, like no one told him this was part of the deal. He looks up at the sampler that the sister of the regional boss did for our office: A MAN KNOWS ONLY AS MUCH AS HE'S SUFFERED—ST. FRANCIS OF ASSISI. He has no answers whatsoever for the form. She's two, he thinks. Housebroken. Some shots. His dad handled all that stuff. She's spayed. Reason for Surrender: she plays too rough.

She smashed this huge lamp, the kid says. Of one of those mariners with the pipe and the yellow bad-weather outfit. His dad made it in a ceramics class.

Rita looks over at me with bright interest. The kid adds, "And she's got this thing with her back legs, she limps pretty bad. The vet said she wouldn't get any better."

"What vet?" I ask. I'm not supposed to push too hard, it's no better if they abandon them on highways, but we get sixty dogs a day here, and if I can talk any of them back into their houses, great. "The vet couldn't do anything?"

"We don't have the money," the kid says.

I ask to see Rita's limp. The kid's vague, and Rita refuses to demonstrate. Her tail thumps the floor twice.

I explain the bottom of the form to the kid: when he signs it, he's giving us permission to have the dog put down if it comes to that.

"She's a good dog," he says helpfully. "She'll probably get someone to like her."

So I do the animal-shelter Joe Friday, which never works: "Maybe. But we get ten goldens per week. And everybody wants puppies."

"Okay, well, good luck," the kid says. He signs something on the line that looks like "Fleen." Rita looks at him. He takes the leash with him, wrapping it around his forearm. At the door he says, "You be a good girl, now." Rita pants a little with a neutral expression, processing the information.

It used to be you would get owners all the time who were teary and broken up: they needed to know their dog was going to get a good home, you had to guarantee it, they needed to make their problem yours, so that they could say, Hey, when *I* left the dog it was fine.

Their dog would always make a great pet for somebody, their dog was always great with kids, their dog always needed a Good Home and Plenty of Room to Run. Their dog, they were pretty sure, would always be the one we'd have no trouble placing in a nice family. And when they got to the part about signing the release form for euthanasia, only once did someone, a little girl, suggest that if it came to that they should be called back, and they'd retrieve the dog. Her mother had asked me if I had any ideas, and the girl suggested that. Her mother said, "I asked *him* if *he* had any ideas."

Now you get kids; the parents don't even bring the dogs in. Behind the kid with the golden/Lab mix there's a girl who's maybe seventeen or eighteen. Benetton top, Benetton skirt, straw-blond hair, tennis tan, she's got a Doberman puppy. Bizarre dog for a girl like that. Chews everything, she says. She holds the puppy like a baby. As if to cooperate, the dog twists and squirms around in her arms trying to get at the penholder to show what it can do.

Puppies chew things, I tell her, and she rolls her eyes like she knows *that*. I tell her how many dogs come in every day. I lie. I say we've had four Doberman puppies for weeks now. She says, "There're forms or something, or I just leave him?" She slides him on his back gently across the counter. His paws are in the air and he looks a little bewildered.

"If I showed you how to make him stop chewing things, would you take him back?" I ask her. The Doberman has sprawled around and gotten to his feet, taller now than we are, nails clicking tentatively on the counter.

"No," she says. She signs the form, annoyed by a sweep of hair that keeps falling forward. "We're moving, anyhow." She pats the dog on the muzzle as a good-bye and he nips at her, his feet slipping and sliding like a skater's. "God," she says. She's mad at me now, too, the way people get mad at those pictures that come in the mail of dogs and cats looking at you with their noses through the chain-link fences: *Help Skipper, who lived on leather for three weeks.*

When I come back from taking the Doberman downstairs there's a middle-aged guy at the counter in a wheelchair. An Irish setter circles back and forth around the chair, winding and unwinding the black nylon leash across the guy's chest. Somebody's put some time into grooming this dog, and when the sun hits that red coat just right he looks like a million dollars.

I'm not used to wheelchair people. The guy says, "I gotta get rid of the dog."

What do you say to a guy like that: Can't you take care of him? Too much trouble? The setter's got to be eight years old.

"Is he healthy?" I ask.

"She," he says. "She's in good shape."

"Landlord problem?" I say. The guy says nothing.

"What's her name?" I ask.

"We gotta have a discussion?" the guy says. I think, This is what wheelchair people are like. The setter whines and stands her front paws on the arm of the guy's chair.

"We got forms," I say. I put them on the counter, not so close that he doesn't have to reach. He starts to sit up higher and then leans back.

"What's it say?" he says.

"Sex," I say.

"Female," he says.

Breed? Irish setter. Age? Eleven.

Eleven! I can feel this dog on the back of my neck. On my forehead. I can just see myself selling this eleven-year-old dog to the families that come in looking. And how long has she been with him?

I walk back and forth behind the counter, hoist myself up, flex my legs. The guy goes, like he hasn't noticed any of that, "She does tricks."

"Tricks?" I say.

"Ellie," he says. He mimes a gun with his forefinger and thumb and points it at her. "Ellie. Reach for the sky."

Ellie is all attention. Ellie sits, and then rears up, lifting her front paws as high as a dog can lift them, edging forward in little hops from the exertion.

"Reach for the sky, Ellie," he says.

Ellie holds it for a second longer, like those old poodles on *The Ed Sullivan Show,* and then falls back down and wags her tail at having pulled it off.

"I need a Reason for Surrender," I say. "That's what we call it."

"Well, you're not going to get one," the guy says. He edges a wheel of his chair back and forth, turning it a little this way and that.

"Then I can't take the dog," I say.

"Then I'll just let her go when I get out the door," the guy says.

"If I were you I'd keep that dog," I say.

"If you were me you would've wheeled this thing off a bridge eleven years ago," the guy says. "If you were me you wouldn't be such an asshole. If you were me you would've taken this dog, no questions asked."

We're at an impasse, this guy and me.

He's let go of Ellie's leash, and Ellie's covering all the corners of the office, sniffing. There's a woman in the waiting area behind him with a bullterrier puppy on her lap and the puppy's keeping a close eye on Ellie.

"Do you have any relatives or whatever who could take the dog?" I ask him.

The guy looks at me. "Do I sign something?" he says.

I can't help it, when I'm showing him where to sign I can't keep the words back, I keep thinking of Ellie reaching for the sky: "It's better this way. We'll try and find her a home with someone who's equipped to handle her."

The guy doesn't come back at me. He signs the thing and hands me my pen, and says, "Hey Ellie, hey kid," and Ellie comes right over. He picks up her trailing leash and flops the end onto the counter where I can grab it, and then hugs her around the neck until she twists a little and pulls away.

"She doesn't know what's going on," I say.

He looks up at me and I point, as if to say, "Her."

The guy wheels the chair around and heads for the door. The woman with the bullterrier watches him go by with big eyes. I can't see his face, but it must be something. Ellie barks. There's no way to fix this.

I've got ASPCA pamphlets unboxed and all over the counter. I've got impound forms to finish by today.

"Nobody's gonna want this dog," I call after him. I can't help it.

It's just me now, at the counter. The woman stands up, holding the bullterrier against her chest, and stops, like she's not going to turn him over, like whatever her reasons are, they may not be good enough.

WRIGHT MORRIS

Victrola

"Sit!" said Bundy, although the dog already sat. His knowing what Bundy would say was one of the things people noticed about their close relationship. The dog sat—not erect, like most dogs, but off to one side, so that the short-haired pelt on one rump was always soiled. When Bundy attempted to clean it, as he once did, the spot no longer matched the rest of the dog, like a cleaned spot on an old rug. A second soiled spot was on his head, where children and strangers liked to pat him. Over his eyes the pelt was so thin his hide showed through. A third defacement had been caused by the leash in his younger years, when he had tugged at it harder, sometimes almost gagging as Bundy resisted.

Those days had been a strain on both of them. Bundy had developed a bad bursitis, and the crease of the leash could still be seen on the back of his hand. In the past year, over the last eight months, beginning with the cold spell in December, the dog was so slow to cross the street Bundy might have to drag him. That brought on spells of angina for Bundy, and they would both have to stand there until they felt better. At such moments the dog's slantwise gaze was one that Bundy avoided. "Sit!" he would say, no longer troubling to see if the dog did.

The dog leashed to a parking meter, Bundy walked through the drugstore to the prescription counter at the rear. The pharmacist, Mr. Avery, peered down from a platform two steps above floor level—the source of a customer's still pending lawsuit. His gaze to the front of the store, he said, "He still itching?"

278

Bundy nodded. Mr. Avery had recommended a vitamin supplement that some dogs found helpful. The scratching had been replaced by licking.

"You've got to remember," said Avery, "he's in his nineties. When you're in your nineties, you'll also do a little scratchin'!" Avery gave Bundy a challenging stare. If Avery reached his nineties, Bundy was certain Mrs. Avery would have to keep him on a leash or he would forget who he was. He had repeated this story about the dog's being ninety ever since Bundy had first met him and the dog was younger.

"I need your expertise," Bundy said. (Avery lapped up that sort of flattery.) "How does five cc's compare with five hundred mg's?"

"It doesn't. Five cc's is a liquid measure. It's a spoonful."

"What I want to know is, how much Vitamin C am I getting in five cc's?"

"Might not be any. In a liquid solution, Vitamin C deteriorates rapidly. You should get it in the tablet." It seemed clear he had expected more of Bundy.

"I see," said Bundy. "Could I have my prescription?"

Mr. Avery lowered his glasses to look for it on the counter. Bundy might have remarked that a man of Avery's age—and experience—ought to know enough to wear glasses he could both see and read through, but having to deal with him once a month dictated more discretion than valor.

Squinting to read the label, Avery said, "I see he's upped your dosage." On their first meeting, Bundy and Avery had had a sensible discussion about the wisdom of minimal medication, an attitude that Bundy thought was unusual to hear from a pharmacist.

"His point is," said Bundy, "since I like to be active, there's no reason I shouldn't enjoy it. He tells me the dosage is still pretty normal."

"Hmm," Avery said. He opened the door so Bundy could step behind the counter and up to the platform with his Blue Cross card. For the umpteenth time he told Bundy, "Pay the lady at the front. Watch your step as you leave."

As he walked toward the front Bundy reflected that he would rather be a little less active than forget what he had said two minutes earlier.

"We've nothing but trouble with dogs," the cashier said. "They're in and out every minute. They get at the bars of candy. But I can't ever remember trouble with your dog."

"He's on a leash," said Bundy.

"That's what I'm saying," she replied.

When Bundy came out of the store, the dog was lying down, but he made the effort to push up and sit.

"Look at you," Bundy said, and stooped to dust him off. The way he licked himself, he picked up dirt like a blotter. A shadow moved over them, and Bundy glanced up to see, at a respectful distance, a lady beaming on the dog like a healing heat lamp. Older than Bundy—much older, a wraithlike creature, more spirit than substance, her face crossed with wisps of hairlike cobwebs—Mrs. Poole had known the dog as a pup; she had been a dear friend of its former owner, Miss Tyler, who had lived directly above Bundy. For years he had listened to his neighbor tease the dog to bark for pieces of liver, and heard the animal push his food dish around the kitchen.

"Whatever will become of him?" Miss Tyler would whisper to Bundy, anxious that the dog shouldn't hear what she was saying. Bundy had tried to reassure her: look how spry she was at eighty! Look how the dog was over-weight and asthmatic! But to ease her mind he had agreed to provide him with a home, if worst came to worst, as it did soon enough. So Bundy inherited the dog, three cases of dog food, balls and rubber bones in which the animal took no interest, along with an elegant cushioned sleeping basket he never used.

Actually, Bundy had never liked biggish dogs with very short pelts. Too much of everything, to his taste, was overexposed. The dog's long muzzle and small beady eyes put him in mind of something less than a dog. In the years with Miss Tyler, without provocation the animal would snarl at Bundy when they met on the stairs, or bark wildly when he opened his mailbox. The dog's one redeeming feature was that when he heard someone pronounce the word *sit,* he would sit. That fact brought Bundy a certain distinction, and the gratitude of many shop owners. Bundy had once been a cat man. The lingering smell of cats in his apartment had led the dog to sneeze at most of the things he sniffed.

* * *

Two men, seated on stools in the corner tavern, had turned from the bar to gaze out into the sunlight. One of them was a clerk at the supermarket where Bundy bought his dog food. "Did he like it?" he called as Bundy came into view.

"Not particularly," Bundy replied. Without exception, the dog did not like anything he saw advertised on television. To that extent he was smarter than Bundy, who was partial to anything served with gravy.

The open doors of the bar looked out on the intersection, where an elderly woman, as if emerging from a package, unfolded her limbs through the door of a taxi. Sheets of plate glass on a passing truck reflected Bundy and the notice that was posted in the window of the bar, advising of a change of ownership. The former owner, an Irishman named Curran, had not been popular with the new crowd of wine and beer drinkers. Nor had he been popular with Bundy. A scornful man, Curran dipped the dirty glasses in tepid water, and poured drops of sherry back into the bottles. Two epidemics of hepatitis had been traced to him. Only when he was gone did Bundy realize how much the world had shrunk. To Curran, Bundy had confessed that he felt he was now living in another country. Even more he missed Curran's favorite expression, "Outlive the bastards!"

Two elderly men, indifferent to the screech of braking traffic, tottered toward each other to embrace near the center of the street. One was wearing shorts. A third party, a younger woman, escorted them both to the curb. Observing an incident like this, Bundy might stand for several minutes as if he had witnessed something unusual. Under an awning, where the pair had been led, they shared the space with a woman whose gaze seemed to focus on infinity, several issues of the *Watchtower* gripped in her trembling hands.

At the corner of Sycamore and Poe Streets—trees crossed poets, as a rule, at right angles—Bundy left the choice of the route up to the dog. Where the sidewalk narrowed, at the bend in the street, both man and dog prepared themselves for brief and unpredictable encounters. In the cities, people met and passed like sleepwalkers, or stared brazenly at each other, but along the sidewalks of small towns they felt the burden of their shared existence. To avoid rudeness, a lift of the eyes or a muttered greeting was necessary. This was often an annoyance for Bundy: the long approach by sidewalk, the absence of cover, the unavoidable moment of confrontation, then Bundy's abrupt greeting or a wag of his head, which occasionally startled the other person. To the young a quick "Hi!" was appropriate, but it was not at all suitable for elderly ladies, a few with pets as escorts. To avoid these encounters, Bundy might suddenly veer into the street or an alleyway, dragging the reluctant dog behind him. He liked to meet strangers, especially children, who would pause to stroke his bald spot. What kind of dog was he? Bundy was tactfully evasive; it had proved to be an unfruitful topic. He was equally noncommittal about the dog's ineffable name.

"Call him Sport," he would say, but this pleasantry was not appreciated. A smart-aleck's answer. Their sympathies were with the dog.

To delay what lay up ahead, whatever it was, they paused at the barnlike entrance of the local van-and-storage warehouse. The draft from inside smelled of burlap sacks full of fragrant pine kindling, and mattresses that were stored on boards above the rafters. The pair contemplated a barn full of junk being sold as antiques. Bundy's eyes grazed over familiar treasure and stopped at a Morris chair with faded green corduroy cushions cradling a carton marked FREE KITTENS.

He did not approach to look. One thing having a dog had spared him was the torment of losing another cat. Music (surely Elgar, something awful!) from a facsimile edition of an Atwater Kent table-model radio bathed dressers and chairs, sofas, beds and love seats, man and dog impartially. As it ended the announcer suggested that Bundy stay tuned for a Musicdote.

Recently, in this very spot—as he sniffed similar air, having paused to take shelter from a drizzle—the revelation had come to Bundy that he no longer wanted other people's junk. Better yet (or was it worse?), he no longer *wanted*—with the possible exception of an English mint, difficult to find, described as curiously strong. He had a roof, a chair, a bed, and, through no fault of his own, he had a dog. What little he had assembled and hoarded (in the garage a German electric-train set with four locomotives, and three elegant humidors and a pouch of old pipes) would soon be gratifying the wants of others. Anything else of value? The cushioned sleeping basket from Abercrombie & Fitch that had come with the dog. That would sell first. Also two Italian raincoats in good condition, and a Borsalino hat—Extra Extra Superiore—bought from G. Colpo in Venice.

Two young women, in the rags of fashion but radiant and blooming as gift-packed fruit, brushed Bundy as they passed, the spoor of their perfume lingering. In the flush of this encounter, his freedom from want dismantled, he moved too fast, and the leash reined him in. Rather than be rushed, the dog had stopped to sniff a meter. He found meters more life-enhancing than trees now. It had not always been so: some years ago he would tug Bundy up the incline to the park, panting and hoarsely gagging, an object of compassionate glances from elderly women headed down the grade, carrying lapdogs. This period had come to a dramatic conclusion.

In the park, back in the deep shade of the redwoods, Bundy and the dog had had a confrontation. An old tree with exposed roots had suddenly attracted the dog's attention. Bundy could not restrain him. A stream of dirt flew out between his legs to splatter Bundy's raincoat and fall into his shoes. There was something manic in the dog's excitement. In a few moments, he had frantically excavated a hole into which he could insert his head and shoulders. Bundy's tug on the leash had no effect on him. The sight of his soiled hairless bottom, his legs mechanically pumping, encouraged Bundy to give him a smart crack with the end of the leash. Not hard but sharp, right on the button, and before he could move the dog had wheeled and the front end was barking at him savagely, the lips curled back. Dirt from the hole partially screened his muzzle, and he looked to Bundy like a maddened rodent. He was no longer a dog but some primitive, underground creature. Bundy lashed out at him, backing away, but they were joined by the leash. Unintentionally, Bundy stepped on the leash, which held the dog's snarling head to the ground. His slobbering jowls were bloody; the small veiled eyes peered up at him with hatred. Bundy had just enough presence of mind to stand there, unmoving, until they both grew calm.

Nobody had observed them. The children played and shrieked in the school yard as usual. The dog relaxed and lay flat on the ground, his tongue lolling in the dirt. Bundy breathed noisily, a film of perspiration cooling his face. When he stepped off the leash the dog did not move but continued to watch him warily, with bloodshot eyes. A slow burn of shame flushed Bundy's ears and cheeks, but he was reluctant to admit it. Another dog passed near them, but what he sniffed on the air kept him at a distance. In a tone of truce, if not reconciliation, Bundy said, "You had enough?"

When had he last said that? Seated on a school chum, whose face was red with Bundy's nosebleed. He bled too easily, but the boy beneath him had had enough.

"Okay?" he said to the dog. The faintest tremor of acknowledgment stirred the dog's tail. He got to his feet, sneezed repeatedly, then splattered Bundy with dirt as he shook himself. Side by side, the leash slack between them, they left the park and walked down the grade. Bundy had never again struck the dog, nor had the dog ever again wheeled to snarl at him. Once the leash was snapped to the dog's collar a truce prevailed between them. In the apartment he had the floor of a closet all to himself.

At the Fixit Shop on the corner of Poplar, recently refaced with green asbestos shingles, Mr. Waller, the Fixit man, rapped on the glass with his wooden ruler. Both Bundy and the dog acknowledged his greeting. Waller had two cats, one asleep in the window, and a dog that liked to ride in his pickup. The two dogs had once been friends; they mauled each other a bit and horsed around like a couple of kids. Then suddenly it was over. Waller's dog would no longer trouble to leave the seat of the truck. Bundy had been so struck by this he had mentioned it to Waller. "Hell," Waller had said, "Gyp's a young dog. Your dog is old."

His saying that had shocked Bundy. There was the personal element, for one thing: Bundy was a good ten years older than Waller, and was he to read the remark to mean that Waller would soon ignore him? And were dogs—reasonably well-bred, sensible chaps—so indifferent to the facts of a dog's life? They appeared to be. One by one, as Bundy's dog grew older, the younger ones ignored him. He might have been a stuffed animal leashed to a parking meter. The human parallel was too disturbing for Bundy to dwell on it.

Old men, in particular, were increasingly touchy if they confronted Bundy at the frozen-food lockers. Did they think he was spying on them? Did they think he looked *sharper* than they did? Elderly women, as a rule, were less suspicious, and grateful to exchange a bit of chitchat. Bundy found them more realistic: they knew they were mortal. To find Bundy still around, squeezing the avocados, piqued the old men who returned from their vacations. On the other hand, Dr. Biddle, a retired dentist with a glistening head like an egg in a basket of excelsior, would unfailingly greet Bundy with the words "I'm really going to miss that mutt, you know that?" But his glance betrayed that he feared Bundy would check out first.

Bundy and the dog used the underpass walkway to cross to the supermarket parking area. Banners were flying to celebrate Whole Grains Cereal Week. In the old days, Bundy would leash the dog to a cart and they would proceed to do their shopping together, but now he had to be parked out front tied up to one of the bicycle racks. The dog didn't like it. The area was shaded and the cement was cold. Did he ever sense, however dimly, that Bundy, too, felt the chill? His hand brushed the coarse pelt as he fastened the leash.

"How about a new flea collar?" Bundy said, but the dog was not responsive. He sat, without being told to sit. Did it flatter the dog to leash him? Whatever Bundy would do, if worst came to worst he had pondered, but had discussed with no one—his intent might be misconstrued. Of which one of them was he speaking? Impersonally appraised, in terms of survival the two of them were pretty much at a standoff: the dog was better fleshed out, but Bundy was the heartier eater.

Thinking of eating—of garlic-scented breadsticks, to be specific, dry but not dusty to the palate—Bundy entered the market to face a large display of odorless flowers and plants. The amplitude and bounty of the new market, at the point of entrance, before he selected a cart, always marked the high point of his expectations. Where else in the hungry world such a prospect? Barrels and baskets of wine, six-packs of beer and bran muffins, still warm sourdough bread that he would break and gnaw on as he shopped. Was this a cunning regression? As a child he had craved raw sugar cookies. But his euphoria sagged at the meat counter, as he studied the gray matter being sold as meat-loaf mix;

it declined further at the dairy counter, where two cartons of yogurt had been sampled, and the low-fat cottage cheese was two days older than dated. By the time he entered the checkout lane, hemmed in by scandal sheets and romantic novels, the cashier's cheerfully inane "Have a good day!" would send him off, forgetting his change in the machine. The girl who pursued him (always with pennies!) had been coached to say, "Thank you, sir!"

A special on avocados this week required that Bundy make a careful selection. Out in front, as usual, dogs were barking. On the airwaves, from the rear and side, the "Wang Wang Blues." Why wang wang? he wondered. Besides wang wang, how did it go? The music was interrupted by an announcement on the public-address system. Would the owner of the white dog leashed to the bike rack please come to the front? Was Bundy's dog white? The point was debatable. Nevertheless, he left his cart by the avocados and followed the vegetable display to the front. People were huddled to the right of the door. A clerk beckoned to Bundy through the window. Still leashed to the bike rack, the dog lay out on his side, as if sleeping. In the parking lot several dogs were yelping.

"I'm afraid he's a goner," said the clerk. "These other dogs rushed him. Scared him to death. He just keeled over before they got to him." The dog had pulled the leash taut, but there was no sign that anything had touched him. A small woman with a shopping cart thumped into Bundy.

"Is it Tiger?" she said. "I hope it's not Tiger." She stopped to see that it was not Tiger. "Whose dog was it?" she asked, peering around her. The clerk indicated Bundy. "Poor thing," she said. "What was his name?"

Just recently, watching the Royal Wedding, Bundy had noticed that his emotions were nearer the surface: on two occasions his eyes had filmed over. He didn't like the woman's speaking of the dog in the past tense. Did she think he had lost his name with his life?

"What was the poor thing's name?" she repeated.

Was the tremor in Bundy's limbs noticeable? "Victor," Bundy lied, since he could not bring himself to admit the dog's name was Victrola. It had always been a sore point, the dog being too old to be given a new one. Miss Tyler had felt that as a puppy he looked like the picture of the dog at the horn of

286

the gramophone. The resemblance was feeble, at best. How could a person give a dog such a name?

"Let him sit," a voice said. A space was cleared on a bench for Bundy to sit, but at the sound of the word he could not bend his knees. He remained standing, gazing through the bright glare at the beacon revolving on the police car. One of those women who buy two frozen dinners and then go off with the shopping cart and leave it somewhere let the policeman at the crosswalk chaperon her across the street.

JERRY BUMPUS

The English and Their Dogs

Does she want tattoos? Bernard has plenty on his arms, neck, palms of his hands, standing there in the amusement arcade he snaps open his fly and out jumps his cock, tattooed too, a great thick thing done blue, green, and red, a flare-eyed dragon. "You should capture that in your little black box," their girl Pol tells Mrs. Huntley and they all enjoy that.

Some of Bernard's tattoos etch scars, giving an embossed effect. "Remarkable," Mrs. Huntley says. "Oh, indeed," they murmur, "remarkable, remarkable," deftly mimicking her, nodding judiciously, their mouths pulled down long and sophisticated. Other tattoos are marred by recent cuts and nicks, these Bernard will have overlaid someday, at his next session perhaps, such as a leafy scroll which will become a boar with a lion's mane, with the center of the boar's eyes twin welty screwdriver gouges. A dewlap from a slash his mates sewed up in a rush became a droopy clit. A white smear of burned flesh across the back of his neck became a dove, and a wide red question mark (undotted) the length of his back, made when he was rudely tied down and branded with a red-hot crowbar—"Oh, rudely indeed"—became the tongue of a lizard sticking its head out Bernard's arse reaching for a mole become a spider crawling on his shoulder. His scalp is tattooed, too, he bends down to Mrs. Huntley and as he runs a hand through his hair she sees the face and yellow-white eyes of a black panther.

The arcade manager appears and tells Bernard he may keep his clothes on or leave the premises.

* * *

The next day they stink of smoke and kerosene. "Don't ask," whispers Thompson, but of course she asks and Bernard says they've been to a fire. "What does that mean?" Mrs. Huntley says.

"That's all he wants to tell us," Thompson says out loud.

Bernard says, "It means we've been to a fire."

"I like your dog," Thompson says. "What's his name?"

Pol's mouth opens slowly, her eyes bulge, Mrs. Huntley and Thompson back away because obviously she is even more drugged than Bernard and Brum, quite sick, and will now erupt.

Instead she entertains them with interior sounds. It's stomach talk, she says later, after Mrs. Huntley wins her trust, and it is something she had always known how to do but only since she has known Bernard, Brum, and Russell, who is the dog, has she given performances. The sounds aren't belches but tight stomach growls so close to words, like the squiggled speech of Donald Duck, that Mrs. Huntley suspects that either Bernard or Brum—or perhaps the dog?—is a ventriloquist. But the longer Pol performs the more Mrs. Huntley is convinced that it is authentic, whatever it is.

Pol clenches herself, her elbows dug into her sides, her hands straight out and open like a singer belting out a song. She shudders, rocking back on her high-heeled shoes, then straining forward as a prolonged passage squeezes out. Then comes a terrible meaty splat deep inside as if she is ripping apart, and Brum says, "Stand back!" and they all move back, including the dog, seconds before Pol indeed erupts.

They go to the other end of the arcade, Brum carrying Pol over his hip, but the manager finds them and tells them to leave and never come back.

"Hey, Bernard," Brum says, "show them the stars of mutt smut."

Not reluctantly but as if thinking of something else, Bernard goes into another room, opening and closing the door carefully so Mrs. Huntley and Thompson can't see in, and returns with a magazine. After one look Thompson goes to the other side of the room. As Mrs. Huntley turns the pages she is careful with her expression because Pol watches her closely.

"It's coming up on five," Brum says.

"*Rrroozl,*" Bernard says. The dog lunges awake, and clattering and sliding across the linoleum he crashes into Bernard. Mrs. Huntley feels Thompson's panic burning on her face as Bernard yanks one of the dog's big front legs from under him. The dog, grinning, plonks down and rolls on his back.

"I really don't think I want to see . . ." Thompson says. Mrs. Huntley frowns his direction without looking at him.

Bernard scratches the dog's belly. It closes its eyes, its tongue lolling. Thompson comments on what a fine dog he is—Bernard shushes him, Brum says, "Shut up," and from the dog comes wristwatch alarm music, "I Just Called to Say I Love You."

The dog opens its eyes, pricks its ears. Sitting up, it hikes a hind leg as if to inspect and lick itself the way dogs do, but instead peers with consternation at the spot the music comes from. Bernard, Brum, and Pol laugh so hard they roll out of their chairs.

When the music stops, Russell gives himself a proper licking. Brum puts his arm around Thompson and nods toward the dog. "Just look at what he's doing. Now tell the truth, don't you wish you could do that?"

Smiling sickly, Thompson says, "Yes."

Brum says loudly, "Did you hear him, Bernard, what he wants to do? Do you think the dog will let him?" Again they laugh so hard they roll around.

The next day Thompson stays at the hotel.

The X rays show a broken bone. Bernard wants to know which is better, the one in which the two pieces are horizontal or the one in which they are perpendicular. Mrs. Huntley can't judge which is better because she doesn't know what the X rays represent. "A cracked cock is what they represent," Brum says. Though Mrs. Huntley admits to never having seen X rays of a penis, she suspects someone is playing a joke on them, for these look like X rays of a broken chicken leg. "That's what it is," Bernard says, "but it's supposed to look like Hopper's knob."

Later Pol takes Mrs. Huntley to her bedroom and shows her Hopper, bound and gagged in a rocking chair. He glances at Mrs. Huntley, then doesn't take his eyes off Pol. She ungags him and talks to him—he doesn't say a word—and introduces him to Mrs. Huntley. "Now you'll be part of her show about us in America," Pol tells him. Aside, she tells Mrs. Huntley, "Watch this," and opens the end of a banana, sticks it in Hopper's mouth, and they watch him eat it. Then she pours a can of lager down him with a funnel.

By messenger they send Mrs. Hopper the X ray of the perpendicular pieces of bone with a note saying this is what they've done to Hopper's knob, and though the rest of him is in passable condition they lack patience and will take all of him apart unless they receive payment.

Later in the day Bernard's father drops by, quite angry about the X ray of the broken knob, word of which has spread like wildfire, and he tells them they are bloody stupid. He glares at Brum and says, "I guess it was the idea of this brainless oaf." Brum delivers a crushing blow to the face of Bernard's father but it's not enough to knock him out or even knock him down. Bernard's father kicks Brum in the stomach, then while he's gasping on the floor Bernard's father kicks him in the ribs.

He explains to Bernard, Pol, Russell, and Mrs. Huntley that sending the X ray was bloody stupid because, though Hopper's wife most certainly believes the X ray is her husband's own knob and will send five hundred quid, she would have come forth with much more if they had sent Hopper's ear with the swastika earring or the thumb with her name on it.

"I see your point," Bernard says, "but we didn't want to hurt him, after all."

"Once you start you must never stop. Once you start you must do the whole thing. Once you start . . ."

Brum, on the floor, starts coughing blood. They agree it's his ribs poking into a lung, it has happened before. Brum's head is sufficiently hard but he has mushy ribs.

Pol tells the camera she wants the world to know it's not half bad with a dog. Mrs. Huntley asks about her childhood, her adolescence. Pol says she had a childhood but she dismisses her past, she has no past.

How did she meet Bernard and Brum? Brum stole her from her pa in

Pontefract and brought her down to Brighton. Bernard came later, and he started her posing. She wants to talk about her life now.

If you and the dog are acquainted, she tells the world, instead of him merely being one you work with in a studio, you can expect complexities afterward. Since posing with Pol and doing what they did, Russell wants her constantly. She points down for Thompson to aim the camera at Russell lying on the floor with his chin on his big paws, staring up at Pol. Anytime she turns around there he is with gleaming eyes, or she'll be sitting with a book and he comes rooting his head between her knees, he is just not subtle at all, and turning him down is hard work because he is so forceful. He's a smart one he is, keeps an eye on the clock and knows when Pol is off to bed and knows what days she has her bath, so undressing is unsafe unless she hooks the door. If she forgets, he reaches up with a paw, turns the knob, and comes right in. She knows he's always looking through the keyhole and more than once has burst in as she is about to step into the tub.

So now there are three permanently in her life, except of course Russell is not the same as Bernard and Brum, not at all the same, and though you might think you can just imagine, imagination falls short. And Bernard watches Russell watching Pol and knows there is a change. He assumes the opposite of the truth, however, believing Russell has a great disgust and is full of hatred of Pol for what she did while posing with him.

Then Bernard doesn't know about Pol and Russell? Of course not, Brum doesn't either, no man must ever know, it would drive them mad with jealous rage. Even though Bernard loves Russell like a son he would kill him if he knew.

Though Bernard had Pol pose with Russell? That was for profit, profit being one thing, love quite another. And he doesn't mind Pol and Brum because that has been from the beginning, or other cocks occasionally, Bernard is not possessive. But with his Russell it is another matter. He must never find out and won't, for Pol easily outsmarts him, both he and Brum being perfect idiots, and Russell with his keen hearing can always hear them coming.

How does Pol feel about her future? She loves Russell. She supposes she loves him. Yes she must say she does. She's certain she loves him in that way because he is so grand and in other ways, too, because he is more true to her than mere men have ever been. And she knows that he will love her on and on, that he will never change. If he runs off for another of his kind it is something he must do and it will only last a while, then he'll come back to her. But Pol assures the world she's not a fool. Russell is a wonderful dog, but he is that, a dog. For conversation and other things she wants Pol turns to humans. Russell is a good dog but all dogs are monotonous.

Is Pol concerned with what other women might think of her? Some of her girlfriends give Russell a try. They think he's very cute and find it an interesting experience because he is a dog and of course because of his proportion. But for most of them once is enough.

Deep in her throat Pol purrs, rising to a murmured *"Rrroozl."* He raises his head, they stare a moment. He stretches, shakes himself all over, and is moving toward her as Thompson switches off the camera.

From a van they steal a shock box stolen from an asylum and use it on each other. They lie about, dozing, their eyes half closed, they agree it's the most ultimate trip, a billion, ten billion times better than the best of dope. Mrs. Huntley and Thompson take care of them, cook, and see that Russell gets his walks. When people come looking for them Mrs. Huntley says that they are ill. A man says he bets it's AIDS, and though Mrs. Huntley denies it, the man backs off, crooking an arm over his face, and no more people come.

Before Bernard stops talking, following his thirtieth or fortieth shock, he talks with Mrs. Huntley before the camera. He regrets his life, what he recalls of it, he also regrets his tattoos and feels they belong on someone else. He calmly says that he now knows that when he looks in the mirror the man he sees is not himself. "Maybe I'm a Frenchman and don't have tattoos. I know I'm here, I'm talking to you, but I'm doubtless other men as well in different places in the world. In time I'll be more them than this one here and that shall be more to my liking."

The door opens and Pol walks in with Russell. Thompson turns the camera as Russell, wagging his tail, comes over and lies at Bernard's feet. Pol wanders around the room and out again.

When the camera returns to Bernard he says he has known that Pol and Russell have been carrying on, he has known all along, and he regrets that, too, but holds no grudges. He pats the dog's big head and Russell smiles, his mouth open, panting, and thumps the floor with his tail.

Pol spends her days trying to find her way out of her seventieth shock, wandering through the rooms, up and down the stairs to the flat where an abundance of furs, televisions, and cameras are stored. After the first dozen or so shocks Pol was euphoric and spent hours before the camera. In one episode Pol puts her face in the camera and immortalized the eating of a packet of pomfret cakes. Then she goes to the sofa, lifts Mrs. Huntley's arm, crawls under it, and snuggles up.

Brum recovers quickly from his shocks, sits in the kitchen drinking ale and smoking, then goes back to give himself another. He ignores the rest of them. When Mrs. Huntley stands in front of him and speaks to him he stares through her stomach. After a hundred or so shocks—Mrs. Huntley and Thompson lose count—there is a great change. Thompson discovers the dial on the shock box had been set up from one to five. Brum moves slowly, very slowly, pushing through the air as if it were thick clear syrup, and sometimes when he is sitting in a chair or lying down he watches his arm rise and his hand slowly open and close.

Mrs. Huntley and Thompson leave them in a convalescent home in Littlehampton. The lady assures Mrs. Huntley that they will receive the best of care. She hasn't a place for Russell, but a gentleman across the way lost his dog to old age, and when Mrs. Huntley goes to inquire, the gentleman and Russell instantly strike up such a warm friendship that neither seems to notice as Mrs. Huntley slips away.

WILLIAM TREVOR

The Penthouse Apartment

"Flowers?" said Mr. Runca into his pale blue telephone receiver. "Shall we order flowers? What's the procedure?" He stared intently at his wife as he spoke, and his wife, eating her breakfast grapefruit, thought that it would seem to be her husband's intention to avoid having to pay for flowers. She had become used to this element in her husband; it hardly ever embarrassed her.

"The procedure's quite simple," said a soft voice in Mr. Runca's ear. "The magazine naturally supplies the flowers. If we can just agree between us what the flowers should be."

"Indeed," said Mr. Runca. "It's to be remembered that not all blooms will go with the apartment. Our fabrics must be allowed to speak for themselves, you know. Well, you've seen. You know what I mean."

"Indeed I do, Mr. Runca—"

"They came from Thailand, in fact. You might like to mention that."

"So you said, Mr. Runca. The fabrics are most beautiful."

Mr. Runca, hearing this statement, nodded. He said, because he was used to saying it when the apartment was discussed:

"It's the best-dressed apartment in London."

"I'll come myself at three," said the woman on the magazine. "Will someone be there at half past two, say, so that the photographers can set up all their gear and test the light?"

"We have an Italian servant," said Mr. Runca, "who opened the door to you before and who'll do the same thing for the photographers."

295

"Till this afternoon then," said the woman on the magazine, speaking lightly and gaily, since that was her manner.

Mr. Runca carefully replaced the telephone receiver. His wife, a woman who ran a boutique, drank some coffee and heard her husband say that the magazine would pay for the flowers and would presumably not remove them from the flat after the photography had taken place. Mrs. Runca nodded. The magazine was going to devote six pages to the Runcas' flat: a display in full color of its subtleties and charm, with an article about how the Runcas had between them planned all the decor.

"I'd like to arrange the flowers myself," said Mrs. Runca. "Are they being sent round?"

Mr. Runca shook his head. The flowers, he explained, were to be brought to the house by the woman from the magazine at three o'clock, the photographers having already had time to deploy their materials in the manner they favored.

"But how ridiculous!" cried Mrs. Runca. "It's completely hopeless, that arrangement. The photographers with their cameras poised for three o'clock and the woman arriving then with the flowers. How long does the female imagine it'll take to arrange them? Does she think it can be done in a matter of minutes?"

Mr. Runca picked up the telephone and dialed the number of the magazine. He mentioned the name of the woman he had recently been speaking to. He spoke to her again. He said:

"My wife points out that the arrangement is not satisfactory. The flowers will take time to arrange, naturally. What point is there in keeping your photographers waiting? And I myself haven't got all day."

"It shouldn't take long to arrange the flowers."

Mrs. Runca lit her first cigarette of the day, imagining that the woman on the magazine was saying something like that. She had a long, rather thin face and pale gray hair that had the glow of aluminum. Her hands were long also, hands that had grown elegant in childhood, with fingernails that now were of a fashionable length, metallically painted, a reflection of her hair. Ten years ago, on money borrowed from her husband, she had opened her boutique. She had called it St. Catherine, and had watched it growing into a flourishing business with a staff of five women and a girl messenger.

"Very well then," said the woman on the magazine, having listened further to Mr. Runca. "I'll have the flowers sent round this morning."

"They're coming round this morning," reported Mr. Runca to his wife.

"I have to be at St. Catherine at twelve," she said, "absolutely without fail."

"My wife has to be at her business at midday," said Mr. Runca, and the woman on the magazine cursed silently. She promised that the flowers would be in the Runcas' penthouse apartment within three quarters of an hour.

Mr. Runca rose to his feet and stood silently for a minute. He was a rich, heavily jowled man, the owner of three publications that appealed to those involved in the clothing trade. He was successful in much the same way as his wife was, and he felt, as she did, that efficiency and a stern outlook were good weapons in the business of accumulating wealth. Once upon a time they had both been poor and had recognized certain similar qualities in one another, and had seen the future as a more luxurious time, as in fact it had become. They were proud that once again their penthouse apartment was to be honored by photographs and a journalist. It was the symbol of all their toil; and in a small way it had made them famous.

Mr. Runca walked from the spacious room that had one side made entirely of glass, and his feet caused no sound as he crossed a white carpet of Afghanistan wool. He paused in the hall to place a hat on his head and gloves on his hands before departing for a morning's business.

At ten to ten the flowers arrived and by a quarter past eleven Mrs. Runca had arranged them to her satisfaction. The Runcas' Italian maid, called Bianca, cleaned the flat most carefully, seeking dust in an expert way, working with method and a conscience, which was why the Runcas employed her. Mrs. Runca warned her to be in at half past two because the photographers were coming then. "I must go out now then," replied Bianca, "for shopping. I will make these photographers coffee, I suppose?" Mrs. Runca said to give the men coffee in the kitchen, or tea if they preferred it. "Don't let them walk about the place with cups in their hands," she said, and went away.

* * *

In another part of the block of flats lived Miss Winton with her cairn terrier. Her flat was different from the Runcas'; it contained many ornaments that had little artistic value, was in need of redecoration, and had beige linoleum on the floor of the bathroom. Miss Winton did not notice her surroundings much; she considered the flat pretty in its way, and comfortable to live in. She was prepared to leave it at that.

"Well," remarked Miss Winton to her dog in the same moment that Mrs. Runca was stepping into a taxicab, "what shall we do?"

The dog made no reply beyond wagging its tail. "I have eggs to buy," said Miss Winton, "and honey, and butter. Shall we go and do all that?"

Miss Winton had lived in the block of flats for fifteen years. She had seen many tenants come and go. She had heard about the Runcas and the model place they had made of the penthouse. It was the talk of London, Miss Winton had been told by Mrs. Neck, who kept a grocer's shop nearby; the Runcas were full of taste, apparently. Miss Winton thought it odd that London should talk about a penthouse flat, but did not ever mention that to Mrs. Neck, who didn't seem to think it odd at all. To Miss Winton the Runcas were like many others who had come to live in the same building: people she saw and did not know. There were no children in the building, that being a rule; but animals, within reason, were permitted.

Miss Winton left her flat and walked with her dog to Mrs. Neck's shop. "Fresh buns," said Mrs. Neck before Miss Winton had made a request. "Just in, dear." But Miss Winton shook her head and asked for eggs and honey and butter. "Seven and ten," said Mrs. Neck, reckoning the cost before reaching a hand out for the articles. She said it was shocking that food should cost so much, but Miss Winton replied that in her opinion two shillings wasn't exorbitant for half a pound of butter. "I remember it ninepence," said Mrs. Neck, "and twice the stuff it was. I'd sooner a smear of Stork than what they're turning out today." Miss Winton smiled, and agreed that the quality of everything had gone down a bit.

Afterward, for very many years, Miss Winton remembered this conversation with Mrs. Neck. She remembered Mrs. Neck saying, "I'd sooner a smear of Stork than what they're turning out today," and she remembered the rather small, dark-haired girl who entered Mrs. Neck's shop at that moment, who smiled at both of them in an innocent way. "Is that so?" said the Runcas' maid, Bianca. "Quality has gone down?"

"Lord love you, Miss Winton knows what she's talking about," said Mrs. Neck. "Quality's gone to pieces."

Miss Winton might have left the shop then, for her purchasing was over, but the dark-haired young girl had leaned down and was patting the head of Miss Winton's dog. She smiled while doing that. Mrs. Neck said:

"Miss Winton's in the flats too."

"Ah, yes?"

"This young lady," explained Mrs. Neck to Miss Winton, "works for the Runcas in the penthouse we hear so much about."

"Today they are coming to photograph," said Bianca. "People from a magazine. And they will write down other things about it."

"Again?" said Mrs. Neck, shaking her head in wonderment. "What can I do for you?"

Bianca asked for coffee beans and a sliced loaf, still stroking the head of the dog.

Miss Winton smiled. "He has taken to you," she said to Bianca, speaking timidly because she felt shy of people, especially foreigners. "He's very good company."

"Pretty little dog," said Bianca.

Miss Winton walked with Bianca back to the block of flats, and when they arrived in the large hallway Bianca said:

"Miss Winton, would you like to see the penthouse with all its fresh flowers and fruits about the place? It is at its best in the morning sunlight, as Mr. Runca was remarking earlier. It is ready for all the photographers."

Miss Winton, touched that the Italian girl should display such thoughtfulness toward an elderly spinster, said that it would be a pleasure to look at the penthouse flat but added that the Runcas might not care to have her walking about their property.

"No, no," said Bianca, who had not been long in the Runcas' employ.

"Mrs. Runca would love you to see it. And him too. 'Show anyone you like,' they've said to me. Certainly." Bianca was not telling the truth, but time hung heavily on her hands in the empty penthouse and she knew she would enjoy showing Miss Winton all the flowers that Mrs. Runca had so tastefully arranged, and all the curtains that had been imported specially from Thailand, and the rugs and the chairs and the pictures on the walls.

"Well," began Miss Winton.

"Yes," said Bianca and pressed Miss Winton and her dog into the lift.

But when the lift halted at the top and Bianca opened the gates Miss Winton experienced a small shock. "Mr. Morgan is here too," said Bianca. "Mending the water."

Miss Winton felt that she could not now refuse to enter the Runcas' flat, since to do so would be to offend the friendly little Italian girl, yet she really did not wish to find herself face-to-face with Mr. Morgan in somebody else's flat. "Look here," she said, but Bianca and the dog were already ahead of her. "Come on, Miss Winton," said Bianca.

Miss Winton found herself in the Runcas' small and fastidious hall, and then in the large room that had one side made of glass. She looked around her and noted all the low furniture and the pale Afghanistan carpet and the objects scattered economically about, and the flowers that Mrs. Runca had arranged. "Have coffee," said Bianca, going quickly off to make some, and the little dog, noting her swift movement and registering it as a form of play, gave a single bark and darted about himself, in a small circle. "Shh," whispered Miss Winton. "Really," she protested, following Bianca to the kitchen, "don't bother about coffee." "No, no," said Bianca, pretending not to understand, thinking that there was plenty of time for herself and Miss Winton to have coffee together, sitting in the kitchen, where Mrs. Runca had commanded coffee was to be drunk. Miss Winton could hear a light hammering and guessed it was Mr. Morgan at work on the water pipes. She could imagine him coming out of the Runcas' bathroom and stopping quite still as soon as he saw her. He would stand there in his brown overalls, large and bulky, peering at her through his spectacles, chewing, probably, a piece of his mustache. His job was to attend to the needs of the tenants when the needs were not complicated, but whenever Miss Winton telephoned down to his basement and asked for his assistance he would sigh loudly into the telephone and say that he mightn't manage to attend to the matter for a day or two. He would come, eventually, late at night but still in his brown overalls, his eyes watering, his breath rich with alcohol. He would look at whatever the trouble was and make a swift diagnosis, advising that experts should be summoned the following morning. He didn't much like her, Miss Winton thought; no doubt he considered her a poor creature, unmarried at sixty-four, thin and weak-looking, with little sign that her physical appearance had been attractive in girlhood.

"It's a lovely place," said Miss Winton to Bianca. "But I think perhaps we should go now. Please don't bother with coffee; and thank you most awfully."

"No, no," said Bianca, and while she was saying it Mr. Morgan entered the kitchen in his brown overalls.

One day in 1952, Miss Winton had mislaid her bicycle. It had disappeared without trace from the passage in the basement where Mr. Morgan had said she might keep it. "I have not seen it," he had said slowly and deliberately at that time. "I know of no cycle." Miss Winton had reminded him that the bicycle had always had a place in the passage, since he had said she might keep it there. But Mr. Morgan, thirteen years younger then, had replied that he could recall none of that. "Stolen," he had said. "I daresay stolen. I should say the coke men carted it away. I cannot always be watching the place, y'know. I have me work, madam." She had asked him to inquire of the coke men if they had in error removed her bicycle; she had spoken politely and with a smile, but Mr. Morgan had repeatedly shaken his head, pointing out that he could not go suggesting that the coke men had made off with a bicycle, saying that the coke men would have the law on him. "The wife has a cycle," Mr. Morgan had said. "A Rudge. I could obtain it for you, madam. Fifty shillings?" Miss Winton had smiled again and had walked away, having refused this offer and given thanks for it.

"Was you wanting something, madam?" asked Mr. Morgan now, his lower lip pulling a strand of his mustache into his mouth. "This is the Runcas' flat up here."

Miss Winton tried to smile at him. She thought that whatever she said he would be sarcastic in a disguised way. He would hide his sarcasm beneath the words he chose, implying it only with the inflection of his voice. Miss Winton said:

"Bianca kindly invited me to see the penthouse."

"It is a different type of place from yours and mine," replied Mr. Morgan, looking about him. "I was attending to a tap in the bathroom. Working, Miss Winton."

"It is all to be photographed today," said Bianca. "Mr. and Mrs. Runca will return early from their businesses."

"Was you up here doing the flowers, madam?"

He had called her madam during all the years they had known one another, pointing up the fact that she had no right to the title.

"A cup of coffee, Mr. Morgan?" said Bianca, and Miss Winton hoped he would refuse.

"With two spoons of sugar in it," said Mr. Morgan, nodding his head and adding, "D'you know what the Irish take in their coffee?" He began to laugh rumbustiously, ignoring Miss Winton and appearing to share a joke with Bianca. "A tot of the hard stuff," said Mr. Morgan. "Whiskey."

Bianca laughed too. She left the kitchen, and Miss Winton's dog ran after her. Mr. Morgan blew at the surface of his coffee while Miss Winton, wondering what to say to him, stirred hers.

"It's certainly a beautiful flat," said Miss Winton.

"It would be too large for you, madam. I mean to say, just you and the dog in a place like this. You'd lose one another."

"Oh, yes, of course. No, I meant—"

"I'll speak to the authorities if you like. I'll speak on your behalf, as a tenant often asks me to do. Put a word in, y'know. I could put a word in if you like, madam."

Miss Winton frowned, wondering what Mr. Morgan was talking about. She smiled uncertainly at him. He said:

"I have a bit of influence, knowing the tenants and that. I got the left-hand ground flat for Mr. McCarthy by moving the Aitchesons up to the third. I got Mrs. Bloom out of the back one on the first—"

"Mr. Morgan, you've misunderstood me. I wouldn't at all like to move up here."

Mr. Morgan looked at Miss Winton, sucking coffee off his mustache. His eyes were focused on hers. He said, "You don't have to say nothing outright, madam. I understand a hint."

Bianca returned with a bottle of whiskey. She handed it to Mr. Morgan, saying that he had better add it to the coffee since she didn't know how much to put in.

"Oh, a good drop," said Mr. Morgan, splashing the liquor on to his warm coffee. He approached Miss Winton with the neck of the bottle poised toward her cup. He'll be offended, she thought; and because of that she did not, as she wished to, refuse his offering. "The Irish are heavy drinkers," said Mr. Morgan. "Cheers." He drank the mixture and proclaimed it good. "D'you like that, Miss Winton?" he asked, and Miss Winton tasted it and discovered to her surprise that the beverage was pleasant. "Yes," she said. "I do."

Mr. Morgan held out his cup for more coffee. "Just a small drop," he said, and he filled the cup up with whiskey. Again he inclined the neck of the bottle toward Miss Winton, who smiled and said she hadn't finished. He held the bottle in the same position, watching her drinking her coffee. She protested when Bianca poured her more, but she could sense that Bianca was enjoying this giving of hospitality, and for that reason she accepted, knowing that Mr. Morgan would pour in more whiskey. She felt comfortably warm from the whiskey that was already in her body, and she experienced the desire to be agreeable—although she was aware, too, that she would not care for it if the Runcas unexpectedly returned.

"Fair enough," said Mr. Morgan, topping up Bianca's cup and adding a further quantity to his own. He said:

"Miss Winton is thinking of shifting up here, her being the oldest tenant in the building. She's been stuck downstairs for fifteen years."

Bianca shook her head, saying to Miss Winton: "What means that?"

"I'm quite happy," said Miss Winton, "where I am." She spoke softly, with a smile on her face, intent upon being agreeable. Mr. Morgan was sitting on the edge of the kitchen table. Bianca had turned on the wireless. Mr. Morgan said:

"I came to the flats on March the twenty-first, nineteen fifty-one. Miss Winton here was already in residence. Riding about on a cycle."

"I was six years old," said Bianca.

"D'you remember that day, Miss Winton? March the twenty-first?"

Miss Winton shook her head. She sat down on a chair made of an ersatz material. She said:

"It's a long time ago."

"I remember the time you lost your cycle, Miss Winton. She come down to me in the basement," said Mr. Morgan to Bianca, "and told me to tick off the coke deliverers for thieving her bicycle. I never seen no cycle, as I said to Miss Winton. D'you understand, missy?" Bianca smiled, nodding swiftly. She hummed the tune that was coming from the wireless. "Do you like that Irish drink?" said Mr. Morgan. "Shall we have some more?"

"I must be going," said Miss Winton. "It's been terribly kind of you."

"Are you going, madam?" said Mr. Morgan, and there was in his tone a hint of the belligerency that Miss Winton knew his nature was imbued with. In her mind he spoke more harshly to her, saying she was a woman who had never lived. He was saying that she might have been a nun the way she existed, not knowing anything about the world around her; she had never known a man's love, Mr. Morgan was saying; she had never borne a child.

"Oh, don't go," said Bianca. "Please, I'll make you a cold cocktail, like Mr. Runca showed me how. Cinzano with gin in it, and lemon and ice."

"Oh, no," said Miss Winton.

Mr. Morgan sighed, implying with the intake of his breath that her protest was not unexpected. There were other women in the block of flats, Miss Winton imagined, who would have a chat with Mr. Morgan now and again, who would pass the time of day with him, asking him for racing tips and suggesting that he should let them know when he heard that a flat they coveted was going to be empty. Mr. Morgan was probably a man whom people tipped quite lavishly for the performance of services or favors. Miss Winton could imagine people, people like the Runcas maybe, saying to their friends: "We greased the caretaker's palm. We gave him five pounds." She thought she'd never be able to do that.

Bianca went away to fetch the ingredients for the drink, and again the dog went with her.

Miss Winton stood still, determined that Mr. Morgan should not consider that she did not possess the nerve to receive from the Runcas' Italian maid a midday cocktail.

Mr. Morgan said, "You and me have known one another a number of years."

"Yes, we have."

"We know what we think of a flat like this, and the type of person. Don't we, Miss Winton?"

"To tell the truth, I don't know the Runcas at all."

"I'll admit it to you: the whiskey has loosened my tongue, Miss Winton. You understand what I mean?"

Miss Winton smiled at Mr. Morgan. There was sweat, she noticed, on the sides of his face. He said with vehemence, "Ridiculous, the place being photographed. What do they want to do that for, tell me?"

"Magazines take an interest. It's a contemporary thing. Mrs. Neck was saying that this flat is well known."

"You can't trust Mrs. Neck. I think it's a terrible place. I wouldn't be comfortable in a place like this."

"Well—"

"You could report me for saying a thing like that. You could do that, Miss Winton. You could tell them I was intoxicated at twelve o'clock in the day, drinking a tenant's liquor and abusing the tenant behind his back. D'you see what I mean, madam?"

"I wouldn't report you, Mr. Morgan. It's no business of mine."

"I'd like to see you up here, madam, getting rid of all this trash and putting in a decent bit of furniture. How's about that?"

"Please, Mr. Morgan, I'm perfectly happy—"

"I'll see what I can do," said Mr. Morgan.

Bianca returned with glasses and bottles. Mr. Morgan said:

"I was telling Miss Winton here that she could report me to the authorities for misconduct, but she said she never would. We've known one another a longish time. We was never drinking together though."

Bianca handed Miss Winton a glass that felt cold in Miss Winton's hand. She feared now what Mr. Morgan was going to say. He said:

"I intoxicate easily." Mr. Morgan laughed, displaying darkened teeth. He swayed back and forth, looking at Miss Winton. "I'll put in a word for you," he said, "no bother at all."

She was thinking that she would finish the drink she'd been given and then go away and prepare lunch. She would buy some little present to give Bianca, and she would come up to the Runcas' flat one morning and hand it to her, thanking her for her hospitality and her thoughtfulness.

While Miss Winton was thinking that, Mr. Morgan was thinking that he intended to drink at least two more of the drinks that the girl was offering, and Bianca was thinking that it was the first friendly morning she had spent in this flat since her arrival three weeks before. "I must go to the WC," said Mr. Morgan, and he left the kitchen, saying he would be back. "It's most kind of you," said Miss Winton when he had gone. "I do hope it's all right." It had occurred to her that Bianca's giving people the Runcas' whiskey and gin was rather different from her giving people a cup of coffee, but when she looked at Bianca she saw that she was innocently smiling. She felt light-headed, and smiled herself. She rose from her chair and thanked Bianca again and said that she must be going now. Her dog came to her, wishing to go also. "Don't you like the drink?" said Bianca, and Miss Winton finished it. She placed the glass on the metal draining board and as she did so a crash occurred in the Runcas' large sitting room. "Heavens!" said Miss Winton, and Bianca raised a hand to her mouth and kept it there. When they entered the room they saw Mr. Morgan standing in the center of it, looking at the floor.

"Heavens!" said Miss Winton, and Bianca widened her eyes and still did not take her hand away from her mouth. On the floor lay the flowers that Mrs. Runca had earlier arranged. The huge vase was smashed into many pieces. Water was soaking into the Afghanistan carpet.

"I was looking at it," explained Mr. Morgan. "I was touching a flower with my fingers. The whole thing gave way."

"Mrs. Runca's flowers," said Bianca. "Oh, Mother of God!"

"Mr. Morgan," said Miss Winton.

"Don't look at me, ma'am. Don't blame me for an instant. Them flowers was inadequately balanced. Ridiculous."

Bianca, on her hands and knees, was picking up the broken stalks. She might have been more upset, Miss Winton thought, and she was glad that she was not. Bianca explained that Mrs. Runca had stayed away from her boutique specially to arrange the flowers. "They'll give me the sack," she said, and instead of weeping she gave a small giggle.

The gravity of the situation struck Miss Winton forcibly. Hearing Bianca's giggle, Mr. Morgan laughed also, and went to the kitchen, where Miss Winton heard him pouring himself some more of the Runcas' gin. Miss Winton realized then that neither Bianca nor Mr. Morgan had any sense of responsibility at all. Bianca was young and did not know any better; Mr. Morgan was partly drunk. The Runcas would return with people from a magazine and they would find that their property had been damaged, that a vase had been broken and that a large damp patch in the center of their Afghanistan carpet would not look good in the photographs. "Let's have another cocktail," said Bianca, throwing down the flowers she had collected and giggling again. "Oh, no," cried Miss Winton. "Please, Bianca. We must think what's best to do." But Bianca was already in the kitchen, and Miss Winton could hear Mr. Morgan's rumbustious laugh.

"I tell you what," said Mr. Morgan, coming toward her with a glass in his hand. "We'll say the dog done it. We'll say the dog jumped at the flowers trying to grip hold of them."

Miss Winton regarded him with surprise. "My dog?" she said. "My dog was nowhere near the flowers." Her voice was sharp, the first time it had been so that morning.

Mr. Morgan sat down in an armchair, and Miss Winton, about to protest about that also, realized in time that she had, of course, no right to protest at all.

"We could say," said Mr. Morgan, "that the dog went into a hysterical fit and attacked the flowers. How's about that?"

"But that's not true. It's not the truth."

"I was thinking of me job, madam. And of the young missy's. It's all right for others."

"It was an accident," said Miss Winton, "as you have said, Mr. Morgan."

"They'll say what was I doing touching the flowers? They'll say to the young missy what was happening at all, was you giving a party? I'll have to explain the whole thing to my wife."

"Your wife?"

"What was I doing in the Runcas' flat with the young one? The wife will see through anything."

"You were here to mend a water pipe, Mr. Morgan."

"What's the matter with the water pipes?"

"Oh, really, Mr. Morgan. You were repairing a pipe when I came into the flat."

"There was nothing the matter with the pipes, ma'am. Nor never has been, which is just the point. The young missy telephones down saying the pipes is making a noise. She's anxious for company. She likes to engage in a chat."

"I shall arrange what flowers we can salvage," said Miss Winton, "just as neatly as they were arranged before. And we can explain to the Runcas that you came to the flat to mend a pipe and that in passing you brushed against Mrs. Runca's flowers. The only difficulty is the carpet. The best way to get that damp stain out would be to lift up the carpet and put an electric fire in front of it."

"Take it easy," said Mr. Morgan. "Have a drink, Miss Winton."

"We must repair the damage—"

"Listen, madam," said Mr. Morgan, leaning forward, "you and I know what we think of a joint like this. Tricked out like they've got it—"

"It's a question of personal taste—"

"Tell them the dog done the damage, Miss Winton, and I'll see you right. A word in the ear of the authorities and them Runcas will be out on the street in a jiffy. Upsetting the neighbors with noise, bringing the flats into disrepute. I'd say it in court, Miss Winton: I seen naked women going in and out of the penthouse. D'you see?"

Bianca returned, and Miss Winton repeated to her what she had said already to Mr. Morgan about the drying of the carpet. Between them, they moved chairs and tables and lifted the carpet from the floor, draping it across two chairs and placing an electric fire in front of it. Mr. Morgan moved to a distant sofa and watched them.

"I used not to be bad with flowers," said Miss Winton to Bianca. "Are there other vases?" They went together to the kitchen to see what there was. "Would you like another cocktail?" said Bianca, but Miss Winton said she thought they all had had enough to drink. "I like these drinks," said Bianca, sipping one. "So cool."

"You must explain," said Miss Winton, "that Mr. Morgan had to come in order to repair the gurgling pipe and that he brushed against the flowers on the way across the room. You must tell the truth: that you had invited me to have a look at the beautiful flat. I'm sure they won't be angry when they know it was all an accident."

"What means gurgling?" said Bianca.

"Hey!" shouted Mr. Morgan from the other room.

"I think Mr. Morgan should go now," said Miss Winton. "I wonder if you'd say so, Bianca? He's a very touchy man." She imagined Mr. Runca looking sternly into her face and saying he could not believe his eyes: that she, an elderly spinster, still within her wits, had played a part in the disastrous proceedings in his flat. She had allowed the caretaker to become drunk, she had egged on a young foreign girl. "Have you no responsibility?" shouted Mr. Runca at Miss Winton in her imagination. "What's the matter with you?"

"Hey!" shouted Mr. Morgan. "That carpet's burning."

Miss Winton and Bianca sniffed the air and smelled at once the tang of singed wool. They returned at speed to the other room and saw that the carpet was smoking and that Mr. Morgan was still on the sofa, watching it. "How's about that?" said Mr. Morgan.

"The fire was too close," said Bianca, looking at Miss Winton, who frowned and felt afraid. She didn't remember putting the fire so close to the carpet, and then she thought that she was probably as intoxicated as Mr. Morgan and didn't really know what she was doing.

"Scrape off the burnt bit," advised Mr. Morgan, "and tell them the dog ate it."

They unplugged the fire and laid the carpet flat on the floor again. Much of the damp had disappeared, but the burnt patch, though small, was eye-catching. Miss Winton felt a weakness in her stomach, as though a quantity of jelly were turning rhythmically over and over. The situation now seemed beyond explanation, and she saw herself asking the Runcas to sit down quietly, side by side with the people from the magazine, and she heard herself trying to tell the truth, going into every detail and pleading that Bianca should not be punished. "Blame me," she was saying, "if someone must be blamed, for I have nothing to lose."

"I'll tell you what," said Mr. Morgan, "why don't we telephone for Mrs. Neck? She done a carpet for her hearth, forty different wools she told me, that she shaped with a little instrument. Ring up Mrs. Neck, missy, and say there's a drink for her if she'll oblige Mr. Morgan with ten minutes of her time."

"Do no such thing," cried Miss Winton. "There's been enough drinking, Mr. Morgan, as well you know. The trouble started with drink, when you lurched against the flowers. There's no point at all in Mrs. Neck adding to the confusion."

Mr. Morgan listened to Miss Winton and then rose from the sofa. He said:

"You have lived in these flats longer than I have, madam. We all know that. But I will not stand here and be insulted by you, just because I am a working man. The day you came after your cycle—"

"I must go away," cried Bianca in distress. "I cannot be found with a burnt carpet and the flowers like that."

"Listen," said Mr. Morgan, coming close to Miss Winton. "I have a respect for you. I'm surprised to hear myself insulted from your lips."

"Mr. Morgan—"

"You was insulting me, madam."

"I was not insulting you. Don't go, Bianca. I'll stay here and explain everything to the Runcas. I think, Mr. Morgan, it would be best if you went off to your lunch now."

"How can I?" shouted Mr. Morgan very loudly and rudely, sticking his chin out at Miss Winton. "How the damn hell d'you think I can go down to the wife in the condition I'm in? She'd eat the face off me."

"Please, Mr. Morgan."

"You and your dog: I have respect for the pair of you. You and me is on the same side of the fence. D'you understand?"

Miss Winton shook her head.

"What d'you think of the Runcas, ma'am?"

"I've said, Mr. Morgan: I've never met the Runcas."

"What d'you think of the joint they've got here?"

"I think it's most impressive."

"It's laughable. The whole caboodle is laughable. Did you ever see the like?" Mr. Morgan pointed at objects in the room. "They're two tramps," he shouted, his face purple with rage at the thought of the Runcas. "They're jumped-up tramps."

Miss Winton opened her mouth in order to speak soothingly. Mr. Morgan said:

"I could put a match to the place and to the Runcas, too, with their bloody attitudes. I'm only a simple caretaker, madam, but I'd see their bodies in flames." He kicked a chair, his boot thudding loudly against pale wood. "I hate that class of person, they're as crooked as a corkscrew."

"You're mistaken, Mr. Morgan."

"I'm bloody not mistaken," shouted Mr. Morgan. "They're full of hate for a man like me. They'd say I was a beast."

Miss Winton, shocked and perturbed, was also filled with amazement. She couldn't understand why Mr. Morgan had said that he and she belonged on the same side of the fence, since for the past fifteen years she had noted the scorn in his eyes.

"We have a thing in common," said Mr. Morgan. "We have no respect whatever for the jumped-up tramps who occupy this property. I'd like to see you in here, madam, with your bits and pieces. The Runcas can go where they belong." Mr. Morgan spat into the chair which he had struck with his boot.

"Oh, no," cried Miss Winton, and Mr. Morgan laughed. He walked about the room, clearing his throat and spitting carelessly. Eventually he strolled away, into the kitchen. The dog barked, sensing Miss Winton's distress. Bianca began to sob and from the kitchen came the whistling of Mr. Morgan, a noise he emitted in order to cover the sound of gin being poured into his glass. Miss Winton knew what had happened: she had read of men who could not resist alcohol and who were maddened by its presence in their bloodstream. She considered that Mr. Morgan had gone mad in the Runcas' flat; he was speaking like an insane person, saying he had respect for her dog.

"I am frightened of him," said Bianca.

"No," said Miss Winton. "He's a harmless man, though I wish he'd go away. We can clean up a bit. We can make an effort."

Mr. Morgan returned and took no notice of them. He sat on the sofa while they set to, clearing up all the pieces of broken vase and the flowers. They placed a chair over the burnt area of carpet so that the Runcas would not notice it as soon as they entered the room. Miss Winton arranged the flowers in a vase and placed it where the other one had been placed by Mrs. Runca. She surveyed the room and noticed that, apart from the presence of Mr. Morgan, it wasn't so bad. Perhaps, she thought, the explanation could be unfolded gradually. She saw no reason why the room shouldn't be photographed as it was now, with the nicely arranged flowers and the chair over the burnt patch of carpeting. The damp area, greater in size, was still a little noticeable, but she imagined that in a photograph it mightn't show up too badly.

"You have let me get into this condition," said Mr. Morgan in an aggressive way. "It was your place to say that the Runcas' whiskey shouldn't be touched, nor their gin neither. You're a fellow tenant, Miss Winton. The girl and I are servants, madam. We was doing what came naturally."

"I'll take the responsibility," said Miss Winton.

"Say the dog done it," urged Mr. Morgan again. "The other will go against the girl and myself."

"I'll tell the truth," said Miss Winton. "The Runcas will understand. They're not monsters that they won't forgive an accident. Mrs. Runca—"

"That thin bitch," shouted Mr. Morgan, and added more quietly: "Runca's illegitimate."

"Mr. Morgan—"

"Tell them the bloody dog done it. Tell them the dog ran about like a mad thing. How d'you know they're not monsters? How d'you know they'll understand, may I ask? 'We was all three boozing in the kitchen,' are you going to say? 'And Mr. Morgan took more than his share of the intoxicant. All hell broke loose.' Are you going to say that, Miss Winton?"

"The truth is better than lies."

"What's the matter with saying the dog done it?"

"You would be far better off out of this flat, Mr. Morgan. No good will come of you raving on like that."

"You have always respected me, madam. You have never been familiar."

"Well—"

"I might strike them dead. They might enter that door and I might hit them with a hammer."

Miss Winton began to protest, but Mr. Morgan waved a hand at her. He sniffed and said: "A caretaker sees a lot, I'll tell you that. Fellows bringing women in, hypocrisy all over the place. There's those that slips me a coin, madam, and those that doesn't bother, and I'm not to know which is the worse. Some of them's miserable and some's boozing all night, having sex and laughing their heads off. The Runcas isn't human in any way whatsoever. The Runcas is saying I was a beast that might offend their eyes." Mr. Morgan ceased to speak and glared angrily at Miss Winton.

"Come now," she said.

"A dirty caretaker, they've said, who's not fit to be alive—"

"They've never said any such thing, Mr. Morgan. I'm sure of it."

"They should have moved away from the flats if they hated the caretaker. They're a psychological case."

There was a silence in the room while Miss Winton trembled and tried not to show it, aware that Mr. Morgan had reached a condition in which he was capable of all he mentioned.

"What I need," he said after a time, speaking more calmly from the sofa on which he was relaxing, "is a cold bath."

"Mr. Morgan," said Miss Winton. She thought that he was at last about to go away, down to his basement and his angry wife, in order to immerse his large body in cold water. "Mr. Morgan, I'm sorry that you should think badly of me—"

"I'll have a quick one," said Mr. Morgan, walking toward the Runcas' bathroom. "Who'll know the difference?"

"No," cried Miss Winton. "No, please, Mr. Morgan."

But with his glass in his hand Mr. Morgan entered the bathroom and locked the door.

When the photographers arrived at half past two to prepare their apparatus, Mr. Morgan was still in the bathroom. Miss Winton waited with Bianca, reassuring her from time to time, repeating that she would not leave until she herself had explained to the Runcas what had happened. The photographers worked silently, moving none of the furniture because they had been told that the furniture was on no account to be displaced.

For an hour and twenty minutes Mr. Morgan had been in the bathroom. It was clear to Miss Winton that he had thrown the vase of flowers to the ground deliberately and in anger, and that he had placed the fire closer to the carpet. In his crazy and spiteful condition Miss Winton imagined that he was capable of anything: of drowning himself in the bath maybe, so that the Runcas' penthouse might sordidly feature in the newspapers. Bianca had been concerned about his continued presence in the bathroom, but Miss Winton had explained that Mr. Morgan was simply being unpleasant since he was made like that. "It is quite disgraceful," she said, well aware that Mr. Morgan realized that she was the kind of woman who would not report him to the authorities, and was taking advantage of her nature while involving her in his own. She felt that the Runcas were the victims of circumstance, and thought that she might use that very expression when she made her explanation to them. She would speak slowly and quietly, breaking it to them in the end that Mr. Morgan was still in the bathroom and had probably fallen asleep. "It is not his fault," she heard herself saying. "We must try to understand." And she felt that the Runcas would nod their heads in agreement and would know what to do next.

"Will they sack me?" said Bianca, and Miss Winton shook her head, repeating again that nothing that had happened had been Bianca's fault.

At three o'clock the Runcas arrived. They came together, having met in the hallway downstairs. "The flowers came, did they?" Mr. Runca had inquired of his wife in the lift, and she had replied that the flowers had safely been delivered and that she had arranged them to her satisfaction. "Good," said Mr. Runca, and reported to his wife some facts about the morning he had spent.

When they entered their penthouse apartment the Runcas noted the presence of the photographers and the photographers' apparatus. They saw as well that an elderly woman with a dog was there, standing beside Bianca, that a chair had been moved, that the Afghanistan carpet was stained, and that some flowers had been loosely thrust into a vase. Mr. Runca wondered about the latter because his wife had just informed him that she herself had arranged the flowers; Mrs. Runca thought that something peculiar was going on. The elderly woman stepped forward to greet them, announcing that her name was Miss Winton, and at that moment a man in brown overalls whom the Runcas recognized as Mr. Morgan, caretaker and odd-job man, entered the room from the direction of the bathroom. He strode toward them and coughed.

"You had trouble with the pipes," said Mr. Morgan. He spoke urgently and it seemed to Mr. and Mrs. Runca that the elderly woman with the dog was affected by his speaking. Her mouth was actually open, as though she had been about to speak herself. Hearing Mr. Morgan's voice, she closed it.

"What has happened here?" said Mrs. Runca, moving forward from her husband's side. "Has there been an accident?"

"I was called up to the flat," said Mr. Morgan, "on account of noise in the pipes. Clogged pipes was on the point of bursting, a trouble I've been dealing with since eleven-thirty. You'll discover the bath is full of water. Release it, sir, at five o'clock tonight, and then I think you'll find everything okay. Your drain was out of order."

Mrs. Runca removed her gaze from Mr. Morgan's face and passed it on to the face of Miss Winton and then on to the bowed head of Bianca. Her husband examined the silent photographers, sensing something in the atmosphere. He said to himself that he did not yet know the full story: what, for instance, was this woman with a dog doing there? A bell rang, and Bianca moved automatically from Miss Winton's side to answer the door. She admitted the woman from the magazine, the woman who was in charge of everything and was to write the article.

"Miss Winton," said Mr. Morgan, indicating Miss Winton, "occupies a flat lower down in the building." Mr. Morgan blew his nose. "Miss Winton wished," he said, "to see the penthouse, and knowing that I was coming here she came up, too, and got into conversation with the maid on the doorstep. The dog dashed in, in a hysterical fit, knocking down a bowl of flowers and upsetting an electric fire on the carpet. Did you notice this?" said Mr. Morgan, striding forward to display the burnt patch. "The girl had the fire on," added Mr. Morgan, "because she felt the cold, coming from a warmer clime."

Miss Winton heard the words of Mr. Morgan and said nothing at all. He had stood in the bathroom, she reckoned, for an hour and twenty minutes, planning to say that the girl had put on the fire because, being Italian, she had suddenly felt the cold.

"Well?" said Mr. Runca, looking at Miss Winton.

She saw his eyes, dark and intent, anxious to draw a response from her, wishing to watch the opening and closing of her lips while his ears listened to the words that relayed the explanation.

"I regret the inconvenience," she said. "I'll pay the damage."

"Damage?" cried Mrs. Runca, moving forward and pushing the chair farther away from the burnt area of carpet. "Damage?" she said again, looking at the flowers in the vase.

"So a dog had a fit in here," said Mr. Runca.

The woman from the magazine looked from Mr. Morgan to Bianca and then to Miss Winton. She surveyed the faces of Mr. and Mrs. Runca and glanced last of all at the passive countenances of her photographers. It seemed, she reflected, that an incident had occurred; it seemed that a dog had gone berserk. "Well, now," she said briskly. "Surely it's not as bad as all that? If we put that chair back, who'll notice the carpet? And the flowers look most becoming."

"The flowers are a total mess," said Mrs. Runca. "An animal might have arranged them."

Mr. Morgan was discreetly silent, and Miss Winton's face turned scarlet.

"We had better put the whole thing off," said Mr. Runca meditatively. "It'll take a day or two to put everything back to rights. We are sorry," he said, addressing himself to the woman from the magazine. "But no doubt you see that no pictures can be taken?"

The woman, swearing most violently within her mind, smiled at Mr. Runca and said it was obvious, of course.

Mr. Morgan said:

"I'm sorry, sir, about this." He stood there, serious and unemotional, as though he had never suggested that Mrs. Neck might be invited up to the Runcas' penthouse apartment, as though hatred and drink had not rendered him insane. "I'm sorry, sir," said Mr. Morgan. "I should not have permitted a dog to enter your quarters, sir. I was unaware of the dog until it was too late."

Listening to Mr. Morgan laboriously telling his lies, Miss Winton was visited by the thought that there was something else she could do. For fifteen years she had lived lonesomely in the building, her shyness causing her to keep herself to herself. She possessed enough money to exist quite comfortably; she didn't do much as the days went by.

"Excuse me," said Miss Winton, not at all knowing how she was going to proceed. She felt her face becoming red again, and she felt the eyes of all the people on her. She wanted to explain at length, to go on talking in a manner that was quite unusual for her, weaving together the threads of an argument. It seemed to Miss Winton that she would have to remind the Runcas of the life of Mr. Morgan, how he daily climbed from his deep basement, attired invariably in his long brown overalls. "He has a right to his resentment" was what she might say. "He has a right to demand more of the tenants of these flats. His palm is greased, he is handed a cup of tea in exchange for a racing tip; the tenants keep him sweet." He had come to consider that some of the tenants were absurd, or stupid, and that others were hypocritical. For Miss Winton he had reserved his scorn, for the Runcas a share of his hatred. Miss Winton had accepted the scorn and understood why it was there; they must seek to understand the other. "The ball is in your court," said Miss Winton in her imagination, addressing the Runcas and pleased that she had thought of a breezy expression that they would at once appreciate.

"What about Wednesday next?" said Mr. Runca to the woman from the magazine. "All this should be sorted out by then, I imagine."

"Wednesday would be lovely," said the woman.

Miss Winton wanted to let Mr. Morgan see that he was wrong about these people. She wanted to have it proved here and now that the Runcas were human and would understand an accident, that they, like anyone else, were capable of respecting a touchy caretaker. She wished to speak the truth, to lead the truth into the open and let it act for itself between Mr. Morgan and the Runcas.

"We'll make a note of everything," Mrs. Runca said to her, "and let you have the list of the damage and the cost of it."

"I'd like to talk to you," said Miss Winton. "I'd like to explain if I may."

"Explain?" said Mrs. Runca. "Explain?"

"Could we all sit down? I'd like you to understand. I've been in these flats for fifteen years. Mr. Morgan came a year later. Perhaps I can help. It's difficult for me to explain to you." Miss Winton paused, in some confusion.

"Is she ill?" inquired the steely voice of Mrs. Runca, and Miss Winton was aware of the woman's metallic hair, and fingernails that matched it, and the four shrewd eyes of a man and a woman who were successful in all their transactions. "I might hit them with a hammer," said the voice of Mr. Morgan in Miss Winton's memory. "I might strike them dead."

"We must try to understand," cried Miss Winton, her face burning with embarrassment. "A man like Mr. Morgan and people like you and an old spinster like myself. We are all standing in this room and we must relax and attempt to understand." Miss Winton wondered if the words that she forced from her were making sense; she was aware that she was not being eloquent. "Don't you see?" cried Miss Winton with the businesslike stare of the Runcas fixed harshly upon her.

"What's this?" demanded Mrs. Runca. "What's all this about understanding? Understanding what?"

"Yes," said her husband.

"Mr. Morgan comes up from his basement every day of his life. The

318

tenants grease his palm. He sees the tenants in his own way. He has a right to do that; he has a right to his touchiness—"

Mr. Morgan coughed explosively, interrupting the flow of words. "What are you talking about?" cried Mrs. Runca. "It's enough that damage has been done without all this."

"I'm trying to begin at the beginning." Ahead of her, Miss Winton sensed a great mound of words and complication before she could lay bare the final truth: that Mr. Morgan regarded the Runcas as people who had been in some way devoured. She knew that she would have to progress slowly, until they began to guess what she was trying to put to them. Accepting that they had failed the caretaker, as she had failed him, too, they would understand the reason for his small revenge. They would nod their heads guiltily while she related how Mr. Morgan, unhinged by alcohol, had spat at their furniture and had afterward pretended to be drowned.

"We belong to different worlds," said Miss Winton, wishing the ground would open beneath her, "you and I and Mr. Morgan. Mr. Morgan sees your penthouse flat in a different way. What I am trying to say is that you are not just people to whom only lies can be told."

"We have a lot to do," said Mrs. Runca, lighting a cigarette. She was smiling slightly, seeming amused.

"The bill for damage must be paid," added Mr. Runca firmly. "You understand, Miss Winter? There can be no shelving of that responsibility."

"I don't do much," cried Miss Winton, moving beyond embarrassment now. "I sit with my dog. I go to the shops. I watch the television. I don't do much, but I am trying to do something now. I am trying to promote understanding."

The photographers began to dismantle their apparatus. Mr. Runca spoke in a whisper to the woman from the magazine, making some final arrangement for the following Wednesday. He turned to Miss Winton and said more loudly, "Perhaps you had better return to your apartment, Miss Winter. Who knows, that little dog may have another fit."

"He didn't have a fit," cried Miss Winton. "He never had a fit in the whole of his life."

There was a silence in the room then, before Mr. Runca said:

"You've forgotten, Miss Winter, that your little dog had a bout of hysteria and caused a lot of trouble. Come now, Miss Winter."

"My name is not Miss Winter. Why do you call me a name that isn't correct?"

Mr. Runca threw his eyes upward, implying that Miss Winton was getting completely out of hand and would next be denying her very existence. "She's the Queen Mother," whispered Mrs. Runca to one of the photographers, and the photographer sniggered lightly. Miss Winton said:

"My dog did not have a fit. I am trying to tell you, but no one bothers to listen. I am trying to go back to the beginning, to the day that Mr. Morgan first became caretaker of these flats—"

"Now, madam," said Mr. Morgan, stepping forward.

"I am going to tell the truth," cried Miss Winton shrilly. Her dog began to bark, and she felt, closer to her now, the presence of Mr. Morgan. "Shall we be going, madam?" said Mr. Morgan, and she was aware that she was being moved toward the door. "No," she cried while the movement continued. "No," whispered Miss Winton again, but already she was on the landing and Mr. Morgan was saying that there was no point whatsoever in attempting to tell people like the Runcas the truth. "That type of person," said Mr. Morgan, descending the stairs with Miss Winton, his hand beneath her left elbow as though she required aid, "that type of person wouldn't know the meaning of the word."

I have failed, said Miss Winton to herself; I have failed to do something that might have been good in its small way. She found herself at the door of her flat, feeling tired, and heard Mr. Morgan saying "Will you be all right, madam?" She reflected that he was speaking to her as though she were the one who had been mad, soothing her in his scorn. Mr. Morgan began to laugh. "Runca slipped me a quid," he said. "Our own Runca." He laughed again, and Miss Winton felt wearier. She would write a check for the amount of the damage, and that would be that. She would often in the future pass Mr. Morgan on the stairs and there would be a confused memory between them. The Runcas would tell their friends, saying there was a peculiar woman in one of the flats. "Did you see their faces," said Mr. Morgan, "when I mentioned about the dog in a fit?" He threw his head back, displaying all his teeth. "It was that amusing," said Mr. Morgan. "I nearly smiled." He went away, and Miss Winton stood by the door of her flat, listening to his footsteps on the stairs. She heard him on the next floor, summoning the lift that would carry him smoothly to the basement, where he would tell his wife about how Miss Winton's dog had had a fit in the Runcas' penthouse, and how Miss Winton had made a ridiculous fuss that no one had bothered to listen to.

JOHN EDGAR WIDEMAN

Little Brother

for Judy*

Penny, don't laugh. Come on now, you know I love that little critter. And anyway, how you so sure it didn't work?

Tylenol?

Yep. Children's liquid Tylenol. The children's formula's not as strong and he was only a pup. Poured two teaspoons in his water dish. I swear it seemed to help.

Children's Tylenol.

With the baby face on it. You know. Lapped it up like he understood it was good for him. He's alive today, ain't he? His eye cleared up, too.

You never told me this story before.

Figured you'd think I was crazy.

His eye's torn up again.

You know Little Brother got to have his love life. Out tomcatting around. Sticking his nose in where it don't belong. Bout once a month he disappears from here. Used to worry. Now I know he'll be slinking back in three or four days with his tail dragging. Limping around spraddle-legged. Sleeping all day cause his poor thing's plumb wore out.

Geral.

It's true. Little Brother got it figured better than most people. Do it till

*My wife and love of my life, to whom this story is dedicated, suggested that my Aunt Geraldine's strange dog needed a biographer.

322

you can't do it no more. Come home half dead and then you can mind your own business for a while.

Who you voting for?

None of them fools. Stopped paying them any mind long time ago.

I hear what you're saying, but this is special. It's for president.

One I would have voted for. One I would have danced for buck naked up on Homewood Avenue, is gone. My pretty preacher man's gone. Shame the way they pushed him right off the stage. The rest them all the same. Once they in they all dirty dogs. President's the one cut the program before I could get my weather stripping. Every time the kitchen window rattles and I see my heat money seeping out the cracks, I curse that mean old Howdy-Doody turkey-necked clown.

How's Ernie?

Mr. White's fine.

Mama always called him Mr. White. And Ote said *Mr. White* till we shamed him out of it.

I called Ernie that too before we were married. When he needed teasing. Formal like Mama did. *Mr. White.* He was *Mr. White* to her till the day she died.

But Mama loved him.

Of course she did. Once she realized he wasn't trying to steal me away. Thing is, she never had that to worry about. Not in a million years. I'd have never left Mama. Even when Ote was alive and staying here. She's been gone all these years but first thing I think every morning when I open my eyes is, You okay, Mama? I'm right here, Mama. Be there in a minute, to get you up. I still wake up hoping she's all right. That she didn't need me during the night. That I'll be able to help her through the day.

Sometimes I don't know how you did it all those years.

Gwan, girl. If things had been different, if you didn't have a family of your own, if I'd had children, you would have been the one to stay here and take care of Mama.

I guess you're right. Yes. I would.

No way one of us wouldn't have taken care of her. You. Ote. Sis or me.

Made sense for me and Ote to do it. We stayed home. If you hadn't married, you'd have done it. And not begrudged her one moment of your time.

Ote would have been sixty in October.

I miss him. It's just Ernie and me and the dogs rattling around in this big house now. Some things I have on my mind I never get to say to anybody because I'm waiting to tell them to Ote.

He was a good man. I can still see Daddy pulling him around in that little wagon. The summer Ote had rheumatic fever and the doctor said he had to stay in bed and Daddy made him that wagon and propped him up with pillows and pulled him all over the neighborhood. Ote bumping along up and down Cassina Way with his thumb in his mouth, half sleep, and Daddy just as proud as a peacock. After three girls, finally had him a son to show off.

Ote just about ran me away from here when I said I was keeping Little Brother. Two dogs are enough, Geraldine. Why would you bring something looking like that in the house? Let that miserable creature go on off and find a decent place to die. You know how Ote could draw hisself up like John French. Let you know he was half a foot taller than you and carrying all that John French weight. Talked like him, too. *Geraldine*, looking down on me saying all the syllables of my name like Daddy used to when he was mad at me. *Geraldine*. Run that miserable thing away from here. When it sneaks up under the porch and dies, you won't be the one who has to get down on your hands and knees and crawl under there to drag it out.

But he was the one wallpapered Little Brother's box with insulation, wasn't he? The one who hung a flap of rug over the door to keep out the wind.

The one who cried like a baby when Pup-pup was hit.

Didn't he see it happen?

Almost. He was turning the corner of Finance. Heard the brakes screech. The bump. He was so mad. Carried Pup-pup and laid him on the porch. Fussing the whole time at him. You stupid dog. You stupid dog. How many times have I told you not to run in the street. Like Pup-pup could hear him. Like Pup-pup could understand him if he'd been alive. Ote stomped in the house and up the stairs. Must have washed his hands fifteen minutes. Running water like we used to do when Mama said we better not get out of bed once we were in the bed so running and running that water till it made us pee one long last time before we went to sleep.

What are you girls doing up there wasting all that water? I'ma be up there in ten minutes and you best be under the covers.

Don't be the last one. Don't be on the toilet and just starting to pee good and bumpty-bump, here she comes up the steps and means what she says. Uh ohh. It's Niagara Falls and you halfway over and ain't no stopping now. So you just sit there squeezing your knees together and work on that smile you don't hardly believe and she ain't buying one bit when she bams open the door and Why you sitting there grinning like a Chessy cat, girl. I thought I told youall ten minutes ago to get in bed.

Ote washed and washed and washed. I didn't see much blood. Pup-pup looked like Pup-pup laid out there on the porch. Skinny as he was you could always see his ribs moving when he slept. So it wasn't exactly Pup-pup because it was too still. But Pup-pup wasn't torn-up bloody or runned-over looking, either.

Whatever Ote needed to wash off, he took his time. He was in the bathroom fifteen minutes, then he turned off the faucets and stepped over into his room and shut the door, but you know how the walls and doors in this house don't stop nothing so I could hear him crying when I went out in the hall to call up and ask him if he was all right, ask him what he wanted to do with Pup-pup. I didn't say a word. Just stood there thinking about lots of things. The man crying on his bed was my baby brother. And I'd lived with him all my life in the same house. Now it was just the two of us. Me in the hall listening. Him on his bed, a grown man sobbing cause he's too mad to do anything else. You and Sis moved out first. Then Daddy gone. Then Mama. Just two of us left and two mutts in the house I've lived in all my life. Then it would be one of us left. Then the house empty. I thought some such sorrowful thoughts. And thought of poor Pup-pup. And that's when I decided to say yes to Ernie White after all those years of no.

Dan. If you want a slice of this sweet-potato pie you better come in here now and get it. Going fast. They're carting it away like sweet-potato pie's going out of style.

It's his favorite.

That's why I bake one every time he's home from school.

Did he tell you he saw Marky at Mellon Park?

No.

Dan was playing ball and Marky was in a bunch that hangs around on the sidelines. He said Marky recognized him. Mumbled hi. Not much more than that. He said Marky didn't look good. Not really with the others but sitting off to the side, on the ground, leaning back against the fence. Dan went over to him and Marky nodded or said hi, enough to let Danny know it really was Marky and not just somebody who looked like Marky, or Marky's ghost because Dan said it wasn't the Marky he remembered. It's the Marky who's been driving us all crazy.

At least he's off Homewood Avenue.

That's good, I suppose.

Good and bad. Like everything else. He can move hisself off the Avenue and I'm grateful for that, but it also means he can go and get hisself in worse trouble. A healthy young man with a good head on his shoulders and look at him. It's pitiful. Him and lots the other young men like zombies nodding on Homewood Avenue. Pitiful. But as long as he stays on Homewood the cops won't hassle him. What if he goes off and tries to rob somebody or break in somebody's house? Marky has no idea half the time who he is or what he's doing. He's like a baby. He couldn't get away with anything. Just hurt hisself or hurt somebody trying.

What can we do?

We kept him here as long as we could. Ernie talked and talked to him. Got him a job when he dropped out of school. Talked and talked and did everything he could. Marky just let hisself go. He stopped washing. Wore the same clothes night and day. And he was always such a neat kid. A dresser. Stood in front of the mirror for days, arranging himself just so for the ladies. I don't understand it. He just fell apart, Penny. You've seen him. You remember how he once was. How many times have I called you and cried over the phone about Marky? Only so much any of us could do, then Ernie said it was too dangerous to have him in the house. Wouldn't leave me here alone with

Marky. I about went out my mind then. Not safe in my own house with this child I'd taken in and raised. My husband's nephew, who'd been like my own child, who I'd watched grow into a man. Not safe. Nothing to do but let him roam the streets.

None of the agencies or programs would help. What else could you do, Geral?

They said they couldn't take him till he did something wrong. What kind of sense does that make? They'll take him after the damage is done. After he freezes to death sleeping on a bench up in Homewood Park. Or's killed by the cops. Or stark raving foaming at the mouth. They'll take him then. Sorry, Mrs. White, our hands are tied.

Sorry, Mrs. White. Just like the receptionist at Dr. Franklin's. That skinny, pinched-nosed *Sorry, Mrs. Whatever your name is* cause they don't give a good goddamn, they just doing their job and don't hardly want to be bothered, especially if it's you, and you're black and poor and can't do nothing for them but stand in line and wait your turn, and as far as they're concerned you can wait forever.

Did I tell you what happened to me in Dr. Franklin's office, Penny? Five or six people in the waiting room. All of them white. Chattering about this and that. They don't know me and I sure don't know none of them but cause they see my hair ain't kinky and my skin's white as theirs they get on colored people and then it's niggers after they warm up awhile. Ain't niggers enough to make you throw up? Want everything and not willing to work a lick. Up in your face now like they think they own the world. Pushing past you in line at the A&P. Got so now you can't ride a bus without taking your life in your hands. This city's not what it used to be. Used to be a decent place to live till they started having all those nigger babies and now a white person's supposed to grin and bear it. It's three women talking mostly, and the chief witch's fat and old as I am. And listen to this. She's afraid of being raped. She hears about white women attacked every day and she's fed up. Then she says, It's time somebody did something, don't you think? Killing's too good for those animals. Looking over at me with her head cocked and her little bit of nappy orange hair, got the nerve to google at me like she's waiting for me to wag my head and cluck like the rest of those hens. Well, I didn't say a word but the look I gave that heifer froze her mouth shut and kept it shut. Nobody uttered a word for the half hour till it was my turn to see Dr. Franklin. Like when we were bad and Mama'd sit us down and dare us to breathe till she said we could. They're lucky that's all I did. Who she think want to rape her? What self-respecting man, black, white, green or polka dot, gon take his life in his hands scuffling with that mountain of blubber?

Geral.

Don't laugh. It wasn't funny. Rolling her Kewpie-doll eyes at me. Ain't niggers terrible? I was about to terrible her ass if I heard *nigger* one more time in her mouth.

Listen at you. Leave that poor woman alone. How old's Little Brother now?

We've had him nine years. A little older than that. Just a wee thing when he arrived on the porch. *Geraldine.* You don't intend bringing that scrawny rat into the house, do you?

And the funny thing is, Little Brother must have heard Ote and been insulted. Cause Little Brother never set foot inside the front door. Not in the whole time he's lived here. Not a paw. First he just made a bed in the rags I set out by the front door. Then the cardboard box on the front porch. Then when he grew too big for that Ote built his apartment under the porch. I just sat and rocked the whole time, Ote hammering and sawing and cussing when the boards wouldn't stay straight or wouldn't fit the way he wanted them to. Using Daddy's old, rusty tools. Busy as a beaver all day long and I'm smiling to myself but I didn't say a mumbling word, girl. If I had let out so much as one signifying I told you so peep, Ote woulda built another box and nailed me up inside. Little Brother went from rags to his own private apartment and in that entire time he's never been inside the house once. I coaxed him, Here, puppy, here, puppy, puppy, and put his food inside the hallway but that's one stubborn creature. Little Brother'd starve to death before he'd walk through the front door.

He about drove Pup-pup crazy. Pup-pup would sneak out and eat Little Brother's food. Drag his rags away and hide them. Snap and growl but Little

Brother paid him no mind. Pup-pup thought Little Brother was nuts. Living outdoors in the cold. Not fighting back. Carrying a teddy bear around in his mouth. Peeing in his own food so Pup-pup wouldn't bother it. Pup-pup was so jealous. Went to his grave still believing he had to protect his territory. Pup-pup loved to roam the streets, but bless his heart, he became a regular stay-at-home. Figured he better hang around and wait for Little Brother to make his move. Sometimes I think that's why Pup forgot how to act in the street. In such a hurry to get out and get back, he got himself runned over.

That reminds me of Maria Indovina. Danny wanted me to walk around the neighborhood with him. He wanted to see the places we're always talking about. Mr. Conley's lot. Klein's store. Aunt Aida's. Hazel and Nettie's. Showed him the steps up to Nettie's and told him she never came down them for thirty years. He said in youall's tales these sounded like the highest, steepest steps in creation. I said they were. Told him I'd follow you and Sis cause I was scared to go first. And no way in the world I'd be first coming back down. They didn't seem like much to him, even when I reminded him we were just little girls and Aunt Hazel and Cousin Nettie like queens who lived in another world. Anyway, we were back behind Susquehanna where we used to play, and there's a high fence back there on top of the stone wall. It's either a new fence or newly painted but the wall's the same old wall where the bread truck crushed poor Maria Indovina. I told him we played together in those days. Black kids and white kids. Mostly Italian then. Us and the Italians living on the same streets and families knowing each other by name. I told him and he said that's better than it is today. Tried to explain to him we lived on the same streets but didn't really mix. Kids playing together, and Hello, how are you, Mr. So-and-So, Mrs. So-and-So, that and a little after-hours undercover mixing. Only time I ever heard Mama curse was when she called Andrea Sabettelli a whorish bitch.

John French wasn't nobody's angel.

Well, I wasn't discussing none of that with Dan. I did tell him about the stain on the wall and how we were afraid to pass by it alone.

Speaking of white people, how's your friend from up the street?

Oh, Vicki's fine. Her dresses are still too mini for my old fuddy-duddy taste. But no worse than what the other girls wearing. Her little girl Carolyn still comes by every afternoon for her piece of candy. She's a lovely child. My blue-eyed sweetheart. I worry about her. Auntie Gerry, I been a good girl today. You got me a sweet, Auntie Gerry? Yes, darling, I do. And I bring her whatever we have around the house. She'll stand in line with the twins from next door, and Becky and Rashad. They're my regulars, but some the others liable to drop by too. Hi, Aunt Gerry. Can I have a piece of candy, please? When they want something they're so nice and polite, best behaved li'l devils in Homewood.

Yes, my friend Vicki's fine. Not easy being the only white person in the neighborhood. I told Fletcher and them to leave her alone. And told her she better respect herself a little more cause they sure won't if she don't. Those jitterbugs don't mean any harm, but boys will be boys. And she's not the smartest young lady in the world. These slicksters around here, you know how they are, hmmph. She better be careful, is what I told her. She didn't like hearing what I said but I've noticed her carrying herself a little different when she walks by. Saw her dressed up real nice in Sears in East Liberty last week and she ducked me. I know why, but it still hurt me. Like it hurts me to think my little sugar Carolyn will be calling people niggers someday. If she don't already.

Did you love Ernie all those years you kept him waiting?

Love?

You know what I mean. Love.

Love love?

Love love love. You know what I'm asking you.

Penny. Did you love Billy?

Five children. Twenty-seven years off and on before he jumped up and left for good. I must have. Some of the time.

Real love? Hootchy-gootchy cooing and carrying on?

What did you say? Hootchy-koo? Is that what you're calling love? To tell the truth, I can't hardly remember. I must of had an operation when I was about eleven or twelve. Cut all that romance mess out. What's love got to do with anything, anyway?

You asked me first.

Wish I'd had the time. Can you picture Billy and Ernie dancing the huckle-buck, doing the hootchy-koo?

Whoa, girl. You gonna start me laughing.

Hootchy-gootchy-koo. Wish I'd had the time. Maybe it ain't too late. Here's a little hootchy-gootchy-koo for you.

Watch out. You're shaking the table. Whoa. Look at my drink.

Can't help it. I got the hootchy-goos. I'm in love.

Hand me one of those napkins.

Gootchy-gootchy-goo.

Behave now. The kids staring at us. Sitting here acting like two old fools.

So you think I ought to try Tylenol?

Two things for sure. Didn't kill Little Brother. And Princess is sick. Now the other sure thing is it might help Princess and it might not. Make sure it's the baby face. Kids' strength. Try that first.

I just might.

No you won't. You're still laughing at me.

No I'm not. I'm smiling thinking about Ote hammering and sawing an apartment for Little Brother and you rocking on the porch, trying to keep your mouth shut.

Like to bust, girl.

But you didn't.

Held it in to this very day. Till I told you.

Hey, youall. Leave a piece of sweet-potato pie for your cousin, Dan. It's his favorite.

ANN BEATTIE

Distant Music

On Friday she always sat in the park, waiting for him to come. At one-thirty he came to this park bench (if someone was already sitting there, he loitered around it), and then they would sit side by side, talking quietly, like Ingrid Bergman and Cary Grant in *Notorious.* Both believed in flying saucers and health food. They shared a hatred of Laundromats, guilt about not sending presents to relatives on birthdays and at Christmas, and a dog—part weimaraner, part German shepherd—named Sam.

She was twenty, and she worked in an office; she was pretty because she took a lot of time with makeup, the way a housewife who really cared might flute the edges of a piecrust with thumb and index finger. He was twenty-four, a graduate-school dropout (theater) who collaborated on songs with his friend Gus Greeley, and he wanted, he fervently wanted, to make it big as a songwriter. His mother was Greek and French, his father American. This girl, Sharon, was not the first woman to fall in love with Jack because he was so handsome. She took the subway to get to the bench, which was in Washington Square Park; he walked from the basement apartment he lived in. Whoever had Sam that day (they kept the dog alternating weeks) brought him. They could do this because her job required her to work only from eight to one, and he worked at home. They had gotten the dog because they feared for his life. A man had come up to them on West Tenth Street carrying a cardboard box, smiling and saying, "Does the little lady want a kitty cat?" They peered inside. "Puppies," Jack said. "Well, who gives a fuck?" the man said, putting the box down, his face dark and contorted. Sharon and Jack stared at the man; he stared belligerently back. Neither of them was quite sure how things had suddenly turned ominous. She wanted to get out of there right away, before the man took a swing at Jack, but to her surprise Jack smiled at the man and dipped into the box for a dog. He extracted the scrawny, wormy Sam. She took the dog first, because there was a veterinarian's office close to her apartment. Once the dog was cured of his worms, she gave him to Jack to begin his training. In Jack's apartment the puppy would fix his eyes on the parallelogram of sunlight that sometimes appeared on the wood floor in the late morning—sniffing it, backing up, edging up to it at the border. In her apartment, the puppy's object of fascination was a clarinet that a friend had left there when he moved. The puppy looked at it respectfully. She watched the dog for signs of maladjustment, wondering if he was too young to be shuttling back and forth, from home to home. (She herself had been raised by her mother, but she and her sister would fly to Seattle every summer to spend two months with their father.) The dog seemed happy enough.

At night, in Jack's one-room apartment, they would sometimes lie with their heads at the foot of the bed, staring at the ornately carved oak headboard and the old-fashioned light attached to it, with the little sticker still on the shade that said, "From home of Lady Astor. $4.00." They had found the lamp in Ruckersville, Virginia, on the only long trip they ever took out of the city. On the bed with them there were usually sheets of music—songs that he was scoring. She would look at the pieces of paper with lyrics typed on them, and read them slowly to herself, appraisingly, as if they were poetry.

On weekends they spent the days and nights together. There was a small but deep fireplace in his apartment, and when September came they would light a fire in the late afternoon, although it was not yet cold, and sometimes light a stick of sandalwood incense, and they would lean on each other or sit side by side, listening to Vivaldi. She knew very little about such music when she first met him, and much more about it by the time their first month had passed. There was no one thing she knew a great deal about—as he did about music—so there was really nothing that she could teach him.

"Where were you in 1974?" he asked her once.

"In school. In Ann Arbor."

"What about 1975?"

"In Boston. Working at a gallery."

"Where are you now?" he said.

She looked at him and frowned. "In New York," she said.

He turned toward her and kissed her arm. "I know," he said. "But why so serious?"

She knew that she was a serious person, and she liked it that he could make her smile. Sometimes, though, she did not quite understand him, so she was smiling now, not out of appreciation but because she thought a smile would make things all right.

Carol, her closest friend, asked why she didn't move in with him. She did not want to tell Carol that it was because she had not been asked, so she said that the room he lived in was very small and that during the day he liked solitude so he could work. She was also not sure that she would move in if he did ask her. He gave her the impression sometimes that he was the serious one, not she. Perhaps *serious* was the wrong word; it was more that he seemed despondent. He would get into moods and not snap out of them; he would drink red wine and play Billie Holiday records, and shake his head and say that if he had not made it as a songwriter by now, chances were that he would never make it. She hadn't really been familiar with Billie Holiday until he began playing the records for her. He would play a song that Billie had recorded early in her career, then play another record of the same song as she had sung it later. He said that he preferred her ruined voice. Two songs in particular stuck in her mind. One was "Solitude," and the first time she heard Billie Holiday sing the first three words, "In my solitude," she felt a physical sensation, as if someone were drawing something sharp over her heart, very lightly. The other record she kept thinking of was "Gloomy Sunday." He told her that it had been banned from the radio back then, because it was said that it had been responsible for suicides.

For Christmas that year he gave her a small pearl ring that had been worn by his mother when she was a girl. The ring fitted perfectly; she only had to wiggle it slightly to get it to slide over the joint of her finger, and when it was in place it felt as if she were not wearing a ring at all. There were eight prongs holding the pearl in place. She often counted things: how many panes in a window, how many slats in a bench. Then, for her birthday, in January, he gave her a silver chain with a small sapphire stone, to be worn on the wrist. She was delighted; she wouldn't let him help her fasten the clasp.

"You like it?" he said. "That's all I've got."

She looked at him, a little startled. His mother had died the year before she met him; what he was saying was that he had given her the last of her things. There was a photograph of his mother on the bookcase—a black-and-white picture in a little silver frame of a smiling young woman whose hair was barely darker than her skin. Because he kept the picture, she assumed that he worshiped his mother. One night he corrected that impression by saying that his mother had always tried to sing in her youth, when she had no voice, which had embarrassed everyone.

He said that she was a silent person; in the end, he said, you would have to say that she had done and said very little. He told Sharon that a few days after her death he and his father had gone through her possessions together, and in one of her drawers they came upon a small wooden box shaped like a heart. Inside the box were two pieces of jewelry—the ring and the chain and sapphire. "So she kept some token, then," his father had said, staring down into the little box. "You gave them to her as presents?" he asked his father. "No," his father said apologetically. "They weren't from me." And then the two of them had stood there looking at each other, both understanding perfectly.

She said, "But what did you finally say to break the silence?"

"Something pointless, I'm sure," he said.

She thought to herself that that might explain why he had not backed down, on Tenth Street, when the man offering the puppies took a stance as though he wanted to fight. Jack was used to hearing bad things—things that took him by surprise. He had learned to react coolly. Later that winter, when she told him that she loved him, his face had stayed expressionless a split second too long, and then he smiled his slow smile and gave her a kiss.

The dog grew. He took to training quickly and walked at heel, and she was glad that they had saved him. She took him to the veterinarian to ask why he was so thin. She was told that the dog was growing fast, and that eventually he would start filling out. She did not tell Jack that she had taken the dog to the veterinarian, because he thought she doted on him too much. She wondered if he might not be a little jealous of the dog.

Slowly, things began to happen with his music. A band on the West Coast that played a song that he and Gus had written was getting a big name, and they had not dropped the song from their repertoire. In February he got a call from the band's agent, who said that they wanted more songs. He and Gus shut themselves in the basement apartment, and she went walking with Sam, the dog. She went to the park, until she ran into the crippled man too many times. He was a young man, rather handsome, who walked with two metal crutches and had a radio that hung from a strap around his neck and rested on his chest, playing loudly. The man always seemed to be walking in the direction she walked in, and she had to walk awkwardly to keep in line with him so they could talk. She really had nothing to talk to the man about, and he helped very little, and the dog was confused by the crutches and made little leaps toward the man, as though they were all three playing a game. She stayed away from the park for a while, and when she went back he was not there. One day in March the park was more crowded than usual because it was an unusually warm, springlike afternoon, and walking with Sam, half dreaming, she passed a heavily made-up woman on a bench who was wearing a polka-dot turban, with a handlettered sign propped against her legs announcing that she was Miss Sydney, a fortuneteller. There was a young boy sitting next to Miss Sydney, and he called out to her, "Come on!" She smiled slightly and shook her head no. The boy was Italian, she thought, but the woman was hard to place. "Miss Sydney's gonna tell you about fire and famine and early death," the boy said. He laughed, and she hurried on, thinking it was odd that the boy would know the word *famine*.

She was still alone with Jack most of every weekend, but much of his talk now was about technical problems he was having with scoring, and she had trouble following him. Once, he became enraged and said that she had no interest in his career. He said it because he wanted to move to Los Angeles and she said she was staying in New York. She said it, assuming at once that he would go anyhow. When he made it clear that he would not leave without her, she started to cry because she was so grateful that he was staying. He thought she was crying because he had yelled at her and said that she had no interest in his career. He took back what he had said; he told her that she was very tolerant and that she often gave good advice. She had a good ear, even if she didn't express her opinions in complex technical terms. She cried again, and this time even she did not realize at first why. Later she knew that it was because he had never said so many kind things to her at once. Actually, very few people in her life had ever gone out of their way to say something kind, and it had just been too much. She began to wonder if her nerves were getting bad. Once, she woke up in the night disoriented and sweating, having dreamed that she was out in the sun, with all her energy gone. It was stifling hot and she couldn't move. "The sun's a good thing," he said to her when she told him the dream. "Think about the bright beautiful sun in Los Angeles. Think about stretching out on a warm day with a warm breeze." Trembling, she left him and went into the kitchen for water. He did not know that if he had really set out for California, she would have followed.

In June, when the air pollution got very bad and the air carried the smell that sidewalks get when they are baked through every day, he began to complain that it was her fault that they were in New York and not in California. "But I just don't like that way of life," she said. "If I went there, I wouldn't be happy."

"What's so appealing about this uptight New York scene?" he said. "You wake up in the night in a sweat. You won't even walk through Washington Square Park anymore."

"It's because of that man with the crutches," she said. "People like that. I told you it was only because of him."

"So let's get away from all that. Let's go somewhere."

"You think there aren't people like that in California?" she said.

"It doesn't matter what I think about California if I'm not going." He clamped earphones on his head.

337

*   *   *

That same month, while she and Jack and Gus were sharing a pot of cheese fondue, she found out that Jack had a wife. They were at Gus's apartment when Gus casually said something about Myra. "Who's Myra?" she asked, and he said, "You know—Jack's wife, Myra." It seemed unreal to her—even more so because Gus's apartment was such an odd place; that night Gus had plugged a defective lamp into an outlet and blown out a fuse. Then he plugged in his only other lamp, which was a sunlamp. It glowed so brightly that he had to turn it, in its wire enclosure, to face the wall. As they sat on the floor eating, their three shadows were thrown up against the opposite wall. She had been looking at that—detached, the way you would stand back to appreciate a picture—when she tuned in on the conversation and heard them talking about someone named Myra.

"You didn't know?" Gus said to her. "Okay, I want you both out. I don't want any heavy scene in my place. I couldn't take it. Come on—I really mean it. I want you out. Please don't talk about it here."

On the street, walking beside Jack, it occurred to her that Gus's outburst was very strange, almost as strange as Jack's not telling her about his wife.

"I didn't see what would be gained by telling you," Jack said.

They crossed the street. They passed the Riviera Café. She had once counted the number of panes of glass across the Riviera's front.

"Did you ever think about us getting married?" he said. "I thought about it. I thought that if you didn't want to follow me to California, of course you wouldn't want to marry me."

"You're already married," she said. She felt that she had just said something very sensible. "Do you think it was right to—"

He started to walk ahead of her. She hurried to catch up. She wanted to call after him, "I would have gone!" She was panting.

"Listen," he said, "I'm like Gus. I don't want to hear it."

"You mean we can't even talk about this? You don't think that I'm entitled to hear about it?"

"I love you and I don't love Myra," he said.

"Where is she?" she said.

338

"In El Paso."

"If you don't love her, why aren't you divorced?"

"You think that everybody who doesn't love his wife gets divorced? I'm not the only one who doesn't do the logical thing, you know. You get nightmares from living in this sewer, and you won't get out of it."

"It's different," she said. What was he talking about?

"Until I met you, I didn't think about it. She was in El Paso, she was gone—period."

"Are you going to get a divorce?"

"Are you going to marry me?"

They were crossing Seventh Avenue. They both stopped still, halfway across the street, and were almost hit by a Checker cab. They hurried across, and on the other side of the street they stopped again. She looked at him, as surprised but as suddenly sure about something as he must have been the time he and his father had found the jewelry in the heart-shaped wooden box. She said no, she was not going to marry him.

It dragged on for another month. During that time, unknown to her, he wrote the song that was going to launch his career. Months after he had left the city, she heard it on her AM radio one morning, and she knew that it was his song, even though he had never mentioned it to her. She leashed the dog and went out and walked to the record shop on Sixth Avenue—walking almost the same route they had walked the night she found out about his wife—and she went in, with the dog. Her face was so strange that the man behind the cash register allowed her to break the rule about dogs in the shop because he did not want another hassle that day. She found the group's record album with the song on it, turned it over and saw his name, in small type. She stared at the title, replaced the record and went back outside, as hunched as if it were winter.

During the month before he left, though, and before she ever heard the song, the two of them had sat on the roof of his building one night, arguing. They were having a Tom Collins because a musician who had been at his place the night before had brought his own mix and then left it behind. She had never had a Tom Collins. It tasted appropriately bitter, she thought. She held out the ring and the bracelet to him. He said that if she made him take them back, he would drop them over the railing. She believed him and put them back in her pocket. He said, and she agreed, that things had not been perfect between them even before she found out about his wife. Myra could play the guitar, and she could not; Myra loved to travel, and she was afraid to leave New York City. As she listened to what he said, she counted the posts—black iron and shaped like arrows—of the fence that wound around the roof. It was almost entirely dark, and she looked up to see if there were any stars. She yearned to be in the country, where she could always see them. She said she wanted him to borrow a car before he left so that they could ride out into the woods in New Jersey. Two nights later he picked her up at her apartment in a red Volvo, with Sam panting in the back, and they wound their way through the city and to the Lincoln Tunnel. Just as they were about to go under, another song began to play on the tape deck. It was Ringo Starr singing "Octopus's Garden." Jack laughed. "That's a hell of a fine song to come on just before we enter the tunnel." Inside the tunnel, the dog flattened himself on the backseat. "You want to keep Sam, don't you?" he said. She was shocked because she had never even thought of losing Sam. "Of course I do," she said, and unconsciously edged a little away from him. He had never said whose car it was. For no reason at all, she thought that the car must belong to a woman.

"I love that syrupy chorus of 'aaaaah' Lennon and McCartney sing," he said. "They really had a fine sense of humor."

"Is that a funny song?" she said. She had never thought about it.

They were on Boulevard East, in Weehawken, and she was staring out the window at the lights across the water. He saw that she was looking, and drove slower.

"This as good as stars for you?" he said.

"It's amazing."

"All yours," he said, taking his hand off the wheel to swoop it through the air in mock graciousness.

After he left she would remember that as one of the little digs he had gotten in—one of the less than nice things he had said. That night, though, impressed by the beauty of the city, she let it go by; in fact, she would have to work on herself later to reinterpret many of the things he had said as being nasty. That made it easier to deal with his absence. She would block out the memory of his pulling over and kissing her, of the two of them getting out of the car, and with Sam between them, walking.

One of the last times she saw him, she went to his apartment on a night when five other people were there—people she had never met. His father had shipped him some eight-millimeter home movies and a projector, and the people all sat on the floor, smoking grass and talking, laughing at the movies of children (Jack at his fourth birthday party; Jack in the Halloween parade at school; Jack at Easter, collecting eggs). One of the people on the floor said, "Hey, get that big dog out of the way," and she glared at him, hating him for not liking the dog. What if his shadow had briefly darkened the screen? She felt angry enough to scream, angry enough to say that the dog had grown up in the apartment and had the right to walk around. Looking at the home movies, she tried to concentrate on Jack's blunders: dropping an Easter egg, running down the hill after the egg, going so fast he stumbled into some blur, perhaps his mother's arms. But what she mostly thought about was what a beautiful child he was, what a happy-looking little boy. There was no sense in her staying there and getting sentimental, so she made her excuses and left early. Outside, she saw the red Volvo, gleaming as though it had been newly painted. She was sure that it belonged to an Indian woman in a blue sari who had been there, sitting close to Jack. Sharon was glad that as she was leaving, Sam had raised his hackles and growled at one of the people there. She scolded him, but out on the street she patted him, secretly glad. Jack had not asked her again to come to California with him, and she told herself that she probably would not have changed her mind if he had. Tears began to well up in her eyes, and she told herself that she was crying because a cab wouldn't stop for her when the driver saw that she had a dog. She ended up walking blocks and blocks back to her apartment that night; it made her more certain than ever that she loved the dog and that she did not love Jack.

About the time she got the first postcard from Jack, things started to get a little bad with Sam. She was afraid that he might have distemper, so she took him to the veterinarian, waited her turn and told the doctor that the dog was

341

growling at some people and she had no idea why. He assured her that there was nothing physically wrong with the dog, and blamed it on the heat. When another month passed and it was less hot, she visited the veterinarian again. "It's the breeding," he said, and sighed. "It's a bad mix. A weimaraner is a mean dog, and that cross isn't a good one. He's part German shepherd, isn't he?"

"Yes," she said.

"Well—that's it, I'm afraid."

"There isn't any medication?"

"It's the breeding," he said. "Believe me. I've seen it before."

"What happens?" she said.

"What happens to the dog?"

"Yes."

"Well—watch him. See how things go. He hasn't bitten anybody, has he?"

"No," she said. "Of course not."

"Well—don't say of course not. Be careful with him."

"I'm careful with him," she said. She said it indignantly. But she wanted to hear something else. She didn't want to leave.

Walking home, she thought about what she could do. Maybe she could take Sam to her sister's house in Morristown for a while. Maybe if he could run more, and keep cool, he would calm down. She put aside her knowledge that it was late September and already much cooler, and that the dog growled more, not less. He had growled at the teenage boy she had given money to, to help her carry her groceries upstairs. It was the boy's extreme reaction to Sam that had made it worse, though. You had to act calm around Sam when he got like that, and the boy had panicked.

She persuaded her sister to take Sam, and her brother-in-law drove into New York on Sunday and drove them out to New Jersey. Sam was put on a chain attached to a rope her brother-in-law had strung up in the backyard, between two huge trees. To her surprise, Sam did not seem to mind it. He did not bark and strain at the chain until he saw her drive away, late that afternoon; her sister was driving, and she was in the backseat with her niece, and she looked back and saw him lunging at the chain.

The rest of it was predictable, even to her. As they drove away, she almost knew it all. The dog would bite the child. Of course, the child should not have annoyed the dog, but she did, and the dog bit her, and then there was a hysterical call from her sister and another call from her brother-in-law, saying that she must come get the dog immediately—that he would come for her so she could get him—and blaming her for bringing the dog to them in the first place. Her sister had never really liked her, and the incident with the dog was probably just what she had been waiting for to sever contact.

When Sam came back to the city, things got no better. He turned against everyone and it was difficult even to walk him because he had become so aggressive. Sometimes a day would pass without any of that, and she would tell herself that it was over now—an awful period but over—and then the next morning the dog would bare his teeth at some person they passed. There began to be little signs that the dog had it in for her, too, and when that happened she turned her bedroom over to him. She hauled her mattress to the living room and let him have his own room. She left the door cracked so he would not think he was being punished. But she knew, and Sam knew, that it was best he stay in the room. If nothing else, he was an exceptionally smart dog.

She heard from Jack for over a year—sporadically, but then sometimes two postcards in a single week. He was doing well, playing in a band as well as writing music. When she stopped hearing from him—and when it became clear that something had to be done about the dog, and something had been done—she was twenty-two. On a date with a man she liked as a friend, she suggested that they go over to Jersey and drive down Boulevard East. The man was new to New York, and when they got there he said that he was more impressed with that view of the city than with the view from the top of the RCA Building. "All ours," she said, gesturing with her arm, and he, smiling and excited by what she said, took her hand when it had finished its sweep and kissed it, and continued to stare with awe at the lights across the water. That summer, she heard another song of Jack's on the radio, which alluded, as so many of his songs did, to times in New York she remembered well. In this particular song there was a couplet about a man on the street offering kittens in a box that actually contained a dog named Sam. In the context of the song it was an amusing episode—another "you can't always get what you want" sort of thing—and she could imagine Jack in California, not knowing what had happened to Sam, and, always the one to appreciate little jokes in songs, smiling.

DONALD BARTHELME

The Falling Dog

Yes, a dog jumped on me out of a high window. I think it was the third floor, or the fourth floor. Or the third floor. Well, it knocked me down. I had my chin on the concrete. Well, he didn't bark before he jumped. It was a silent dog. I was stretched out on the concrete with the dog on my back. The dog was looking at me, his muzzle curled around my ear, his breath was bad, I said, "Get off."

He did. He walked away looking back over his shoulder. "Christ," I said. Crumbs of concrete had been driven into my chin. "For God's sake," I said. The dog was four or five meters down the sidewalk, standing still. Looking back at me over his shoulder.

> gay dogs falling
> sense in which you would say of a thing,
> it's a dog, as you would say, it's a lemon
> rain of dogs like rain of frogs
> or shower of objects dropped to confuse enemy
> radar

Well, it was a standoff. I was on the concrete. He was standing there. Neither of us spoke. I wondered what he was like (the dog's life). I was curious about the dog. Then I understood why I was curious.

345

wrapped or bandaged, vulnerability but also
aluminum
Plexiglas
anti-hairy materials
vaudeville (the slide for life)

(Of course I instantly made up a scenario to explain everything. Involving a mysterious ((very beautiful)) woman. Her name is Sophie. I follow the dog to her house. "The dog brought me." There is a ringing sound. "What is that ringing?" "That is the electric eye." "Did I break a beam?" "You and the dog together. The dog is only admitted if he brings someone." "What is that window he jumped out of?" "That is his place." "But he comes here because . . ." "His food is here." Sophie smiles and puts a hand on my arm. "Now you must go." "Take the dog back to his place and then come back here?" "No, just take the dog back to his place. That will be enough. When he has finished eating." "Is that all there is to it?" "I needed the beam broken," Sophie says with a piteous look ((Sax Rohmer)). "When the beam is broken, the bell rings. The bell summons a man." "Another man." "Yes. A Swiss." "I could do whatever it is he does." "No. You are for breaking the beam and taking the dog back to his place." I hear him then, the Swiss. I hear his motorcycle. The door opens, he enters, a real brute, muscled, lots of fur ((Olympia Press)). "Why is the dog still here?" "This man refuses to take him back." The Swiss grabs the dog under the muzzle mock playfully. "He wants to stay!" the Swiss says to the dog. *"He wants to stay!"* Then the Swiss turns to me. "You're not going to take the dog back?" Threatening look, gestures, etc., etc. "No," I say. "The dog jumped on my back, out of a window. A very high window, the third floor or the fourth floor. My chin was driven into the concrete." "What do I care about your flaming chin? I don't think you understand your function. Your function is to get knocked down by the dog, follow the dog here and break the beam, then take the dog back to his place. There's no reason in the world why we should stand here and listen to a lot of flaming nonsense about your flaming etc. etc. . . .")
I looked at the dog. He looked at me.

who else has done dogs?
Baskin, Bacon, Landseer, Hogarth, Hals

with leashes trailing as they fall

with dog impedimenta following:
bowl, bone, collar, license, Gro-pup

I noticed that he was an Irish setter, rust-colored. He noticed that I was a Welsh sculptor, buff-colored (no, really, what did he notice? how does he think?). I reflected that he was probably a nice dog from a good home (bourgeois dog) but with certain unfortunate habits like jumping on people from high windows (rationalization: he is a member of the television generation and thus—)

Well, I read a letter, then. A letter that had come to me from Germany, that had been in my pocket. I hadn't wanted to read it before but now I read it. It seemed a good time.

Mr. XXXX XXXX
c/o Blue Gallery
Madison and Eighty-first St.
New York, N.Y.

Dear Mr. XXXXXXXX:

For the above-mentioned publishers I am preparing a book of recent American sculptors. This work shall not become a collection of geegaws and so, it tries to be an aimed presentation of the qualitative best recent American sculptors. I personally am fascinated from your collected Yawning Man series of sculptors as well as the Yawning lithographs. For this reason I absolutely want to include a new figure or figures from you if there are new ones. The critiques of your first show in Basel had been very bad. The German reviewers are coming from such immemorial conceptions of art that they did not know what to do with your sculptors. And I wish a better welcome to your contribution to this book when it is published here. Please send recent photographs of the work plus explanatory text on the Yawning Man.

Many thanks! And kindest regards!

> Yours,
> R. Rondorfer

Well, I was right in not wanting to read that letter. It was kind of this man to be interested in something I was no longer interested in. How was he to know that I was in that unhappiest of states, between images?

But now something new had happened to me.

> dogs as a luxury (what do we need them for?)
> hounds of heaven
>
> fallen in the sense of fallen angels
> flayed dogs falling? musculature
> sans skeleton?

But it is well to be suspicious. Sometimes an image is not an image at all but merely an idea. People have wasted years.

I wanted the dog's face. Whereas my old image, the Yawning Man, had been faceless (except for a gap where the mouth was, the yawn itself), I wanted the dog's face. I wanted his expression, falling. I thought of the alternatives: screaming, smiling. And things in between.

> dirty and clean dogs
> ultraclean dogs, laboratory animals
> thrown or flung dogs
> in series, Indian file
>
> an exploded view of the Falling Dog:
> head, heart, liver, lights
>
> *to the dogs*
> *putting on the dog*
> I am telling him something which isn't true

and we are both falling

dog tags!
but forget puns. Cloth falling dogs, the
gingham dog and the etc., etc. Pieces
of cloth dogs falling. Or quarter-inch
plywood in layers, the layers separated
by an inch or two of airspace. Like old
triple-wing aircraft

dog-ear (pages falling with corners bent back)

Tray: cafeteria trays of some obnoxious brown
plastic
But enough puns

Group of tiny hummingbird-sized falling dogs
Massed in upper corners of a room with high ceilings,
14–17 foot
in rows, in ranks, on their backs

Well, I understood then that this was my new image, The Falling Dog.
My old image, the Yawning Man, was played out. I had done upward of two
thousand Yawning Men in every known material, and I was tired of it. Images
fray, tatter, empty themselves. I had seven good years with that image, the
Yawning Man, but—
But now I had the Falling Dog, what happiness.

> (flights? sheets?)
> of falling dogs, flat falling dogs like sails
> Day-Glo dogs falling
>
> am I being sufficiently skeptical?
> try it out

die like a
dog-eat-dog
proud as a dog in shoes
dogfight
doggerel
dogmatic

am I being over-impressed by the circumstances
suddenness
pain
but it's a gift, thank you

love me, love my

Styrofoam?

Well, I got up and brushed off my chin, then. The silent dog was still standing there. I went up to him carefully. He did not move. I had to wonder about what it meant, the Falling Dog, but I didn't have to wonder about it now, I could wonder later. I wrapped my arms around his belly and together we rushed to the studio.

MICHAEL BISHOP

Dogs' Lives

All knowledge, the totality of all questions and all answers, is contained in the dog.
    —Franz Kafka, "Investigations of a Dog"

I AM TWENTY-SEVEN: Three weeks ago a black Great Dane stalked into my classroom as I was passing out theme topics. My students turned about to look. One of the freshman wits made an inane remark, which I immediately topped: "That may be the biggest dog I've ever seen." Memorable retort. Two of my students sniggered.

I ushered the Great Dane into the hall. As I held its collar and maneuvered it out of English 102 (surely it was looking for the foreign language department), the dog's power and aloofness somehow coursed up my arm. Nevertheless, it permitted me to release it onto the north campus. Sinews, flanks, head. What a magnificent animal. It loped up the winter hillock outside Park Hall without looking back. Thinking on its beauty and self-possession, I returned to my classroom.

And closed the door.

TWENTY-SEVEN AND HOLDING: All of this is true. The incident of the Great Dane has not been out of my thoughts since it happened. There is no door in my mind to close on the image of that enigmatic animal. It stalks into and out of my head whenever it wishes.

As a result, I have begun to remember some painful things about dogs and my relationships with them. The memories are accompanied by premonitions. In fact, sometimes I—my secret self—go inside the Great Dane's head and look through its eyes at tomorrow, or yesterday. Every bit of what I remember, every bit of what I foresee, throws light on my ties with both humankind and dogdom.

351

Along with my wife, my fifteen-month-old son, and a ragged miniature poodle, I live in Athens, Georgia, in a rented house that was built before World War I. We have lived here seven months. In the summer we had bats. Twice I knocked the invaders out of the air with a broom and bludgeoned them to death against the dining room floor. Now that it is winter the bats hibernate in the eaves, warmer than we are in our beds. The furnace runs all day and all night because, I suppose, no one had heard of insulation in 1910 and our fireplaces are all blocked up to keep out the bats.

At night I dream about flying into the center of the sun on the back of a winged Great Dane.

I AM EIGHT: Van Luna, Kansas. It is winter. At four o'clock in the morning a hand leads me down the cold concrete steps in the darkness of our garage. Against the wall, between a stack of automobile tires and a dismantled Ping-Pong table, a pallet of rags on which the new puppies lie. Everything smells of dog flesh and gasoline. Outside, the wind whips about frenetically, rattling the garage door.

In robe and slippers I bend down to look at the furred-over lumps that huddle against one another on their rag pile. Frisky, their mother, regards me with suspicion. Adult hands have pulled her aside. Adult hands hold her back.

"Pick one up," a disembodied adult voice commands me.

I comply.

The puppy, almost shapeless, shivers in my hands, threatens to slide out of them onto the concrete. I press my cheek against the lump of fur and let its warm, faintly fecal odor slip into my memory. I have smelled this smell before.

"Where are its eyes?"

"Don't worry, punkin," the adult voice says. "It has eyes. They just haven't opened yet."

The voice belongs to my mother. My parents have been divorced for three years.

I AM FIVE: Our ship docks while it is snowing. We live in Tokyo, Japan: Mommy, Daddy, and I.

Daddy comes home in a uniform that scratches my face when I grab his trouser leg. Government housing is where we live. On the lawn in the big yard between the houses I grab Daddy and ride his leg up to our front door. I am wearing a cowboy hat and empty holsters that go *flap flap flap* when I jump down and run inside.

Christmas presents: I am a cowboy.

The inside of the house gathers itself around me. A Japanese maid named Peanuts. (Such a funny name.) Mommy there, too. We have a radio. My pistols are in the toy box. Later, not for Christmas, they give me my first puppy. It is never in the stuffy house, only on the porch. When Daddy and I go inside from playing with it the radio is singing "How Much Is That Doggy in the Window?" Everybody in Tokyo likes that song.

The cowboy hat has a string with a bead to pull tight under my chin. I lose my hat anyway. Blackie runs off with the big dogs from the city. The pistols stay shiny in my toy box.

On the radio, always singing, is Patti Page.

DOGS I HAVE KNOWN: Blackie, Frisky, Wiggles, Seagull, Mike, Pat, Marc, Boo Boo, Susie, Mandy, Heathcliff, Pepper, Sam, Trixie, Andy, Taffy, Tristram, Squeak, Christy, Fritz, Blue, Tammi, Napoleon, Nickie, B.J., Viking, Tau, and Canicula, whom I sometimes call Threasie (or 3C, short, you see, for Cybernetic Canine Construct).

"Sorry. There are no more class cards for this section of 102."

How the spurned dogs bark, how they howl.

I AM FOURTEEN: Cheyenne Canyon, Colorado. It is August. My father and I are driving up the narrow canyon road toward Helen Hunt Falls. Dad's Labrador retriever, Nick—too conspicuously my namesake—rides with us. The dog balances with his hind legs on the backseat and lolls his massive head out the driver's window, his dark mouth open to catch the wind. Smart, gentle, trained for the keen competition of field trials, Nick is an animal that I can scarcely believe belongs to us—even if he is partially mine only three months out of the year, when I visit my father during the summer.

The radio, turned up loud, tells us that the Russians have brought back to Earth from an historic mission the passengers of Sputnik V, the first two animals to be recovered safely from orbit.

They, of course, are dogs. Their names are Belka and Strelka, the latter of whom will eventually have six puppies as proof of her power to defy time as well as space.

"How 'bout that, Nick?" my father says. "How'd you like to go free-fallin' around the globe with a pretty little bitch?"

Dad is talking to the retriever, not to me. He calls me Nicholas. Nick, however, is not listening. His eyes are half shut against the wind, his ears flowing silkenly in the slipstream behind his aristocratic head.

I laugh in delight. Although puberty has not yet completely caught up with me, my father treats me like an equal. Sometimes on Saturday, when we're watching Dizzy Dean on *The Game of the Week,* he gives me my own can of beer.

We park and climb the stone steps that lead to a little bridge above the falls. Nick runs on ahead of us. Very few tourists are about. Helen Hunt Falls is more picturesque than imposing; the bridge hangs only a few feet over the mountain stream roaring and plunging beneath it. Hardly a Niagara. Nick looks down without fear, and Dad says, "Come on, Nicholas. There's a better view on up the mountain."

We cross the bridge and struggle up the hillside above the tourist shop, until the pine trunks, which we pull ourselves up by, have finally obscured the shop and the winding canyon road. Nick still scrambles ahead of us, causing small avalanches of sand and loose soil.

Higher up, a path. We can look across the intervening blueness at a series of falls that drop down five or six tiers of sloping granite and disappear in a mist of trees. In only a moment, it seems, we have walked to the highest tier.

My father sits me down with an admonition to stay put. "I'm going down to the next slope, Nicholas, to see if I can see how many falls there are to the bottom. Look out through the trees there. I'll bet you can see Kansas."

"Be careful," I urge him.

The water sliding over the rocks beside me is probably not even an inch deep, but I can easily tell that below the next sloping of granite the entire world falls away into a canyon of blue-green.

Dad goes down the slope. I notice that Nick, as always, is preceding him. On the margin of granite below, the dog stops and waits. My father joins Nick, puts his hands on his hips, bends at the waist, and looks down into an abyss altogether invisible to me. How far down it drops I cannot tell, but the echo of falling water suggests no inconsequential distance.

Nick wades into the silver flashing from the white rocks. Before I can shout warning, he lowers his head to drink. The current is not strong, these falls are not torrents—but wet stone provides no traction and the Lab's feet go slickly out from under him. His body twists about, and he begins to slide inexorably through the slow silver.

"Dad! Dad!" I am standing.

My father belatedly sees what is happening. He reaches out to grab at his dog. He nearly topples. He loses his red golf cap.

And then Nick's body drops, his straining head and forepaws are pulled after. The red golf cap follows him down, an ironic afterthought.

I am weeping. My father stands upright and throws his arms above his head. "Oh my dear God!" he cries. "Oh my dear God!" The canyon echoes these words, and suddenly the universe has changed.

Time stops.

Then begins again.

Miraculously, even anticlimatically, Nick comes limping up to us from the hell to which we had both consigned him. He comes limping up through the pines. His legs and flanks tremble violently. His coat is matted and wet, like a newborn puppy's. When he reaches us he seems not even to notice that we are there to care for him, to take him back down the mountain into Colorado Springs.

"He fell at least a hundred yards, Nicholas," my father says. "At least that—onto solid rock."

On the bridge above Helen Hunt Falls we meet a woman with a Dalmatian. Nick growls at the Dalmatian, his hackles in an aggressive fan. But in the car he stretches out on the backseat and ignores my attempts to console him.

My father and I do not talk. We are certain that there must be internal injuries. We drive the regal Lab—AKC designation Black Prince Nicholas—almost twenty miles to the veterinarian's at the Air Force Academy.

Like Belka and Strelka, he survives.

SNAPSHOT: Black Prince Nicholas returning to my father through the slate-gray verge of a Wyoming lake, a wounded mallard clutched tenderly in his jaws. The photograph is grainy, but the huge Labrador resembles a panther coming out of creation's first light: he is the purest distillation of power.

ROLL CALL FOR SPRING QUARTER: I walk into the classroom with my new roll sheets and the same well-thumbed textbook. As usual, my new students regard me with a mixture of curiosity and dispassionate calculation. But there is something funny about them this quarter.

Something *not right*.

Uneasily I begin calling the alphabetized list of their names: "Andy . . . B. J. . . . Blackie . . . Blue . . . Boo Boo . . . Canicula . . . Christy . . . Frisky . . ."

Each student responds with an inarticulate yelp rather than a healthy "Here!" As I proceed down the roll, the remainder of the class dispenses with even this courtesy. I have a surly bunch on my hands. A few have actually begun to snarl.

". . . Pepper . . . Sam . . . Seagull . . . Squeak . . ."

They do not let me finish. From the front row a collie leaps out of his seat and crashes against my lectern. I am borne to the floor by his hurtling body. Desperately I try to protect my throat.

The small classroom shakes with the thunder of my students' barking, and I can tell that all the animals on my roll have fallen upon me with the urgency of their own peculiar blood lusts.

The fur flies. Me, they viciously devour.

Before the lights go out completely, I tell myself that it is going to be a very difficult quarter. A very difficult quarter indeed.

* * *

I AM FORTY-SIX: Old for an athlete, young for a president, maybe optimum for an astronaut. I am learning new tricks.

The year is 1992, and it has been a long time since I have taught freshman English or tried my hand at spinning monstrously improbable tales. (With the exception, of course, of this one.) I have been too busy.

After suffering a ruptured aneurysm while delivering a lecture in the spring of 1973, I underwent surgery and resigned from the English Department faculty. My recovery took eight or nine months.

Outfitted with several vascular prostheses and wired for the utmost mobility, I returned to the university campus to pursue simultaneous majors in molecular biology and astrophysics. The GI Bill and my wife and my parents footed the largest part of our expenses—at the beginning, at least. Later, when I volunteered for a government program involving cybernetic experimentation with human beings (reasoning that the tubes in my brain were a good start on becoming a cyborg, anyway), money ceased to be a problem.

This confidential program changed me. In addition to the synthetic blood vessels in my brain, I picked up three artificial internal organs, a transparent skullcap, an incomplete auxiliary skeletal system consisting of resilient inert plastics, and a pair of removable visual adaptors that plug into a plate behind my brow and so permit me to see expertly in the dark. I can even eat wood if I have to. I can learn the most abstruse technical matters without even blinking my adaptors. I can jump off a three-story building without even jarring my kneecaps. These skills, as you may imagine, come in handy.

With a toupee, a pair of dark glasses, and a little cosmetic surgery, I could leave the government hospitals where I had undergone these changes and take up a seat in any classroom in any university in the nation. I was frequently given leave to do so. Entrance requirements were automatically waived, I never saw a fee card, and not once did my name fail to appear on the rolls of any of the classes I sat in on.

I studied everything. I made A pluses in everything. I could read a textbook from cover to cover in thirty minutes and recall even the footnotes verbatim. I awed professors who had worked for thirty-forty years in chemistry, physics, biology, astronomy. It was the ultimate wish-fulfillment fantasy come true, and not all of it can be attributed to the implanted electrodes, the enzyme inoculations, and the brain meddlings of the government cyberneticists. No, I have always had a talent for doing things thoroughly.

My family suffered.

We moved many, many times, and for days on end I was away from whatever home we had newly made.

My son and daughter were not particularly aware of the physical changes that I had undergone—at least not at first—but Katherine, my wife, had to confront them each time we were alone. Stoically, heroically, she accepted the passion that drove me to alter myself toward the machine, even as she admitted that she did not understand it. She never recoiled from me because of my strangeness, and I was grateful for that. I have always believed that human beings discover a major part of the meaning in their lives from, in Pound's phrase, "the quality of the affections," and Katherine could see through the mechanical artifice surrounding and buttressing Nicholas Parsons to the man himself. And I was grateful for that, too, enormously grateful.

Still, we all have doubts. "Why are you doing this?" Katherine asked me one night. "Why are you letting them change you?"

"*Tempus fugit.* Time's winged chariot. I've got to do everything I can before there's none left. And I'm doing it for all of us—for you, for Peter, for Erin. It'll pay off. I know it will."

"But what started all this? Before the aneurysm—"

"Before the aneurysm I'd begun to wake up at night with a strange new sense of power. I could go inside the heads of dogs and read what their lives were like. I could time-travel in their minds."

"You had insomnia, Nick. You couldn't sleep."

"No, no, it wasn't just that. I was learning about time by riding around inside the head of that Great Dane that came into my classroom. We went everywhere, everywhen. The aneurysm had given me the ability to do that—when it ruptured, my telepathic skill went too."

Katherine smiled. "Do you regret that you can't read dogs' minds anymore?"

"Yes. A little. But this compensates, what I'm doing now. If you can stand it a few more years, if you can tolerate the physical changes in me, it'll pay off. I know it will."

And we talked for a long time that night, in a tiny bedroom in a tiny apartment in a big Texas city many miles from Van Luna, Kansas, or Cheyenne, Wyoming, or Colorado Springs, or Athens, Georgia.

Tonight, nearly seventeen years after that thoughtful conversation, I am free-falling in orbit with my trace-mate Canicula, whom I sometimes call Threasie (or 3C, you see, short for Cybernetic Canine Construct). We have been up here a month now, in preparation for our flight to the star system Sirius eight months hence.

Katherine has found this latest absence of mine particularly hard to bear. Peter is a troubled young man of twenty, and Erin is a restless teenager with many questions about her absent father. Further, Katherine knows that shortly the *Black Retriever* will fling me into the interstellar void with eight other trace-teams. Recent advances in laser-fusion technology, along with the implementation of the Livermore-Parsons Drive, will no doubt get us out to Sirius in no time flat (i.e., less than four years for those of you who remain Earthbound, a mere fraction of that for us aboard the *Black Retriever*), but Katherine does not find this news at all cheering.

"*Tempus fugit*," she told me somewhat mockingly during a recent laser transmission. "And unless I move to Argentina, God forbid, I won't even be able to see the star you're traveling toward."

In Earth orbit, however, both Canicula and I find that time drags. We are ready to be off to the small Spartan world that no doubt circles our starfall destination in Canis Major. My own minute studies of the "wobble" in Sirius' proper motion have proved that such a planet exists; only once before has anyone else in the scientific community detected a dark companion with a mass less than that of Jupiter, but no one doubts that I know what I am doing.

Hence this expedition.

Hence this rigorous, though wearying, training period in Earth orbit. I do not exempt even myself, but dear God, how time drags.

Canicula is my own dark companion. He rescues me from doubt, ennui, and orbital funk. He used to be a Great Dane. Even now you can see that beneath his streamlined cybernetic exterior a magnificent animal breathes. Besides that, Canicula has wit.

"Tempus fugit," he says during an agonizingly slow period. He rolls his eyes and then permits his body to follow his eyes' motion: an impudent, free-fall somersault.

"Stop that nonsense, Threasie," I command him with mock severity. "See to your duties."

"If you'll remember," he says, "one of my most important ones is, uh, hounding you."

I am forty-six. Canicula-Threasie is seven.

And we're both learning new tricks.

I AM THIRTY-EIGHT: Somewhere, perhaps, Nicholas Parsons is a bona fide astronaut-in-training, but in this tributary of history—the one containing me now—I am nothing but a writer projecting himself into that grandiose wish-fulfillment role. I am an astronaut in the same dubious way that John Glenn or Neil Armstrong is a writer. For nearly eleven years my vision has been on hold. What success I have achieved in this tributary I have fought for with the sometimes despairing tenacity of my talent and a good deal of help from my friends. Still, I cannot keep from wondering how I am to overcome the arrogance of an enemy for whom I am only a name, not a person, and how dangerous any visionary can be with a gag in the mouth to thwart any intelligible recitation of the dream.

Where in my affliction is encouragement or comfort? Well, I can always talk to my dog. Nickie is dead, of course, and so is Pepper, and not too long ago a big yellow school bus struck down the kindly mongrel who succeeded them in our hearts. Now we have B.J., a furrow-browed beagle. To some extent he has taken up the slack. I talk to him while Katherine works and Peter and Erin attend their respective schools. B.J. understands very little of what I tell him—his expression always seems a mixture of dread and sheepishness—but he is a good listener for as long as I care to impose upon him; and maybe when his hind leg thumps in his sleep, he is dreaming not of rabbit hunts but of canine heroics aboard a vessel bound for Sirius. In my capacity as dreamer I can certainly pretend that he is doing so. . . .

A SUMMER'S READING, 1959: *The Call of the Wild* and *White Fang* by Jack London. *Bob, Son of Battle* by Alfred Ollivant. Eric Knight's *Lassie Come-Home. Silver Chief, Dog of the North* by someone whose name I cannot recall. *Beautiful Joe* by Marshall Saunders. *Lad, a Dog* and its various sequels by Albert Payson Terhune. And several others.

All of these books are on the upper shelf of a closet in the home of my mother and stepfather in Wichita, Kansas. The books have been collecting dust there since 1964. Before that they had been in my own little gray bookcase in Tulsa, Oklahoma.

From the perspective of my thirty-eighth or forty-sixth year I suppose that it is too late to try to fetch them home for Peter and Erin. They are already too old for such stories. Or maybe not. I am unable to keep track of their ages because I am unable to keep track of mine.

In any event, if Peter and Erin are less than fourteen, there is one book that I do not want either of them to have just yet. It is a collection of Stephen Crane's short stories. The same summer that I was blithely reading London and Terhune, I read Crane's story "A Small Brown Dog." I simply did not know what I was doing. The title lured me irresistibly onward. The other books had contained ruthless men and incidents of meaningless cruelty, yes, but all had concluded well: either virtue or romanticism had ultimately triumphed, and I was made glad to have followed Buck, Lassie, and Lad through their doggy odysseys.

The Crane story cut me up. I was not ready for it. I wept openly and could not sleep that night.

And if my children are still small, dear God, I do not want them even to *see* the title "A Small Brown Dog," much less read the text that accompanies it.

"All in good time," I tell myself. "All in good time."

* * *

I AM TWELVE: Tulsa, Oklahoma. Coming home from school, I find my grown-and-married stepsister's collie lying against the curbing in front of a neighbor's house. It is almost four in the afternoon, and hot. The neighbor woman comes down her porch when she sees me.

"You're the first one home, Nicholas. It happened only a little while ago. It was a cement truck. It didn't even stop."

I look down the hill toward the grassless building sites where twenty or thirty new houses are going up. Piles of lumber, Sheetrock, and tar paper clutter the cracked, sun-baked yards. But no cement trucks. I do not see a single cement truck.

"I didn't know what to do, Nicholas. I didn't want to leave him—"

We have been in Tulsa a year. We brought the collie with us from Van Luna, Kansas. Rhonda, whose dog he originally was, lives in Wichita now with her new husband.

I look down at the dead collie, remembering the time when Rhonda and I drove to a farm outside Van Luna to pick him out of a litter of six.

"His name will be Marc," Rhonda said, holding him up. "With a *c* instead of a *k*. That's classier." Maybe it was, maybe it wasn't. At the time, though, we both sincerely believed that Marc deserved the best. Because he was not a registered collie, Rhonda got him for almost nothing.

Now I see him lying dead in the street. The huge tires of a cement truck have crushed his head. The detail that hypnotizes me, however, is the pool of gaudy crimson blood in which Marc lies. And then I understand that I am looking at Marc's life splattered on the concrete.

At supper that evening I break down crying in the middle of the meal, and my mother has to tell my stepfather what has happened. Earlier she had asked me to withhold the news until my father has had a little time to relax. I am sorry that my promise is broken, I am sorry that Marc is dead.

In a week, though, I have nearly forgotten. It is very seldom that I remember the pool of blood in which the collie's body lay on that hot spring afternoon. Only at night do I remember its hypnotizing crimson.

* * *

175 YEARS AGO IN RUSSIA: One night before the beginning of spring I go time traveling—spirit faring, if you like—in the mind of the Great Dane who once stalked into my classroom.

I alter his body into that of a hunting hound and drop him into the kennels on the estate of a retired Russian officer. Hundreds of my kind surround me. We bay all night, knowing that in the morning we will be turned loose on an eight-year-old serf boy who yesterday struck the general's favorite hound with a rock.

I jump against the fence of our kennel and outbark dogs even larger than I am. The cold is invigorating. My flanks shudder with expectation, and I know that insomnia is a sickness that afflicts only introspective university instructors and failed astronaut candidates.

In the morning they bring the boy forth. The general orders him stripped naked in front of his mother, and the dog-boys who tend us make the child run. An entire hunting party in full regalia is on hand for the festivities. At last the dog-boys turn us out of the kennels, and we surge across the estate after our prey.

Hundreds of us in pursuit, and I in the lead.

I am the first to sink my teeth into his flesh. I tear away half of one of his emaciated buttocks with a single ripping motion of my jaws. Then we bear the child to the ground and overwhelm his cries with our brutal baying. Feeble prey, this; incredibly feeble. We are done with him in fifteen minutes.

When the dog-boys return us slavering to our kennels, I release my grip on the Great Dane's mind and let him go foraging in the trash cans of Athens, Georgia.

Still shuddering, I lie in my bed and wonder how it must feel to be run down by a pack of predatory animals. I cannot sleep.

APPROACHING SIRIUS: We eight men are physical extensions of the astrogation and life-support components of the *Black Retriever*. We feed on the ship's energy; no one must eat to stay alive, though, of course, we do have delicious food surrogates aboard for the pleasure of our palates. All our five senses have been technologically enhanced so that we see, hear, touch, smell, and taste more vitally than do you, our brethren, back on Earth.

Do not let it be said that a cybernetic organism sacrifices its humanity for a sterile and meaningless immortality. Yes, yes, I know. That's the popular view, but one promulgated by pessimists, cynics, and prophets of doom.

Would that the nay-sayers could wear our synthetic skins for only fifteen minutes. Would that they could look out with new eyes on the fierce cornucopian emptiness of interstellar space. There is beauty here, and we of the *Black Retriever* are a part of it.

Canicula-Threasie and the other Cybernetic Canine Constructs demonstrate daily their devotion to us. It is not a slavish devotion, however. Often they converse for hours among themselves about the likelihood of finding intelligent life on the planet that circles Sirius.

Some of their speculation has proved extremely interesting, and I have begun to work their suggestions into our tentative Advance Stratagem for First Contact. As Threasie himself delights in telling us, "It's good to be ready for any contingency. Do you want the tail to wag the dog or the dog to wag the tail?" Not the finest example of his wit, but he invariably chuckles. His own proposal is that a single trace-team confront the aliens without weapons and offer them our lives. A gamble, he says, but the only way of establishing our credibility from the start.

Late at night—as we judge it by the shipboard clocks—the entire crew gathers around the eerily glowing shield of the Livermore-Parsons Drive Unit, and the dogs tell us stories out of their racial subconscious. Canicula usually takes the lead in these sessions, and my favorite account is his narrative of how dog and man first joined forces against the indifferent arrogance of a bestial environment. That story seems to make the drive shield burn almost incandescently, and man and dog alike—woman and dog alike—can feel their skins humming, prickling, with an unknown but immemorial power.

Not much longer now. Sirius beckons, and the long night of this journey will undoubtedly die in the blaze of our planetfall.

* * *

I AM FIFTEEN: When I return to Colorado Springs to visit my father the year after Nick's fall from the rocks, I find the great Labrador strangely changed.

There is a hairless saddle on Nick's back, a dark gray area of scar tissue at least a foot wide. Moreover, he has grown fat. When he greets me, he cannot leap upon me as he has done in past years. In nine months he has dwindled from a panther into a kind of heartbreaking and outsized lapdog.

As we drive home from the airport my father tries to explain. "We had him castrated, Nicholas. We couldn't keep him in the house—not with the doors locked, not with the windows closed, not with rope, not with anything we tried. There's always a female in heat in our neighborhood and he kept getting out. Twice I had to drive to the pound and ransom him. Five bucks a shot.

"Finally some old biddy who had a cocker spaniel or something caught him—you know how gentle he is with people—and tied him to her clothesline. Then she poured a pan of boiling water over his back. That's why he looks like he does now. It's a shame, Nicholas, it really is. A goddamn shame."

The summer lasts an eternity.

TWENTY-SEVEN, AND HOLDING: Behind our house on Virginia Avenue there is a small self-contained apartment that our landlord rents to a young woman who is practice-teaching. This young woman owns a mongrel bitch named Tammi.

For three weeks over the Christmas holidays Tammi was chained to her doghouse in temperatures that occasionally plunged into the teens. Katherine and I had not volunteered to take care of her because we knew that we would be away ourselves for at least a week, and because we hoped that Tammi's owner would make more humane arrangements for the dog's care. She did not. She asked a little girl across the street to feed Tammi once a day and to give her water.

This, of course, meant that Katherine and I took care of the animal for the two weeks that we were home. I went out several times a day to untangle Tammi's chain from the bushes and clothesline poles in the vicinity of her doghouse. Sometimes I fed her, sometimes played with her, sometimes tried to make her stay in her house.

Some days it rained, others it sleeted. And for the second time in her life Tammi came into heat.

One night I awoke to hear her yelping as if in pain. I struggled out of bed, put on a pair of blue jeans and my shoes, and let myself quietly out the back door.

A monstrous silver-black dog—*was it a Great Dane?*—had mounted Tammi. It was raining, but I could see the male's pistoning silhouette in the residual glow of the falling raindrops themselves. Or so it seemed to me. Outraged by the male's brutality, I gathered a handful of stones and approached the two dogs.

Then I threw.

I struck the male in the flank. He lurched away from Tammi and rushed blindly to a fenced-in corner of the yard. I continued to throw, missing every time. The male saw his mistake and came charging out of the cul-de-sac toward me. His feet churned in the gravel as he skidded by me. Then he loped like a jungle cat out our open gate and was gone. I threw eight or nine futile stones into the dark street after him. And stood there bare-chested in the chill December rain.

For a week this went on. New dogs appeared on some nights, familiar ones returned on others. And each time, like a knight fighting for his lady's chastity, I struggled out of bed to fling stones at Tammi's bestial wooers.

Today is March the fifth, and this morning Katherine took our little boy out to see Tammi's three-week-old puppies. They have a warm, faintly fecal odor, but their eyes are open and Peter played with them as if they were stuffed stockings come to life. He had never seen anything quite like them before, and Katherine says that he cried when she brought him in.

I AM AGELESS: A beautiful, kind-cruel planet revolves about Sirius. I have given this world the name Elsinore because the name is noble, and because the rugged fairness of her seascapes and islands calls up the image of a more heroic era than any we have known on Earth of late.

Three standard days ago, seven of our trace-teams descended into the atmosphere of Elsinore. One trace-team remains aboard the *Black Retriever* to speed our evangelical message to you, our brethren, back home. Shortly we hope to retrieve many of you to this brave new world in Canis Major.

Thanks to the flight capabilities of our cybernetic dogs, we have explored nearly all of Elsinore in three days' time. We divided the planet into hemispheres and the hemispheres into quadrants, and each trace-team flew cartographic and exploratory missions over its assigned area. Canicula and I took upon ourselves the responsibility of charting two of the quadrants, since only seven teams were available for this work, and as a result he and I first spotted and made contact with the indigenous Elsinorians.

As we skimmed over a group of breaktakingly stark islands in a northern sea, the heat-detecting unit in Canicula's belly gave warning of this life. Incredulous, we made several passes over the islands.

Each time we plummeted, the sea shimmered beneath us like windblown silk. As we searched the islands' coasts and heartlands, up-jutting rocks flashed by us on every side. And each time we plummeted, our heat sensors told us that sentient beings did indeed dwell in this archipelago.

At last we pinpointed their location.

Canicula hovered for a time. "You ready to be wagged?" he asked me. "Wag away," I replied.

We dropped five hundred meters straight down and then settled gently into the aliens' midst: a natural senate of stone, open to the sky, in which the Elsinorians carry on the simple affairs of their simple state.

The Elsinorians are dogs. Dogs very like Canicula-Threasie. They lack, of course, the instrumentation that so greatly intensifies the experience of the cyborg. They are creatures of nature who have subdued themselves to reason and who have lived out their apparently immortal lives in a spirit of rational expectation. For millennia they have waited, patiently waited.

Upon catching sight of me, every noble animal in their open-air senate began wagging his or her close-cropped tail. All eyes were upon me.

By himself Canicula sought out the Elsinorians' leader and immediately began conversing with him (no doubt implementing our Advance Stratagem for First Contact). You see, Canicula did not require the assistance of our instantaneous translator; he and the alien dog shared a heritage more fundamental than language.

I stood to one side and waited for their conference to conclude.

"His name translates as Prince," Canicula said upon returning to me, "even though their society is democratic. He wishes to address us before all of the assembled senators of his people. Let's take up a seat among them. You can plug into the translator. The Elsinorians, Nicholas, recognize the full historical impact of this occasion, and Prince may have a surprise or two for you, dear Master."

Having said this, 3C grinned. Damned irritating.

We nevertheless took up our seats among the Elsinorian dogs, and Prince strolled with great dignity onto the senate floor. The IT system rendered his remarks as several lines of nearly impeccable blank verse. English blank verse, of course.

PRINCE: Fragmented by the lack of any object
Beyond ourselves to beat for, our sundered hearts
Thud in a vacuum not of our making.
We are piecemeal beasts, supple enough
To look upon, illusorily whole;
But all this heartsore time, down the aeons
Illimitable of our incompleteness,
We have awaited this, your arrival,
Men and Dogs of Earth.
    And you, Canicula,
We especially thank for bringing to us
The honeyed prospect of Man's companionship.
Tell your Master that we hereby invite
His kinspeople to our stern but unspoiled world
To be the medicine which heals the lesions
In our shambled hearts.
    Together we shall share
Eternity, deathless on Elsinore!

368

And so he concluded. The senators, their natural reticence overcome, barked, bayed, and bellowed their approval.

That was earlier this afternoon. Canicula-Threasie and I told the Elsinorians that we would carry their message to the other trace-teams and, eventually, to the people of Earth. Then we rose above their beautifully barbaric island and flew into the eye of Sirius, a ball of sinking fire on the windy sea's westernmost rim.

Tonight we are encamped on the peak of a great mountain on one of the islands of the archipelago. The air is brisk, but not cold. To breathe here is to ingest energy.

Peter, Erin, Katherine—I call you to this place. No one dies on Elsinore, no one suffers more than he can bear, no one suffocates in the pettiness of day-to-day existence. That is what I had hoped for. That is why I came here. That is why I sacrificed, on the altar of this dream, so much of what I was before my aneurysm ruptured. And now the dream has come true, and I call you to Elsinore.

Canicula and I make our beds on a lofty slab of granite above a series of waterfalls tumbling to the sea. The mist from these waterfalls boils up beneath us. We stretch out to sleep.

"No more suffering," I say.

"No more wasted potential," Canicula says.

"No more famine, disease, or death," I say, looking at the cold stars and trying to find the cruel one upon which my beloved family even yet depends.

Canicula then says, *"Tempus?"*

"Yes?" I reply.

"Fug it!" he barks.

And we both go to sleep with laughter on our lips.

TWENTY-SEVEN, AND COUNTING: I have renewed my contract for the coming year. You have to put food on the table. I am three weeks into spring quarter already, and my students are students like other students. I like some of them, dislike others.

I will enjoy teaching them *Othello* once we get to it. Thank God our literature text does not contain *Hamlet*: I would find myself making hideous analogies between the ghost of Hamlet's father and the Great Dane who haunted my thoughts all winter quarter.

I am over that now. Dealing with the jealous Moor again will be, in the terminology of our astronauts, "a piece of cake."

Katherine's pregnancy is in its fourth month now, and Peter has begun to talk a little more fluently. Sort of. The words he knows how to say include *Dada, juice,* and *dog. Dog,* in fact, is the first word that he ever spoken clearly. Appropriate.

In fifteen years—or eleven, or seventeen—I probably will not be able to remember a time when Peter could not talk. Or Erin, either, for that matter, even though she has not been born yet. For now all a father can do is live his life and, loving them, let his children—born and unborn—live their own.

"Dog!" my son emphatically cries. "Dog!"

Acknowledgments

"Where Is Garland Steeples Now?" from *Strangers in Paradise* by Lee K. Abbott. Copyright © 1985, 1986 by Lee K. Abbott. Reprinted by permission of the Putnam Publishing Group.

"Molly's Dog" from *Return Trips* by Alice Adams. Copyright © 1984 by Alice Adams. Reprinted by permission of Alfred A. Knopf, Inc.

"The Falling Dog" from *City Life* by Donald Barthelme. Copyright © 1970 by Donald Barthelme. Reprinted by permission of International Creative Management.

"Distant Music" from *Secrets and Surprises* by Ann Beattie. Copyright © 1976, 1977, 1978 by Ann Beattie. Reprinted by permission of Random House, Inc. First published by *The New Yorker*.

"Black and Tan" from *Barking Man* by Madison Smartt Bell. Copyright © 1990 by Madison Smartt Bell. Used by permission of the author and John Farquharson Ltd. First published by *The Atlantic*.

"Dog" from *Town Smokes* by Pinckney Benedict. Copyright © 1987 by Pinckney Benedict. Reprinted by permission of Ontario Review Press.

"Dogs' Lives" from *Close Encounters with the Deity* by Michael Bishop. Copyright © 1984 by Michael Bishop. Reprinted by permission of the author. First published by *The Missouri Review*.

"Heart of a Champion" from *Descent of Man* by T. Coraghessan Boyle. Copyright © 1974 by T. Coraghessan Boyle. Reprinted by permission of Georges Borchardt, Inc., and the author. First published by *Esquire*.

"The English and Their Dogs" by Jerry Bumpus. Copyright © 1988 by Jerry Bumpus. Reprinted by permission of the author. First published by *The Greensboro Review*.

ACKNOWLEDGMENTS